Denton
Elliot
Finn

Hathaway House, Books 4–6

Dale Mayer

HATHAWAY HOUSE, BOOKS 4–6
Beverly Dale Mayer
Valley Publishing Ltd.

This is a work of fiction. Names, characters, places, brands, media, and incidents are either the product of the author's imagination or are used fictitiously. Any resemblance to actual events, locales, or persons, living or dead, is entirely coincidental.

ISBN-13: 978-1-773364-29-2
Print Edition

Books in This Series:

About This Bundle

Welcome to Hathaway House, a heartwarming military romance series from USA TODAY best-selling author Dale Mayer. Here you'll meet a whole new group of friends, along with a few favorite characters from Heroes for Hire. Instead of action, you'll find emotion. Instead of suspense, you'll find healing. Instead of romance, ... oh, wait. ... There is romance—of course!

Welcome to Hathaway House. Rehab Center. Safe Haven. Second chance at life and love.

Aaron

Navy SEAL Denton Hamilton has checked himself into Hathaway House, hoping for a fraction of the results his friends have gotten at the rehab center. Now missing a rib, muscles and a portion of his stomach, as well as suffering from PTSD, Denton would be happy to have his physical self healed. He's not so sure he'll ever get his mental health back, and finding a woman who'll have him now—as his friends have been lucky enough to do—is out of the question. Who would be willing to love a man like him?

Administrative Assistant Hannah Forsythe helps Dani run Hathaway House. A loner at heart, she's drawn to Denton's struggle and dismayed at his belief that no one could ever love him. But when an ill-advised observation she makes has unexpected consequences for Denton's recovery,

Hannah's only choice is to separate herself from him to help him progress without her.

As time passes, Hannah wonders if her choice has cost her everything she's ever wanted or whether Denton can work through his feelings to give them both their happy ending at Hathaway House.

Elliot

Former Navy SEAL Elliot Carver came to Hathaway House to get help with the lingering repercussions of a mission gone bad. His body is dealing with the physical trauma of a spinal cord injury, while his mind is caught in a loop of painful memories that he can't sideline, and both won't let him heal the way he'd like.

Former ER Nurse Sicily Lawrence has just made her way out of a difficult relationship, and the quietness of the night shift at Hathaway House gives her peace of mind. The last thing she needs is to get involved in another volatile union. But she has seen injuries like Elliot's before, and she knows that a certain type of therapy can help. One Elliot isn't interested in trying.

Now, for Elliot's sake, Sicily must push him toward the progress he needs, even it means losing him. And, with time and luck, maybe they can cross the hurdle and find each other at Hathaway House.

Finn

Navy SEAL Finn MacGregor arrives at Hathaway House not only with half of one leg but with a stoma, one that necessitates the use of a colostomy bag. While it's nice to once again see his old friend Dani Hathaway and her father, the Major, it's tough to feel like the least sexy man on the face of the earth. Especially after he meets the pretty nurse in charge of his care …

Fiona Smithers has seen practically everything when it comes to the human body, and Finn's physical problems don't faze her. Emotionally she's wary though. Once before, one of her patients had confused the gratitude he felt for her as love. … That scenario left Fiona devastated to know her friendliness had been misunderstood. Whether deemed love or friendliness, those emotions directly effected that patient's initial healing and then his setbacks of body as well as of heart and of mind, making her more determined not to run the same risks again.

Yet, this time, she may not be able to help herself. She wants Finn in her life on a permanent basis, but, after seeing his obsession with her in his artwork, is that even possible?

Sign up to be notified of all Dale's releases here!
https://geni.us/DaleNews

Denton

Hathaway House, Book 4

Dale Mayer

Prologue

DENTON HAMILTON STARED at his email in disbelief.
He'd heard so much about Hathaway House from Brock and Cole that Denton had been living in a fantasy world, hoping a miracle would happen and he'd have a chance to join his friends at the same center.

But the costs … they were horrific.

He'd applied anyway. Made his case, knowing they took on a certain number of pro bono cases, and had hoped and waited.

He pulled out his cell phone and called Brock. It rang several times, then went to voice mail. He tried Cole.

"Denton, what's up?"

The curiosity in his friend's voice was justified. They'd been on the phone only a few minutes earlier. "I got in," Denton croaked, his voice clogging up. He cleared his throat several times, then repeated, "I got into Hathaway House. They have a bed for me." His voice rose at the end as the words in front of him finally settled in. "I'm coming there, Cole. I'll be there next week. We'll be together again."

"Holy crap, are you serious? That's the best news I've heard in a long time," Cole said warmly. "Wait until you see this place. You'll love it." He paused, then added in a teasing voice, "And you'll love the women."

"Nah, I'm not coming there for that. Besides, just because you and Brock found the perfect ladies for your lives, that doesn't mean Cupid is smiling in my direction. No, I'm happy to know I'm coming to Hathaway House and getting my best chance at regaining my strength and my health."

"Maybe so, but in this place, miracles do happen. I got mine. I know there is one here just for you."

Chapter 1

DENTON HAMILTON COULDN'T believe his luck. His life had a tendency to go off the rails on a regular basis, so when good things happened, he always tried to stop and make a point of recognizing the moment. In this case, arriving at Hathaway House was beyond good luck. He hadn't had the funds to pay his own way, so when the benefactor money had been offered, he'd been over the moon. Both Brock and Cole were already there, and that made the trip all that much sweeter.

His brothers in arms were no longer big strapping men, ready to take on the world, like when they had first met. Now both of them were broken and damaged, nowhere near the men they were when they had first signed up for the military to train as SEALs. Still, Denton knew they had improved at Hathaway, and he was fully prepared to do what he could to improve his own physical health.

He was missing a ton of muscles, and his right calf was a mess. He would likely never do any heavy lifting again because he'd lost some back muscles to rebuild those calf muscles, plus, he was missing a bottom rib and part of his stomach. Food sensitivities were now a thing of everyday life as were blood sugar issues … Life could be a whole lot worse. The right calf muscles … those were traumatizing.

Waking up the first time with his right leg a mess had

been a hell of a shock. Who knew so many muscles were required to get that leg moving properly, not to mention doing simple things like climbing stairs? On top of that, he had also lost the baby toe on his left foot. He felt like a real idiot anytime he complained about it. The doctor had just chuckled and told him that missing toes meant relearning to walk again. But he had lost just one, and it shouldn't cause him that much trouble.

So, for now, a cane was his best friend. In the meantime, his goal was to return to be as fit as he could. He had to build up his right leg, and he had to build up his back. But he still counted himself lucky. He would do his best to make sure that whoever paid for him to come to Hathaway House wouldn't regret choosing him.

"Thank you so much for the ride," he said to the man beside him.

Dr. Wiseman smiled. "You're welcome. I'm always happy to deliver somebody here. It doesn't happen often enough. You're blessed that you are here."

"And I know it." He shook his head. "I'm not even sure how I made the cut. I don't have any money. Apparently, the center has donors, and one of them paid for my transfer and medical costs. The military said I'd been through everything they could do, but my leg is still useless. I hope all this is worth it."

"Not useless." The doctor shook his head. "It needs a lot of work, and the latest round of surgeries will take a lot of effort on your part to rebuild that leg. But the necessary muscles have been reattached. They need time to heal." Wiseman parked the car, exited, came around to Denton's side and opened the door. "This is only my second visit here," he said. "I'm looking forward to seeing the place again."

"I do appreciate the ride. I wasn't sure how all this would work."

"Sometimes the world works in mysterious ways," Dr. Wiseman said. He gave Denton a big smile. "Don't knock it. You're here. Make the most of it."

"I promise I'll do that much."

If Denton's reply was a little too emphatic, it was to be expected. He felt a little overwhelmed, truth be told. All those months and months of surgeries and the recoveries thereafter, seemed like a never-ending road where standing on his own two feet would be not only impossible, but also something that only the truly rich could afford. Not even the military had that much when it came to ongoing medical assistance. If Denton had stayed at the VA Hospital, he could have had all kinds of assistance, but none of it would have been as specialized as offered here at Hathaway House. Unlike some other people, he didn't have a problem being a charity case.

As Dr. Wiseman opened his car door, Denton struggled to his feet with the doctor's assistance. The front door to the medical center opened, and an orderly came toward them, pushing a wheelchair. Denton looked at it and sighed. "I'd hoped my wheelchair days were over."

Dr. Wiseman laughed. "You should be grateful that there is even a wheelchair for you. No overdoing it."

Once in the wheelchair, Denton turned to look up at Dr. Wiseman. "I don't have a problem accepting help. I was raised by a single mom. I learned from her. When she needed something done or when she needed something for me, she didn't care. She would ask people for help, or she would barter for what she needed. She was an expert at that.

Pride was never an issue for her." He shook his head. "Pride will never be an issue for me. I'm just too damn grateful to be alive."

"Good." Dr. Wiseman squeezed Denton's shoulder and walked beside him as the orderly pushed the wheelchair along the ramp. "There's a lot of people here. They come from all walks of life, all suffering traumatic events. Make sure you talk about your nightmares."

He nodded. "Will they ever go away?"

"PTSD is something a lot of men and women deal with. Military veterans are all over the world. Anybody who's been through the sort of traumatic experiences you have, well, it's to be expected. Let's just say, it's not necessarily forever. Having the right attitude and finding a strong positive support system are ways to improve your life and to help ease the traumatic stress of what you've been through."

At the front doors, he pushed a button, and both glass-paneled doors opened wide to allow the wheelchair through.

"Ah. There she is—Dani Hathaway."

Dani came around the front counter and shook the doctor's hand. "I'm so glad you came back for a visit."

"Thought I'd visit a couple of my favorite patients while I'm here."

Dani turned her gaze to Denton, and he shook her hand.

"Welcome to Hathaway House, Denton," she said brightly.

He answered simply and honestly. "Thanks. I'm glad to be here."

She smiled. "I believe two men are here who can't wait to see you."

Denton brightened. "I was so afraid they'd be gone before I got here, and I wouldn't get to see them," he confessed.

"Nope. They're waiting for you. However, we do have to get you through a quick orientation before you have time for yourself and them. So let's get you to your room."

She spoke to the orderly pushing his wheelchair. "George, would you take Denton to Room 73, please?" She looked back at Denton. "I'll be there shortly."

As he was wheeled away, he called over his shoulder, "Thanks again for the ride, Dr. Wiseman."

"No problem," he replied. "Good luck!"

As they rolled through wide, spacious hallways, Denton twisted around to look up at George. "How long have you worked here?"

"Forever," the orderly replied wryly. "It seems like forever."

Denton winced. That wasn't what he'd hoped to hear. "It's that bad?"

George's laughter rolled free. "No, not at all. I've been here since the place first opened. I came on board when Dani's father was still figuring out how to make this place into a working, viable business. That was ten years ago, at least, and I'm still here. I don't plan on leaving anytime soon."

Ten years. Denton sighed in relief. "That's good to know. I thought for a minute there you were saying this wasn't a good place to be."

He chuckled. "Just the opposite. You'll see a lot of people who have been here a long time." He turned a corner. "You're down on this side. I believe your buddies are on the other side though."

"Is that a big issue? Surely we can go back and forth to

see each other?"

"Absolutely not a problem. They're more mobile than you are."

"And I'll be catching up real fast—at least as fast as I can," he vowed, eager to get started.

"Not too fast though," George cautioned. "That's the worst thing you could do. Talk to Cole about that. You'll end up with a setback that'll take you even longer to recover from."

Denton's excitement disappeared. "So how do I do this? I want to make the most of my stay. I don't want to go too fast and have a setback, and I don't want to go too slow so that whoever pitched in to bring me here feels like they made the wrong choice."

"Don't you worry about that," George said. "Everybody here has an equal chance. There's no report card. There is no better or best. You must listen to your doctors and your body. And everybody's system, injuries, and mental state are all different. It's really important that you be true to yourself."

On that note, George pushed Denton through an open door. "This is your private room, with your own bathroom and a full shower. And your view overlooks the horse pastures."

"Cole said something about horses, and we can spend time with them," Denton said, enthralled. "And Brock talks about being with the animals in the vet clinic all the time." Denton shook his head. "Is that true?"

George nodded. "Stan runs the veterinary clinic on the lower level. We have a lot of animals in similar situations as our human patients. Some are in need of prosthetic limbs and special surgeries, and they are religiously cared for. Stan and Dani also do special rescues, and we keep the animals until we get them adopted out. You'll find several dogs visiting upstairs. They're comfort animals, so they will come around to make you feel not quite so alone. When you're capable physically, you can go downstairs to see Stan and meet the other animals. He's always got an animal that needs a hug. Because, like you, they've suffered enough."

Denton nodded, feeling a bit emotional.

George motioned to the bed. "Do you need any help getting on the bed?"

He spoke in such a commonplace tone of voice, Denton didn't take offense. "I think I should get there just fine. I have been doing decently enough, but my progress has slowed."

"That's fairly typical. Everyone plateaus at one point or another." George walked to the closet and opened the door. "Extra blankets and towels are here, and you have a couple drawers and the clothes hangers to put away some personal items. The desk is right here if you need it for your laptop, and as you can see beside the bed, you have one of those tables you can swivel over and back as need be." He glanced around the room. "I think that's all you need to know about in here. If you don't have any other questions, I'll let you settle in. Hannah should be here soon. She'll give you a tablet with further instructions and a timetable for your daily schedule."

Denton nodded. "I think I'm fine for the moment. Thank you so much."

He watched George leave. He hated to say he was a little nervous, but he was. Still, he was here. He made his way out of the wheelchair and sat down on the bed. He could walk but not far. Instead of walking around the bed, he rolled on his back and flipped his legs over, getting to the other side. Using the bed for support, he made the few steps to the window so he could look out. He smiled. A little filly was outside with a couple older horses in one great big pasture. Beautiful rolling hills. He shook his head and smiled widely. "This place is fantastic," he murmured.

Hearing a noise behind him, he turned a little too fast and had to grab hold of the window ledge.

"Easy there, tiger." Dani Hathaway stood in the doorway, her gaze concerned. Beside her was a tall, slim woman, holding a manila file folder and a tablet, wearing dark dress pants and a fitted white shirt.

"I'm fine." He smiled reassuringly. "You startled me."

Moving carefully, he took a few steps to the bed and sat down. With a lot of effort, he shifted back to lean against the headboard.

Dani smiled. "This is Hannah. She's here to get you settled in. I'll stop by a little later."

Hannah handed him a tablet and a notebook. "The notebook is for you, if you want to jot down any goals, any progress you want to keep track of, notes for yourself, whatever you like," she said. "Here is a pen and more are always at the front desk. The tablet gives you information on your team and your daily schedule. We have quite a system here. You don't have one practitioner. You will have five."

Denton's eyebrows rose at that thought. Then he looked at the screen and saw not only a short biography but a photograph along with the list of experiences and specialties of each medical professional. Dani was thorough, if nothing else.

Hannah continued. "If you check the Schedule tab at the top, you will see your daily events. It is not the same for everybody. The same team works on multiple patients a day and sometimes twice as many as that in a week. Everybody shuffles now and again, when we make changes. Also, you won't have the same physiotherapist. You will have several."

He glanced at her. "Is there a reason for that?"

She nodded. "That way, fresh eyes can see from different perspectives what a patient needs."

He nodded. "That makes sense."

She smiled at him, then handed him a cell phone. "This is yours. It has all your team members' numbers programmed in. Anytime you need any of us, including myself," she said, "you can call. It doesn't matter what time of day or night. Your team, in particular, happens to all live on-site."

He nodded and scrolled through the list. "Brock's on my team though, right?"

She laughed. "No, Brock's not on your team. Only employees are on your team. I understand that you, Brock and Cole are great friends." Something strange flickered through her voice as she said that.

He glanced at her, wondering what that was about. "We are. The three of us were inseparable."

"Good. Feel free to call them any time. If you look, you'll see both their numbers programmed in your phone on a secondary contact list. Okay, I'll explain the meals and how that works for you, but I'm sure they'll fill you in with a lot more as soon as they get a chance to see you."

So much information tumbled out of Hannah's mouth, Denton struggled to keep up. His expression must have given him away because she laughed when she came to a stopping point.

"I know I've dumped a lot on you, but it's not that bad. Everything I said is also written in here." She handed him a folder.

"Oh, thank God," he said. "I was so afraid I wouldn't remember."

"Not at all."

They shared grins.

She turned and walked toward the door. "I suggest you take a little time to get accustomed to your surroundings," she said. "In that folder is a map of the ground floor. Downstairs is a vet clinic. The public comes and goes on a regular basis to see the vet, to visit the animal patients. Some of the animals are permanent residents, and some are here for only short-term help. But all of them need as much loving care as any of the people in this place can give."

"Just like the patients." He liked the sound of that. "And I can go down there?"

"Eventually. Brock or Cole can take you in a day or two." At the doorway she stopped and faced him. "I do want to caution you. Please don't rush anything. Take your time. The move alone to transfer you here is hard on your body. You need time to adjust, so please honor that and give your body the time it needs."

He nodded soberly. "I can do that. I wouldn't want anything to set back my progress."

She gave him the sweetest smile. "I know you'll do your best."

And damn if there wasn't something special about her that made him want to do just that.

Chapter 2

HANNAH STEPPED INTO the hallway. Denton appeared to be a little overwhelmed with all the information she'd given him. She decided to come back later to see how he was doing. It was a lot to take in. This kind of medical center was a new experience for everyone, including the staff. Adjustment took a while. Patients needed time to settle in, as soon as possible, and to get into a routine.

She walked to the front desk and poked her head into Dani's office. "I'm done with Denton but will check again later today. The poor guy looked a little lost. Maybe if you get a chance, stop by this afternoon."

Dani looked up and smiled. "I can do that. You have definitely been helpful, taking over some of this work for me."

"Anything I can do to help. You're overworked. You should have a full-time assistant for yourself." Hannah smiled and withdrew.

Dani worked harder than anybody she'd ever seen before. Of course, it was her place, so it made sense. And she probably worked the hardest at keeping the staff and the patients happy. Obviously, there would always be personality conflicts and the occasional butting of heads, but in general, this place worked relatively smoothly.

Hannah had had experience in other medical offices,

including a doctor's office and a medical clinic in Houston. She certainly preferred working here. She'd only been at Hathaway House one year, and it had taken a few weeks to get into the Hathaway House mind-set and a few more weeks to realize how freeing it was to be here. The fact that the animals were here as well helped tremendously.

Thinking of the animals reminded her of something. She quickly jotted a note to herself. The next time she went shopping, she'd get a couple dog beds. That way she could have a few more of the animals upstairs on a regular basis. The patients appreciated having them around, and it wasn't always easy for patients to go downstairs. One of her jobs was to bring various animals from the clinic to visit the patients upstairs. She tended to use her various scheduled breaks throughout the day to find people who needed a one-on-one animal visit. This was especially true for the animals. Seeing too many people all at once was often stressful for them.

Hannah had three animals that she looked after on a regular basis and tracked when they were picked up by patients and taken away. If she'd had the chance, she'd have kept them all for herself. But understanding the animals were doing a very important job here made it easier to share them.

Some animals—like Chickie, the tiny partially crippled dog that appeared to get around in everyone's arms rather than walking—were a good example of that. He had water and food and a bed at the front counter and in the back area of the ground floor. But he was often cuddled up with somebody who needed it. And it was probably better that way as Chickie was very small and didn't move very well. The worst thing would be to have animals running loose, tripping up people on crutches or getting in the way of wheelchairs. Hathaway House employees didn't want any of the humans or the animals to get injured on-site either.

But something was very special about Chickie. He also had a supersensitive stomach, and although they warned everybody not to feed him, somehow his tummy was always a little upset. She wasn't sure if he was nibbling on crumbs off the floor or if somebody was secretly feeding him.

Helga was another example. She was a beautiful young Newfoundland, missing a leg. Her prosthetic limb was constantly undergoing design upgrades, everybody coming up with suggestions to make it work better for her. Helga herself didn't seem to care. The joint moved and rolled as she needed it to, and other than that, she was happy.

This group had been amazingly helpful in getting animals back on their feet. Chickie didn't have prosthetic limbs because his legs were quite crippled, and he had nowhere near the mobility that a lot of the other animals did. Being small made it easier as he required a lot more assistance.

Helga was huge, and as such she was appreciated by the men who were a little too afraid of hurting Chickie. The ones who loved Chickie simply carried him around like a baby.

Chickie belonged to the center, and Stan kept up regular medical treatments to keep him healthy. Hannah didn't understand how Dani had the time or the influx of funds to funnel monies in so many different directions, but she managed to get enough to cover what was needed. Hannah knew finding donors was a constant challenge, but Dani did it. She had a lot of benefactors who she could call in to get assistance for people who needed specialized medical help but couldn't afford to come here. And when one healed and moved on, then she opened the waiting list and brought in the next person needing their special rehabilitation efforts. It was a good system.

Dani also kept horses on the property. Most were refugee rescue horses. Some were damaged, but some were older and had no place in the regular world anymore. Dani was a horse lover, and Hannah didn't think Dani would ever turn away a horse. They had six right now. But unlike the dogs with a life expectancy of about twelve to fifteen years, horses often lived to their mid-twenties. The commitment was a lot longer.

Hannah had the title of administrative assistant, but really she was a jack-of-all-trades. She was a cross between Dani's assistant and the substitute front receptionist, plus she did some bookkeeping. And truth be told, she was good with that. There was certainly nothing boring about this job.

Her phone was ringing as she walked behind the front counter.

"Hey, Hannah. Do you have a moment?"

"Sure Stan, I'll be right down."

She hung up the phone and checked to see where Chickie was. He was curled up in his bed, looking darn tired. She decided to leave him where he was. He had done the rounds this morning with her, and he was certainly entitled to a nap. She grabbed a coffee cup, filled it and headed downstairs to see Stan.

The vet clinic was a mess. Several dogs in the reception area were struggling with their owners. In the center of the chaos was a cat, glaring at everybody.

Hannah stared at the cat. "So who's this guy?"

"We're not exactly sure."

Hannah looked at the vet's receptionist. "What? Didn't he have an appointment?"

Rebecca stood behind her desk. "No, and I didn't see who he came in with either. I have no idea. He doesn't look to be injured in any way."

Stepping between the dogs and cat, Stan crouched down. The cat took one look and jumped onto Stan's shoulders. Stan laughed. "Well, he's a friendly fellow."

"Very." Hannah studied the cat for a moment. "He's not scared of the dogs, and he seems to like the noise."

Stan glanced over at her with a knowing look. "You've been trying to get a therapy cat upstairs since forever."

She shrugged sheepishly. "It seems hardly fair that we have therapy dogs, but no cats."

He nodded. "We'll have to give this wonderful cat a checkup before we can let him around the human patients. But I was thinking of you and upstairs."

She stroked the feline, who seemed to like all the humans so far. "He's a beauty. He's almost bobcat size, isn't he?"

Stan nodded. "I wouldn't be surprised if something wild was in his heritage. He is really big."

She gently scratched behind his ears, and the huge cat's rumble filled the room.

"Good Lord," Stan said. "That's quite the engine."

She smiled. "You have to check him out real fast, Stan. I could use him upstairs." She turned to look at all the dogs sniffing the cat. She smiled. "Looks like you have a full day as it is."

Stan nodded, lifted the cat off his shoulders and handed him to Hannah as his temporary assistant. "Isn't that the truth?"

Hannah stepped out of Stan's way as he led one of the dogs with its owner into a treatment room. The cat gracefully jumped from Hannah's arms and onto the reception desk. Hannah smiled at the big cat, busy inspecting Rebecca's workspace.

"Is it usual to have them this calm at the clinic?"

Rebecca shook her head. "No. Usually they come in hissing at everything in sight."

"Well, this guy is certainly not doing that."

Rebecca stood and picked up the cat. "I'll take him to the back. That'll help the dogs calm down."

Hannah nodded and watched as the huge cat stared at her, his eyes glowing until he was out of the room.

She turned to the other people sitting in the waiting room. "Did any of you see the cat arrive?"

Two people shook their heads.

"No, suddenly he was just here. With all the chaos with the dogs, I didn't notice where the cat came from," the older woman replied.

Hannah looked down the long hallway. "It's possible he came in from the barn area." She headed that way to look, but the stalls were all empty, and the doors were closed. Mystified, she headed upstairs. She popped into Dani's doorway and explained the scenario.

Dani laughed. "So the center is so good that animals are coming in on their own now, are they?"

The two women laughed, and then Hannah returned to her office. They never knew what the next unusual scenario would be at this crazy job. And she wouldn't change it for anything.

Her cell phone rang within minutes of her sitting down. She groaned. "Good thing my workload is easier today."

She glanced down to see the caller was Denton. "Denton Hamilton, what can I do for you?"

His hesitant voice came through. "I hate to be a bother, but I've tried calling Brock and Cole, but neither call appears to be going through."

She frowned. "That's odd. I'll bring the numbers down myself, and we can double-check them." She grabbed her checklist and headed toward Denton's room.

He sat on his bed, his legs hanging over the edge. He had switched to shorts, perhaps for some of the medical tests or physical therapy or just to feel more comfortable. But to see his calf mangled like that, she fought back a wave of sympathy. His foot was also completely covered in scar tissue, and it appeared to be missing part of a joint. She glanced at his face and realized he had watched her reaction.

He kicked out his bum leg. "What do you think?"

She shrugged and sent him a gentle smile. "I've seen worse."

He looked at her, his gaze searching her face until he realized she was serious, and he relaxed. "I guess I don't have to hide it, do I?"

She shook her head. "Never. Please do not hide anything. Find a level of comfort, and learn to live with it. You can relax. We've all seen much worse injuries. We'll do the best we can to help you get back to a normal life."

He smiled. "And part of that is contacting my friends." He held out his phone.

She checked to see if she'd switched some of the digits. "I'm so sorry. I'm mildly dyslexic, and phone numbers are sometimes a challenge." She carefully brought up each of the numbers, then checked her list, and together they watched as she put in the right numbers.

"Try that now." Inside, she winced at her mistake. She hadn't done that for a while. But when she got tired or busy, her brain automatically switched numbers on her. It was frustrating.

Denton tried Brock first, and when the man answered, she watched happiness bloom across Denton's face. He waved at her and mouthed the words, *Thank you.*

She nodded, gave him a smile and turned to leave. Behind her, she could hear him chatting with Brock. There was such love and friendship in his voice, and she was happy for them. It also reminded her how lacking her own life was in those two areas. Love, well, she hadn't found it yet. However, she'd made more friends since arriving at the center than she had ever had in her life. But she didn't have any friends from school or from college. She didn't have any long-term friendships beyond this last year. She'd tried hard enough to make some, but it never seemed to work out. She never had the knack for it. Apparently, of all the things wrong with Denton, his ability to make and keep friends was not one of them.

"HEY, BUDDY ... Guess who's finally landed?" Denton asked when Brock answered.

Brock laughed and cheered. "What room are you in? I'll come to you."

Denton gave Brock the room number and ended the call. Denton thought about the look he'd seen on Hannah's face when she exited the room. Something in her voice, something in her expression, he didn't quite recognize.

Something akin to hesitation, as if she wanted to stay longer. He wished he could call her back. He didn't know what, if anything, was wrong. But he'd spent a lot of time alone himself, wishing that somebody would talk to him. Sometimes he had to admit the last few months at the hospital had been hard. He'd been inundated with people. But not one of them had been a friend. Not one of them had been a Brock or a Cole. His friends had been here, dealing with their own rehab, and Denton had been there, dealing with his. However, now he'd passed through one stage and had made it to the next. Although he was following in their footsteps, he knew that these guys would always give him a helping hand. That was what friends did. And he never doubted them.

Together they'd seen some pretty ugly things. They'd been on some dangerous missions. They'd done some incredibly grueling training and had pushed themselves to the limit, and still they'd survived. Not just that but they'd excelled. He wasn't ashamed or worried about anything he'd done in his past. That his future was unknown, and therefore a little unnerving, was true. But he hoped he didn't have to face that alone either. And again, Brock and Cole were there ahead of Denton to show him the way.

He could hear footsteps coming down the hallway. He wasn't sure if someone was headed toward him or not, but he got excited nonetheless.

Suddenly a familiar head popped around the corner of his doorway, and with a big grin on his face, Brock stepped into the room. "I am glad to see you're here finally!"

Denton shook his head. "I tried to get here earlier, honest. But recovering from my surgeries was a never-ending process, and I couldn't seem to get clear of it."

Brock nodded in understanding. "We've been there, done that." He motioned at the bare leg Denton had hanging off the edge of the bed. "Looks pretty gnarly, man."

Denton laughed at his slang. "It is gnarly. But hopefully here we can build it up. Who knew they could take muscles off your back and reattach them somewhere else?"

"Modern medicine is a beautiful thing, man." Brock's back and side were severely damaged. "My injuries weren't much better. Half my body is scar tissue, with half a cheek missing." But he said it with a big grin and a shrug, as if to say, *What the hell? It's what the cards are, and we must live with them.*

Brock had always been like that, until his accident. Denton nodded. "It's not exactly where I thought we'd end up though."

"We should have. The lives we led, the situations we were in, if we'd had even a basic understanding of how many of our fellow soldiers ended up like this, it wouldn't seem so odd."

"Maybe we chose not to look too closely?"

"Absolutely." Brock glanced around the room. "This place is great. You'll love it here. If you work hard, you will excel, and in no time, you'll see a huge difference."

"I'm counting on it," Denton said in a quiet voice. "A lot of extra funding had to be put into place to get me here. I'm looking to make the most of the opportunity."

Brock stared at him for a long moment, before giving a sharp nod. "You've always been the one who showed gratitude and understanding about how lucky you were. While I was griping about circumstances, you'd put that sunny smile on your face and say, *We are good.*" He shook his head. "Honestly, that'll hold you in good stead here."

Denton laughed. "Look what I got." He held up the map in his hand. "Hannah gave this to me."

"Hannah? Not Dani?"

Denton shook his head.

"Hannah's been here for a while, but she's stepping up to take some of Dani's extra workload apparently."

"Both of them made sure I was settled into my room."

"Well, lucky you. Hannah's a sweetie."

"And Dani isn't?"

"Oh, she is too, but she's taken. Hannah's single."

Denton rocked back slightly and looked up at Brock. "What? Is there a matchmaking service here too?"

"No, but once you're past that intensive medical level, and you're back on your feet, it's automatic for your mind to return to other activities besides getting from point A to point B without the help of crutches and a wheelchair."

Denton smirked. "And you are always one to lead the pack in that direction." He studied Brock for a long moment, assessing the impish grin but also the warm light in his gaze. "So spill then. Who is she?"

Brock looked at him sheepishly. "Her name is Sidney. She's one of the massage therapists here."

"Is it serious?"

Brock nodded. "Serious as I can make it. I've got another month here, then I'm graduating forward."

Inside, Denton took that as a visceral hit. He winced. "I was kind of hoping for more than a month, if not six months."

"I won't be far way," Brock said. "I'll be staying in Dallas. Sidney will continue working here, and I'm looking for a job in town. We'll see what we can do about living arrangements."

"Wow, that is serious."

Brock nodded. "When you find the right woman"—he took a deep breath—"and you come so close to losing your life, you don't mess around. I love her. Like, I *really* love her." He opened his arms and grinned sheepishly. "And after I was injured, I never thought I'd see such a day come. But she doesn't mind the scars. She doesn't care about the broken body. She's truly special."

"Then you are very lucky," Denton said. "I think we all go through that stage, thinking we're done with relationships, especially when we wake up in bed, broken, screaming in the middle the night with flashbacks causing our bodies to swim in sweat and the fear raging up our throats."

"My nightmares were never as bad as yours. I get a few, but they don't torment me quite so bad. Make sure you talk to the therapist about that. Post-traumatic stress syndrome is nothing to fool around with."

"I know. I've been keeping it under control, but sometimes ..."

"Sometimes life gets to be too much." He nodded in understanding. "Like I said, make sure you talk to the therapist about it. Everybody here does such a marvelous job in their own field. It's amazing how much progress we're all making."

"What about Cole? Where is he? Is he still playing catch-up?"

"Hell no," Brock said. "He's doing much better now too. He had a rough beginning, but he's come a long way."

"*Lovely.* I'm so far behind both of you that there is no point in playing catch-up."

Brock stepped into the hallway, returning a moment later with a wheelchair. "That's not important. What matters is understanding your limits and sticking to them. I was always leapfrogging ahead, doing too much, too fast. Cole was always playing catch-up, scared that what he did wasn't enough. Yet, you need to be content to do what you can do so you can be happy with yourself for the rest of your life."

He smiled. "While you're here, follow that same pattern. You will progress at a pace that's right for you. Don't worry about anyone else. Progress of any kind might look like a complete impossibility—particularly when you see so many people months ahead of you into their rehab. But when you look back on your own progress, you'll be amazed." He patted the wheelchair. "One of the things you don't want is to overdo it. That lesson I learned from Cole, who ended up back in the hospital only a few days after he got here. Hop on, and let's go for a ride."

Slowly, but under his own strength, Denton made his way to sit in the wheelchair, his legs on the footrests, and with a sense of finally coming home that he hadn't had in so long, he let his best buddy take him from his room for a tour of the place.

As they turned a corner, Hannah came toward them down the hallway. She grinned. "Now that looks like a perfect idea for this morning. Make sure you don't take him too far or make him do too much," she cautioned Brock.

He gave her a smile. "I would never do anything to hurt this guy."

Denton twisted to look behind them as she continued on.

Brock leaned down and whispered in his ear, "See? Like I said ... Hannah's hot. She's smart, and you're definitely interested."

Denton sank back into the wheelchair. "I might be interested, but I don't plan to do anything about it. I'm here to heal, and that's where I'll put my focus."

Brock whistled a light, happy tune but then paused for a

moment. "You can do what you want, but when life smacks you upside the head, you can't ignore it. All you can do is let fate play a hand and see where you land."

Chapter 3

A T THE END of the hallway, Hannah stopped and looked over her shoulder to see the two men chuckling together. She smiled and murmured, "If nothing else, just having friends around would help."

"Talking to yourself, Hannah?" Shane's voice came from behind her. "That's not a good sign at your age." He shook his head. "Of course, if you're talking about the two strapping men who went down that hallway, then maybe your comment was about something important."

She flushed and shook her head. "I was saying how having friends around would help Denton heal faster. To have them as role models and to have their support."

"We all need friends."

She nodded. "I can't say I've had a ton in my lifetime. And to see what these men have together is a unique experience for me."

"I think their circumstances, coupled with what they've been through, have helped build a bond most of us can't access."

"And yet his buddies, Cole and Brock, found partners here at the center," she said slowly. "And so, either they opened that existing relationship to let others in or they had the capacity to have more than just one or two friends."

He stopped and studied her for a long moment. "You've

made friends since you've been here, right?"

She laughed. "Yes, absolutely." Of course, they weren't close friends. "I don't have friends from grade school. I barely remember anybody I went to college with. Some people have friends who span twenty to thirty years. How did they do that? How do you find people you're willing to stay in contact with all those years? That's such a gift. I think these three have it. And maybe, I realize I wish I had something like that."

He seemed to follow her rambling thoughts without any trouble. He smiled and nodded. "I've seen that happen myself. My parents have friends spanning fifty years. But I never had any long-term friends either. I made friends in college, and I've stayed in contact with a few of those but more for networking, in case I ever need another job. That way, I always know who to contact and can say, 'Hey, what's happening in your corner of the world?'" He grinned at her. "My real friends are here. I've been here for close to six years straight now, and I've certainly made more friends in those years than from before. You've only been here a year. I've seen you make friends, but they don't necessarily meet the criteria of long-term friendship."

"I hear you. It would be nice to see where I am in five or seven years. I'd like to have a friend so I can look back when I'm old and gray and smile because I've known somebody else for all that time. And they know me as well as I know them."

"I think a lot of times those become partners. It's not that we can't have male friends or female friends, but often a friend like that is the person who we fall in love with. The person who we plan to stay with, the person who we want to be with for the rest of our lives. To become a best friend.

And that's who you get to spend your time with and smile at and hold hands with when you're in your rocking chairs, many years down the road."

She grinned. "That's a nice picture. I know a lot of people would cringe at the thought, but imagining sitting on a rocking chair fifty years in the future and holding my husband's hand makes me smile and sigh. To think that somebody could know me and love me and want to be with me for that length of time—well, that's just special."

"I think Dani's found that with Aaron," Shane said. "I think Brock and Sidney have found that." He smiled. "I'm not too sure yet, but Sandra may have found the exact same thing in Cole too." He glanced up and down the hallway. "It's something I've never seen here before, but definitely a love bug is going on. Maybe Cupid moved in." He shrugged. "I don't know what it is, but there's been a change. Maybe you need to stay open to the idea, and you'll find somebody to love yourself."

He wrapped an arm around her shoulders and gave her a gentle hug. And then he walked away, leaving her alone with that thought.

She realized one thing—Shane was one good friend she'd made while here.

IT WAS HARD to find anything more perfect than this morning. Finally seeing Brock. Finally being at the center, a place Denton had tried so hard to get into for so long. Denton's heart was overwhelmed with joy and satisfaction. He'd achieved this. No, not all on his own. But that didn't matter. He was here now. Brock was here now and hopefully would be for another couple months. But like he had said, he would stay close. And that was like having family all over again.

Denton gave a happy sigh and settled back for the tour. Brock took him through the upstairs, which was the ground-floor level, showing him the nurses' station and all the physiotherapy rooms. Brock kept up his rambling conversation that was both easy and lighthearted. And it did a lot to help Denton relax. They bypassed Dani's office—whether on purpose or not, Denton didn't know—but Brock did wheel Denton past the front reception where Hannah was. The two men smiled at her.

"What's this?" She grinned and said teasingly, "Is the reception desk a tourist stop now?"

Brock nodded. "I figured I'd better show him all the places on limits and off-limits," he joked.

Denton raised an eyebrow. "I haven't heard about the off-limits places."

"That's because there aren't very many." Hannah shook her head. "How come you haven't taken him to pick up a cup of coffee for the tour?"

Denton looked up at his buddy. "What? You're gypping me out of a cup of coffee?"

With a chuckle, Brock turned the wheelchair in the opposite direction. "I was getting there—honest. I was getting there."

Denton watched as they came to a massive open dining-area space. A set of large retractable doors were open, creating one giant room with a massive deck outside, merged seamlessly together. Brock stopped right at the dining room entrance, so Denton could get a good look.

"This is the main hub of this place," Brock said. "Drinks

and snacks are always available. If you're on a special diet, then talk to your team about getting specific snacks available for you. There are three set mealtimes, but if you miss a meal and you're hungry, you can always talk to Dennis."

A large male behind the counter lifted his head and waved. He smiled and called out, "Hey, Brock … did we get a new one?"

Brock laughed as he wheeled Denton closer. "Denton, this is Dennis. Anytime you need food, whether it's mealtime or not, he'll hook you up."

Dennis came around and shook Denton's hand. "Welcome."

Appreciating the camaraderie and openness of the place, Denton shook Dennis's hand. "Hannah said something about coffee?"

Dennis chuckled. "Where would we be without that brew?" He pointed to the side wall. "Brock can take you to our snack station. There's always coffee and tea, black and herbal. Hot chocolate too and juice. If you want something that we don't have, let me know, and I'll do my best to get it for you."

Brock wheeled them slowly through what was mostly an empty room. Some staff appeared to be having a meeting at a table at one end of the room, papers strewn across the tabletop, and a couple of patients sat at a table outside.

"The property looks unbelievable," Denton commented. "It's a unique setting."

"You don't know the half of it. Once you see the animals, you'll understand how special this place is."

They made it to the coffee bar where Brock poured two cups, set them on a tray and handed the tray to Denton to carry. "You hungry? There are cookies, cinnamon buns, or fruit."

Denton said, "I want a cinnamon bun," then laughed as Brock had already picked up two and added them to his tray.

"Now the only question you must answer is, sit inside or outside?"

"Is the tour over?"

"Nope. This is a midway stop."

Laughing and joking, the two moved outside to one of the largest tables on the deck. The sunshine and fresh air were spectacular. As Brock moved a dining chair so the wheelchair could pull right up to the table, Denton carefully lifted the tray to the table without any spills. He glanced up at Brock. "I was sure I would dump it."

"You wouldn't be the first to do that. It took me a long time to learn how to carry a tray while on crutches."

Denton shook his head. "I'm so not ready for that."

"I wasn't either," Brock said cheerfully.

Denton relaxed in his chair, enjoying an atmosphere that felt more like a vacation resort than an actual medical facility. "Staff and patients mingle all the time?"

"They can. They do have offices, and they have some separate meeting rooms, but they might as well come here, have fresh coffee and something to eat while having their meeting."

"And visitors?"

"They come too. All visitors must pass through the front doors, and they must sign in. You have to arrange for your visitors ahead of time to avoid interrupting your rehab schedule."

"That makes sense." Denton asked a few more questions but then fell silent as he took the first bite of his cinnamon bun. He shook his head and moaned. "Oh my God, this is so good."

Brock nodded. "Wait until you get to the meals. I will miss the food here."

Denton stared at him in astonishment. "Are you serious? Usually, in any kind of medical facility, the food is crappy."

"Not here." Brock ripped off a huge piece of cinnamon bun from the outside of his roll and ate it.

"There you are," a woman called out.

Brock glanced up, and the look in his eyes—a warm, almost melted look—had Denton studying Brock in surprise. A tall beautiful woman came around the table and reached out a hand. Brock grasped it.

Denton turned to the woman. "I gather you're Sidney."

Laughter rolled from her, and she nodded. "Nice to meet you. You must be the Denton I've heard so much about."

Denton winced. "All good things, I hope."

"Of course," she said with a smile. "I see Brock's giving you the tour."

Denton nodded. "I'm still hoping to meet up with Cole soon."

"You will," she said confidently. "He's doing his sessions right now. Maybe another half hour to forty-five minutes." She glanced at her watch. "Wow. Okay, it's almost lunchtime. The morning has disappeared faster than I expected." She glanced at Brock. "Are you two staying here for lunch, or are you giving him a tour down below after your coffee and then coming back?"

"We'll have our coffee and cinnamon buns, finish the tour and then we'll hopefully meet up with Cole for lunch here. I'll text him and make sure he'll be here." Brock looked up at her hopefully. "Can you join us too?"

"I have a meeting with the other therapists. If it runs late, then I won't make it. But if I finish on time, then I'll be happy to." She gave him a warm smile and then switched her gaze to Denton. "I trust you're here for all the right reasons. Be sure you make the most of your stay," she said cryptically, and then she pivoted and walked off.

Denton couldn't help but watch her as she left. She was beautiful and confident. His gaze flew back to Brock, who had a foolish smile on his lips. "You got it bad, don't you?"

"I got it bad. And for the first time in my life, I've found a partner whom I'm quite happy to spend the rest of my life with."

"Wow." Denton picked up his coffee mug and took a big drink. So many new and different things going on here. His mind had trouble grasping it all. His impression of Brock was still like the good old times before their trio had been injured. Though Denton had visited Brock when he was broken and then again just out of surgery, now he was a completely new man. "I'm really happy for you."

Brock grinned. "Hey, you probably haven't heard Cole's hooked up too."

Denton stared at him. "Cole?"

Brock nodded. "But that's Cole's tale to tell. So I'll let him fill you in." Brock bounced to his feet. "Drink up your coffee. We'll finish the tour and then come back for lunch."

Eager and still stunned by everything he'd seen and learned, Denton polished off his bun and washed it down with the last of his coffee. He looked at the tray. "Where do we put the dirty stuff?"

"You grab it, and I'll take you there." Once they'd dropped off their dishes, they headed into a wide hallway and stopped outside a large elevator door. Brock pushed the button.

"The animal clinic's downstairs, along with some other fun things."

Inside the elevator, Denton's mind spun. *Animals? Other things?* When the elevators opened, the hallway teemed with dogs.

Brock chortled. "Well, what's going on here?"

The receptionist glanced at them. "Hi, Brock. A property seizure was completely overrun with dogs in poor condition. We're waiting on another vet to come in, but the rescue people brought in all the animals at once. We're still sorting them out."

Sadness washed over Denton at the sight of the maltreated animals. Each one's fur was matted and dirty, and he could see scabs and sores. None appeared to have much spirit left within them. He glanced at the receptionist. "Are these all from the seizure?"

"We have twelve from the seizure, but over seventy animals were rescued."

He shook his head. "Is there anything we can do to help?"

The woman looked at him. "Have I seen you here before?"

"I'm Denton." He waved. "I just arrived."

She looked at him. "You probably shouldn't be doing very much then." She glanced at Brock for confirmation.

"He might not do very much yet, but he can certainly reach out a hand and help a scared animal," Brock said. He moved Denton into the center of the room. "Hang on. Let's see what Stan's up to and if he needs more volunteers."

Just then an older man in scrubs stepped from one of the rooms. His gaze landed on Denton and Brock and lit up.

"Hey, guys. Sorry, it's a bit chaotic right now." He turned to the receptionist. "Put these two into the cages. They've been checked over. Let's go through the rest of them one by one and get some treatments started."

Two other women came out of the back rooms. Denton watched as the assistants carefully moved several more dogs into the treatment rooms. He reached for a smaller one—some sort of shaggy-looking crossbreed that could barely see from the mop over its eyes—and smiled sadly when the dog cowered away. Denton immediately pulled back, then let the dog gather its courage just to sniff him on his own. The dog returned again after a few minutes, watched his fingers, and then a tiny tongue came out and licked them. He stroked the animal. "He's trembling in fear."

"Yes. It's been a long day for them already, and they've gone through a lot of trauma and shock. But now that they are here, they'll get fixed up and taken care of, and hopefully they'll all be fine."

As they watched, the vet techs came out again and led the bigger dogs into two different treatment rooms.

Brock reached for a German shepherd, lying on its side, and Denton could see bald patches and scars along its side. The shepherd lay there, staring at Brock with huge eyes. Brock scratched him gently behind the ears. "You'll be fine now, boy. You'll be just fine."

For Denton, it was one more shock to his system. He adored animals, all of them. And to see so many hurting, well … he could feel a lump rising in his throat. "I want to help."

The receptionist stood from behind her desk, shuffling folders. She gave him a gentle smile. "And you certainly can. But one of the best things you can do is get strong enough so you can help yourself. And then you can take on as many volunteer hours in the vet clinic as you want to give."

He nodded. The woman had a valid point.

"The first batch is getting their checkups now," she said. "The rest of the day will be full of shampooing, a lot of fur clipping and many medical treatments. Now that the triage is essentially done, we know who needs treatment first."

Brock nodded. He and Brock stayed for another twenty minutes, gently petting and calming the animals still in the larger room. And while they waited, several other animals were switched out and collected. When they finally left to go upstairs, only four dogs were left that still needed to be checked over. "We'll come back later and see how they're all doing." He glanced down at Denton. "You ready to go?"

Swallowing hard, Denton gave a sharp nod. "Yes."

Quietly the two headed toward the elevator. As he was about to push the button, Brock stopped. "Oh, I got so caught up with the dogs, I forgot to show you what else is down here." He pushed the wheelchair farther down the hall and took a left. As he went, he pointed out the stalls, access to the barns, and the double doors that led out to the pastures. "But we want to go this way." And he took Denton in the other direction. There the double doors opened up to a huge patio and a massive pool.

Denton sat back and stared. A huge smile crept over his face. "Oh, wow. All I want to do is go in there, like, right now."

"And you will. As soon as you get the green light from your health team," Brock said. He pointed out the changing rooms and the hot tub.

Denton could see all the modifications on the pool to help people get in and out—even a motorized seat that moved up and down for those who needed it. "You don't see a pool like this in very many places."

"No. We certainly put it to good use though."

Denton scanned the water, watching three people splashing around. A man was doing laps, a woman sat on the pool's edge, and the other woman was treading water. Denton wasn't sure, but it looked like she didn't have any arms. He stared down at his bad leg and realized, yet again, how lucky he was. He wasn't helpless. And knew he could tread water in the pool without too much trouble. Then he remembered how some of his back muscles had been replaced in his right leg and wondered how that would affect his swimming.

"Don't worry about it."

It was as though Brock had read his mind.

"You'll do what you can do as fast as you can do it, and then you'll improve from that point on." Brock turned him around. "The stairs over there go up to the deck, where we were sitting for coffee before."

Denton nodded. "Too bad there isn't an elevator right here."

"You're right, there isn't, but we use the one back down the hall where we came downstairs. There is also a service elevator, but we're not allowed to use it unless there are exceptional circumstances."

"I guess there isn't that much need for another elevator. Because people don't use one for the vet clinic, correct?"

"Correct. The clinic has its own door on this lower level, and that's what the vet clients use."

Back at the elevator, Brock got them inside and upstairs. "I haven't heard from Cole, but I suggest, given the hour, that we pick a table."

"I'd like to see Cole over lunch, if we get the chance."

"You will, if Cole's in any physical shape to make it. If he's not, then we'll hit his room afterward."

At that thought, Denton fell silent. Because of course, what *he* wanted was only part of the equation. What Cole wanted and what Cole could do—well, that was a whole different story.

They made it back to the same table they'd used before, but now the room had filled up by half. Denton could smell delicious aromas as big bins of food were brought out for the buffet. "I can't believe I'm hungry."

"You need the food to rebuild. They do not cut corners here, and it's all good stuff."

"Denton? Is that you?" Cole raced toward Denton.

Tears stung his eyes. He opened his arms, and Cole threw his arms around him and gave him a huge hug. When he stepped back, Denton looked his buddy up and down.

"Oh, my God, I'm so glad to see you here," Cole said. "I was afraid you couldn't make it."

Denton was completely surprised to see Cole looking as well as he was. He wasn't as fit or as big or as strong and obviously not quite as healthy as Brock. But Cole was still miles away from where Denton currently was. He shook his head. Seeing his two buddies was like a look into his own future, where he might be in a month or two as compared to where he'd be in six months. "Damn. You look good, man."

Cole grinned at him. "It's you who looks good. We're so glad to have you here."

Chapter 4

HANNAH WONDERED WHAT it was about her new awareness that made her see the missing element in her life everywhere. She remembered, back in college, a pregnant woman saying that ever since she found out she was pregnant, all she saw was pregnant women around her. Maybe that was a good thing. Maybe it made her realize she wasn't alone in whatever condition she was in. Hannah seemed to understand how much her lack of friends had impacted her life now that all she saw were other groupings of friends.

Denton may have started this new process that she hadn't noticed earlier, after she'd seen him with Brock. And now Cole was with them. She sat at the far end of the deck, all alone like always. The other staff, although friendly, weren't necessarily friends. And when they did come together, it was usually over meetings or because they had patients to discuss and needed advice from one another. Still meetings but more informal.

After a year of being here, she hadn't made *close* friends. Sure, there were guys like Shane. Stan downstairs. She was friendly with Dani. But not to the point where Hannah arranged to have lunch with them every day. Maybe that was on her. Maybe she had messed up. Maybe she sent out some sort of vibe that said, *Stay back. I want to be alone.*

It's what she knew. And change was hard. Being alone was comfortable. At least it had been up until now. She didn't like it, but she wasn't sure that she *disliked* it enough to make the effort to change it.

Laughter came from the side of the deck where Denton and Brock and Cole sat, which brought her attention once again to the three men. They'd been friends since forever. Been through some of the most grueling training anybody had been through. When they saw one of their friends fall, the others had been there to help. But now that all three had fallen—physically injured, yet on the way to recovery—they were all here to help each other get through this chapter of their lives. It was incredible. It was amazing. It was uplifting.

It was also heartbreaking.

If she were in a car accident right now or some disease or illness overtook her system, who would help her get through the day?

She'd lose her job, and she wouldn't be able to pay her bills. Sure, she had decent medical insurance here, and she would get medical care, but she couldn't continue to live here. She'd have to find another place, and she'd be alone. She had no other friends in town or even close to town, and she would go through whatever healing process was required, either to recovery or to death ... alone.

It was a terrifying thought.

As she'd never faced a major trauma, her lack of friends and family wasn't exactly something she'd had to face. But now that she looked at it closer, she didn't like the gap in her world. Unlike some people, who filled the emptiness in their lives with work and hobbies, she'd just closed the door and acknowledged that that part of her life didn't even exist. That wasn't good either. She stared at the coffee cup in her hand, studying the swirls of coffee at the bottom of the mug. Aimless. Confused. Insecure. Because throughout all this was the question: Why didn't she have friends? And that brought up the next question, which was: What was wrong with her?

She gave a heavy sigh, leaned back in her seat, raised her coffee cup and stared over it at the pasture. Many a day she'd sat here and smiled at the animals, enjoying the view, loving being part of this place. But right now it was hard to see the beauty. All she saw was a single horse in the pasture, which made her instinctively feel there should be two horses. Because, in her mind, she was certain the horse was lonely.

And if she felt the horse was lonely, clearly she was projecting her own loneliness onto the animal. And clearly she felt lonely because she was alone. The two didn't always go together. Often she enjoyed her own company, just have silence around her, that sense of comfort in her own space, but right now, she admitted she was lonely. But for how long had this been? As she kept the door closed on that whole compartment within herself, she wasn't exactly sure she had an answer. Now that she was wondering, however, it seemed like forever. She'd had various friends in school. But not friends she did anything with on the weekends or ones who discussed every detail of their lives with her.

She'd had a couple boyfriends but none lately. Most people preferred to be with a partner so they weren't alone. Her last relationship had only been so-so, and when it had broken off, she hadn't been upset. It was also why she hadn't been too worried about finding another relationship until she found somebody she was really attracted to. No more settling.

So far, that hadn't happened. Until now. Until Denton. Hannah had to wonder if her interest was merely because of that vibrant energy, that sense of gratitude, that sense of *I can do this* which surrounded him and how he had attracted two such good friends. She saw no hint of ego or arrogance, which she was accustomed to seeing from so many people. Neither was there that brokenness inside that she'd seen a lot of. It was like he walked carefully through the middle of all that maze of emotions and did it very successfully. He had charisma. Was that why he had friends? Did he send out a welcoming energy to say, *You're a friend I haven't met yet?*

She wanted to know. At the same time, she was scared to become too friendly with him in case that spark of attraction wasn't mutual. What was it he had that allowed him to make and keep friends? And the people she worked with? What did they have that enabled them to have such good friendships?

Because they did. She saw the staff groupings but hadn't really *seen* them until now. She glanced at Denton once more to see the three men full of joy and laughter with such a sense of welcome and delight in being in each other's company. They'd all been through such hardships, and she was proud of them. Amazed at how well they had handled life when it had reached up and smacked them down.

Insight struck her like a lightning bolt. She wanted to be part of that circle.

As she watched them, Sidney joined them, placing a hand on Brock's shoulder. He looked up at her, and his smile didn't brighten, but it changed. It became more intimate, more loving. Sidney got inside that circle. Sidney had a bright, sunny personality, whereas Hannah was quietly reserved. She was happy to be around others but quite content to retire to her room all alone.

Sidney called out to somebody. Hannah watched as

Sandra walked over, for Cole. Sandra accepted his hand. He tugged her down and tucked her closer and whispered something in her ear. The other men chuckled, and Sandra blushed and rolled her eyes. Hannah was close enough to see the intimacy yet far enough to not hear the conversation. As she studied the five of them, she saw another aspect of Denton that she didn't understand.

He was clearly content to simply be there, content to watch his friends find partners. He didn't show any sign of being jealous or of feeling left out. Instead, his huge expanse of a smile said he was so grateful to be included.

Maybe that was it. Maybe she wasn't happy with her friend world as she wasn't included in much. She knew many people here, but she wasn't part of any inner circles. She was happy to be here—thankful even. But she wasn't particularly grateful for something special in her life. And that was sad.

In fact as she watched Denton for a while longer, she realized how empty her life truly was.

"YOU GUYS LOOK great together," Denton said warmly. "I never thought to see the two of you pair up with such beautiful women."

Brock smiled. "These women are beautiful on the inside as well as beautiful on the outside. I've thought about this. Maybe we had to get so empty inside so that there was room for them. I guess our lives were so full of people before, so many orders, so many routines, so many instructions, and so many things to do in a day that although we had time for relationships, there wasn't nearly as much room for them then as there is now."

"It's not just that," Cole added. "We weren't as welcoming of something at this level because of all the other stuff that filled our days. Our relationships were more superficial as well. That was all we had time for. But now look at us. It's a whole new world out there. And I, for one, want to make the most of it. I feel like I didn't lose ten years of my life but more like my life had gone by so fast I almost missed those ten years. I know the next ten will disappear almost as quickly. And I don't want them to go by in a blur, not knowing anything about what happened. I want to look back and know they were the foundation for the rest of my life. I want them to be happy years. I want to wake up in the morning and smile. I want to go to bed at night with peaceful dreams, not nightmares."

It was hard to miss the whisper of concern across Sandra's face. She squeezed Cole's shoulder gently.

He reached out and patted her hand. "I'm fine. Don't worry. The nightmares haven't started up again."

Denton could see the relief on her face.

"Just checking," she said quietly.

Denton nodded and smiled. "Sounds like nirvana, what you all have."

"That doesn't mean it's not available to you too, Denton," Sandra said. "Maybe you're not at the point yet where you can see the joy of what's to come."

He glanced down at his mangled leg and gave a shrug. "That's possible. It's hard to see anything yet." He raised his gaze and caught sight of Hannah sitting all alone on the other side of the deck. He had assumed she awaited somebody joining her. But now that her meal was done, she sat there alone, her mug in her hand, staring out over the pasture. It was the lonely look on her face that caught his attention. Surely she had friends here. He couldn't imagine working in a place like this without making lots of friends. Then again, he was an extrovert. He made friends easily, always had. He understood some people had to work at it. He always thought that was a shame. But the world was full of all kinds of people. He watched as she put the cup on the table, then pulled her knees to her chest and wrapped her arms around them. As if holding herself in and keeping the rest of the world out.

"Hey, Denton? You there, buddy?"

He pulled away his gaze and glanced at Brock. "I'm here. What did I miss?"

A knowing gaze crossed Brock's face, as he looked where Denton had been staring.

Denton shook his head. "Nothing there, Brock."

"There could be, if you want it to be," Brock said with a big grin.

Cole piped up. "I feel like I'm missing something now." His gaze slipped from one buddy to the other, as if looking for answers.

Denton smiled. "You're not missing anything, yet."

At that point the two women said goodbye to their partners and headed inside the dining hall and back to their various workstations. The men stuck to their schedules and were able to spend their free time however they wanted. But both women were employed at the center. That was a whole different story for them.

Suddenly Brock pounded the table with his palm. His grin widened. "Damn, it's good to have you here, Dent. Who'd have thought all three of us would have made it like this?"

Cole grinned. "Hey, we all survived. That's the most

important part. I'm happy to be alive and with whatever health and physical ability I have now. I know it'll get better—especially with Sandra at my side."

Denton had no one at his side, but he had his friends, and he hoped that, in time, their new partners would become his friends too. The three guys had all had girlfriends in the past and at no point had those relationships been allowed to break up the three men's friendships.

And instinctively he knew that these women wouldn't come between them either. Content in knowing that he had friends who would be there with him through thick and thin, a clan of like-minded people who would grow and develop as their relationships and families grew, he smiled.

He was truly blessed. Denton studied his friends' faces and nodded. "And I'm damn glad to be here too."

Chapter 5

F OR THE NEXT week and a half, Hannah went about her job but constantly noticed groups of people paired up in discussions, both professional and personal. Also, a lot of visitors came back and forth as several families checked out the facilities to see if it was the right place for their loved ones. Other family members came to visit loved ones. Everywhere Hannah looked, she saw togetherness. To combat being overwhelmed by her feelings, she focused on the people who were single at Hathaway. Shane and Stan came to mind, and there were certainly lots of others. Stan had a life downstairs with his own staff. She didn't know a whole lot about them. But as she gravitated away from the friend groups, she realized she was gravitating more toward people who were single.

As if singles would be more likely to become her friend, instead of trying to make friends with groups of people who were already linked together. She felt like she was on the outside, figuring out a way to get inside. That was wrong. It felt like high school all over again. She'd hated that time. She didn't want to fall into that same kind of mentality.

She walked to her office, sat down at her desk and worked through some patient files. Medical updates were to be entered manually into the computer. Bills needed to be processed, and there was always paperwork.

Dani walked in, a cup of coffee in hand, and sat down in Hannah's visitor chair. "Okay, so tell me what's wrong."

Hannah glanced at her in surprise. "What do you mean, *what's wrong?*"

"You," Dani said, her tone light. "The last few days you've been different."

Hannah winced. "Has it been that obvious?"

Dani nodded. "For someone who knows you and works with you every day, yes."

"Sorry. I've been thinking a lot about friends and friend groups and not having friends." She gave a weak half laugh. "The minute your mind picks up on a problem around you, all you see are the things that you don't have."

"Haven't you made friends here?" Dani asked carefully. "Everyone has lovely things to say about you and your performance."

Hannah smiled at her. "And that's all great because we also live here and work here. It's important that we also have a life that includes more than a working relationship. Friends are everywhere here. And I'm not one of them, it seems." She forced a smile. "Is anything wrong with me?" Dani's eyebrows rose in surprise, and Hannah quickly added, "I've been more introspective lately."

"There's nothing wrong with a little introspection at times," Dani said slowly, "but don't let it get carried away. I don't think there's anything wrong with you, Hannah. It may be that you're still fairly new here, and you're a hard worker who spends a lot of time on her job."

"I certainly understand that," Hannah said in relief. "Since I arrived at Hathaway House, I haven't taken the time to grow close to anybody else here." She smiled ruefully. "And that's probably not healthy either."

Dani nodded. "It does make sense that, if your entire life is wrapped up here, you should have other friends off the property or make friends here so that you can do things away from work. Just because you live here, it doesn't mean you have to be completely focused on this place."

"That's what I was thinking. But I don't know how to meet the people who do other things." She studied Dani. "And if I'm feeling that way, are others? Like, some of the patients maybe too?"

Dani glanced around the small office thoughtfully. "Maybe we need to organize more outings. For the ambulatory patients especially. Let's plan a social trip to town. See if we have a group of ten who we can take to the mall and out for lunch to the park ... maybe pick out a few sightseeing or shopping places that people want to go to."

"That's not a bad idea," Hannah agreed. "It might help to develop relationships for those patients who are isolated or only briefly get hugs. It can be lonely here," she admitted. "I hadn't realized how lonely I was until the last few days."

"Because of Denton's arrival?" Dani asked.

Hannah nodded. "And that's silly. Denton, Brock and Cole were friends long before they came here."

"True enough." Dani smiled. "And since you came here, we've also seen a surge in other relationships developing. Of which Aaron and I are a prime example. And the trend is continuing. Seeing that can make people want more than what they have."

"Exactly," Hannah said, deciding she'd whined enough. "A field trip next week sounds like fun."

Dani stood. "Put together a basic proposal. Give me some ideas of where and what people would like to do. Go talk to the ambulatory patients. We'll start with them.

Otherwise we'd have to bring a whole staffing crew with us to help out."

"Can do. But maybe we could do something modified for the less ambulatory patients. Just getting them out on the grounds, around the horses. And a picnic for them too. Regardless, how about I start small with the trip to town, and we'll see how it goes?"

"Sounds good. Let me know what you come up with." With that, Dani left Hannah's office. Surprisingly Hannah felt better. For the moment at least.

Notebook in hand, Hannah made her way to some of the patients, looking for suggestions and those wanting to participate in a field trip. When she got to Denton's room, she found him sitting slumped on his bed, his face flushed and sweaty.

She knocked and hesitantly stepped inside. "How are you, Denton? Looks like you've had a rough day so far."

He wiped his face with the towel in his hand. "I'm pretty tired," he admitted. "Who knew that recovery from an injury could be so harsh? In the military, we went through all kinds of physically strenuous exercise. We were constantly in training, constantly running, constantly doing feats. To be honest, it was harder than anything we'd ever done before." He shook his head. "There were times when I was taken to the edge of my endurance. My spirit was so low I felt I was done. That I was physically finished." He gave her a wan smile. "But I hit that point faster than I ever thought possible here."

She crossed her arms and stepped into his room. "Remember though, you are just starting out so don't be hard on yourself. What got you through those tough times in the military?" she asked curiously.

"My friends," he said. "Brock and Cole. They got me

through the tough times. There was one time where I quit. I was done for. I knew I couldn't take one more step. They wouldn't listen to me. They grabbed me by the arms and dragged me forward. Because if I could take one more step on my own, then several more steps would help me get there. I let them help. That was a huge wakeup call for me. I was letting somebody else help me make my dreams happen. It's hard to admit when you need help. Yet, it's a great thing to understand that when you need help, somebody is there who cares." He collapsed backward on the bed and groaned. "Holy crap, I'm tired."

"Did you get lunch?" she asked.

He shook his head. "I'm trying to motivate myself to get something to eat. I need to. I'm really hungry, but I'm so tired."

"I'd suggest that you use the wheelchair, but I don't want to hurt your feelings."

He raised his head and looked at her. "If I could get into the wheelchair, I could probably help myself." He pushed himself into a sitting position, clearly wincing as he moved sore muscles. He glanced at the wheelchair and then at her. "Is it too late to eat?"

She glanced at her tablet. "It's one-thirty. You still have time." She walked to the wheelchair parked in the corner of his room and pushed it toward him. When it was right beside him, she said, "It's your choice."

He smiled and slowly made his way into the chair. Once he was seated, he collapsed and relaxed. "Lord, that feels better. Just the thought of forcing that leg and foot into any more exercise today is beyond me."

She hesitated. "Can you get yourself there, or would you like me to help?"

"YOU KNOW? I'M so tired I won't be too proud to accept the offer of help." He inclined his head in her direction. "If you have a few moments, thank you. I could use a push."

She grinned. "It's nice to see you won't be stubborn."

He chuckled. "Oh, stubbornness I got in spades. The learning to give ... the wanting to accept ... remembering to be appreciative?" he said. "That's a talent."

She stepped behind the wheelchair and pushed him forward through the doorway. "Well, from what I can see, you got that talent down pat. I wish I did." Her voice had a serious tone to it.

He twisted to look up at her. "What do you mean?"

"I mean, you have the ability to make friends and keep friends. I was talking to Dani about it today. The three of you—Brock, Cole and you." She upped the wattage of her smile. "I, on the other hand, don't. Not real friends. Although if I had, would they become something I'd depend on now? I don't know."

He settled in as they rolled down the hallway toward the dining hall. "Something about being in BUD/s training instinctively let the three of us know that we had to help each other to make it through. It wasn't that anybody could make you run the miles when you wore down. You had to find that strength within yourself. But what about when you couldn't find it? That's when your friends pushed you, urging you to keep up, to dig deep. It helped knowing that you weren't alone. Knowing they were struggling too. It's hard when it looks like you're the only one who's not doing so well. The self-confidence takes a hit, and it's hard to recover from that."

"I can imagine," she said quietly. "You have a lot to be proud of in your life."

He nodded. "Just because my life went in a different direction, that doesn't mean it isn't full of good things."

She gave a light laugh that sounded false. "Maybe and maybe not. I can't see myself feeling terribly overjoyed by what I've accomplished so far."

"Particularly with friends, I gather?" He wanted to twist and look up at her again, but that was awkward and pretty hard on his back. But he could tell from the silence as she pushed him down the hallway and from the wheels silently spinning beneath them that he had hit the target. "I don't mean to hurt you," he said hesitantly. "I'm not sure that making friends is such a talent as much as it's the opportunity in accepting and taking up opportunities from crossing paths."

She stayed quiet, so he tried again.

"Meaning that it takes the right people at the right time under the right circumstances to click. And probably a lot of good people are here, and you're all doing the same things, but it can be a little easier to be friends and coworkers at the same time when you live here."

"Quite possibly." At that, she stopped at the large door-way. "Where do you want to sit?"

"Outside," he said. "Any chance I get, I like to be outside."

She pushed the wheelchair to the start of the buffet line.

He turned to look up at her. "Thanks for the assist." He gave her a big grin. Then seeing the uncertain look on her face, he asked in a gentle voice, "Have you eaten?"

She shoved her hands into the pockets of her long sweater and shook her head. "No, I guess time went by so fast this morning that I missed it," she confessed.

"In that case, this is one of those times where the right circumstances and the right people have come together, and they clicked." He grinned at her. "Come have lunch with me."

She hesitated, and he watched her inner struggle play out on her face. But then she stepped up behind him and said, "I might eat a little. I'm not terribly hungry." She grabbed two trays and put one in front of him and hers behind.

"You should eat. Particularly if you're worried about something. Stress is a killer on your stomach. Something I already know. I worried myself crazy for a long time and developed ulcers. Not fun."

"Normally I'm not a worrywart. But now, some of these self-revelations are a little harder to accept."

They stopped in front of the hot food. He couldn't see all the dishes, but he could read the labels on top.

"Let me help. What would you like?" she asked quickly.

It was Asian-fusion day. She efficiently filled his plate with a selection of foods that fit into his diet. They carried on past the others as she loaded up coffee and drinks for both of them. With the cutlery now on her tray, she looked around the room. "Left or right?"

He wondered, confused for a moment, then realized a pathway led to a set of tables on other side of the room. "The path of least resistance," he joked.

"That means right." She looked at his tray. "You ready to try this on your lap, or do you want me to take my tray and come back and get yours?"

A voice beside them piped up. "Not to worry, I'm right here," Dennis said. "I'll follow along with Denton's tray."

Together, the trio made their way to one of the larger

tables sitting in the sun. Denton pulled up to the end where there were no chairs, and Dennis placed Denton's tray in front of him. They quickly removed everything off the tray and waited while Hannah unloaded hers. Then Dennis took the empty trays.

"Thank you, Dennis," both Denton and Hannah said in unison.

Denton lifted his face to the sun and closed his eyes. "This is simply wonderful," he murmured.

"We don't get that attitude very often in the first few days here," she said.

"That's too bad. People need to be more thankful for the simple things in life." He picked up his fork and speared a large piece of broccoli. He popped it into his mouth and smiled. "Perfect. Crunchy, fresh with a beautiful sauce." On that note, he dove into the rest of his meal. He watched as she picked her way through a much smaller portion of everything.

When he was halfway done, he motioned at her plate. "Eat up."

She glanced at him with a smile. "Isn't that my line?"

He chuckled. "Nobody's had to tell me to clean my plate since I was able to sit up on my own."

At that, she laughed out loud.

He was delighted to hear it. Her laughter was light and musical, turning heads and raining down across the deck. He doubted she had any idea how lovely she was. "You should do that more often."

She raised an eyebrow at him. "What? Laugh?"

He nodded. "Yes, exactly that." He gave her a wicked smile. "That sound lights up the whole room." And he picked up his fork and finished his meal.

Chapter 6

WHEN SHE FINISHED eating, Hannah pulled her coffee toward her, tucked her legs underneath her and settled back against the bench. She leaned one arm on the top of the railing and looked out over the pasture. "Dani's done such a beautiful job with this place."

"She has, indeed. I haven't gotten to meet the Major though. I understand he's quite a character."

She glanced at Denton, surprised. "Major hasn't come by to say hi?"

Denton shook his head. "But then again I haven't been here very long."

"True enough. He is quite a character, like everyone says."

"And the reason Dani started this place, right?" He looked up as if to assess Hannah's answer.

Hannah nodded. "Her father was an injured veteran and in rough shape. As he slowly improved, he and Dani created this business."

Denton raised his eyebrows. "Now that's having a passion and a purpose." He pushed away his empty plate and rubbed his tummy. "That feels a whole lot better."

She chuckled. "Nothing like good food to change your attitude."

"In this case, it was more about needing food to give me

some energy before I collapsed."

"Too much of a workout this morning?"

"I don't think so. Some days are better than others."

She studied him and realized he had no intention of saying more. He wasn't the kind to whine about something he couldn't change. He focused on what he could do, being appreciative of everything that was here and available for him. "I could learn a lot from you," she admitted. "You seem to have your priorities straight."

He shot her a piercing gaze. "So do you. You're here. You're helping people—that's huge."

"I don't have the skills I would like to have," she said, "and although I like this job and I like living here, it's been a little lonely."

He tilted his head to the side to watch her curiously. "And yet, you're surrounded by people."

"Back to that ... not sure I have what it takes to make good friends."

He shook his head. "You are really friendly. I haven't noticed anything odd in that way."

She chuckled. "How could you? You barely know me."

He lifted a finger and waggled it at her. "Not true. I've known you for what, ten days now?" He grinned. "In some parts of the world, that's long enough to get married."

At that, she laughed out loud again. "Well, I've never been married, so I wouldn't know."

He nodded. "Neither have I." That wicked grin flashed once more. "See? Now we've got all the preliminaries out of the way."

"You're incorrigible." She picked up her coffee cup, surprised to find her cheeks felt hot. Was she blushing? Was he flirting with her? How long had it been since she'd had a man do that? When she'd come here, she'd been happy to focus on helping others as she'd had such a hard time getting to know very many people at her old job. She had worked in a large legal firm, and it had been a lot of work with not a whole lot of time off, and all she'd done was return to her empty place and repeat the next morning. Here, her job was people more so than papers. And it was a good thing because it was making her a little more social, a little more comfortable in her own skin. And maybe that was the trick. She'd been intimidated at the law office. She'd done her best, but when she'd seen this job advertised, she had applied and had no trouble walking away from the other one.

She'd been here a year, and although she certainly didn't feel the way she had before, she hadn't warmed up to others and quickly found the group of friends that she'd secretly hoped for. And yet, she knew that was her fault. When her shifts were done, she ate—usually alone, sometimes with others—and then went to her room. She went for a lot of solo walks and drove by herself into town on a regular basis, but she hadn't reached out either. She hadn't asked any of the staff to accompany her on those excursions. She was always friendly but never a friend.

"Heavy thoughts?"

She raised her head to meet his gaze and smiled. "Just a further realization that, although I've been friendly, I haven't been terribly welcoming or inviting of others into my life."

"Maybe that's a good thing," he said. "It takes time to settle in, and it takes time to trust those around us. To know who they are. Don't settle into a new place too quickly or jump in to make friends right away. Sometimes it's better to understand who they all are and decide which ones you want to make friends with first."

"Oh, I've done that. But sadly it's time to stretch a little more."

"So why not go around and ask people if they want to ride to town with you and what they like to do?"

She studied his face suspiciously, but he seemed genuinely curious. "We're organizing a trip to town for the more mobile patients," she said. "Depending on where and what people would like to do, we'll run several such trips. For people who like to go shopping we will do a trip to the mall. Some people might want to get out and do something at the parks if that's possible."

"Although I have challenges, I wouldn't mind seeing more of the area. A day trip sounds great."

She smiled. "I'll put your name down on the list then, pending your medical team's approval. What is it you'd like to do? Go for a drive to get away, or do you need to go shopping for something in particular?"

He frowned. "I don't think I have anything I *need* to do. Although, if a bank is close by, I could use an ATM machine."

"Okay." She nodded. "I'll let you know what days we set up and which places we'll go to." She stood. "Do you need a hand back to your room?" She picked up their two coffee cups and waited for his answer.

He shook his head. "I have another fifteen minutes until my session with the doctor this afternoon. I think I'll stay right here and enjoy the sun a little while longer."

She held up his coffee cup. "You want a refill?"

He glanced at it and shook his head. "Nope, thanks. I'll sit here, relax, close my eyes, and I'll take my time getting back to my room." He glanced at her. "But thank you for your help."

She shrugged. "Anytime." She walked back inside and deposited the dirty cups on the appropriate cart.

Dennis winked at her. "Is this another shipboard romance happening?"

She shook her head. "Not likely."

He studied her intently for a long moment. "Not so sure about that. Looks to me like a nice pairing."

She flushed again, made her excuses and hurried off to her office. His chuckle followed. She winced. The last thing she wanted was for anyone to know how much she liked Denton. But apparently, it was already obvious.

Inside though, the thought of a romance between the two of them was enough to make her heart smile. Nothing would come of it, of course, but that didn't mean she couldn't enjoy the moment.

Then she'd need to move back to reality—and fast.

DENTON WAS LUCKY. Luckier than he thought. So many things came easily for him. But talking with Hannah made him realize that, for some people, making friends was hard. She appeared to be a lovely person. But friendships developed over time. Good friends were there through the hard times, not just the good times. Of course, the BUD/s training had brought him and Brock and Cole together. It was the worst time of his life, but it was also one of the best. And if someone didn't have an experience like that in their life, with people at their side, Denton could imagine it would be hard to bond at that level. He also had to remember that, just because he had friends here, the work was still his to do. His friends would be there to cheer him, but Denton was the one who had to take those steps.

He was the one who had to do the work and to show the progress. He was the one who had to go from point A to point B, and if he didn't make it, it was all on him. And that was one thing he knew he avoided really looking at. He was trying hard to be here, trying hard to do whatever needed to be done, but there was a lot of pressure. It wasn't that they used the pressure to make him advance—it was pressure he was putting on himself. It didn't have to be that way. But he didn't want to be less of a success story than his friends were. He didn't want them to look at him and point out his performance. He didn't want to lose their respect because he fell and gave up.

Was he worrying too much about their opinion? They were friends but still ... he'd always been his own man. At least in his head, but things were different here ... he hated the feeling but insecurity ate at him. And he found himself questioning everything he did.

That was something about having friends. You wanted them to admire what you'd done. You wanted them to feel proud of you. But when they didn't feel proud of you, you also needed them to get in your face and say, *Buck up and go on. No room here for slackers.*

If recovery had taught him one thing, it was that a whole group of people in rehab gave up early on. These people said the work was too much. They achieved a certain level of health, and that was okay. It was an acceptable level for them, and then they didn't try anymore. Because the rest of it was hard. It was *really* hard. The pain was incredible for the level of physicality that they were expected to do.

The delving into psychological issues and fears was equally as hard. And he knew that bothered him the most.

He'd barely even touched the surface with his group counselor. Denton had so much to be grateful for that he got impatient at himself for being so afraid. Even if it was natural. As if he expected to be above that. Unlike a lot of people, he didn't have a network of business associates ready to offer him jobs or money. He didn't have a wife to go home to or children who didn't care what kind of shape he was in, yet were simply happy that he came home.

He was alone. His mother had passed away a few years back. His friends were here, but they also had their own lives. And for the first time, Denton realized that with them having partners, those relationships could easily end up in marriage. His friends could end up developing families and different lives away from him. He'd never considered that.

Even while they were all doing their military thing, Denton knew there was a possibility of all of them going in opposite directions once they left the military. But that was sometime out in the distant future. When it came sooner than expected and in an unlikely way, they all were doing their best to get back on their feet, and automatically that meant getting back together again. That they came together to heal was huge. But as they healed, the faster they moved on with their individual lives. The others were moving at a faster rate than Denton was. But it wasn't the rate that bothered him. It was the fact that, as they moved on, they might move far away.

People had a lot more opportunities to maintain friendships over long distances because of the Internet, but it wasn't the same as having the guys right next door—barbecues in the backyard, slinging beer on a Friday night, closing the day down.

Denton was tired, but he still had to return to his room

to deal with the next item on his schedule.

He needed his appointment with the shrink today. She appeared to be very knowledgeable and very intuitive. Almost too intuitive. He slowly made his way to his room. This session would be in his room, and that was a darn good thing. The only good thing about the whole appointment was being able to get out of the chair and up onto the bed, maybe even put a blanket over his legs. He already felt chilled now because he knew the next session would be hard emotionally.

It was also hard to rip yourself apart, figuring out what was wrong on the inside and what was stopping you from being the best you could be in handling all the things thrown at you. You had to get away from the guilt of getting injured and to stop playing the blame game—both difficult to walk away from.

Why had it been him? Why hadn't it been someone else? Why had he been the one in the unit assigned to this post? Why had he been asked to drive that truck? And the blame just continued. He hadn't thought he held very much of that inside. But the more his therapist dug in, the more she prodded, and the more she poked, he realized that, indeed, although he may not have had much of his anger visible, he still held a lot of it inside. He knew it was also necessary to get rid of it, but purging one's soul was darn hard.

He was grateful when he got to his room and realized the psychologist hadn't arrived yet. He made his way to the side of the bed, and using the bed for support, he slowly stood up, again hating the shakiness of his limbs. He sat down, shuffled his butt until he was leaning against the headboard and pulled up the blanket from the end of the bed over his legs. As he studied his damaged calf, a tremor rippled up and down the muscles. He pulled the calf toward him and gently massaged it. He had a cream the therapist had given him. He opened that tube, put some cream on his fingers and slowly worked it deep into the muscle. He knew it was better than before, but it was hard to see any improvement from ten days ago.

In fact, the improvements were all about pain. He was digging deeper, and that was an improvement. He was pushing himself harder, and that was an improvement. But he wasn't seeing the results he wanted to see. He was becoming impatient. After a ton of hard work and time, he wanted to see the results. And he understood in his own mind how hard Brock must have worked because Denton had seen how Brock had been right after his accident.

Brock had been flat on his back and in terrible shape. To see the man now, well, there was absolutely zero comparison. The same for Cole. Denton understood a lot about what had happened to Cole when he'd first arrived. He had teased him about it gently because Cole had always felt like he was playing catch-up. Denton hadn't felt the same way. But in one way, he did understand Cole's competitiveness, Cole's need to prove himself in light of Brock's rehab success.

Raised with little money, and often with government subsidies or charity, Denton always had a sense of *I don't deserve this. People are doing this because I'm injured.* It was the same as when he was growing up—people would be nice to him because his mother was poor, and his life must, therefore, really suck. It was hard to argue with that logic.

But this left an underlying fear that he hadn't gotten anywhere on his own. Case in point, like it had taken others to get him here to Hathaway House.

A lot of things about his life hadn't been easy. But he

had loved his mom. They'd been very close. The two of them had as much fun as any father, mother and son combination could have, but no doubt, there had been hard times. It was difficult to see other families operate in a typically normal way versus what he had experienced. When she'd died, he'd turned to Brock and Cole. And they'd been there for him.

As he lay here, tired, worn out and with a full tummy, he heard a knock at the door. He rolled his head to the side and smiled when he saw Dr. Hutchinson. "Good afternoon, Doc."

She smiled and waved at him. "Considering you're in bed, maybe I should say *good evening*. Are you ready to sleep? Had a tough morning?"

Her gaze was intense, and he knew her eyes understood so much more than he would like. That was one thing about the people here—it didn't matter which staff member was helping him, it was like they all could see into his soul.

"I am more tired than usual." He stretched out his bad leg, closed the tube of cream and pulled the blanket back over it. "That doesn't mean I don't have enough energy to talk with you though."

She chuckled. "Our sessions don't always have to be difficult."

"So you say," he said, knowing he sounded slightly cynical. "But it hasn't exactly been easy so far."

"It's not like you're in tears and angry about any of it."

He shrugged. "What good would that do?"

She nodded, then pulled up a chair and sat down beside him. "So, tell me the truth. How do you feel about being here?"

He had to think about it for a long moment, and then

he was as honest as he could be. "I'm very pleased to be here."

"Would you have gotten the same care, the same advantages, the same improvements elsewhere?"

He nodded. "Quite likely I could have. But here I have the added benefit of having both my buddies with me."

"How does that make you feel?"

He smiled. "Loved, secure, happy and grounded."

And damned if she didn't come at him with another dozen questions. He did his best to answer everything. As he'd found out with her, every time they had a session, a little bit more of himself was revealed. Sometimes that was good, sometimes bad.

"Do you feel that your friends are responsible for your improvement?"

He shook his head. "No. They created their milestones ahead of me, and they're cheerleaders, but when the work is there in front of me, only one person has to do it, and that's me. They have their own work to look after. It's up to me to deal with mine."

"Good answer. Have you made any attempt to meet new friends?"

He frowned at her. "You asked that last time, and I thought it odd then too."

She shrugged. "I need to know that you aren't closing yourself off from other people. You came here with the expectation of having friends already in place, and often we find that means people aren't open to making new connections."

Her words somewhat echoed Hannah's earlier comment, and he settled back and considered that. "I'd like to think I am open to making new friends. But you may be right. I came knowing I had friends and a friend group already in place, and I didn't worry about anything else."

"And you think that's good for you?"

He shrugged. "I don't know what's good for me anymore. And I can only handle so many self-improvement things on a day-to-day basis, and if that's not one of them, then that's not one of them. I have to do what's best for me right now, not what might be good for other people." He studied her carefully. "Has anybody complained that I've been unfriendly?"

"I have no idea," she said. "I haven't heard any. I wondered if you were feeling open to making new friends or if you feel you're complete with the two you have."

He shifted uncomfortably on the bed. Once again Hannah's face and her comment about having difficulty making friends rose to the forefront. "I don't know," he said, his tone short.

"Well, think about it over the next few days, and let me know if anything comes to mind." She checked her watch. "I'm afraid we'll have a short session today. I have to deal with a couple patients coming and going."

He hated that his insides jumped for joy. He hoped it wasn't something he had said or one of his answers. Because it would make him feel like he needed to work on something else. What he wanted was to relax and not work on anything. He wanted to have a normal day.

She stood. "I understand they are arranging some trips into town. Are you interested in going?"

"Hannah already signed me up." He waited, wondering if that was all she would ask. But she smiled and nodded and wrote something down on her tablet that worried him. She made her way to the door.

He couldn't help himself. "What did you just write down?"

She raised an eyebrow. "A note about you wanting to go into town." She gave him a brighter smile and then left.

And for the first time in a long time, he wasn't sure he believed her.

He hated the worry, the doubts. That was one thing about his medical team. They were here for him, but at the same time, he wanted to know what they saw when they looked at him.

He thought he was doing fine—or was he deluding himself?

Chapter 7

IF HANNAH HAD known how much fun it would be setting up trips to town, she would have proposed the idea ages ago. Over the next few days she found herself enjoying having the chance to talk to all the different patients, to see what it was they were looking for in an outing—to shop and to visit people. Some wanted to get out because the walls were closing in on them, and they needed a change of scenery. Some had brought up activities, like bowling or seeing a movie. Several wanted to go to the mall because they needed clothing or stuff that they hadn't had a chance to pick up themselves, and others needed to replenish personal hygiene items. She made extensive notes, then a couple days later met with Dani. She sat down in the visitor's chair and smiled at her boss.

"That was fun and a little frustrating."

Dani's grin widened, and she leaned back in her chair.

"We have fourteen requests to go to town. Of those, ten would like to go on the first trip, if possible."

"Well, we were looking for ten. So that works."

"Sure, but none of them agree on what they want to do. One wants to see a movie. Another wants to visit the dentist." Hannah raised her eyebrows as she glanced over at Dani. "Never even occurred to me that somebody here might need to go to the dentist, but of course, you don't have a dentist or hygienist coming here, do you?"

Dani chuckled. "Nope, we sure don't. We arrange for the dentist or optometrist trips as required. Some must go in for the prosthetic engineering, et cetera. We set these visits up all the time. But I'm not sure that should be part of a social outing."

Hannah agreed. "Several want to go shopping. Some need shaving gear. Some need a couple more T-shirts, underwear, socks—that type of thing. Everybody was excited at the idea of getting out."

"Good. So, if we remove the one who needs to go to the dentist—I'll make arrangements for him on his own—that leaves nine, correct?"

"Yes, but I'm thinking Roger might still want to go out for the day. A dental trip can be handled separately, but I don't think he should come off the list."

"Okay, we can take ten but half that would be better. We also wanted to keep this as a fun social trip, not for shopping, but might manage to combine it. We'll have the driver and some other staff, depending on the ambulatory level of those going," she said. "Let me see the list."

Hannah handed over the sheet of paper.

Dani took a few moments to peruse it. "These people are all good candidates for this field trip. Every one of them can handle their own wheelchair or crutches. They are all ambulatory. We will go to a park if that's what they want. We can even arrange to have either a picnic with food from the kitchen or we can pick up food in town and take it to the park."

"What about the movie?"

Dani shrugged. "We can certainly drop off some people at the movie theater, but it would have to be a matinee, and while they are at the movie, the others could be shopping." She glanced up at Hannah. "See if you can get the movie-goers to agree on a movie at the Theodore."

"Also several of the patients asked who was paying for this."

Dani glanced up and frowned. "The center will absorb the cost of the gas, the driver, lunch if it's a picnic basket from here and providing the staff. But the individual patients will be required to look after things like their own movie theater tickets and their shopping purchases and if we choose lunch out."

"Okay, that's more than fair. That'll make several of them quite happy."

Dani gave her a sharp look. "Are you hearing any concerns about money from anybody?"

Hannah sat back and thought for a moment. "I think a couple people were grumbling a bit about not having enough. But in this case, I would be a little more concerned if people didn't have the money to get things like socks and underwear," she confessed.

After talking with Dani, Hannah took her notes back to her desk. One of the best things about this job was the variety of the tasks she got to do. And the people she had a chance to work with. The atmosphere here was different. Sometimes it was sober, sometimes it was a delight. Every-body cheered and joined in each other's personal successes. But it was equally hard when there were difficulties. There had been quite a kerfuffle when Cole had had to go back to the hospital. There was a lot of soul-searching going on in the staff meetings, to see if they could've done something better.

So far, she'd been blessed to see so many people improve

to the point of leaving and to watch new people arrive. There was nothing quite like watching the progress of someone doing something as simple as getting a cup of coffee. They struggled in the beginning and within a few months had no problems whatsoever. Attitude, physical ability and perception of their life completely changed in a short period of time.

Of course that brought her mind right around to Denton again. She decided to sweep through the dining hall and get a coffee rather than any of the other spots in the building that housed coffeemakers. She knew she wasn't fooling anyone, least of all herself.

If he just so happened to be there, she could walk over to say hi. And it would give her a chance to talk to him about the outing as planned. She thought he would like to go no matter what the trip entailed. She well understood the need to get out once in a while—to see something different, do something out of the routine. She just had to see if his medical team approved this day trip.

She entered the dining hall, her notepad tucked under her arm, and headed toward the coffee bar. Her cup poured, she stood there for a long moment, and then surveyed the space.

Dennis was there, cleaning tables. She smiled at him. "How's your day going, Dennis?"

He looked up and beamed a smile at her. "It's going great. How about you?"

She nodded. "It's good. It's one thing about being here—most of the days are good."

He nodded and laughed. "There are a lot of good things about this place. But that sense of hope and achievement, those are hard to beat. We are lucky enough to get the benefit of everybody else's hard work." He shook his head as he walked past. "It's hard to not feel proud when seeing so many other people achieve things in their lives."

Hannah carried her coffee out to the deck and stood for a moment, letting the sun bathe her face. Dennis was right. Being here was a hell of an achievement, and she was lucky to witness all of the patients' successes. As she turned to head back to her office, she saw Denton making his way on his crutches toward Dennis. There was a short conversation, and then Dennis quickly disappeared into the back. She wondered what was up.

Denton made his way to the closest table and sat down heavy and hard. He looked completely wiped out. Immediately she headed for him. "Denton, are you okay?" She didn't mean to sound so worried, but she was.

The look on his face was just awful.

DENTON GAVE HER a brief smile. "I'm fine, but my blood sugar's completely wiped out. I tell you, there are days when I have to wonder if I am diabetic."

"Have you been tested?"

He nodded. "I have a super high metabolism and have to watch the balance of sugars versus proteins. Dennis is getting me some food." He gave her a boyish smile that was more cheerful than the first one he'd attempted. "The good news is, I get to eat a lot."

That moment Dennis came back with a tray he placed in front of Denton. The plate was filled with an assortment of fresh fruit and nuts.

"Not bad ... protein, fats, carbs and fruit for easy sugar," she said, studying his snack.

"Exactly." He lifted the fork, and she was amazed to see how much of an effort it appeared to be for him. A tremor ran through his hand as he took several bites.

She figured it would probably take ten to fifteen minutes before his system realized food was coming. She pulled out a chair. "Would you mind company?"

He waved at her. "Please, sit. I'm so sorry. I should've invited you to join me. My manners now are nonexistent."

She chuckled softly. "You have a lot more things to worry about than your manners." She watched him eat for a minute. "How about I get you a cup of coffee to go with that?"

He glanced at her, and his face broke into a grateful smile. "Thank you. But I can get it myself. You know you don't have to wait on me, right?"

She shook her head, rose and brought over the coffee. "Sometimes it's nice to help people."

He was obviously feeling better because his grin deepened. "Besides, that's what friends do."

She chuckled, remembering their early discussion. "Absolutely."

He polished off his food and pushed back his plate with a happy sigh. "Now that's a whole lot better."

"Does this happen a lot?"

He shook his head. "I didn't have enough for breakfast. My mistake. I won't do that again."

She nodded, watching him carefully as the color returned to his face, and the absolute sheer fatigue slipped off his features. "It's amazing how quickly that helped."

"I'll be back to normal within another few minutes." He studied her for a long moment. "You know? I have been thinking a lot about the discussion we had the other day. About friends. I realized there's one thing that you do very well that I need to learn to do."

She looked at him in surprise. "What's that?"

"Stand on my own two feet when I need to—without friends to support me."

Chapter 8

H ANNAH STARED AT him in surprise. "Why is that an issue?"

He toyed with his coffee cup for a long moment before he looked at her and gave her the ghost of a smile. "Well, Brock is leaving in only two to three weeks or so. But only because I was talking to you did I consider it. One of the reasons I was so excited to come here was because my friends were here. Friends who have always been part of my adult life, helping me get through the tough times. Not sure I would have gotten through it without them."

She sat back. "I'm sure you could have," she said warmly.

"But I don't *know* that I could," he said with a gentle smile. "It's not been something I've ever had to do. It's not that I've ever been tested to be sure."

"What about growing up?"

He shrugged. "A rural high school and elementary school was normal." He chuckled. "I know I had friends. It's one of the reasons why, when I was at BUD/s training, it was easy for me to sort through and pick out people who I knew were my kind. And teamwork has always been a big part of military life. Particularly in my case. Our unit was tight. We are brothers, and we always had each other's back. And that hasn't changed, even though the three of us are out of the navy now. That we're all injured and that we're all here adds to the fact that we're helping each other."

"Are you afraid that if Brock and Cole weren't here, you wouldn't do as well?"

He winced, then nodded. "Maybe a little."

She tilted her head and considered the issue. "For myself, I've always been mostly alone. I kept trying to look for people who were of my mind-set, but I never really succeeded."

"I keep coming back to a fundamental question. If I had been injured first and if I'd have come here alone, would I have done as well as Brock?"

She stared at him, seeing the earnestness, the determination, the absolute knowledge that he'd had a helping hand when Brock didn't. And the worry that Denton couldn't have done as well on his own.

"I don't know, but I believe you would have. It's not that you had friends to help you do the actual rehab here, but they were a kind of a security blanket, knowing that, if you ever needed somebody to call on or someone to talk to, they were there."

"Absolutely. But Brock had to do it himself. Brock had to stand on his own two feet to make this happen. Cole came in, and he was so busy playing catch-up with Brock he almost lost his way. But because Brock was here and the others were here to help Cole slow down and to give him a chance to be here on his own, he picked up and is doing well. But now I've arrived, and of course, already this whole group was here waiting for me, like a safety net. That made it easier on me."

"What's wrong with that?" she exclaimed. "This isn't meant to be a battle of the toughest or a test for the best-mental-fitness-single-performance. Every one of you has different challenges and issues to overcome. It's not been easy for anybody."

He settled back, staring at his coffee.

She leaned forward and gently placed her hand on top of his. "I'm so sorry if I made you doubt yourself. That's not what I intended at all."

His gaze lifted, and he studied her. "You had nothing to do with me doubting myself. I think a part of me says I'm not as good as the other two because this wasn't easier for me."

She shook her head. "Why does any of this matter? This is hard enough for all of you." She glared at him. "If you need to have some kind of a test to see how you do without your friends, pick something that doesn't matter quite so much. This is when you *need* your friends. Be grateful you have them."

"I am grateful," he said sincerely. "Don't get me wrong. It makes me wonder how I would fare on my own. It's not that I'm being competitive because I'm not."

It never occurred to her that he would question such a thing. She'd been alone so much of her life, looking on the outside of all these groups, wondering how to become part of them, and instead he was inside one of the groups, wondering if he could stand without support from that same group. She shook her head. "I can't say it's anything I ever wondered about."

"That's because you have yourself. When things get down, you know you can buck up."

"So can you." She leaned forward earnestly. "More than most people. You did what was necessary—you made it. And now you're lucky enough to have friends on your side to help you get through another difficulty. Don't ever doubt that you're incapable of doing it on your own."

He gave her a sheepish grin and nodded. "Maybe you're right. But it started eating away at me today, thinking that I've always had help, that someone was always there, giving me assistance. Just even being here," he said. "I didn't have money and the financial backing." He lifted his arms and opened them wide. "Why me? Because I have friends? Because I know people?"

She shook her head. "Because you're in need." She grinned. "Talk to Dani about that one. She has several people on tap who she contacts on a regular basis when she sees people in need who don't have the funds to come to Hathaway. She has a rotating system. She always has somebody who cannot pay the full price. Does that make a difference to her? Not at all. Should it make a difference to you? Absolutely not."

He leaned forward. "That's what I mean. See? I couldn't get here on my own. It took her. It took her financial backers to get me here, whoever they were."

She opened her mouth and then closed it. "I think you're going about this from a completely skewed perspective. It's not that you're not grateful for all you've been given, but you're questioning whether you deserve any of this. There are so many other things you could sit here and question. This doesn't need to be one of them. When you get a gift like financial backing, it should have you thinking of how best you can make them not regret giving it to you."

Denton sat there and stared at her, a huge smile building on his face. "You know? That was a promise I made to myself when I got here—to do a damn good job of everything for everyone who had done something to get me here," he said. "Somewhere along the line, I had forgotten that promise."

She smiled. "It doesn't need to be brought up every moment of the day. Every day it's a challenge to step up and do what you can do. It's doing and knowing that you've done your best, day after day, that counts. And that is hard to do. Hard to maintain."

He chuckled. "You'd make a hell of a cheerleader."

"I was never a cheerleader. I never made the team." She sat back in her chair. "I was always average at a lot of things but never great at anything."

His eyebrows shot up. "The one thing you are not is average," he said. He reached across the table this time and cupped her hand with his. His strong fingers closed gently around her much smaller hand. "You are very special."

She wanted to withdraw her hand, but he wouldn't let her.

He continued quietly. "And you're not used to compliments. You're not used to people saying good things about you because you're not used to having friends."

She tilted her head to the side. "Most of the friends I thought I once had used to insult each other rather than compliment them," she said, attempting to keep her voice light rather than share that pain. She loved the feel of his much rougher skin against hers. They were just so different. His hand was strong, lean and masculine—hers was softer, rounder, slim. And so very feminine in comparison. She stared at their joined hands, spreading her fingers out to line up with his. "You're right. I'm not used to compliments. That makes me feel socially awkward."

"You're not socially awkward. You're a very good person on the inside, so maybe you're one of those people who likes to have one or two good friends instead of a whole pile of acquaintances."

She nodded. "The one good friend I had died. Way back when I was twelve. She died in a car accident with her mom." She bit her lip at the memory. "It was hard for me, but my parents ... I don't think they understood how absolutely destroyed I was."

"Was that your first experience with death?"

She nodded. "It was. And it was a hell of a lesson."

He gave her a gentle, knowing smile. "Maybe it's time for you to examine that. Because what we tend to learn from our first major tragedy is an awareness that people do disappear forever. People who we love and care about from one moment to the next are gone. And a lot of people close off their feelings because they think if they care again and lose that person too, it would be devastating. I've seen this happen time and time again," he said. "They choose not to have good friends to save themselves the pain of losing them in the future."

She sat back and stared at him. "You know? I had totally forgotten about that accident. It was so long ago." She cast her mind back and winced. "In fact, I'd even changed schools around that time. I couldn't stand being around the same people and the same places, the school breaks and recesses I'd spent with her. I figured, in a new school, I would have new experiences, new friends, but I was still so hurt and in so much pain I closed myself off."

He nodded in a slow, compassionate way. "Chances are that's what this is all about. Open yourself up to a little bit of trust in your life, and you'll be just fine."

She chuckled. "I don't think it's quite that easy."

"Why don't we put it to the test over the next few days?"

he suggested. "We work hard at me standing on my own two feet without always thinking about my friends, and you doing something every day to make new ones."

She chuckled. "Well, that's easier on me probably."

"The people you have to pick from are all around you, but that doesn't mean you want to make friends with all of them." He waggled his eyebrows at her. "So, what do you think?"

She held out her hand to shake on it. "Sure. But you'd better take good care of yourself because if I find you lapsing, forgetting food throughout the day, then I win," she said with a mild threat.

His grin widened. "Deal."

THERE WAS NO reason for Denton to be bothered about his friendships, but at the same time, they did concern him. Because as his friends headed off into their futures, on their own paths, Denton was afraid the shock of losing them both would be a bit much. It wouldn't be at the same time so he'd have a chance to adjust to the loss but ... He hated to think that that would even come into question because he wanted them to be happy. It didn't mean they would necessarily separate, but their relationships would change.

Hannah was right about something else. He'd allowed his blood sugar to drop, weakening him. That shouldn't have happened. Normally he kept snacks with him all the time to pick up his energy level. It had something to do with his muscles dumping the glycogen after working out way too fast. He didn't quite understand it. But he knew that if he didn't take care of himself, his blood sugar levels would drop.

He had a full afternoon ahead. It was the mental stuff that was rough, but he was determined to do as good a job as he could. He pushed himself away from the table and slowly positioned his crutches under his arms, noting his legs were not quite so shaky, and headed toward his room. Once there, he realized he was still feeling the fatigue. Normally it wouldn't come back this fast. But then again, he'd wiped himself out. The workout this morning had been brutal. He probably shouldn't have been on the crutches but in his wheelchair. And he also hadn't had a chance to get to his massage after his physiotherapy session because Shane had been called away.

In this weak moment, he was forced to face the psychologist. That would have scared any man who didn't want to talk about his feelings as much as the shrinks wanted them to. He knew he would do just fine with his life. So what if he was missing his little toe from his left foot and the bulk of his hamstrings on his right leg? His back was a bit more of an issue, but he'd come a long way just to get to this point. His medical team had worked magic. And being here had mentally worked magic too.

There was a knock at the door, and he looked up to see Shane.

The physio walked into his room. "I heard you crashed."

Denton nodded. "Nothing to worry about. I'm prone to swinging blood sugar levels. I did too much this morning and didn't have a snack." Shane opened his mouth, but Denton held up a hand. "I know you told me to make sure I grabbed something. But I think I got lost on my phone for a bit and didn't have time."

Shane fisted his hands on his hips and glared at him in mock anger. "Well, that'll be the last time I'll let you get away with that."

Denton rolled his eyes and grinned. He knew Shane cared. And that was one of the things that made this place so special. "Don't worry. It's the last time I'll do it too." He shuffled back on the bed where he could lay against the headboard. "Also I'm paying for it because I didn't get a massage."

"How is your schedule this afternoon? Do you want to do that now?"

"I have a visit with Dr. Hutchinson about now." He leaned across the bed, pulled his tablet toward him and studied his schedule. "Yes, that's next. I also have a checkup with the doctor this afternoon as well, but after that, I would be free." He lifted his head to look at Shane. "Unless that doesn't work for you?"

Shane scrolled through his own tablet. "I'll be back before four. You could have a good massage and then dinner."

"Unless I fall asleep and sleep through dinner." He chuckled. "I have to admit, I'm pretty tired." He watched as Shane made several notes. "I don't think I overdid it badly today. I think it was the combination of the blood sugar and the workout," he rushed to say. "The workout wasn't too hard. It was just the combination."

Shane nodded. "Still, we'll adjust your schedule to make sure you get your snack and see how that works going forward."

With that, he took his leave. As he walked out, the psychologist walked in. They spoke in the doorway for a couple minutes. Denton wondered if they were discussing him, but it wasn't for him to worry about.

He had enough in his life to worry about without adding to it.

He didn't want his friends to know about his worries either. He didn't want them to be hurt by his fear he couldn't stand up without them, but he knew that if they heard the discussion, they'd probably feel exactly that. He pasted on a smile as the doctor walked in.

She pulled up a chair. "I'm pretty sure we met like this the other day too."

He gave her a half laugh. "This time it was due to my own stupidity."

She nodded. "Then tell me about it."

Chapter 9

T HE FIRST SOCIAL trip, minus Denton, went off without
a hitch, making it a twice-monthly event to the delight
of everyone. For the next several days, Hannah focused on
being a little friendlier to a few more people around her. She
felt uncomfortable picking one person, so she decided she
should be friendlier with everyone. She could work with
that. She overheard a couple people saying she was in a much
better mood these days, and they were wondering what was
going on. Of course, she'd already heard her name linked
with Denton's, and that bothered her. When she stopped to
check in with him on the fourth day, she brought up her
concerns.

"I don't know if my attempts are working or not."

"It's not something you can ask about or quantify,"
Denton replied. "It's something we have to judge for
ourselves."

She shrugged. "But I'm trying to be much friendlier."

He stopped and looked at her. He put down the towel
he'd been folding among the clothes he'd been putting away
when she came in. "You can't just be friendlier. Because they
don't realize you're purposefully being friendlier to them but
think you're simply happier in general." He returned to
folding his clothes, thankfully not seeing the color rise on her
cheeks. "This can always be something situational. You have

to pick out one person, maybe one person per day, and do something very friendly for them."

"Well, that hardly seems fair. Isn't it better if I'm friendlier with everyone, rather than picking and choosing individual people?"

"But then you don't possibly hurt people, and you don't chance getting hurt if they don't pick you back."

She stared at him. "Oh, my God. That's what I'm doing, right?"

He walked over carefully, on his own steam, and he gave her hand a squeeze, then stepped back. "Maybe. But that doesn't make it wrong. It's a learning process. You have to open yourself up to them, the same as you're hoping they will to you."

She nodded slowly. "Well, so far I think I've failed then." She shook her head. "I thought this would be easy. So, enough about me. What about you? How did you do for the last few days?"

"I've been so damn busy," he said, now sitting on the side of the bed. "Between one meeting and appointment and another, it's been easier to not think about my friends."

"And how are you feeling about that?" she asked. "How do you rely less on your friends but not have them feel like you're cutting them out of your life?"

He stared at her and raised an eyebrow. "Now that's a damn good question. Just because I'm being independent doesn't mean I make them feel like I don't want them around." They exchanged sad smiles.

"It's not quite as easy as you thought, is it?" she asked.

He shook his head as his phone buzzed. He pulled it out and studied the screen. "It's Brock. He says he hasn't seen me in a few days."

She nodded. "That would be your cue. Have coffee with them. See how you feel. See how your response is to see him. He's contacted you independently, and you're feeling more independent and self-sufficient. Then go meet him on equal terms. If you're approaching this from a perspective of feeling needy, then wait a little longer until you feel more grounded and prefer standing on your own feet."

He stared at her for a moment. "It didn't take you long to pick that up."

She chuckled. "I suggest we check back in a couple more days."

"Sure ... but does that mean we don't get to see each other for a couple mornings?"

She spun around, knowing that the tingle in her cheeks meant she had turned bright pink. She hoped her voice didn't sound too girlish. "Absolutely not. We could do coffee sometime even?"

He shook his head. "I'd like that. Inside or outside, that would be lovely."

Hannah smiled from ear to ear. "Good, let's try for that soon." Not believing she'd flirted with him, she hurried out. She pressed her hands to her cheeks as she rushed down the hallway, feeling the heat in her palms. She prayed she wouldn't run into anybody who would do nothing but raise eyebrows and ask questions she had no intention of answering. She dashed into her office and plunked herself down at her desk.

Somehow that relationship had moved from the casual level up to the level of a special friend. She couldn't be happier. Then she remembered how she'd kept herself separate over the years to avoid being hurt. She'd missed out on opportunities like these. She definitely needed to branch out in finding friends. Who interested her? Who did she want to be friendlier with? She really liked Dani. She liked Sandra. And well, if she was getting together with Denton, there were always his friends, Brock and Cole. That thought felt a bit tenuous. How could she make friends with Denton's friends on the off chance she and Denton had made a connection? She pushed that thought from her mind and focused on her work.

Several hours later Hannah glanced at the clock and realized the lunch hour was almost over. She wasn't terribly hungry, but she could use a coffee break. And some fresh air would absolutely help. She picked up her coffee cup and wandered into the dining hall. There she filled up her mug and turned to see Dennis.

"You didn't eat lunch today?" he asked.

She smiled up at him as she was reminded what a nice man he was. "With all the people around here, how could you possibly notice I didn't come in and eat?" she teased.

His grin was wide and happy. "I always keep track of my favorite people," he announced. "And you don't eat enough."

"That's not fair," she protested. "I eat very well."

He motioned toward the buffet table. "I was about to pack it away. Can I get you something?"

She stopped and looked at what was offered. "The Greek salad looks so lovely."

"Well, it was lovelier when I first put it out there. Right now it's looking a little sad. I can freshen it with a little more cheese though." He walked away and returned with a bowl of Greek salad topped with more feta cheese. He put it on a tray and pulled out a plate. "Let's see what we have to go with it."

She knew she wouldn't get away without adding something to it. "I'll have a little chicken."

Instead, Dennis placed a good-size chicken breast on her plate and added a bit of seasoned brown rice.

"That's about the right amount for you, I think." He motioned to an empty section of the buffet. "I just put away the fruit platter. Give me a second." He scurried into the kitchen and came back with the large platter. "It's been picked over, but there are still lots of berries, if you'd like."

Hannah took a small serving bowl and pulled out blueberries, raspberries, strawberries and some blackberries. Then, with a big smile of thanks for Dennis, she grabbed a knife and fork and headed to a table out in the sunshine. She hadn't sat down for more than a few minutes when Sandra walked to her table.

"May I sit with you?"

Surprised and pleased, Hannah nodded. "Of course."

Sandra sat in the opposite chair. "You know? We've worked together for the last year, but it seems like because we work together, we never get the time to socialize."

"Isn't that the truth?" Hannah took a big bite of her Greek salad and smiled while she chewed. After the swallowed, she pointed at her plate. "Dennis fixed this for me. I do so love the food here."

Sandra nodded. "And Dennis always makes those of us here as happy as we can be."

"True enough." It took Hannah a few minutes to realize Sandra sat almost uncomfortably, as if waiting for something. Hannah glanced around. "Is something wrong?"

Sandra slumped a little bit in her chair. "I wanted to ask you something, as you seem to be the closest with Denton." She hesitated. "Has he said anything about why he might be upset with Cole?"

Hannah's eyebrows shot up, and she vigorously shook her head. "Oh, my goodness, no. I don't think there's anything wrong." And then she realized what he was trying to do and the rebound effect. She slowly lowered her fork to her tray. "There was something, but it wasn't Cole himself. It was more ..." And she stopped. She didn't know if she should say anything. This was Denton's issue. Lamely she added, "It's not my place to discuss it, but I know he was being a little more independent and not quite so dependent on his friends."

Sandra studied her face. "You think that's all there is to it?"

Hannah nodded gently. "Absolutely."

Relief washed over Sandra's face. "That would be good to know. It felt a little bit like he'd been cut off. This isn't a place to be cut off from your friends."

"That's so very true. And I certainly don't think Denton wants Cole to feel in any way that he wasn't still his best friend or at least one of his two best friends." She'd have to mention to Denton how his silence and his goal for more independence had affected the others. And if Cole was feeling the change, Brock likely was too.

"Thanks for that, Hannah. I'll let you enjoy the rest of your food."

Hannah watched as Sandra got up and walked away. She'd been friendly. She wasn't sure that counted in her quest for friendship as she hadn't initiated the contact, but it was still nice.

She finished off her lunch, her thoughts swirling around closely entwined old friendships and how the different dynamics worked. After she returned her dirty dishes, she detoured to Denton's room. She knocked, but there was no answer. Feeling torn between happiness and concern, she headed to her office.

WHEN A KNOCK came at the door, it opened before Denton could greet his visitor, and he raised his head and frowned. Then his gaze lit up as Brock walked in.

He waited at the doorway for a moment, then nodded. "That's why I didn't wait for an answer," Brock said. "You've never been able to hide your feelings on your face, so I wanted to see if you have an issue with us or are genuinely glad to see us. No one knows what the hell is going on."

Denton winced. "Brock, I will always be glad to see you guys."

"Really? So how come you've been putting us off for days now? We usually meet for coffee or a meal, but lately, when we've stopped by, the door's often locked. You aren't initiating any contact." He walked in, pulled up a chair, turned it backward and sat down. "So what gives?"

Denton stared at him, feeling speechless.

"This sure as hell better not be the two of you having an issue with me," Cole declared from the doorway. "We've always been able to talk. We've always been able to deal with our issues, so what the hell is going on?"

Brock motioned for Cole to come in. "He was fine when I entered, a welcoming expression on his face, so I'll take that as a good sign."

Cole grabbed a second chair and sat. "Then why the hell have you been avoiding us?"

"Not so." The guys staring at him made Denton feel

bad. "I wasn't avoiding you."

"Okay, so what gives?"

He opened his mouth and then closed it, not sure how to start.

Brock jumped in. "Is it Hannah? You don't want to say anything to us because you found a girl?"

"Hell no. That's not the way we roll, and you know that." Denton hated to think his friends would blame Hannah. Like she didn't have enough problems making friends on her own already.

Cole nodded. "We've never had a problem before. But something is definitely going on, and one of the big changes that we see is that you and Hannah appear to be spending a lot of time together and getting pretty close."

"I sure hope we are," he blurted out, then stopped. "And wow, I didn't expect that answer."

"This is a good surprise?" Cole asked. "Because we've all been blindsided by the women who work here. It's not that we expect you to be any different. That means we've seen the signs that you couldn't see yet. We didn't see them at the beginning either. Not until our respective women had gotten in trouble or had issues, one way or another." Cole laughed. "You should be thanking us. Especially Brock, as he's been paving the way for the rest of us."

"Our leader once again," Denton said teasingly. But he had a big grin on his face, and his heart was warm and feeling so damn fine. "Okay, so the funny thing is, she and I talked about the fact that she's never had real friends. And how envious she was that we have the kind of friendship we have. It got me to thinking. What I liked about Hannah was the fact that she wasn't dependent on anyone. She stood strong even though she was alone, and it never seemed to bother her. Now I realize, of course, it bothers her, and I also realize she's had to do things in some ways to stand on her own to feel a little more secure."

The men sat back and stared at him.

"That's garbage," Cole said. "I'm sorry for Hannah if she doesn't have friends or hasn't experienced what it's like to be in something like our group, but to consider that she was better off alone or maybe had learned certain things you hadn't …" He shook his head. "Well, I don't see that."

Brock tilted his head and studied Denton. "There's more to it than that. Does it go back to your perception of yourself as a charity case for most of your life, and you're still afraid you are?"

"Dammit, Brock." Irritation flared in Denton's gut. "I got over that a long time ago."

Brock raised one eyebrow. "Did you?"

"Of course I did." He waved his arms wide. "I'm here. I'm delighted to be here. I'm not paying a penny for this. Somebody else is forking over that money. That's not my issue."

"Tell us—like it or not—how this could be deemed a charity case, how you feel like you never pulled your own weight because you've had so much help. And now you're afraid you won't stand on your own two feet because you have us?" Cole asked shrewdly.

Denton sat back and groaned. "It's not even like that so much. I noticed Hannah had an air of independence about her. Because she hasn't had friends and family around her. She's done everything herself. I'm not sure I would've made it through without you guys."

"So you're afraid that you can't do what she's doing? You can't do it on your own because you have friends?"

Denton felt pinned in place, like a bug under a magnifying glass. "I guess. I know it's kind of twisted around and upside down. Could you guys not make a big deal out of this? I wanted to see how I would do if I wasn't texting a dozen times in a day or seeing you guys every day."

Silence fell over the room.

Brock stared at him. "And so? What was the result?"

Cole gave Denton a lopsided grin, encouraging him to share with them.

"I understood a little bit about what she's going through," Denton said. "That loneliness that she's always had in her life. I didn't have the same experience she did, since I do know what it's like to have good friends. Friends who barge in my door to make sure I'm not hiding from them. Friends who understand how important our relationship is."

"So how does she feel about what you're doing?" Brock asked.

This time Denton chuckled. "Well, it's part of the challenge for me to separate slightly this last week and for her to step forward. To see if she could make some friends and be a little friendlier every day."

"I never noticed her not being friendly," Brock said with a frown.

"Exactly. But if you didn't see her with me, would you see her at all?"

The two men looked at him and then chuckled.

"Maybe not," Cole answered. "But then we are both seeing just one woman. And maybe that's why you see her. Because she's for you."

"No idea yet if she is or not. But I'd like to find out. However, I don't want to collect another friend because they need that relationship, and I don't want to be collected because she needs a relationship."

"Now we come to the crux of it all," Brock mused. "I think that's a very valid point. Enough so we can understand you figuring out this whole relationship thing. We're on board. I promise you."

"All the power to you," Cole added. "None of this relationship thing is easy. We've seen that she's sincere, honest and real. And you know how we feel about those qualities."

"Absolutely," Denton said. "And maybe that's why we had this initial attraction. Because she is all that. The sense that I can trust her. That she'd be there for me. And if she can accept what she sees now, then it can only get better, and yet, if I relapse, she'd take it in stride."

"So, it is that serious?" Cole grinned.

Denton shrugged and smiled too. "I'd like to think so, but I also think we have to wait and see."

Brock chuckled. "I feel like we should bring other single buddies of ours here. There is something magical about Hathaway House."

Cole laughed. "Don't tell Dani that. If she thought we were using this place as a matchmaking service, she'd run for the hills."

Denton shook his head. "Are you sure about that? From what I understand, she's the one who blazed this trail. I've heard Aaron always was a bit of a trailblazer. I'm sorry he's not here right now. I'd love to get to know him."

The men exchanged grins.

"Aaron is at school right now. According to Dani," Brock said, "he just finished a set of tough exams. He should be home soon."

"Good. Let's meet up with him when he's back."

Chapter 10

HANNAH CONTINUED TO go out of her way for the next few days to be friendly to everyone, even though she knew this general approach defeated her purpose to be a little more social and to do something for someone specific every day. If she did end up doing things with Denton, then it was a sure thing she would be doing things with the men around him. And that meant their women as well. That Hannah might become a part of their group, with her becoming the sixth member, had her feeling fuzzy inside.

Maybe the whole thing wasn't as much of an issue as she'd thought. It had taken a few days, but she'd noticed a shift. Everybody seemed friendlier toward her. It wasn't so much that she was making friends but that she was more open and welcoming and was getting the same kind of response back. Even the kitchen staff had noticed.

"Something must be good in your life right now," Dennis had said with a laugh, teasing her. "I've never seen you with so many smiles on your face."

"Really?" She winced. "Was I that unfriendly?" She trusted him to give her a truthful answer since Dennis was a straight shooter.

He shook his head. "Nope, not unfriendly, just not over-ly friendly. You've always had an air of reservation about you, as if you weren't quite sure if you were welcome."

That startled a laugh out of her. "That's exactly how I felt. I never attracted friends before, and I was always worried about my welcome. This is kind of an experiment," she admitted. "To see if I can work on making some friends. So I have to be friendlier."

"I wouldn't worry about that," he said with a shrug. "You're good people, and good people always find friends."

"I've never felt like I was *good people*."

"Listen," Dennis said, his expression serious. "Sometimes you choose the wrong group, or sometimes it's hard to meet people. When you've been hurt, it sometimes seems impossible. It's hard not to keep looking at everyone in the same negative way."

She stared at him in wonder. "And here I thought you worked in the kitchen. I didn't know you were a shrink. You've got real talent there."

That big grin of his flashed. He waved his cup of coffee, motioning to a fresh pot brewing right beside them. "It's just a matter of standing behind the counter, watching people day in and day out and understanding how much our existence here is simply a small view of the real world out there. People grow. People change, and sometimes you can't see who they are. As a staff member, I see how people treat me. In a supposedly lower-paying job like this one," he said, "you see people's true colors. But for the most part, those who are here have been very good to me."

"Good. I'd hate to think you were being slighted in any way. You've always got a smile for everyone, and you're one of the most helpful people on staff. I would be lost without you."

He chuckled as he gave the counter a wipe. "And that's very kind of you to say. The thing is, I don't think you see yourself as you really are. I've never seen you *ever* have a sour word for anyone. You always have a smile on your face, and you're always here ready to do the job, regardless of the night you had or how someone spoke to you. It's not an easy job. None of this is. But there are rewards"—he shook his head—"and those rewards are tremendous. It's not about the money in your bank account. It's about your day-to-day experiences and that little bit of yourself offered to everyone else. Don't try so hard to make friends or to be friendly. Just be yourself."

"That'd be terrific, but I haven't made many friends so far," she pointed out to him.

"Because you weren't open to it. That's one of the biggest things—you will make friends if you are open to the concept. That is a matter of how many people walk in front of you. Do you see them or not?" He gave her a small wave with his towel and headed back into the kitchen.

Hannah wasn't sure what happened, but it felt like she'd gotten a lecture on life.

"Wow," a man behind her murmured.

She spun in surprise to see Shane behind her. "Right? Who knew Dennis was so deep?"

Shane shook his head. "I didn't know, and I've been working with him for six years."

"He is very good at what he does, and obviously he understands people in a way we don't." She frowned slightly. "You know? It'd be very good for every one of us to stand on the other side of that counter for a few days and watch the world walk past—the good, the bad and the ugly."

"Do I have to?" Shane asked. "I wouldn't want my hands so near the food. I'd gain forty pounds in a month."

She burst into laughter. "You? Overweight? That would

be something to see."

He gave her a mock look of horror. "Bite your tongue. I work hard to keep all that lovely food prepared here for us off my waistline."

"So far, I haven't had to do too much work in that area. I do eat, but I have a high metabolism."

"True, but one day your metabolism will slow down. And you will pay the price."

It was her turn to look at him. "Now *you* bite *your* tongue," she snapped laughingly. "I wouldn't know what to do in a gym. I've never felt comfortable in those places."

"Never say never," Shane said. "Many of us workout here. You are more than welcome to join us anytime."

She shook her head. "Oh, no thank you. That would be incredibly awkward for me."

He stopped, studying her for a moment. "I guess if you've never been in there, it's intimidating."

"Very intimidating. I wouldn't know what to do or where to start. I'd be afraid of hurting myself on the first day."

He nodded. "Let's do something about that. Normally I do a forty-minute workout at the end of the day. Why not meet me? We can go through something very basic, very simple, that you can do on your own without any awkward-ness."

She wanted to refuse. But then her brain poked at her. It was one of the few invitations she'd ever received at Hatha-way. She wrinkled her nose up at him. "Is getting sweaty a requirement?"

He burst into laughter. "It's a definite requirement."

She sighed. "Okay. I'll try it once, and if it's too ..." She was at a loss for words.

"Too what? Too heavy? Too painful? Or too sweaty to return to work?"

At her nod, he wrapped an arm around her shoulders. "The gym can be adapted for whatever you need and whatever you feel comfortable with. Nothing is written in stone. Just pick a day and join me." He poured himself a cup of coffee and took a bite of his cinnamon bun. "I work out so I can have these. That's the only reason why."

"Because you love food."

His eyes lit up. "Exactly." He grinned at her and gave her a wink before disappearing down the hallway.

Well, now she'd done it. She'd gotten herself signed up for a workout with Shane. Suddenly, she was afraid the whole thing would be a huge disappointment, and she'd make a fool of herself.

But at least he had offered. Which was a success.

Suddenly feeling happier at the concept, she returned to the coffee pot. She refilled her mug and after a moment, poured a cup for Dani too. As she placed the mugs on a tray, she glanced at the fresh hot cinnamon buns and decided she and Dani both needed the treat. She grabbed the laden tray and headed to Dani's office.

As she walked toward the main office, she caught sight of a horse trailer pulling down the driveway. She paused outside Dani's office and watched as the trailer made its way to the far end of the building. She glanced at Dani. "You've got more horses coming?"

Dani lifted her head from her desk and looked at her in confusion. "Horses? I don't think so. Why?"

Hannah put the tray down on her desk. "Well, a horse trailer pulled up the drive and headed toward Stan's end of the building."

Dani hopped up and walked to the front door to take a look. "As soon as I've had coffee and that treat—thank you, by the way," she said, "I'll head down there to see what that's all about."

"Do you mind if I come with you?" Hannah offered. "I've seen the horses here but only from afar."

"You're kidding, right?" Dani's expression was one of disbelief.

Hannah chuckled. "Nope. I never had the opportunity to ride a horse before. I haven't been around a real horse."

After finishing their coffee and pastries, Dani headed down the hallway. "That'll change right now. Come with me."

DENTON ROSE, FINISHING the last set of calf raises, his muscles shaking with the effort. The workout today had been hard and demanding, and he was so done.

"That was a great effort," Shane said approvingly. "You pushed that movement to the max. Don't forget to have your snack as soon as you get back to your room."

Denton laughed wryly. "It seems nobody lets me forget about my little lapse."

Shane shook his head. "Hell no. Not in a place like this. Dennis won't blab about it, but he's certainly on top of things too. And if it looks like you're suffering or struggling in any way, he will mention it to one of us on your team."

"Considering it's all done in my best interests, it's a little hard to get upset about it."

"That's the spirit."

"How is it that even missing a toe is such a major injury?

How can it have such a brutal effect on my body?"

"It's pretty amazing how much something like that affects everything else."

Denton's hamstrings were killing him as he did one more muscle exercise. "Another question—how can muscles that are no longer there hurt?"

"Are you hurting badly today?" Shane gave him a crooked grin and said, "If not, pick it up."

At that, Denton laughed out loud. "I guess you've heard all the excuses and procrastination delays anybody can give."

Shane nodded his head. "When you work at a place like this, you don't run short on those. Remember to dig in to work on the slow, controlled movement. For that burn that says something is happening. You're building muscles, which means you must make tiny micro tears into the existing muscle, so it can rebuild bigger and stronger. If the muscles are new, they must be fired awake again. Nerve endings can be painful. You know perfectly well how this works. When it all comes together, it's a piece of art."

"I'm a work in progress." Denton closed his eyes, feeling the pain shoot up his legs, the back of his ankle, even his knees. Missing a hamstring muscle made it harder. But it wasn't bad. It could be so much worse. At least he had his legs. From what he'd seen here, a lot of guys were way worse off. When he finally finished his set, his body was completely drenched in sweat.

"There you go," Shane said. "Nice job."

"Am I supposed to be so worked up over this?"

"Absolutely. It's like hitting a wall. You feel like it's taken everything out of you right now. When you rebuild, you come back stronger and bigger and better than ever."

Denton nodded. "Good to know."

They went to work on other muscles, focusing on balancing both sides of his body. By the time his session with Shane was done, Denton was drenched. He shook his head. "I'm hitting the showers."

Shane nodded. "Or you can go to the pool."

Denton lit up like a firecracker. "Really? I thought it would be longer before I hit the pool."

"You've been cleared, so how about today? You worked hard. Your body could do with the cooldown."

"Sounds even better," Denton said. "I'll get my swim trunks and meet you down there."

"I'll be with you for about twenty minutes, and then I have another physiotherapy session in the pool. So I can't keep an eye on you while I work with the other person. That okay?"

Denton knew what Shane was asking. "Yes, I'm perfectly capable of going in the water on my own. I'm ecstatic to have a chance to hit that hot tub. And thank you for the confidence in my ability and independence."

With a high-five, they separated. Denton had a new surge of energy at the thought of the pool and the hot tub, and he made his way quickly to his room. His shirt clung to his back as sweat dripped from his scalp. But knowing where he was going made all the difference. Deciding the wheelchair might be more prudent, he sat down and wheeled his way to the elevator, his towel wrapped around his shoulders. He slowly made his way to the pool deck and wondered what the protocol was.

Shane appeared at his side. "First things first. Because you came from a workout, you need a quick shower before you get into the pool. Afterward you can get right in the water."

Denton realized Shane was already in his own bathing trunks. Fit and lean, he was a great role model. Denton was seriously excited. Containing his exuberance, he made his way to the changing room and parked the wheelchair outside. Denton rinsed off and then made his way very slowly to the pool's edge, surveying all the amenities disabled people might need, including a motorized lift for getting in and out. "No money spared here, huh?"

"No, when it came to putting in the pool, Dani and the Major did it right."

"And we all get the benefit of that." He stood for a moment, struck with hesitation. What was the easiest way for him to get in?

"Don't worry about it. Just jump in," Shane said, chuckling.

Denton flashed him a big grin and fell sideways into the water. Cool waves wrapped around his body. He'd always been a water baby, and he couldn't believe how much he'd missed it. As he slowly sank, his body instantly reacted, bending and swerving, kicking and waving, the motion so damn natural it almost brought tears to his eyes. When he broke the surface, he closed his eyes for a long moment, enjoying the sensation of once again being back in his natural environment.

"Glad to see I don't need to worry about you in the water," Shane said jokingly.

"I *was* a Navy SEAL," he said with a grin. For him that said it all. He closed his eyes and floated in joy.

Life could be a lot worse.

Chapter 11

O NCE AGAIN, HANNAH marveled at the joys of her job. How many people got to spend an hour visiting with horses in the middle of their workday? She met Maggie and Molly, the baby, who stood in attendance. Hannah watched as a new arrival was unloaded.

"This is Sir Raleigh," Stan said. "He's a racehorse. Destined for the factory."

Dani's face turned grim. "And will he fit in with the other horses?"

Stan chuckled. "The last time we talked, you told me to rescue any horse I knew of. He's still intact. I figured we could give him a quick surgical procedure and put him out to pasture along with the others."

Dani's face broke into a beautiful smile. "So very glad to hear that. I was a little concerned about the stallion aspect, but if we can castrate him, then that's fine."

"Should've been done a long time ago, after his stallion days were well and truly gone. He's very old, so in that aspect, they wouldn't bother with the surgery. Yet, it would've made him a lot easier to handle. I'm equipped here to perform the surgery, so I will take care of that in the next couple of days, and then he'll be fine to be pastured with the mares, particularly given his age."

Stan was right. Hannah watched the two men maneuvering Sir Raleigh into a stall. He blew and stomped slightly in outrage but more for show. He wasn't rearing back, and he wasn't kicking anybody, so he had been well trained. "He doesn't appear to be adjusting too badly."

"He might already have a good idea what's happening too," Dani replied.

Hannah winced, thinking about the glue factory. "I'm sure he'll have a lovely life here."

Once Sir Raleigh had settled, Stan stepped in and did a quick exam. The horse stood quiet. But by the way he stood, Hannah could see he was proud. Every inch a stallion.

"I'm surprised they would get rid of him."

"The stallion is only good for one thing," Dani murmured. "And if his offspring aren't showing the promise they had hoped for, then it's not worth even that."

"It's a tough life."

Dani stepped inside the stall and held out her hand. Hannah watched from the safety of the gate. The stallion smelled Dani and then blew gently on her hand. She stroked his long nose. "You'll be just fine here, boy. We'll make sure you get another ten to fifteen years of good living."

Hannah watched in amazement as the horse calmed down under the tender care of Stan and Dani. Within minutes, Sir Raleigh was led to fresh hay and water. He started to eat and drink. "When will you let him out to feed on the green grass?" Dani asked.

"It'll be much easier to deal with him confined here," Stan answered. "After the procedure, we will give him a day out in the pasture on his own, and then we'll slowly introduce him to the mares."

"There are only females in the pasture. Right?"

"That's correct. I have only one gelding, the others are

mares. But once he's gelded and calmed down slightly, he'll blend in."

"Gelded?" Hannah asked.

Dani chuckled. "Stallions tend to maintain their personalities, even after being gelded. He will remain somewhat aggressive and hard to handle, and he will still think the mares are his."

"So, a male is a male?" Hannah asked.

Stan shot her a mock look while Dani chuckled. "Exactly."

"Dani, you have built something special here. I can't imagine where these animals would've ended up without your help," Hannah said.

"Not just the animals. Think of all the injured people upstairs." Stan shook his head. "Even staff members who don't work out so well in other places do better here."

Hannah laughed. "Dani collects cast-off animals, injured patients and cranky staff."

"I don't collect anything," Dani protested. "I'm just trying to help."

"And a fine job she does too," Denton said.

Hannah turned to see Denton in his wheelchair. His hair was wet, and although he looked tired, he also had a very happy smile on his face.

"Don't you look like you've had a great day," she said in a teasing voice.

"Oh, I did, indeed. I got in the pool for the first time today."

"Now that makes sense. I don't use it enough," Hannah said.

"No time like the present," Denton said. "Although, if you want company in the water, it won't be me. I'm tired today. About to go up and change and head for dinner."

The group slowly broke up as everyone returned to the main building. Hannah took the opportunity to walk with Denton to the elevator and upstairs.

"I'll be a little bit. I still have some work to do in the office," she confessed. "Dani had a new horse arrive, so I came down with her to see him."

"Are you a horse-crazy girl too?"

"No." She shook her head with a startled laugh. "I haven't been around them at all. I find them fairly intimidating," she confessed.

"I get that. They're large animals. Lots of people here look after them. But I know some of the staff and the patients go down and visit with them all the time."

"I get down to Stan's stomping grounds to bring certain animals to integrate with the patients. Chickie and Helga are two of my favorites. But it's part of my job, so I don't get to linger down there."

"And I haven't spent much time with them at all."

"Stop by the office. When I left, Chickie was sleeping on his bed."

"Sure. I can stop by there first."

Together they walked into her office, and sure enough, Chickie was curled up in a ball. As soon as they walked in, he lifted his head and gave a small yelp. She picked him up, and he snuggled close. She glanced over at Denton.

"I'm soaking wet," he said wryly. "I need to rinse off and change, and in the meantime, it looks like Chickie could use some loving." His smile flashed. "Give me twenty minutes, and I'll be back. Maybe he'll sit with me."

Hannah sat in her chair and carefully tucked Chickie into her lap and quickly went through the rest of her work for the afternoon. In the back of her mind she wondered if maybe she'd get an invitation to have dinner with Denton too. If nothing else, for coffee before.

She gently stroked Chickie's head. "You're a lucky thing. You get to visit with him." When she heard slow footsteps approaching, she looked up to see Denton arriving at the doorway. She smiled. "No wheelchair?"

"That was the easy way. I was thinking that maybe, if I could walk to dinner and then make the trip back again, I could rest in my room for the remainder of the evening. I hate to take the easy route, but at the same time, I worry about overdoing it."

"And without the wheelchair, do you want to hold Chickie?"

He flashed her a grin and gave her a bashful look. "I was kind of hoping you'd be done for the day and could have coffee with me."

She laughed out loud and hopped to her feet, holding Chickie gently in her arms. "And here I was hoping to have dinner with you."

The two stared at each other, feeling that instant rapport.

"Then how about we do both, and you can tell me how you're getting on." He glanced around the room. "Are you done here?"

She nodded and shut down the computer. With Chickie in her arms, the two of them walked to the dining hall.

"Inside or out?"

"Outside right now. We can always find a seat closer to the food when it's ready."

"You sound like you're hungry," she teased.

"That I am."

When they found seats in the sun, he sat down, and she delivered Chickie to him before walking to the coffee bar. She picked up a tray with two cups filled with black coffee and returned to the table.

"I couldn't remember if you take creamer in your coffee or sugar or both."

"Cream is good, thanks."

Chickie looked up and sniffed the air as Hannah placed the creamer tubs and sugar packets on the table.

"It must be hard not to have everybody feed him," Denton said, scratching the pup behind his ears.

She nodded. "Especially with Chickie. His system is very touchy. If he has anything other than his dietary food, it causes him a great deal of pain."

She watched as Denton gently stroked Chickie's small tan-colored body. Chickie shifted slightly to sit deeper in Denton's lap and closed his eyes.

"Unlike a lot of dogs," she said, "he spends a lot of time sleeping."

"Maybe that's best for him at this stage." He lifted his gaze and looked at her. "So, give me an update on how your friend thing is working out."

She winced. "Maybe good? Maybe I'm doing it for all the wrong motives, and that's not so good." She shrugged, not wanting to share how wrong her motives could be related to him. He was quickly becoming someone she wanted to be so much more than a friend with, and yet she didn't know what he wanted. What if he just wanted to be friends? How did that work? For her it wouldn't work at all. "I want to be a little more relaxed about it."

"Everything is negotiable. And you're right. You can't force it to work either." He studied her for a long moment.

"So … is there anybody who you decided to befriend?"

She winced. "Well, there is somebody I'd like to be a little friendlier with, but I don't know how that will work out."

He sent a sharp glance her way. "Friendlier? Or like really friendly?"

She flushed. "It's kind of personal."

"Personal's what friends do," he said. "But I didn't realize you were sweet on anybody here."

"I didn't realize it either." She stared at her coffee cup and wrinkled her nose. "But that's the thing about opening yourself up, looking at other people as friends. It tends to open you up to other feelings at the same time."

An awkward silence followed. She raised her gaze to look at him, wondering how he took her news. She had been deliberately vague about it.

He continued to study her intently.

She could feel her flush deepen and darkened. She raised an eyebrow. "What?"

He leaned forward. "Who?"

HE WATCHED AS she settled back in her chair, shaking her head.

"Not sure I'm ready to say anything about it yet," she confessed. She dropped her gaze instead of staring at him directly.

Why was he pushing her again? He'd been hoping he was the one she was sweet on. If she wouldn't say anything, how the hell was he supposed to know? That was what he liked about his buds. They were all direct—they spoke up when they had something to say. And Denton never had to finesse anything nor figure out the rules of dating. But it had seemed to him that he and Hannah were working toward something that wasn't just friendship.

"Do you consider me your friend?" she asked.

He raised an eyebrow and nodded. "Certainly, the beginning of a friendship anyway."

"Not in the same vein as Brock and Cole of course," she added. "I wondered how that worked."

He settled in his seat, holding on to Chickie as he shifted. "We were already working on being friends. I want you to find somebody else to do something nice for every day."

"No, I am," she rushed to reassure him. "Every day I'm spending more time around people. I spent quite a bit of time with Stan and Dani today. Which was nice and unusual at the same time. But it was fun."

He relaxed slightly. "Is it Shane?" He hadn't meant to come right out and ask who she was sweet on, but it was disturbing and would eat at Denton until he knew for sure. He had hoped that something was between them, not that she was looking for someone else. He wondered if he should encourage her to choose him for her acts of kindness. At least then he'd know she cared. He hadn't made any claims or presumed to be so forward as to throw his hat into the ring, so she had no idea of his feelings.

"*Is it Shane* what?"

"The guy you're sweet on?"

"Oh, my goodness, no." She leaned forward and grasped Denton's hands. "Not at all. Shane's a sweetheart. But we're friends. And I like that."

Relief settled inside him. Still Denton frowned. "Now you have me thinking about every male in the place, wondering who it is."

She gave him an odd look, then picked up her coffee cup and took a drink. "Maybe it isn't anything anyway. Just a passing fancy. How does one even begin to know?"

He couldn't stop thinking about who the person could be. "Whenever they come into the room, it's like the room lightens and brightens and becomes so much warmer and cozier. You look up to see if they are walking into the room, even though you know there's absolutely no way they could be here because they are away. But you can't help yourself, hoping they'll be here." He gave her a crooked grin. "They're the last thing on your mind when you go to sleep, and they're the first thing on your mind when you wake up because they've been in your dreams all night with you."

Her mouth opened ever-so-slightly, her eyes going wide. "Oh my, that sounds wonderful."

"It is," he said, unsettled. Because only one person was always on his mind. And it was her. He watched Hannah, wondering what the hell just happened to his world. And how cruel could the world be if that was how he felt, and she had chosen somebody else.

Then Brock and Cole walked in. Denton waved at them, relieved to see this distraction from his tortuous thoughts.

She took a cue from that and stood.

"You're not staying for dinner?" he asked. He was disappointed to see her leave, particularly when she had said she'd hoped to have dinner with him. "I thought maybe you wanted to talk about something."

She cast a sideways glance at the men approaching. "Another time." And she walked to the rack of dirty dishes and placed her cup with them, then came and took Chickie from him.

He watched as she made her escape from the dining room. He frowned. His buddies plunked down on chairs beside him.

"We didn't mean to chase her away. Sorry for intruding on your private moment."

He glanced at Brock. "I'm not sure what you intruded on."

"What do you mean by that?" Cole asked.

Denton explained the odd conversation they'd had as he gazed from one friend to the other. "But she left. We were supposed to have dinner together, but you guys showed up, and she walked out." He shrugged. "Not sure what to make of any of it." First came silence at the table, and then Brock and Cole chuckled.

Denton frowned at them both. "What's up?"

"The mysterious person she's sweet on is you. And when you didn't pick up on her cues, she didn't know quite what to make of it."

He stared at them and frowned. "What? What was I supposed to say? I asked if she was sweet on Shane."

At that Cole laughed. "Everybody here loves Shane, but I don't think he has anybody special."

"But maybe that's who she has feelings for," Denton argued. Inside, he wondered if they were right. He tried to think back on the odd conversation as if he'd missed something, and maybe a second pass would show him what it was. "I'd like for you guys to be right, but I don't see it."

"We'll find out from our ladies if Hannah's been spending time with anyone," Cole said. "But I don't believe it's anyone else but you. You have to give her the right cues and let her know where she stands, that's all."

"Okay." But he wondered, "If that's what she meant,

then I've screwed up. Because I didn't give her any kind of response to that."

"Do you want to?"

Denton looked down at his broken body still on the mend. "It's hardly the best timing."

"I understand why you say that," Brock said slowly, "but I think you're wrong. I think if ever we needed to show up as the people we truly are, then today is the day for it." Brock shrugged. "If there's one thing I've learned in my new relationship, it's how she wants honesty on all levels. I'm no longer the big warrior I was. I'm no longer a SEAL. But what I am is a lot more realistic for her. I'm a lot more me. My integrity is intact. My ethics, my moral code all are intact, and I'm still the warrior even today. Just another variety."

Cole nodded. "That's so very true. We aren't the people we once were. But who we are now is authentic. Don't try to be anything else, and don't wait to be any better. Don't wait till your body heals and you're as good as you can be. Because there can always be setbacks. You'll live life now with a whole different set of health issues. We can be stronger, more vibrant, able to take on the world, but that doesn't mean when we have an issue or get set back, that we don't want somebody who'll be there for us, knowing what we were like before. You don't want to go into a relationship looking for perfection or expecting it. It doesn't exist. You can't have it, and the last thing you want to do is to present yourself in that light. The reality is, this is who you are."

Denton stared at the table. "So how do I fix this?"

The other two men shared a glance, then shrugged. "That's up to you," Brock said. "You'll find a way. And on that note, are we eating dinner together?"

Denton nodded. "I got stood up, so I guess so."

Cole patted him on the shoulder. "The food's ready, so come on. Let's get in line before everyone else joins in."

Denton nodded, and with the others ahead of him, he slowly made his way to the buffet. But inside his head, he kept remembering how she had said she was hoping to have dinner with him. When his buddies came, something had changed. He had figured that, maybe afterward, he and Hannah could go for an evening swim and have coffee and dessert. He stood in the line with the guys and pulled out his phone to send her a text.

I wish you had stayed, but I'm eating dinner with the guys. Meet me for coffee and dessert at the pool later?

He held his phone tightly in his hand as he studied the food, waiting for her answer. Finally, when it came, she'd included a happy face.

Sure. One hour?

A grin whispered across his face. **Yes**, he typed. **That would be perfect.**

Brock edged toward him. "By that expression on your face, I'm guessing your love life is better?"

Denton nodded. "If it's my love life, then it's better. But if she's after somebody else …" He shook his head. "It might be time to find out for certain."

"So where will the romantic evening be?"

"I'll tell you, but make sure you guys are going in the opposite direction," he said. "We're meeting by the pool for coffee and dessert."

Brock rolled his eyes. "That pool has a lot to answer for."

The men chuckled. Denton followed slowly as they walked along the buffet, collecting everything they could possibly want to eat—a huge delicious-looking baked ham, brown rice, and lots of vegetables. Denton was tired, and he remembered Shane's suggestion to eat a lot of protein. With a slice of hot ham on his plate and a couple scoops of sides, Denton grabbed his cutlery and slowly made his way to the table. He would enjoy his dinner.

But he would enjoy the rest of his evening more.

Chapter 12

HANNAH DECIDED SHE'D go for a swim before meeting Denton. She'd done a lot of thinking about her life since his arrival. Figuring out what it was that had changed so much. Because something had indeed changed—she just wasn't exactly sure what. She'd met literally dozens of people here in the last year—patients, staff, support workers, family members—and then all the delivery vehicle drivers, etc. And in all that time, none of them had influenced her the way Denton did. Partly because she could see their friendship blossom. Partly because she had noticed some friendships were debilitating. As somebody who had spent so much time thinking about friends, that wasn't an easy thing to watch— it made her feel terrible.

She could never have explained why she worried about it. She had mentioned it earlier to Denton but hadn't gone into detail. It wasn't her place, but as soon as the opportunity presented itself, she would consider telling him. There was nothing wrong in finding security in numbers.

All she wanted was to have more friends. She finally realized that having friends was an important part of life.

Friendships were also important for their own healing abilities. Life was such a surprising mix of people; she couldn't help but wonder if she hadn't screwed up somewhere along the line. Screwed up in a way she had no right to.

She didn't want to be the girlfriend who split up her boyfriend's long-term group of male friends.

She wasn't a psychiatrist, a medical doctor, a therapist, or counselor. Maybe her comment to Denton about distancing himself from his friends was taking Denton too far from Brock and Cole. She didn't want that. Not in any way. She owed Denton an apology. As she slowly swam from one end of the pool to the other, taking her time, diving and floating, her mind kept running over the issues, feeling the pain and the regret. And the worry. Why hadn't she considered this evolution earlier?

There was more to work on, but she hadn't given it much thought. It hadn't hit her until she saw his two friends walking toward him and realized the distance Denton had put between the three of them was wrong because Brock and Cole didn't do anything wrong. She had. She now realized the impact her words had on people. The impact her being here had on people. She shouldn't have separated Brock and Cole from Denton. She shouldn't have had anything to do with that. She should've kept her mouth shut, and the fact that she hadn't was incredibly disturbing.

When she broke through the surface of the water, she had a newfound sense of resolve.

She knew what she needed to do, but it wouldn't be easy. And if it turned out badly, she could change her mind. That wouldn't be good because it could end up with her losing her job. But she'd rather lose her job than have Denton lose his friends. Because it wasn't just Denton who was affected but also Brock and Cole. And that was not good. She walked to the shallow end of the pool, her heart heavy.

"There you are." Denton stood nearby smiling down at her.

"Hi. Did you have a good dinner?"

He nodded. "It's always good to spend time with my friends."

She nodded, but inside she hurt. Because of course, he hadn't been spending time with his friends because of her. She grabbed her towel and slowly made her way out.

"Did you eat?" Denton asked.

"I had some salad. I wanted a swim first. I'll grab something more now." She dried off, grabbed her beach cover-up and threw it over her bathing suit. She didn't have any issues with her body, but she was extremely unhappy with who she was inside right now. And that sense of vulnerability hurt. She walked beside him. "You want to grab a table for coffee?"

He grinned and said cheerfully, "Dennis is bringing it over."

She chuckled. "Good. That saves me a trip, and Dennis is a sweetheart."

"I heard my name," Dennis called out from the stairs.

She glanced over to see him enter the pool area, a large tray in his hand. The evening sun was setting, and they chose a table off to the side, still bathed in the sun's glow.

Hannah sat in one of the chairs, still rubbing her hair with her towel. "This looks lovely."

"Well, I knew you were coming down here, and you didn't eat much earlier," Dennis said. "So this is a hot beef sandwich and a Greek salad—which I know you love—and coffee and desserts for you both. Enjoy." Then he turned and walked upstairs.

"Thank you," Hannah and Denton said together.

Denton chuckled. "Some of the people here seem so perfect for their roles. Like they really enjoy their lives and what they do for everyone."

"Isn't that the truth?" She stared at the roast beef sandwich and smiled. "And you know something? He's right. I am hungry." She dug into her sandwich and ate it without taking a break.

"You were hungry."

She grabbed a napkin, wiped her fingers and then her face and nodded. "I didn't think I was at first, but there's nothing quite like swimming and a little bit of worry to get somebody's appetite going."

"Not me. When I get worried, I can't eat."

"I'm the opposite," she said. "When I'm worried or upset, food becomes therapy."

"And yet, you are still slim."

She shrugged. "Metabolism. Apparently it's gonna catch up with me later." She gave him a smile. "But so far, I've been lucky."

"Besides, what can you possibly be worried about?"

She shook her head and stayed quiet, choosing to sip her coffee instead.

"Is it something that you can't share with a friend?" he teased.

"It's not that so much as I'm afraid I've done something wrong. I'm finally realizing the impact my words have on other people."

He slowly lowered his own cup of coffee. "Wow, that sounds serious."

She settled back into her chair. "It is. I just don't know how serious."

"Well, I'm here, available to listen, anytime you want to

talk."

She winced. Should she? Or should she talk it over with somebody else first? Had she done something to harm him? At the same time she didn't know if it had affected him at all. "Maybe I'm worrying for nothing."

"So tell me, and then I can help you."

She stared down at her coffee on the table. "It concerns you."

There, she had said it. She took a deep breath and let it out slowly, watching his reaction. He lowered his cup of coffee, his gaze darkening. She didn't know what was going on behind his gaze—she was afraid he'd get mad at her.

He leaned forward slightly in his chair. "Tell me."

She gave a small shrug. "I'm worrying that my comments about you being too dependent on your friends had a negative effect and gave you a bad reason to distance yourself from them."

He settled back into his chair and studied her for a long moment.

She felt the silence. She wasn't entirely comfortable with that, but until he spoke up, she couldn't do a lot. She wanted to rush in and fill the void with nonsense or make excuses, but something told her to hold her peace.

"And you're worried about that?"

She nodded.

"The thing is, you were correct. I was extremely dependent on my friends, and it never even occurred to me until you said that."

She winced. "But I didn't want to come between you and your friends."

He chuckled. "See? That's where your inexperience with how good friends work comes into play." He lifted his mug again. "Just because I needed some space and distance to figure out how much my neediness was affecting my own healing and my ability to move forward, it didn't affect their relationships with me."

"Yes, it did. Sandra came by and asked about you, wondering why you would distance yourself."

"Of course they were worried *for* me and *about* me. But they weren't worried I didn't care about them anymore. Their worry was that something was going on outside of me that they didn't know about, and they didn't know how to help. They were offering me support then they backed away and let me do my thing."

"Did they ask you what you were upset about?"

He nodded. "To some extent. The result was that they understood, but they thought I was being foolish."

"And are you?"

He shrugged. "Maybe. But I needed to examine it. I needed to look back on the situation from childhood to see if it was true or false. And for that, I thank you."

She stared at the table for a long moment, wondering if it really was that simple. She gave a sigh. "Thank you. I'm still not sure you understand the effect this could have on you and your friends. And I'm afraid that I may have caused a problem that isn't so easily resolved."

"You didn't cause a problem. You created an awareness of something I needed to look at. I decided I was extremely dependent, and I have spoken to my counselor and my shrink about it extensively in the last few days. And I know you're probably worried I'm upset and angry at you for pointing it out, but I'm delighted you did."

She sat back in surprise. "Well ..."

He chuckled. "Right? And here you were, worried about

it all for nothing."

She shook her head. "I was thinking about all the people I've met since I arrived here last year and how a few of them have made an impact on me. I've seen inner strength in others who have surmounted incredible obstacles. Obstacles I've never been challenged to overcome. I found some incredible people who have done some incredible things. Their attitudes have been phenomenal. And it's made me look at who I am. Made me realize how lucky I am and how grateful I am to be here. To meet these wonderful people and learn about the reality of living an authentic life from them. I have a lot to learn," she admitted. "But the people I've met here have taught me more than I realized."

"Absolutely. That's one of the big things I have always said. When I woke up in the hospital and saw the extent of my injuries, I knew I got away lucky. I still had all four limbs. I still had a body that could stand upright. That was a powerful motivator to do some of things I had never had a chance to do before. And I felt truly blessed. There were days when I was dark and angry and hating life, wondering why this had happened to me in the first place. But there were so many good things about it I quickly moved on."

She nodded. "That's one of the things I like about you. Your ability to see the sunshine. Most people here don't get there for quite a while."

He leaned forward. "Don't forget. I recuperated in the hospital for a long while. I was late coming here compared to the others. Brock's injuries were much more severe than mine. His recuperation has been longer and harder. Yet, he did it in such a fine style I had to stand up and do my best to face my injuries with the same courage."

AS HE SAID the words, he could feel the truth of them rippling through him. Words he never expected to say. He'd never been one to analyze things like that. There were just so many things he could do without having to stop and spend time in deep thinking. And yet, he thought about all the benefits of having friends. Benefits he had depended on when he first got here. Emotions and needs he hadn't even discussed or contemplated before, and having nothing to do with him getting injured but from way back in his childhood. Okay, maybe his childhood issues influenced his initial emotions about his injuries. So, she had been right to bring it all up. In fact, he was glad she had because he'd had no way of seeing it without her comment.

He'd taken his relationships with Cole and Brock for granted.

And that wasn't good. What she wanted for him, and what he wanted for himself, was to know he could do this without his friends, a complete either/or situation. Either fully engaged with his friends or not engaged at all unless Brock or Cole reached out to Denton. To know that his healing would come about whether Cole and Brock were here or not. They were damn good people, and he was proud to call them friends. But he also knew he couldn't afford to let something happen to that friendship. Which, considering they both had partners, was possible.

"Denton, you seem awfully somber. Are the worries of the world sitting on your shoulders?"

He lifted his head, then shrugged. "No, not at all. I'm blessed to have friends in my life, but I need to know I can handle whatever comes my way, even if they're not here.

They are great people, and I'm honored, but time changes everything. Maybe that's why I was desperate to come here. Because, after my accident, I knew I'd do well here because they were here. We were all injured within months of each other, which seemed to be part of that same ongoing theme. But I also needed to know I could recover here without them."

"Well, that time is now, is it not? Isn't Brock moving on soon?"

Denton nodded. "He is. He's hoping to find a job working in Dallas. He still has to find a place to live, so I'll see him for a while, but he won't be here every day after that."

She nodded. "That sounds like progress. A necessary progress in a whole different way for him as well."

Denton smiled. "Absolutely. And once again he's leading the way. He always did in our relationships. With every group of friends you have different strengths, and Brock was always a good one for charging forward and letting us know what the weather would be like up ahead."

"I think that's a lovely thing," she said warmly. "And just because you're considering all this, it does not mean you aren't capable of doing everything you want to."

He sat back and chuckled. "It's interesting how you have minimal friends and have been alone most of your life while I come from a large SEAL family, a big support group, lots of friends. We each have something the other would like to have."

"I can't say too many people have said that to me before," she said. "Most of the time people see me as standoffish, reserved, maybe even cold."

"All of which are completely different and have no bearing on who you really are. They might think you're reserved, and you could be because you don't present yourself as super friendly. Hence what you're working on. And yet, at the same time, you're independent, and that can be threatening to people. As if you don't need anybody, and if you don't need them, a lot of times they are not sure what their role is in a relationship with you."

"That's a harsh way to look at relationships."

He shook his head. "Not at all. They are bringing something different than what you have to offer into a friendship. That's normal. We each offer something different. We each need something different. As you're making me see that I've needed that support. To know that somebody was there for me. To know I wasn't alone handling what I had to handle."

She winced.

He rushed to reassure her. "I'm not saying it's a bad thing. You are so capable of handling your problems alone. This is a good thing."

She laughed. "I'm not sure how it can be. But if you say so."

"It's a very good thing, if you think about it. Look at how much more you've learned about yourself. That's important. What I've learned about me doesn't change my friendship with Brock and Cole, and it doesn't change how much I need or want them in my life. It helps in a different way. It helps me grow as a person. Part of me came here feeling like I didn't belong. I wasn't as badly hurt as so many I see, including my friend Cole, who has a harder road to travel. But I'm here to help him. I was thinking that their presence helps me."

"And you've given me a great reminder that friendship is about giving and taking. And although I was saying the words, I wasn't following up with the actions."

Chapter 13

"AND YOU ALSO have to remember," she said, "you are injured. Several times you said you aren't as badly injured as the others. There is no comparison here. You came because you needed help. You came because this was the place to get your physical body back as good as it could be, and along with that comes the work to make the mental and psychological aspects of yourself whole as well. It doesn't matter how you are when you arrive. You still deserve to be here. You still deserve to have your friends around you, pulling for you, rooting for you. It's almost like you've been overly friendly all this time because you feel guilty."

He tilted his head, frowned. "Guilty?"

She nodded. "Yes. You are feeling guilty you weren't as badly injured as the others. Guilty that Cole was suffering more than you. That Brock suffered and that so many others here are suffering. Look at you. Can you focus on your own healing as much as you focused on helping everyone else? It's not that you're purposely running yourself ragged, but how many times, at the end of the day, do I come see you, and you're exhausted? Sure, I know Shane's workouts take a toll on you. All of your rehab does. But I'm sure you are also popping into almost every room to give words of encouragement to others."

His eyebrows rose. "And that can't be just my natural personality?"

This time a note of defensiveness was in his tone. One she recognized. "Of course it can," she said gently. "But it's also important to make sure you're not doing it to absolve yourself of any guilt because these men are suffering more than you ever did."

His pinched face meant she had crossed the line. She still hadn't learned to keep her mouth shut. She said, "I didn't mean to take the conversation in that direction. You can take the parts that fit and disregard the rest."

She gave him a quick smile. "And now I'm getting chilled, so I'll take these dishes to Dennis and go to my room for the night." She stood, collected all the dishes, and headed to the stairs with her tray. When she was halfway up, she glanced back. He hadn't moved.

He sat there, staring at the table.

"Have a good night," she called out.

Back in the dining hall, she placed the tray onto the rack of dirty dishes and then headed to her studio apartment.

If she felt bad before, she felt terrible now. She had a quick hot shower, dried off, and changed into her pajamas. Then she crawled into bed and turned off the light.

"You're a fool, Hannah. A complete fool," she whispered to the darkness.

She rolled over and tried to fall asleep. But before long, she knew there would be no sleep for her. She was filled with guilt. What she'd said ate at her. Finally, she grabbed her phone, pulled up his Contact and wrote a quick text.

I'm so sorry.

And she sent it. Instantly, she felt better. She wasn't a mean person. She hated to hurt anybody, yet there was no way to ignore the fact she had hurt him.

There was no immediate response, and she realized he'd probably gone to bed. That was exactly what she should do too. She pulled up her blankets and closed her eyes and fell into an uneasy sleep. When her phone jingled, she came out of her doze and fumbled for the device.

It was Denton.

"Don't be sorry. You spoke the truth. It wasn't easy to swallow some of it. That doesn't mean it was the wrong thing to do. I only hope the reason you saw that in me wasn't because you see something similar in yourself. Because that would mean you had suffered and that's not something I would want for you."

She burst into tears. Even now he was only thinking of her.

"No, I didn't, other than losing my best friend," she quickly replied through her tears, "and what I've seen in my years of observing. Maybe I better learn to keep my mouth shut."

He replied, "Not an issue. So don't make it one and definitely don't consider quitting."

She sniffled. "It might be better if I do."

"If it's the job, that's one thing," he said. "But please stay in touch. I don't want to lose you too."

She cocked her head at the odd phrase. "What do you mean by *me too?*"

"Being in the military," he said, "we lost a lot of people I worked with. Some died. Others were too badly injured to continue, and some couldn't handle the pressure, and they just left. That's one of the reasons why I work hard to be a good friend—because I've lost so many. I don't want to lose any more."

"Are we friends? Is that what this is?" she asked. "It seems like it's so much more." She took a deep breath, then let the words out. "And yet, at the same time so much less."

"I'M SORRY," HE said in a low voice. "I'll take the blame for that."

There was silence, and he winced. This wasn't quite how he'd wanted the conversation to go. He wanted things between them to be light and heartwarming. And then he realized what he had told her, about him being friends with her. Should he correct that now? Maybe it would be easier over the phone to not see any rejection on her face.

"I want this to be so much more," he said. "It has the makings to be more. It can be warm and caring and loving. But I understand that you already have somebody else in your life who you are attracted to. And that's not something I want to interfere with."

Her broken laugh made his wince deepen.

"Sure, and that person is you. But I felt like I was nothing more than a friend, and isn't that ironic? Because what I wanted was to be more than friends. Seeing you and your friends, I wanted to be a part of that. And in a way, you have become my friend. Once I realized that, I wanted so much more."

He grinned. "Then why are we having this conversation over the phone?" he said in a bright tone. "We could be sitting together, having coffee, or curled up in bed, discussing our feelings."

"I'm not very good at discussing my feelings," she said with a note of defiance.

"Neither am I." He gave a laugh. "You do realize how ridiculous this conversation is? Like we're dragging this information out of each other."

"You should be getting some sleep. You need to heal tonight so you have a good day tomorrow."

"What? Are you hanging up on me? This is a perfect opportunity to have a little bit of intimacy."

"It is?"

He could hear the cautious question in her voice. "It is," he said affirmatively. "Only somebody who's been posted on missions all over the world understands how important it is to keep a relationship going over long distances. Only somebody like that can understand how important it is to use whatever medium is available to stay in touch, to keep that connection alive, even though they're miles away."

"Oh."

He shook his head, smiling to himself. "You really are sweet."

That startled a laugh out of her. "That's the last thing I am. Pragmatic, yes. Realistic, yes, and reserved, yes."

"Sweet, yes. Innocent in so many ways, yes. Caring, yes. Even now you're telling me to go to sleep so I have a better day tomorrow."

"It's important. That's what you're here for."

"I'm here for a lot of reasons. Physical healing is one of them. But that doesn't mean I should turn my back on something else that's so very important."

"What is that?"

"You." He heard her gasp, and then her voice became soft and tender.

"You mean that?"

"Absolutely."

"Oh. Well, in that case, you still need to get some sleep, and I think we should meet for breakfast. See if you wake up with a completely different mind-set. I'm sure the light of reality and the bright day will change your mind."

He shook his head and gave a bark of laughter. "Skittish, I like that." He had no idea why because, in many ways, it was foolish. But something about her always pulling back from a relationship with him was refreshing. It wasn't that he wanted to give chase, but she wasn't just diving in, happy to have known him for five minutes.

He'd seen a ton of relationships like that. Short-term. He'd always planned on growing old with somebody, planned on staying with the right person for the rest of his life. He couldn't imagine anything nicer than taking the next sixty years and exploring the world around them but also the world between them. There was so much to learn when you were with somebody new. Their perspective was different. Their feelings were different. Just the way they comprehended life around them was different. So many people tried to make those perceptions bend and twist to fit their own ways, but he was the opposite.

He wanted to see what the other person had to offer and to learn from it. There was such joy, such freedom, in that. With a smile on his face, he said his goodbyes, hung up the phone and snuggled under the covers. He was reminded once more that coming here had been the best decision he'd ever made. And for once, that decision had nothing to do with Brock and Cole.

Chapter 14

HANNAH WOKE WITH a smile on her face and a bounce to her step. Inside, however, she had a case of nerves. And then she realized she'd overslept. She raced through her shower and got dressed, and by then, it was time to meet Denton for breakfast, and she felt rushed and panicked. Not the cool, calm, capable woman she preferred to present. Instead, she bolted for the dining room in a mad rush. The last thing she wanted him to think was that she had stood him up.

Of course, he was already there, sitting at a table for two out in the sunshine. He had a cup of coffee in his hand and a smile on his face. She grinned and made her way to him. She sat down. "Sorry I'm late."

He raised his eyebrows. "You're not late. I'm early."

She glanced at her watch and realized she was five minutes early too. She settled back in her chair. "Well."

He chuckled. "I'll take that as a good sign on both our parts."

She leaned over and held out her hand. He picked hers up in his and entwined their fingers. She stared down at them. "Are we thinking that something might be here?"

"I never had a problem with the whole friendship thing. I needed to understand my motivations behind my actions," he admitted. "And now I have to take another look at my motivations for maybe not working quite so hard. So I can stay here longer to spend more time with you."

He had said the words in a joking manner, but she realized he was at least partially serious. She laughed. "I don't want you doing that. But after you've healed and no longer live here, if you were to find a job or a vocation not too far away, then I won't object to that."

He nodded. "I'm giving serious thought to that."

"Any ideas?"

He shook his head. "No, not yet. But I have some friends I can talk to. One is a developer in town. He tried to recruit me before."

"In Dallas?"

He nodded. "Yes. He does those large multi-building, multi-floor apartments and business high-rises."

"What would you do?"

He shrugged. "One of the things I was well-known for in the military, and even before, was getting the job done. So I think he sees me as not quite a project manager but maybe the manager over project managers."

She whistled. "Wow, starting right at the top."

He shook his head and grinned. "What I get to do is kick butt. Only not military style anymore."

"I'm beginning to see how different that is," she said seriously. "The navy and all the other military branches have a pretty tough regimen when it comes to forcing people to do what needs to be done. The fact that you were a US Navy SEAL, well, that adds to my admiration for what you went through."

He shook his head. "But now I have to deal with something different. And that's a whole other story."

She chuckled. "Nope, you are one of those bright friendly guys in every light."

"Until I'm the one who takes your job away because you can't do the job yourself."

She winced. "Okay, I haven't seen that side of you, but I don't doubt it's there. I couldn't do it. I'd have trouble firing anybody. But I make a great team player."

"That's one thing I do understand—teamwork. So it's an interesting prospect."

"It would keep you close?"

He nodded. "Thomas has ten years of work ahead of him at least. He's really buried. He could use an extra hand."

"But can't he hand over control to somebody else?"

He shot her a look of respect. "That's the problem I was thinking about. Thomas has the tendency to be scatter-brained, and he needs somebody to keep him organized too. Anyway, he might come by to talk to me in a week or two. I need more details about the job itself, the hours, and of course, the paycheck."

"For something like that, it would probably be at least twice what you were paid in the military."

His eyebrows shot up. "I know the private sector pays a lot more money, but I doubt it would be anything like that."

"Developers will pay big bucks from what I hear. Particularly if you're any good, then you can write your own ticket. Because having capable managers who can get the job done will save them time—stop them from having to step in and deal with the crap—and save them money for delays and overruns." She studied him carefully. "You know? I think you'd do well at that. You're personable, but you have an iron will." She gave him a nod. "You'd excel at that."

"I don't have any training though. I may have to take some courses or something." He shrugged and stared down at his coffee cup. "Not sure yet."

"And no need to rush forward into a decision. You're here for at least another two months, and then decision time will happen. But not today, not right now."

"Exactly." He lifted his coffee cup in a toast. "Well, should we get some food?"

She glanced over at the buffet, showing some signs of activity. "Sure. You know? I think we both should go." She glanced back at him. "Are you coming?"

"Absolutely."

Together they walked over and selected their breakfast foods. Hannah grabbed a coffee while she was there and then deliberately turned her back on Denton, letting him know she could give him the space he needed to be independent, and returned to their table. And as she had expected, he had followed behind her with his own tray, encountering no problems.

"You're getting very adept at handling independence."

He nodded. "I'm more confident about that now. I may have always been fairly good at it."

"Plus making friends," she teased.

"Friends have always been a major part of my support group." He took several bites of scrambled egg, then lifted his head. "By the way, I'd like to be included in those day trips into town."

"We're doing two a month. I'll put you down for the next one if you like. They've become hugely popular. People making friends all over the place," she added with a smile.

He chuckled. "Fun trips will do that."

They settled into an easy camaraderie and finished breakfast. Both Cole and Brock walked over and sat down with them, their elbows on the table, glancing from Hannah to Denton. She could feel the heat climbing her neck. She pushed her chair back. "I'll go grab more coffee." She looked at Denton. "Shall I refill yours?"

He handed her his cup, and she walked away. She didn't know why she was uncomfortable with Brock and Cole, except for her earlier motivations and thinking maybe getting close to the women would allow her into that group too—and of course, they likely blamed her for Denton cooling his relationship with Brock and Cole.

So very twisted of her. And her mind acknowledged—so very human. As she looked over her shoulder, the men still sat there. She wasn't sure what to think about that, but she knew she needed to get used to it. These three were all very close. And of course, it was natural for them to want to check her out and make sure she was good enough for Denton. Something that she probably failed at right from the beginning.

With both cups refilled, she returned to the table, surprised and a little unsettled to join all three of them there.

She gave Brock and Cole as friendly a smile as she could muster. "How are you two doing?"

Cole answered. "Good. We're checking to make sure our buddy here is doing as well as he can."

She nodded and kept her voice neutral. "As you can see, he's doing well," she said warmly, her gaze darting to Denton and back again.

He reached across the table and covered her hand with one of his.

The men's gazes went from one to the other, and then Brock spoke up. "We're glad to see this."

She glanced at him in surprise. "Why? I thought you were upset over the relationship."

Brock shook his head. "Only when we thought you were trying to separate him from us." He gave her a boyish grin. "But we understand now, and so we think you two will do well together."

Totally surprised at his unexpected response, she stared at him. "Why would you think that?" she asked cautiously.

He grinned. "Because he's very friendly, and you're very reserved, so you'll help tone down the puppy in him, and he'll help bring out the puppy in you."

Her jaw dropped. And then she chuckled. "I'm not sure if that sounds like an adult relationship or not, but it does sound like fun."

"And more fun is definitely required. Something about this place encourages effort, serious determination and focus, but we all need to let our hair down sometimes, and we all need someone to do that with."

How true. And yet, she wanted so much more. As she glanced over at Denton, she squeezed his hand and watched his gaze light up.

She wondered if she'd ever get tired of seeing that look in his eyes. That sense that they were on the same page, connected in ways she didn't understand. Lord, she hoped she wouldn't.

Then he dropped her hand. "There is nothing quite so special as friends."

And *wham*, she'd been friend-zoned—again.

DENTON CAUGHT AN odd look on Brock's face and realized he had said the wrong thing. Had she noticed? Did she understand?

Brock and Cole were his friends, but that didn't mean Denton wanted his buddies to know how close he was getting to Hannah. For that reason he had pulled back, dropping her hand.

Hannah stood then, collected her coffee cup and said, "Back to work for me." She smiled in farewell and walked away, placing her dirty cup on the dish rack.

Denton glanced at Brock. "What was that earlier look on your face for?"

Brock settled back. "I thought I understood the relationship was much more serious than I first considered. But then you made it sound like you two were just friends, so that confused me. But maybe it's not me who is confused. It's you."

Cole spoke up. "Exactly what I would say. It's like you're hot, then cold."

Denton leaned back. "I didn't back off that badly."

Both men snorted.

"Yes, you did," Brock said. "You dropped the relationship to being just friends."

Denton glanced at his hands, realizing if that was how his actions looked to the men, it was also how it would look to her. The opposite of what he had wanted. He understood why he'd done it, but he didn't want to explain it to his buddies.

"I guess I'm a little confused." He tried to joke it off lightly.

"Understandable. Nothing like a young love to remind us that there's so much else in life, and maybe she isn't the right person for you after all." Cole shrugged. "No way to tell but to go forward and see what comes from it."

Denton thought about all the things he knew about

her—the way she acted, her honesty and caring, her integrity and he was pretty darn sure of the return of emotion. He nodded. "I'm sure she's right for me."

"You've only known her for like three weeks at most." Brock shook his head. "Don't push it."

Denton laughed. "Is that you saying that? I know you're another few months down the relationship road with the love of your life, but it didn't take you long to figure out what you wanted. I'd hate to think I'm that slow." The thing is, he wasn't. He knew what he wanted—Hannah.

But it was new and not something he wanted to share or have his friends criticize.

"It's not that you're slow, but I think it has to do with all this friends stuff that she's got you thinking about. That appears to confuse the issue for you."

Good point. He frowned. "How do I know if her friendship is more than friendship?"

"You already know you're more than friends. The question is, how much more? The thing is, you don't have to answer that now. You take a few steps down that road and see how it feels, see what develops, see how it grows."

"We've been dancing around the issue of coming together, separating, coming together … It's been a unique time."

"Partly because you're injured, partly because she works here. So you have a lot of different issues that will be affected. Have you discussed the future at all?" Brock pressed.

Denton nodded. "We were talking about me hooking up with Thomas's company in Dallas." They already knew about his friend, had met him over the years.

"Did that make her happy?" Cole asked.

Denton smiled and nodded. "Yes."

"Good," Brock said. "Then don't analyze it too much. Just let it happen. You'll do fine." He stood up and grinned at Denton. "I'm really happy for you."

The men left soon afterward. Inasmuch as Denton appreciated their parting words of wisdom, he couldn't stop the feeling that he'd done something very wrong. Or that Hannah would take his actions the wrong way.

He stared at his phone. Nope. It would be better to explain in person. He should go to her office, which was something he rarely did. He thought about that for a long moment and realized he avoided her work environment. He didn't want to intrude with her work the same way she didn't intrude on his life here because he was one of the patients.

Decision made, he got up and walked to her office. "You left rather abruptly," he said quietly. "I came to see if something was wrong."

If he hadn't been watching her face so closely, he wouldn't have seen the hurt whisper across her features.

"I didn't mean to hurt you or make it seem to you like we were only friends, *only* to my buddies," he quickly added. "I didn't think about how you'd perceive it until you got up and left." Wisely, he withheld mentioning Brock and Cole's responses.

She shot him a shuttered look.

He sighed. "I don't want a relationship where I constantly have to worry about what I say, afraid you will take it the wrong way. I would never do anything to hurt you, and I would never do anything deliberately to make you feel bad. If you feel like I relegated our relationship back to friends, I'm sorry because that hadn't been my intention."

She studied him for a long moment. "Yet, that's what it

seemed like. And here I'd thought we'd moved past that."

He nodded. "We have. And it feels ... I don't know ... special."

At her start of surprise, he tried to explain. "I wanted to keep it between us. Enjoy knowing we're together. They are my friends, but I don't tell them every single thing. I was afraid that if I told them about us, about how I felt, in some way it would take away the intimacy, the uniqueness of what we have."

Her gaze warmed. She sat back in her chair and stared at him in surprise. "So, you were trying to distance them, not me?"

He thought about that for a long moment, then nodded. "That's probably a good way to look at it." He shrugged and gave her a sheepish look. "They know so much about me that they already understand how close we are. But I didn't want to discuss it with them. I wanted to keep it just for us, something between us for as long as I could."

Slowly a smile dawned across her face, and he relaxed, but his gaze was caught on how special her smile was. And he was so damn glad it was just for him.

"It's probably the one excuse any woman would accept—and be delighted with." She chuckled. "And in this case, you're completely forgiven."

He laughed and mimicked wiping sweat off his face. "I fully expect I will make more mistakes, you know?" he warned. "Please don't hold them against me and walk away hurt. I will do my best not to blunder, and I will do everything in my power to not make the same mistakes again."

Chapter 15

HANNAH SMILED UP at him. She had been hurt, but his explanation more than made up for it. "Apparently," she said, "I have more to learn in this relationship than you do."

He grinned at her. "Then how about we teach each other?"

Denton opened his arms, and Hannah stood and stepped into them. For the first time, she didn't care if anybody could see. She didn't worry what others might think or about getting into trouble. Or raised eyebrows at her unorthodox behavior. This was good. And she'd do a lot to fight for it.

Actually, she'd do anything. He was the one man for her. The road wouldn't be calm or straightforward, but she'd never been one to take the easy road in anything she did.

Over Denton's shoulder, she caught Dani glancing up to see the two of them hugging. A big smile flashed across her face, and she gave Hannah the thumbs-up sign.

Hannah pulled back slightly. "Don't look now, but our relationship is no longer a secret."

Denton twisted slightly. Several people were peering through the open doorway, wide grins on their faces, followed by Dani, who got up and walked from her office with a wave and a smile.

Hannah chuckled. "My vote is to give them something really juicy to look at. Then no one will have any doubts we're together."

"I'm all for that." He tilted up her chin and pulled her into his arms for a passionate kiss.

She threw her arms around his neck and kissed him back.

A kiss full of promise. A kiss full of love. A kiss not just for the moment but forever.

Epilogue

E LLIOT CARVER STARED at the letter on his lap. He'd avoided opening it for the last thirty minutes. It was from Hathaway House and—with any luck—Aaron Hammond himself.

He still wasn't sure he should go, even if a room was available. He'd come to realize that nothing anyone could do would likely help him out. A change of scenery would be good, and if he could make a change, then this would be the best option.

If it was an option.

He'd known Aaron in the military, and like Elliot, Aaron had been injured. Hathaway House had turned his life around to the point that he was now engaged to Dani Hathaway, part owner and manager of the rehabilitation center.

Aaron had been instrumental in bringing in other people, others of the US Navy SEAL brotherhood who were in need. Then the men who served helped each other rehab. And if you were a SEAL, then the hand was held out even farther.

But what if Elliot wasn't qualified or didn't fit or failed to meet their medical requirements? So many aspects could mess this up for him. Including his own doubts …

"Aren't you going to open your mail?" Finn asked, rolling to his side. He was a maverick, like Elliot. Only Elliot felt washed up and thrown away. Finn was new to rehab. New to being injured. He was in a holding pattern, but he had a mess of surgeries coming up. If he kept his positive outlook on life after all that, then Elliot would be happier for Finn. As it were, if Elliot himself could get some sleep, then maybe life would turn around for him.

Right now that looked doubtful.

He shook his head and said, "Maybe later."

"Hell, no way. You open that. If this works out for you, then maybe I'll give the place a try. We have to stick together. This is a battle we didn't train for, so it'll take all the intel we can get to make it through."

A groan escaped. Finn was right. Elliot suddenly reached down and snatched up the envelope. If he got an invitation to go, yeah, he would go. All the rest was his fear talking.

And he'd had enough of that crap. *All in, all the time.* The SEAL motto he now used like a mantra.

He ripped it open and pulled out the letter.

His heart slammed against his ribs as he read the first line out loud.

"Elliot, we'd like to invite you to Hathaway House for the rest of your rehabilitation …"

"Hot damn," Finn crowed with envy. "Go and then tell me how it is. I'll get started on my own request."

Elliot stared at his friend and knew Finn was right about one thing. This journey was one none of them had experienced before. They had to learn from those who had gone before.

"Do it," Elliot said, waving the acceptance letter in his hand. "I'll meet you there, and we'll both beat this."

And the two men shook hands about their future.

Elliot

Hathaway House, Book 5

Dale Mayer

Chapter 1

E LLIOT CARVER WOKE with his heart pounding and his mind screaming at him to run while his frozen body lay on the bed, completely soaked in sweat. He shuddered as awareness returned, and he tried to relax. Cream-colored walls and brightly hued curtains stared back at him. The same walls he'd seen before going to sleep. He was still at Hathaway House. It had been another nightmare, another horrifying event that drove through his brain and refused to leave him in peace.

They called it PTSD—post-traumatic stress disorder. Frankly he didn't give a crap what they called it. There was no cure, there was no getting away from this and there was no improvement. It didn't matter what they did. He had tried everything from medication to counseling to yoga. So far with no effect.

Of course, every time he woke up, the sudden jerk of the fight-or-flight response immediately sent his engines firing into overdrive and his back into painful spasms. He'd broken his back. Yet, he was one of the lucky ones—his spinal cord hadn't snapped. That didn't matter to his pain receptors though. His spinal cord had been inflamed and swollen. The muscles and the nerves had been badly damaged. The subsequent surgeries had set him even further behind. Several plates were put in up and down his spinal column, just to hold the vertebrae together.

However, there was no doubt about it, the doctors had done a wonderful job. He knew that. He wished they could do something about his nightmares. Sometimes he'd be sitting still and the flashes would come. He would hear bombs going off and see bits of his friends flying around him. The last thing he wanted was to mentally revisit the accident over and over again. He figured, after the hell he'd been in for months, there would've been some improvement. But instead of improving, it seemed his condition was worse. More little pieces of memories shot through him at too-frequent intervals, and whether he liked it or not, suddenly he was reliving more and more of his past. In no way did he want to relive six years of SEAL missions—going through it once had been bad enough. But it was as if once the memories started they couldn't stop. And he'd relive other harsh times as well.

It was as if his mind didn't want to give him a break. His brain was constantly on a loop. He didn't know how to turn it off as he didn't know how it had started. He had gone so far as to contact a naturopath about it, and they had said his dopamine levels might have something to do with it. He understood the explanation they had given, but he didn't understand how it would help. He might contact the naturopath again or seek out even more avenues if things didn't improve soon.

The doctors *said* his condition would improve. They predicted that as his muscles strengthened his depression would reduce.

He hated the depression. It hit without warning, without any kind of logic. Sure, he had survived his accident, but he wouldn't be in as good a shape as before. He might not do as many yoga moves as he once did, but then he now had steel bars in his spine, so what did he expect? He wouldn't get upset because he couldn't jump or play volleyball anymore since he could do all kinds of other things. Like walk. If he couldn't do some activities, well, that was just life.

He was alive, he was well and he was not going back into the military. That was out forever, and maybe that was okay too. There'd been an edge to him before, reminding him time was running out. That he needed to make some decisions about how long he would do this. He loved his work and loved his job. He'd been good at it, loving the challenge and daily training. But he had been in inner turmoil for a while, as if knowing something would blow up in his face. And it had happened way sooner than he thought it would.

"Is it bad tonight?"

He turned his head to the side and smiled at Sicily Lawrence, his night nurse and hopefully a friend. "No. It's not too bad."

She gave him a knowing smile that said she understood he was lying, and that was okay. She had gained a lot of experience working with various patients at Hathaway House over her five years here. It was understandable she'd see right through him. Now if only she had answers for what ailed him.

"And no, I don't need something to help me sleep. I'll go back under eventually."

She nodded. "Can I get you anything?"

He thought about that for a moment and realized his throat was dry, scratchy. "Would you mind fetching me some fresh water?"

"Of course not. I'll be back in a moment." She flashed

him a bright smile and disappeared.

He could hear her soft footsteps moving down the hall. It had taken him a long time to feel connected here. He still wasn't there yet, but he didn't feel quite so standoffish anymore, so maybe things were getting better. He'd known several men who'd come to Hathaway House and had done fabulously well. He'd desperately wanted the same for himself. He'd connected to Sicily first.

Somebody was always on watch here. But he usually saw Sicily at this hour. She had this uncanny sense about his condition. He almost never saw her during the day. But when his guard went down and the nightmares came around, it was Sicily who followed them. Her bright-pink cheeks and creamy skin gave her a farm-girl complexion that spoke of being raised with lots of fresh air and sunshine. She was slim and fit, but he liked her smile the best. Maybe because it was always directed at him, with what seemed like a little special something behind it. Not too many men could resist that.

Of course, he'd been single for a long time, and that wouldn't change any time soon. How was he supposed to sleep with a woman if he woke up screaming and shouting every night? It wasn't what he wanted. It wasn't what he needed. No way in hell he'd ever consciously hurt a woman—but the possibility of hurting her in his sleep was now there. So that meant no woman in his bed for a long time to come. He'd had relationships in the past—even one he thought might make it to the altar—but things usually broke off before too long because he was always on missions. Either he was out of town too much or they simply couldn't stand the thought of not knowing whether he was alive or dead, and they'd start to have misgivings. That was usually the beginning of the end.

But that wouldn't happen anymore. There would be no more missions for him. No more leaving the country in the middle of the night. His life had changed. Still, with some slight improvements, he could move to his own place and enjoy an independent—albeit lonely—lifestyle.

A special camaraderie was here at Hathaway. He hadn't known anything about it until he had transferred over. Another SEAL Elliot knew had recommended he come here. Aaron had been here as a patient and was now an integral part of the place. That was all it took for Elliot. If it was good enough for one SEAL, it was good enough for another. The thought made him smile. Even now, broken and a mess, he still counted himself as part of the SEAL brotherhood. There were a whole lot worse things to belong to.

Sicily had told him three other SEALs were in residence now as well. Denton, Cole and Brock. Elliot had known them by name. They were a tight group, but Elliot didn't know them at all personally. He should step up and intro-duce himself, but he hadn't so far. He wasn't even sure why except he was tired and frustrated and didn't want to deal with any new stressors. Yet he could certainly use more people in his life, his new team to be a daily influence in his life—to replace the SEAL brotherhood he no longer shared in that way.

He'd mentioned them to Finn in an email. He'd known of them too. Finn was holding off to see if Elliot got the results he'd been hoping for. So far he hadn't.

Those with support did better than those without. Elliot hardly had any family left. Only his father. His parents had divorced when he was younger, and he'd stayed with his dad, who had remarried a woman with a ready-made family. And that marriage hadn't lasted either. He wasn't even sure he remembered their names. How sad was that? Still, he was close with his dad, and now his dad didn't have anyone else either.

His dad had been Elliot's champion as Elliot made it through the surgeries. And frankly Elliot wouldn't have been surprised if his father had done something to get him into Hathaway House. Although there wasn't anything technically wrong with the previous place, his father thought for sure Elliot would show more improvement just from being here.

Physically he was improving—emotionally and spiritually, not so much. His counselor was good. Elliot had opened up about some of his fears and past experiences, but there was no cure for PTSD—at least not yet. His counselor kept him digging, wondering if there was anything else in his psyche compounding the issue.

So far it was a big fat no.

Sicily walked in the door, holding a large glass of ice water. Moving slowly, he propped himself up on the bed, so his head was higher.

"How's the pain?" she asked. "You need anything else?"

He took a long thirsty drink of the cold water. When he put down the glass, he shook his head. "I'm fine. I need to sleep." He tried to get comfortable in the bed, feeling the muscles in his back threatening to cramp with his movements. He froze and then took several deep breaths, trying to relax.

"I can work on a couple of the muscle cramps in your back if you'd like?" she asked, concern in her voice.

As this was something she had offered in the past, he wasn't shy about accepting her help now. The surgeons had warned him about this problem. It took both Elliot and Sicily to get him rolled to his stomach so she could access his muscles. Until the muscles and nerves reconnected and healed and his body physically strengthened, spasms would be the norm. He could do certain things to alleviate them, but sudden sharp movements were not among them.

Of course, he was tired and worn out in the middle of night, and he forgot. But Sicily knew what she was doing. Before long, the tension in his back had eased. He propped himself up on his elbow and grabbed the water again. He took another long drink and then turned out the light.

"Thank you. I think I will sleep now." He relaxed on the bed and closed his eyes, grateful sleep was reaching for him. He barely heard Sicily's quiet tread as she left the room. His last thought was *What a lifesaver she is.*

Chapter 2

S ICILY LAWRENCE HEADED to the nurses' station. She flexed her fingers and reached for the tube of cream she kept there. She squeezed some onto her hand and rubbed it in.

The other night nurse, Jenna, looked up, a question in her eyes.

Sicily shook her head. "It wasn't as bad as some nights," she said.

The nurse nodded. "But it's every night still, isn't it?"

"Yes, but there's progress," Sicily said quietly. Most patients were asleep on their floor, so she was used to speaking in low tones. In fact, during the daytime shift, she had to remember to speak up. "According to his chart, he was having a lot of these episodes during the day too. At least that appears to have stopped."

"Then again he's not sleeping as much during the day," Jenna pointed out. She was very pragmatic.

Sicily smiled. "You're right. But as long as he doesn't need to sleep during the day, we will take that as a step forward too." She pulled up his file, wrote a quick note and closed it down again. She'd talk to the doctor about the situation. Elliot preferred not to take drugs as they left him groggy and unfocused. She didn't have a problem with that, except she hated to see anybody suffer unnecessarily.

Jenna said, "It's surprising we don't have more patients with PTSD in here."

"I think we probably do, but I don't believe it's as big an issue for some as it is for Elliot."

Jenna nodded. "That's possible."

"And don't forget. A lot of the other men and women here are on various medications, which have been known to suppress the PTSD symptoms. At some point, when they taper off their meds, that's when their symptoms show up."

"I can't imagine what some of our patients went through. No wonder they have nightmares."

Sicily couldn't agree more. She grabbed her mug and went to the coffee station where she poured herself a fresh cup. She'd mostly worked nights since she'd been here. But in all those nights and with all those patients, something about Elliot tugged at her heart. She made a point of walking past his door on a regular basis. He was the kind who hated to ask for assistance. If he needed anything, most times he did it for himself. But sometimes he suffered when there was no need. When she caught him in one of those moments, she always made a point to step in and help. Life was tough enough when you were alone. It didn't have to be twice as hard because you were stubborn too.

Of course most of the men and women here were stubborn, driven and incredibly capable due to their very natures. They had been placed in a position of having to reorient themselves to this new reality of physical injuries. In Elliot's case, she understood how close he came to being a paraplegic. She knew he understood that as well. There was always a sense of being grateful for as far as he'd come. But at the same time, he was exhausted. His sleep patterns were constantly disrupted with the PTSD, so his medical team readjusted Elliot's rehab schedule day to day, not wanting to wake Elliot from any sleep he got—sleep was the primary goal for him. That kind of long-term drain on his energy wasn't good either. But she had no permanent solution for him. She wished she did.

Originally he'd taken sleeping pills, but he hated the way they made him feel. Instead of him waking up a dozen times, he woke up a half-dozen times, but each was horrific enough that his nightmares ripped him into wakefulness through the sleeping pills. Often he never got back to sleep. So Sicily understood that was not an improvement either. During the day, he worked himself to the bone during his physical therapy routines, and sometimes he did collapse, but often that was a short-term solution only.

"His counselors are working through the emotional aspects," Jenna said. "But post-traumatic stress isn't something anybody can deal with overnight."

If he could get some sleep, that would help. But like so many times before, she was at a loss as to how to handle that or otherwise help him. In cases like this, possibly traditional medicine wasn't the answer. She was open to the idea of alternative therapies, but she'd yet to hear of any that worked either.

She checked her watch. It was after five a.m., almost time for her shift to end. She rose from her chair and began her rounds again. She went the long way around, coming to Elliot's room last. As she passed his room, she slowed with her ear cocked to hear how he was doing. An odd sound came from within, and she poked her head around the open door to see him lying in bed, chanting something in a very low tone. She hesitated to interrupt because she wasn't sure if he was awake or asleep. He'd been known to talk in his sleep before and even to carry on a complete conversation. As she went to withdraw, he turned his head and stared at her.

"Good morning, Sicily."

She froze and hesitantly took a step inside. "I didn't want to disturb you, if you were sleeping or doing something."

He smiled. "Well, I got some sleep, so I'm feeling a little better."

Her eyebrows shot up. "A little sleep is good. But the fact that you're awake at this hour isn't."

"I've been trying to meditate. It's supposed to be good for my soul. Slow down the thoughts in my mind, reduce the stress going through my system."

She nodded. "Meditation is good for all of us."

"Do you do it?" he challenged.

"No. Not anymore. I used to, but like so many routines, it fell by the wayside," she confessed.

He nodded. "It's so much easier if you have somebody to do it with. I was speaking to Shane about adding yoga to my schedule, but no yoga teacher is on staff."

"Several people here are comfortable enough with yoga to show you some moves," she said lightly. "It's something I do myself every morning."

"Every morning, as in your 'morning' before you go to work, or as in right now as you come off shift?"

She chuckled. "Normally I head to my room, switch out of my uniform and sleep for a few hours. When I wake up, I do some yoga."

"I rarely see you during the day."

"I'm here. But I'm not on shift, so I usually don't come upstairs. I help downstairs a lot. I have a bike, and I like to go riding every day. I do a lot of walking too." She shrugged.

"It's hard getting used to the night shift, but once you're in the routine, it does leave the bulk of the day to do the things you want to do."

"Yeah, like sleep."

She grinned. "Sure, but I start work at ten p.m., so considering I'm off at six a.m.—in another ten minutes or so—I've got all morning to sleep. I usually get a solid six-and-a-half to seven hours, and then I have most of the afternoon and the evening to myself."

"Then why don't you stop by and visit when you're off?"

"Maybe I will," she said lightly. "It's kind of hard to visit my work area and not have it feel like it's my job."

"True enough. Even when I was an active SEAL, I hung out with my SEAL buddies in my time off. Hard to know sometimes when a workday started and a workday ended. Could you show me a few yoga poses?"

His leer and suggestive waggling eyebrow movements made her laugh. "I could," she said, crossing her arms. "But would you listen to me?"

"It depends on what body contortions you're able to do," he said with a big grin. "I might get a little sidetracked."

She rolled her eyes at him. "I do have a couple moves that might help you sleep."

He raised his eyebrows at her. "Hell, those I'd like to try." He motioned to the space beside the bed. "Care to demonstrate?"

She shot him a suspicious look, but seeing only curiosity in his gaze, she nodded. She glanced down at the watch on her wrist. "Technically my shift is done. So here's a ten-minute yoga lesson. If you're interested, we can do more when I come back on tonight."

She slowly went through several moves meant to destress, unwind and relax the muscles from a long day. It occurred to her she should do her yoga before she went to bed instead. That would most likely be of more value to her too.

She took her time and showed him the different arm and hand positions. "It's important to work on your breathing. Every movement you make, you inhale and exhale. Don't focus so much on getting through the exercises but on sinking into each position and getting your breathing right."

"Right. We work on the breathing for physiotherapy as well."

She nodded. When she had done her ten minutes, she slowly stood up, stretched high to the sky and let out a deep breath. "That's my morning workout. It's simple. It's fast, but it makes me feel so much better."

When she turned to look at him, he stood by his bed in his boxers, stretching for the sky as if imitating her movements.

She stared at him, bemused. "Have you been following along?"

"Only for the last position. But if you want to repeat from the beginning," he said, "I'd like to give a couple of those a try."

She stepped back a little farther and went through the first couple of exercises with him as he did his best to get into the positions—adapting his damaged body as best as he could. She pointed out where he'd overextended his knees and elbows, touching where the muscles were tense.

"Breathe. Let the tension release and relax."

By the time he'd gone through the ones he could do easily, or at least capably, another fifteen minutes had gone by. He sat down on the bed, his expression one of surprise.

"I do feel better. It's like the tension always strumming through me has eased back, and it's not quite so taut."

"Exactly." She grinned at him. "Now the dining hall's open, and it's breakfast time."

"Have breakfast with me?" he wheedled. "I hate eating alone."

She smiled. "Fine, let's get breakfast, but you are not going out in that state of undress. Get some clothes on, and then we'll go down together."

"Where will you be then?" He walked gingerly to the closet and pulled out a pair of lightweight jeans and a T-shirt.

"I have to return to the office and sign out. I'll be back here in five minutes."

Suddenly feeling like a giddy schoolgirl, she slipped from the room and raced to her office. She'd left her computer on. She logged off and shut down her station. She walked over to the board and signed out at her normal time.

Then Sandra walked in to start her day. "Don't you look spry this morning? I don't know how you do the night shift. And for so long."

"I don't mind it. There are advantages."

"You can always ask to have your shift switched. So you know, we'll be hiring some new people. It's a good time for you to switch to daytime if you want."

"It's something to consider, but it hasn't been an issue for me."

"Your choice." Sandra studied the shift board for a moment and then looked at the big chalkboard where they put up any alerts and notices. "Quiet night?"

Sicily nodded. "Very much so," she confirmed. "Even Elliot didn't have a terrible night."

"That's good news, indeed," Sandra said.

Sicily walked from the room and headed toward Elliot's. He sat on the side of his bed with his tablet in his hand.

"Are you sure you can fit in breakfast?" she teased.

He looked up with a grin. "I was the one waiting for you."

She nodded at the crutches beside him. "Are you using those today?"

"I thought I would try. I was checking my schedule, to see how arduous it'll be. If I do too much first off ..." He shook his head. "Well, I'm sure you have a good idea what happens then."

She chuckled. "Indeed, I do." She turned on her heel and led the way to the dining hall. She slowed her pace slightly, so she didn't appear to be racing away. But neither would she make it too easy on him. If he was giving the crutches a try, then she would see how well he handled them.

BY THE TIME he made it to the large open dining room, Elliot was wondering at the wisdom of the crutches. They did force him to keep his back straight. He wasn't using his brace and hadn't worn it for the last couple weeks. He loved being free of the constriction. At the same time, there was a certain comfort in knowing his back would be safe and secure with it on. It was kind of a toss-up sometimes. But as his back strengthened, it was just as important that he used his core muscles to help his balance. As he slowly improved, everything integrated. He couldn't strengthen one part of his body and ignore the rest.

He stared at the long line of people with their trays, and

he realized with his crutches, it would be that much harder to carry his food.

Sicily stepped up beside him. "You fill it, and I'll take it to the table."

He nodded his head. "I won't argue with that."

He loaded his plate with sausages, ham, eggs, and hash browns, grabbing toast and a bowl of fresh fruit for good measure. As he walked along the buffet, he realized one of the differences in being here, with the women around, was that there were no secrets. Something was very freeing about that. Before he'd felt as if he had to keep up a front. Keep up the big strong man appearance. As a SEAL, he was one of the best fighters in the country. That meant he always had a certain image to project and to maintain.

But now things were different. Sicily saw into him and saw who he was inside better than most women he'd ever met. He did not want to let go of that. He wanted to deepen it, to make it more … so much more.

He wasn't sure that was kosher. Although he would have to be blind not to see the various relationships between staff and patients at Hathaway House. Not the protocol of most medical facilities, but he had seen friendships blossom and relationships grow. Even Dani, the owner, was engaged to Aaron, one of the former patients. Elliot was happy for them. Dani was a beautiful woman, inside and out, and Aaron, well, Aaron was a former SEAL. They had friends in common. At the same time, it was good to know Aaron had found love in a place like this, and it underscored what Elliot was considering himself.

The people here saw who the patients were at a level most other people never had the chance to see. They saw the patients face trauma, nightmares, physical injuries and imperfections that only showed up under these circumstances. Most of the time, nonmedical individuals didn't deal with this stress or emotional baggage, except for spouses and other family members of injured veterans.

Many relationships existed on the surface only and never touched the deeper layers. There was no need to unless somebody was involved in some sort of major trauma. Most people never found out who they were on the inside at that level. Once a trauma happened to one half of a pair, then the other partner was pulled in, whether they wanted to be or not. They couldn't avoid seeing what the injured person was going through.

The best relationships grew out of times of stress, when you saw how the other person acted at the worst point in their life. If you still respected that person and still loved and appreciated who they were at that point, then the relationship had every reason to flourish. But so many other people would take one look and crack. They couldn't handle seeing the other person in pain, realizing they didn't have it in them to be supportive or to be there for that person during the hard times.

"Shall we sit over there?" Sicily pointed to the sunny side of the deck, interrupting his musings.

"Sure." He let her lead, then followed.

He always figured when he was in a relationship he was there not for a good time but for a long time. But he'd been the first to admit that hadn't worked out so well. Now maybe that would change. He was no longer leaving the country on a regular basis, and his work was no longer dangerous. Hell, he didn't even have a job. That was a real issue. Sure, he had a pension, but it wasn't the same thing. He still intended to be a fully functioning member of society, paying taxes and putting money away for retirement. That had not changed. He just didn't know what he wanted to do. Although he was leaning toward business. He just had no idea what facet. He was who he was on the inside, and he was the same person he'd always been. Now the person on the inside was a little stronger. He was a little wearier, and he'd seen a whole lot more of the world and of himself than he'd have liked, but it was all good. He could do this. Most of the time.

"Thanks for the invite," Sicily said.

Given a choice, he'd do this every day. "You're welcome." If Sicily was his, he could do this all the time.

Until all those memories came out of the shadows and attacked him, like some enemy who he knew existed but had never seen. One of the most frustrating things for him was that he didn't necessarily know when or how the attacks would happen or from what corner. He knew that they were coming, and they would give him hell.

He'd been through a battery of psychological tests. He knew who he was on the inside, so when he'd hit the bottom, there hadn't been any ugly surprises. The biggest surprise was how deep and bottomless that well of falling seemed to be. But as soon as he landed, he took stock and got back on his feet and then crawled up again. It was not easy, not fast and certainly didn't happen without help, but he had made it.

As he looked around at the people beside him, he realized this was exactly where he needed to be. Everyone here was in the same place mentally. Sure, there were ups and downs and some differences, but they were all on the path to recovery. They had all turned the mental corner and were doing what they needed to do for their own sakes. Not that they didn't care about their friends, family, children or spouses, but the rehab patients had to do what they had to do right now. So they were here, doing what they did best, and that was dealing with life. A new life.

He settled in to enjoy his meal.

Chapter 3

WHEN BREAKFAST WAS over, Sicily walked alongside Elliot to his room. They exchanged a quick goodbye, and after seeing one of his medical team arriving, Sicily left him, fatigued but restless. Smiling to herself, she went to see Stan at the vet clinic. She was too wired-up and excited for sleep. That was so unlike her.

As she walked into the clinic, Stan was at the front counter, studying the appointment book for the day. He looked up and flashed a smile her way. "Hey, don't you look great? But aren't you supposed to be in bed now?"

"Just had breakfast and I'm still a little too wired to go to bed. I thought maybe you could use a hand for an hour or two." She gave him a sly look. "Or rather I was hoping an animal or two might need a cuddle."

"That's more like the truth. There are always cages to clean, stalls to muck out and dogs to walk."

She grinned. "Bunnies to cuddle, dogs to brush and cats to comb?"

He nodded. "Always those too." He led her into the back room. "We have six rescues. Mom had kittens as soon as she landed. Smart mom. She knew exactly where she was safe."

Sicily fell in love as soon as she saw them. The mom was a huge black medium-haired cat, and the look in her eye was one of gratitude that she was, indeed, safe and sound. She let Sicily stroke her for a long while. When the cat started to squirm, Sicily headed back to the waiting room at the front counter.

"Now those are adorable kittens."

Stan smiled. "They are cuties."

"Do you have more people at reception these days?" Sicily asked curiously. "Every time I'm here, somebody new seems to be at the desk."

"We've started some job-sharing initiatives, and since we've increased our hours, we have more shifts to cover," Stan said with a big smile. "We are open on Saturdays now too. It's not so much that you see a lot of new people. There are five of us now, working throughout the week."

"Wow. Good for you." As she watched a great big German shepherd walked in on the end of a leash, its regal head high, ears pointed and nose up. "How lucky you guys are."

Stan chuckled. "I love being around the animals, but it can be tough when the news isn't good."

"I know that feeling well."

"I hear you used to work in an ER in Detroit," Stan queried.

"I did for a couple years. But after a while, I couldn't do it anymore. So much death and fighting, shootings and violence," she said quietly. "Hathaway House is much more my style."

"At least everyone upstairs wants to be here, but when it comes to the patients down here, that's not always the case," Stan said slowly.

"I get that. Thanks for the pet therapy. I'll see you later." Sicily headed to the stalls, seeing if any large animals were inside. The stalls were all empty, so she carried on outside and walked around to look at the pastures. Old Maggie was there with the young filly, Molly, at her side, plus a couple other new horses. A gelding had arrived since she'd last been down here.

She walked over to greet all the horses, ambling over to have their noses rubbed. A few minutes later, she headed around the building, passing the pool area. It was empty, but the water twinkled so beautifully in the sunlight she wondered if she should indulge in a morning swim. Making a quick decision, she returned to her place and changed into her suit. She grabbed her cover-up and a towel and walked back out.

At this point, two people were at the far end of the pool. She headed to one of the lanes and dove in. Even though she lived here and the staff had full use of the place as well, her nighttime shift made it a little harder for her to partake of Hathaway House's exercise benefits during the day. While she had a lot of available options, she tended to leave all the equipment for the patients. She did fifty laps in the pool before she stopped and floated, letting her heart return to a normal pace. She bobbed toward the steps before slowly climbing out. She found a chair in the sunshine and sat to dry herself off.

"Good morning. How are you today?" Dani asked, climbing out of the pool and wringing out her long hair. "It's nice to see you in the water."

Sicily laughed. "I'm still a little too keyed up to sleep, but I should try."

Dani smiled. "Night shift is hard on the system."

"Everybody keeps saying that, but I'm not so sure it's true in my case," she said. "But at the same time, it's not exactly conducive to relationships."

"Not if both of you are on night shift." Dani grabbed her towel and rubbed her hair. "Do you have a boyfriend?"

Sicily flushed and shook her head rapidly. "No, I don't."

"But you must be sweet on somebody if you're considering the difficulties of night shift on a relationship," Dani teased.

Sicily flushed deeper. "No, I was looking around and seeing so many new couples," she said, inspired by the thought. "Wondering how I'd handle it."

"You can ask to switch to daytime shifts," Dani said cheerfully. "Unless you like night shifts, then you'll find a way around it."

"True. And thanks for the offer." As she sat there with the warm sun on her, she realized the combined efforts from her swim and the heat were having the desired effect. "I think I can sleep now." She got up, grabbed her towel and with a small wave to Dani, made her way out of the pool area.

"Sleep well," Dani called out.

Once inside her apartment, Sicily had a shower and slipped into her nightie, then crawled into bed. One of the reasons she'd taken the night shift position was to avoid getting into any complicated relationships, yet that too had stemmed from her earlier stressful lifestyle. Her last one had been very volatile as they'd both worked at the same hospital in the same environment. The move here had let her improve so many elements in her life and night shift had been one of them. This way, she wasn't available for any relationship. For the first time in the five years since, she wondered if she could make a relationship work or if she'd need to switch shifts. Other people made it work, but she wasn't other people. Elliot was special. While she had her night shift schedule, that gave them a special connection, but if their relationship was to move forward, would she continue working nights? She wasn't sure.

But what about after he left? Or was she worrying over nothing? Because there was nothing between them. Yet.

By the end of the morning, Elliot was exhausted. Physiotherapy had been hard, and without much sleep, it was even harder.

Shane shook his head. "You looked like you had a pretty rough night when you walked in here."

"Yeah, the nightmares were bad again last night."

Shane nodded but didn't say anything. The two were accustomed to Elliot's PTSD symptoms, and so far there didn't appear to be anything that could help Elliot get through it. Particularly as he was so reactive to most medications. Shane stood back and looked at Elliot. "Time for a nap? Or a massage?"

"Massage. My back's crappy after last night."

Shane nodded. "That's a good idea. Maybe we can get you knocked out while I'm working on you. So let's set it up for your room." He glanced at his watch and said, "Eat something before we start, and that way if you sleep through lunch, you won't be starving when you wake up. I'll talk to Dennis, and he'll get you something special."

"If I could sleep all afternoon, that would be good too," joked Elliot.

"If that's what works for you. We always try to accommodate our patients," Shane said, picking up his tablet. "I have to go to my office. I'll meet you back in your room in ten."

Elliot nodded. "Looking forward to it."

"I'll check out your back. You can tell me where your spasms are coming from. We may need to adjust your bed and see if we can find a way to stop the knots. If I can figure out which muscle groups are affected, we can work on strengthening them. Yet not so hard that they end up cramping on you, mind you."

"Thanks." Tired as he was, Elliot slipped into the wheelchair and let his body collapse with gratitude. When he was this exhausted, there was no point pushing his body further. That was reserved for mornings, after he woke. Not for noon when his body was ready to crash for eight hours. Slowly he wheeled his way down and around the hallways until he came to his room. He pushed open the door and headed inside. Food would have to wait. He had enough time and barely enough energy to change before Shane arrived. After that, he hoped he could sleep the rest of the afternoon away.

If he was that lucky.

Chapter 4

S ICILY WOKE UP to bright sunshine in her bedroom. She lay tucked under the covers, cozy and happy and feeling rested. She was blessed with good sleep patterns, unlike Elliot. She couldn't imagine not sleeping on a regular basis. Even after she had one bad night, she felt worn down. How miserable he must feel after months of sleep deprivation. He'd adjusted well, even though his ongoing lack of sleep could have extremely detrimental effects on his healing. Hell, even if you weren't healing, lack of sleep made it difficult to get through the day. It was like an enduring weariness that took over your soul. You put in the time, but you weren't refreshed. There was never any sense of renewal.

Whereas she could go to bed upset and tired, but after seven hours of good sleep, she woke up bright and happy. She hopped out of bed and walked to her small patio. The double French doors were locked in an open position. They were wide enough that the fresh air could come in and closed enough to keep out ninety-nine percent of the critters. She clicked the lock and opened the patio doors wide, staring out at the pastures in front of her. These apartments were on the ground floor. They were more studios—small, without full kitchens—but they were perfect for the staff as they had access to all the food they needed in the main building. She walked back inside and put on a pot of coffee. She went into the bathroom, brushed her teeth and her hair. When the coffee had dripped through, she poured herself a cup, walked onto her patio and sat down in a chair.

It was after four o'clock. She still had lots of time before she started work. She wondered about taking a trip into town. She definitely had a few things on her Need to Buy list. She wasn't sure if she wanted to do a trip today. She had friends in town, and she often arranged to have dinner with them after her shopping and before she came home. She glanced at her watch and realized Martha would still be at work. Normally Sicily set up things like this a couple of days in advance. Maybe she'd sit and relax today. She had some cleaning and laundry to do and a good book waiting for her. She stretched in her chair and relaxed. When her phone buzzed beside her, she picked it up and grinned. Clicking the Answer button, she said, "Hello, Elliot. How are you doing?"

"Since I slept the afternoon away," he said, his voice sounding much brighter than she had heard it sound in a long time, "I'm doing much better."

"How nice," she said in surprise. "What was the magical recipe?"

"Hard physical work in the morning and then Shane's deep-tissue massage. If you can survive the painful parts, he has a soothing touch. I fell asleep, and he threw a blanket over me and walked out. By the time I woke up, I realized it was almost four."

"There is nothing like a massage to help take away some of the stress. Any more bad dreams?"

"Not this time."

"Awesome." She smiled, loving that he had called. "I'm just up myself. Of course I did get a lot more sleep than you did."

"Sure, but you need it more than I do."

There was an odd pause down the line.

"Did you have a particular reason for calling?" she asked.

"I did, but I forgot what it was," he confessed. "I hate that."

She laughed. "It happens to me all the time."

"Really? I figured it was from my injuries."

"Nope, it happens to all of us. I was contemplating running into town—to the grocery store and the drugstore. Did you need anything?"

"Not right now. Hannah's been arranging day trips. I went on one a couple weeks ago, but I wouldn't mind going back into town again. Although I can't sit for long in those bus seats. And I don't really need to buy anything. Trips out are a nice break though."

"You're somewhat mobile. Dani's taken a couple people out occasionally, but I'd have to get permission."

"Shane made a similar offer," Elliot said. "I have to think about what I need and how high my energy level is. Actually a spur-of-the-moment trip works better for me than those planned future excursions. Can't say I'm wanting to plan too much right now."

"Maybe your day trips should be more about the drive and a chance to get out of Hathaway House for a little bit."

"Maybe." He shrugged. "You said you have to go grocery shopping. Don't you eat here?"

"I do, but I still need things like coffee and snacks. I don't always go to the cafeteria. And occasionally I have my breakfast here in my room."

"That makes sense with your night shift hours. Now that I think about it, I wouldn't mind a few things along that line myself. My wheelchair can go in the back of the car."

"Let me talk to Dani about what the protocol is. I'll add it to my list of things to discuss. I just don't know if and when we can make a trip like that happen."

"Okay, you do that. I can talk to Hannah about when the next group trip is planned. It's not that I'm against going as a group, but they're busy trips. That's not quite what I'm up for. Plus I won't know if I'm up for it until the day of the trip."

"No worries. If I walk over before five, I should catch her today. No guarantee though."

"Don't rush. You don't work until ten o'clock, so maybe you can leave her a note. You can talk to her tomorrow." Then he gave a snort. "Why the hell am I asking you to talk to her when I can call her myself?" He groaned. "It's a case of being a patient for too long. I seem to be losing the ability to think and to act on my own. I'm not impressed with that. Give me five." And he hung up.

She stared down at her phone, put it back on the coffee table and picked up her coffee. She wouldn't mind taking him into town. If they could get the wheelchair into her car, that would work. She understood liability issues were involved. It was a sanctioned trip by Hathaway if they took Hathaway's minibus and the driver was an employee … She shook her head. Surely he could do a couple short trips into town instead of these full-day adventures.

She understood how nice it was for some of the patients to have the outings, but it was too much for some. She didn't know how Elliot would handle sitting in a car for a couple hours either.

He should be doing more back exercises that would allow him to cope with this type of mobility. Even a little bit of horseback riding every day would be a huge help. She frowned. Lots of horses were here at Hathaway House, but she wasn't sure any were appropriate for disabled riders. Maybe Dani should consider that. Sicily thought about it, then she snatched up her phone and sent Dani a text.

Maybe Sicily should talk to Stan. Medical training would be required for the person handling the horses. What they needed would be a therapist trained to work with the special rehab-compatible animals *and* with the people needing rehab. They had that combination going on here, but they didn't necessarily have somebody who could facilitate a better interaction between those animals and people. It could be a huge addition to the place.

A text came back immediately from Dani. **We could consider it. It's hard to find the right personnel.**

Sicily nodded. That made sense.

Dani sent another text. **Good idea though. If you know anyone ...**

Right, the staffing issues. Still, that didn't mean it wasn't an option. She pulled up Stan's number and sent him a text, asking if he knew anyone. She didn't expect to hear back anytime soon because he was busy. She wondered idly if she shouldn't spend some time with him in the clinic. He could always use a hand at the end of the day. And she certainly had some time right now.

She glanced down at her nightie. She got herself a second cup of coffee and wandered into the bedroom area where she found clothes for the day. She'd come back and change for work before her shift started. In the meantime, she had several hours to enjoy first. She locked up her place and pocketed her phone and then headed to the clinic.

Chaos reigned. Sicily stared, openmouthed, at five dogs barking and yowling in a melee that nearly raised the roof off the room. Owners struggled with leashes and leads, and suddenly Sicily spotted the source of all the trouble. She waded her way into the middle of the pups to find a huge orange tabby staring down all the dogs. Sicily picked him up and cuddled him. The dogs calmed down once the cat was out of their immediate range. She shook her head and laughed at the owners. "This guy is causing quite a fuss, isn't he?"

Rebecca, the receptionist, separated from the chaos and grinned. "He is."

"It wasn't so bad until one dog started to bark, and then that was it. They all had to get in on the action," an older woman said. Her small Maltipoo dogs still yapped at Sicily's heels.

She rearranged the cat to drape over her shoulder and headed to the back of the vet clinic. There she put the big cat on the examining table. "I guess you haven't eaten anything yet today, have you, buddy?"

A vet tech on the far side called back, "He got breakfast early, but he hasn't had a second meal. Was that him causing a commotion up front?"

"Oh, yeah."

The vet tech went out to the front, her arms full of bags. "The day has been nuts."

"I'm here to help out for an hour or two, so tell me what I can do."

As the vet tech turned, using her back to open the swing door, she said, "If you could clean up in here, that would be a huge help." And then she disappeared.

Sicily looked around at the mess. Feed bags had been ripped open, and it seemed as if nobody had had a chance to sweep up the kernels. That's where she would start. An hour later, she was still tidying up the room. At least the cat was fed, his bowls rewashed and he sat on the floor again. He licked himself for a while, then stretched out on his side, dozing off. Stan walked in a few minutes later, took one look at her and grinned.

"Are you sure you don't want to work here full-time?"

"I work upstairs full-time," she said with a smile. "I work down here for free part-time."

He nodded amiably. "That's why I want you full-time. Especially for free."

She laughed. "Crazy day?"

"You don't know the half of it."

She saw the wrinkles on his forehead and the fatigue pulling on his chin. "Anything else I can do to help?"

He glanced at his watch. "I have a couple more to see so would love the help. I need to check on the surgeries from this morning, and we have a few overnight visitors to work with." He glanced around. "Four dogs are in the cage. How about taking them for a walk? They haven't been out to lift a leg in ages, and they could really use it. Take them one at a time though."

"Right. I can do that." She turned to the kennel area of the clinic. Four dogs were in the large cages, all of varying sizes. She clipped the first one onto a leash and led him through the back and out to the pastures.

The sun was easing off a little bit, and there were trees—lots of them. She let the dog wander around and sniff each one, and then she scratched him and gave him a little bit of human attention. He had a cast, which looked to be fresh, and stitches across his hip bone. Maybe he'd had an argument with a vehicle. If that was all he had for injuries, he'd done well.

After twenty minutes, she slowly led him back to his cage and then took the next one out. As she came back inside with the third dog, she heard a noticeable silence and much more peace and quiet inside. Stan was checking over the surgeries for the day. "I have one more dog to take out."

He turned and looked at her in surprise. "I didn't realize you were still here."

"The dogs needed more than a few minutes. I gave them a chance to walk around and have some fun and little bit of loving."

He grinned. "Hey, that's what a lot of us need. Thank you very much."

She chuckled. "Did you get to read my text?"

"I haven't had two seconds to look."

"I wondered if you knew anybody who had horses for horseback riding for the disabled. Dani said she'd tried to get somebody on staff to put a program like that together but couldn't find anybody qualified."

"We have tried several times," Stan said. "It's always about getting the right people. I don't know of anybody now, but I've got my ear to the ground in case. Some people here definitely could use equine therapy."

"I was thinking about Elliot. With his back injury, that would be a great way for him to build up his sitting muscles. He struggles with that a lot."

"Sounds like a great idea. Let's keep on it."

ELLIOT LAY ON the bed, biting his lip as Shane worked on his back. He'd taken extra courses to help with some of the specialized cases here. He had a magical touch.

"It's not supposed to hurt this much."

Elliot winced. "I'm not sure if it hurts, or if I'm clenching against the potential hurt."

Shane chuckled. "Understood. But you're undoing all my work, being tense and waiting for something bad to happen. The world's not like that. You can't repair some things."

Elliot relaxed his hands and dropped them to the side of his body. His mind was stuck on the wisdom of that thought. "I guess that's true in every area of life."

"I think so." Shane's strong hands glided up and down Elliot's back, massaging the injured muscles, untwisting and untying knots until the muscles draped over his body in a state of peace. Elliot was so tired he wanted to sleep, but at the same time, his mind was spinning.

"Do you know any of the other guys here?" Shane suddenly asked.

Elliot frowned. "I know of several but haven't gone out of my way to be friendly. Although I should make a greater effort."

"We have one group of three best friends here. Brock is done with rehab, but he is back and forth now because he's in a relationship with one of our ladies. Cole is in his last month, and he's showing massive improvement. And of course you might know Denton as he's been around a little more often."

Elliot smiled. "Yeah, I've seen him falling all over the place. But hey, he's working hard, and that's huge. I do know Aaron slightly. But that is one busy guy."

Shane moved his hands to the back of Elliot's neck and gently worked the muscles leading into the base of the skull, around the ears and down the jawline. When he was done,

Elliot lay there, feeling boneless and wishing this feeling could go on forever. His mind drifted over his body, and he closed his eyes, willing his system to shut down to get the rest he needed. In the background, he could hear Shane collecting his things and moving from the room.

Elliot wanted to say thank you. But his mouth wouldn't move, and his brain didn't have that much energy. Besides, he also knew Shane didn't need it. He understood how much Elliot appreciated the work. He lay quietly, letting his thoughts drift through his system.

The nightmares were building and getting stronger. He hadn't told anybody on his team, and because of that, he found it almost impossible to fall asleep these days. He'd done lots of research online and understood many kinds of subconscious events must be brought to the surface so he could deal with them and move on. He had no idea how to do that because as far as he knew, he'd relived that same event repeatedly at least one thousand times.

The nightmare was always the same. He was in the village in the middle of combat, searching for the hidden insurgent. Elliot's adrenaline was high because at any moment a bullet could hit him in the back or a rifle butt to his face or a knife to his gut. But he had been trained to do this. Crouching down low, he slipped around the clay wall to the side of the dilapidated structure. He heard no sound. He peered around the corner and saw a little girl lying like a broken doll on the floor.

Without making his way over, he studied her to see if she was still alive. He hoped so, but he also knew the insurgents used children to lure in soldiers. He didn't know any soldier who wouldn't protect a lone child or woman, but the insurgents had no such qualms. They set them up as victims and then cheerfully took out both the victim and the soldiers with a bomb.

As Elliot watched, the child's chest rose ever so slightly and drifted down again. She appeared to be unconscious. No way was she sleeping—her leg lay at an odd angle, clearly broken.

From the far side of the clearing, he saw Jordan's head pop over the top of the wall. With one look, they communicated an entire set of instructions before they both slipped behind the walls again. Regardless of any orders, Jordan had children of his own. No way he would leave that child there. Elliot knew this was a trap, but he also knew there would be no talking to Jordan about it. Elliot peered around the corner again to see if anybody else was close, shifting his rifle into position. He waited for Jordan's move. At the very least, he could cover Jordan. Elliot's heart raced, and his breath pounded in the back of his chest. The night was silent, and still he waited.

Elliot drifted in and out of the nightmare state as the scene replayed in his head, returning to the beginning right through to where he'd stepped around the building. He never quite got past that point. He never saw who shot him. He never saw who threw a grenade at him and never found out the fate of the child. He never saw Jordan again.

The explosion that day took everything from him. Hot anger rose from his stomach to his heart, and then tears poured from his eyes. He never made a sound though, and the pain of everything he'd seen, everything he'd done, welled out through his eyes as if the cleansing could heal the soul and rid him of his past.

He needed to know what happened that day. He needed to know what had happened to his friend and to that little girl. But his friend was dead, and there was no sign of the little girl. The incomplete scene was killing him, not knowing if Elliot had caused it. Had he alerted the insurgents to their presence? Had he gotten Jordan killed? Did the child die too? All these questions rolled around in his head with no answers. What could the navy say? Nobody could tell him anything. They said Jordan was killed in action. That would've been what the label on his file said. The grenade that brought the shelter down on him had also toppled onto Jordan. That explosion … first the grenade then the shelter … He was never going to forget it. Mixed into all of it was rapid gunfire before he partially crushed by cement falling from the building. His body had taken a hit from the original blast and the cement.

No one ever talked about the actual damage a grenade could cause. They hit the soft tissue of a person's organs with such force the damage was often unsurvivable. They'd found Jordan under the rubble of what was left of the building. Elliot had woken up to the rest of his team trying to get them both out from underneath the debris. They had found Jordan, but it was too late. Elliot told them about the little girl, but there was no sign of her. He knew in his heart it had been a trap. He knew it was something that those animals would do.

Jordan had gone down, trying to rescue a little girl, and he had died on the spot. But Elliot was terrified he hadn't done everything he could to help Jordan.

With a deep gasping breath, his thoughts returned to the reality of where he lay. He knew he was undoing all of Shane's work. But those memories, those flashes, the emotional pain kept rolling through his system without end. Ever since he had woken up in the hospital, it had been like this. His body was searching, seeking and fighting for answers that would never come because nobody had them. As such, the unknowns crept into his subconscious, stealing away the sanity in his life.

Chapter 5

S ICILY WALKED BACK up to her quarters. She needed to shower and change for dinner. Even then, she was late for her normal dinnertime. She loved spending time with Stan and really enjoyed spending some time with the horses. She was going to do some research and see if she could find a horse therapist somewhere in the vicinity. Maybe they could organize some trips out for a couple of the patients. She'd heard it was a big movement in other parts of the country, so she couldn't imagine it being any different here. Still, they needed people to be close enough for the patients to travel back and forth. Or maybe they could afford to bring in a therapist here instead.

She took a quick shower and dressed in a light sundress before heading out to dinner. On the way, she checked in at the office to make sure everything was okay. The afternoon receptionist had a big smile on her face, telling her to go get dinner and relax. Sandra was going to be on until ten. As many medical staff lived in the residence they were on call in case emergencies occurred overnight.

The only plus side to being late for dinner was that the room was mostly empty, and there were plenty of choices of where to sit. Sicily looked around for Elliot, but there was no sign of him. As she walked over to the buffet and the spicy roast beef, Dennis stepped up with a big smile.

"Have you seen Elliot yet tonight?" she asked.

Dennis shook his head. "No, but that doesn't mean much. I haven't been here the whole time. Just the last twenty minutes."

She nodded, glanced down at the delicious selection of foods and began to fill her plate. Finally, she added a glass of milk and headed outside to sit in the sunshine. She pulled out her phone, found Elliot's number and sent him a text.

Have you eaten?

She didn't wait for his answer but dove into her own dinner. He'd been extra tired lately and might not have felt up to the trip. She could deliver a plate if he responded.

By the time she'd finished her meal, there was still no answer. She decided to have some coffee and then check in again.

Sicily sat, relaxing and sipping her coffee in the evening sun, and her thoughts turned to all the things Dani had managed to accomplish at Hathaway. Her partner, Aaron, had been accepted into vet school after having completed his extra courses to get into the program. His marks were high enough, and his interview had gone so well, that the vet school had let him into the September term. He was working his way through the latter half of the first term now.

She was delighted for Dani, and for Stan. They both worked so hard, and if there was anybody that could help them, it would be a huge benefit. Everyone played an important role here. Even Sicily was happy to help out beyond the scope of her nursing duties.

When she'd finished her meal, she walked back toward Elliot's room. The doors were closed. She checked her phone to see if there had been an answer, but there wasn't. She gave a light knock on the door. She wasn't due to start work yet for a couple more hours, but that didn't mean she wasn't concerned about the patients.

At the quiet response from within, she opened the door and stuck her head into the room.

"Did you get my message?" she asked.

Elliot shook his head. She could see the fatigue and pain on his face. She opened the door wider and stepped inside. Her medical training immediately kicked in.

She frowned at the lines bracketing his mouth. That usually meant a rough night coming.

"Are you feeling okay?"

He gave her a half-smile. "I'm fine. Just a rough day."

"Did you have an evening meal?"

He shook his head. "No."

"They were just starting to put the food away. I can either help you get into the wheelchair and take you down, or I can go pick you up a selection of food and bring it back for you," she suggested. "Or we can call the kitchen and have a plate sent up."

He glanced at her in surprise. "I'd really love to not have to go there, but I am hungry," he confessed.

"Understandable. There was roast beef with gravy, and the Yorkshire puddings were divine."

"Okay, so now I'm really hungry."

She nodded. "Back in a bit."

Sicily turned and headed back over to the dining room. She grabbed a tray. Dennis approached from the opposite side, his eyebrows raised.

"I need this for Elliot," she said. "He's not getting out of bed right now."

Dennis dished up a large serving of roast beef and piled up the mashed potatoes and the gravy. He tossed a Yorkshire pudding on the side. "What vegetables does he like?"

She looked at the tray and shrugged. "I have no idea. Just give him a selection."

Dennis added both corn and broccoli, and then grabbed a second plate, filled it with chocolate cake for dessert. Finally, Sicily poured a large glass of ice water. With a very heavy tray, she carefully walked back to Elliot's room. She found the door closed.

"Shit."

She hadn't bothered with a cart, so moving slowly, she carefully squatted and placed the tray on the floor before opening the door. She checked to make sure all was okay and found him lying down with his eyes closed. She picked up the tray and carried it inside. He had a small table that swung over the bed. She placed the meal there, then turned to study his face. Was he asleep?

In a low whisper she said, "Elliot?"

His eyes flew open. He smiled. "I'm not sleeping, honest."

"I kind of wish you were," she said with a smile. "But that's okay. You also need to eat." She hit the buttons on the bed to help him sit up.

When he was comfortable, she moved the swing table into position. He looked at the food, and his eyes lit up.

"I have to admit you guys never starve us here."

"No starving allowed." She grinned. "Now, eat. Good food is essential for healing."

She sat in the visitor's chair to keep him company while he ate. People did better when they had others around. And she was totally okay with spending more time with Elliot.

WAS SHE JUST doing her job? No, surely not. She'd leave if that was the case. To know she'd been thinking about him made him smile inside. Until it occurred to him that maybe it was just part of her duties. That took some of the joy out of it. He slowed down the pace of his bites.

"Getting full?" she asked cheerfully.

He nodded. "A little. Still, I really appreciate you bringing me the food."

She hopped to her feet, picked up his water glass and filled it for him. "Some things are just habits," she said. "Some patients you just become more attached to than others."

He eyed her carefully. "Too attached?"

She laughed. "I didn't mean that in a bad way. It's like any profession. For example, a teacher will always remember a couple of students over the others. So the nurse will always remember some patients over the others."

He dropped his gaze to his food and nodded, a sinking feeling in his gut. So he was just a job to her.

As if wondering if she'd said something wrong, she walked back over to the bed and sat down beside him.

"In your case, I figured we've become friends," she said carefully. "That means that I can worry about you."

He glanced up, caught her gaze and a slow smile dawned on his face. "I like the sound of that." He cut another slice of roast beef and popped it into his mouth. He couldn't believe the way the conversation was going, but it was adding extra enjoyment to his meal.

"I'm glad we're becoming friends. It's a hard enough stage in my life to go through. It's much harder to go through it alone."

"There is no point in going through it alone," she said

seriously. "There are lots of people here who would like to be friends. Open up and meet people."

"Right. Still not the easiest thing to do."

She shook her head. "No. But it's worth it."

Friends would be nice. He'd isolated himself since arriving. Been too tired to care, really. Sicily, though ... she made him think of more than friendship. The thought made him smile. Except the last thing he was looking for right now was a partner. Not now. He was a mess. His nightmares would terrorize any woman who shared his bed.

"What are you smiling about?"

He shook his head. "Something that's not very funny," he said shortly. He paused, then added quietly. "My nightmares and how they will affect my future."

"In what way?"

He could feel her gaze on his face, and he refused to look in her eyes. He took another bite of his food. "Can you just imagine some poor woman sleeping beside me? When I wake up screaming and yelling, she will be terrified."

"Possibly. But she will also get used to it. You might find that having her there with you would be a calming influence. Maybe your PTSD symptoms would lessen. Maybe you wouldn't have as many nightmares."

He lifted his gaze to stare at her. "Is that possible?"

She shrugged. "It's not impossible. Many people suffer like you do and still manage to have a relationship."

He put his fork down and swiped his hand across his face. He reached for his water and drank down the glass with a couple of big swallows. Leaning back against his headboard, he said, "Thank you for that. I really was too tired to make it for dinner."

She stood and grabbed the empty tray. "I'm not on shift

for another few hours. I'll see you later tonight. I'll try not to wake you if you are sleeping." With a last smile over her shoulder, she turned and walked out of the room.

Taking some of the light with her.

He moved the small swing table out of his way to walk to the window. He'd been tired earlier, but the food had invigorated him. Fresh air would be lovely, but his body was struggling. Not wanting to give in to his physical weakness, but knowing there was only so much he could push himself to do, he settled into the wheelchair and slowly rolled his way outside to the elevators. There he took the short drop down to the vet clinic. But instead of heading toward the clinic, he made his way down the long hallway, through the stalls and over to the big, double doors that would take him outside. There was a paved walkway, close to the building and all the way around the property, so he knew he could do a perimeter circle. He wanted the fresh air more than he needed the exercise.

Outside, he pushed his way over to the corner of the building. He stopped for a moment and stared at the horses. He wanted to be closer, but there was no way in hell he could. This was his secret shame. A fear that went back to his childhood that he'd never beaten. Maybe that was why he'd excelled at so many other things in his life—to compensate for the one fear he couldn't face. One huge, black female came to the fence and nickered in his direction. He loved to see them, but from a distance.

After saying goodbye to the black mare, he slowly rolled his way around the rest of the building, lifting his face to the evening sun and the breeze that coasted around the property. It really was beautiful here.

He came around another corner and ended up in the

open-air pool area. A number of other patients were sitting outside by the water. He thought about what Sicily had said about making friends. Two men sitting together looked up at him and smiled. He took that as a good sign, and he slowly wheeled his way over to them and introduced himself.

The two men nodded. "I'm Cole and this is Denton."

Elliot nodded toward the pool. "Hope I can get into that soon."

"It's beautiful," Cole said. "I felt like I had made a huge leap forward when I was finally allowed in the water. It's up to your team to give the word, though."

Elliot nodded. "I was wondering about that." He studied the water for a moment and then looked back to the men. "I don't have a bathing suit, though."

"They have them in the change room here for patient use. When you're allowed to swim, you will be assigned some."

Elliot pulled his phone out and texted Shane. **Any chance I can go in the pool for a swim.**

Shane's response was immediate.

Yes. Have you got trunks and towels?
No.
You want to go now?
Sure, that would be very nice.
I'm free. I'll meet you there in five.

He looked up from the phone to the two men. "That was easy. Shane said he'd meet me here, and that I can go in."

He nodded his goodbyes to Denton and Cole and slowly made his way around to the change room. In the time it took to make it there, he saw Shane striding toward him.

"Have you done much swimming since your accident, Elliot?"

Elliot shook his head. "No, but I was a strong swimmer before. I doubt that's changed."

"Perfect. Let's get you some trunks and some towels, and I'll hang around for a few minutes, just to make sure you don't get in trouble when you're on your own."

A few minutes later, he was changed and hanging onto the railing, working his way to the edge of the pool. The pool was completely empty now, and the surface was like glass. He glanced over at Shane and smiled. Taking a deep breath, he just fell in, without making any attempt to dive or buffer the fall. The distance wasn't very big, and the sensation of the water closing over his head was so great that he wanted to shout with joy. When he was completely submerged, he rolled and swam, turning like a dolphin and enjoying the freedom that the water gave and the absolute ability to move the way he always used to. When he finally surfaced, it was to see Shane standing beside the pool, a satisfied look on his face.

"See? I can swim. Remember, I was a SEAL."

Shane smiled. "Right you are. Don't do too much, though," he cautioned. "Just try to do a little bit of work, and I'll have a look tomorrow to see how we can fit this into your schedule. Then you can come down here on a regular basis." He glanced at his watch, and pointed to the clock up on the far wall. "Thirty minutes only today."

Elliot nodded. In truth, he was already getting tired. But being in the water was such a joy, he didn't want to cut it short. Still, he didn't want to overdo it his first time. He wanted to be able to come back down here again. He rolled over onto his back, and stretching out, he floated on the surface of the water. Now, *this* was perfect.

Chapter 6

B Y THE TIME Sicily walked into the nurses' station, she was only two minutes ahead of her shift. Sandra was just coming off shift. Jenna should be here already.

"Good evening."

"Hey, glad to see you. I can go home now." Sandra laughed.

Together, the two went over the day's notes. They caught each other up on a few of the patients and went over any irregularities and conflicts, but it had mostly been a simple day, and it looked to be another simple night.

Sicily sat down and went over the caseload. She had one new patient in today, and she had several that would be checking out this week.

As soon as the check-outs left, there were going to be intakes, the following day, and they'd need to prep for those. That was the way the system worked. Checking out was always a good sign. It was lovely to see the people who came to Hathaway move on with their lives, and get back to the reality of living with their families and friends.

Their patients' quality of life was so important. When patients left Hathaway House, they were physically stronger, more flexible and more capable. And most of all, they were also happier. Psychologically, they had gone through difficult times. She always smiled at those successes. Sure, there was the odd person who didn't make the same gains others did. Those cases were harder to deal with, but with perseverance, success still happened. People generally arrived angry, hurt and terrified, but they usually left strong and capable, and that gave Sicily a real sense of satisfaction. A sense of knowing that what she did had value and the people around her needed her. The patients absorbed everything their teams had to offer them and turned that into something good. She hoped Elliot would have the same experience.

But his case was different. PTSD was unfortunately common enough that they always had cases, and everyone's experience was different. In Elliot's case though, it seemed he had a memory block. As the nightmares and the symptoms got worse, she knew he would come to a crunch period where he would either remember the truth or find a way to block it to the point where he couldn't remember anything. There was no "normal" way for this to work its way out.

He needed a breakthrough one way or the other. Even if that meant just accepting where he was for the moment. As it was so very hard to heal when the body didn't get the rest it needed.

She wrapped up her charts and walked to her medicine room to carefully prepare for her evening rounds. Sandra took care of medications for the day shift, but Sicily and Jenna split that job at night for some of the patients who took their medications as soon as Sicily got on shift. Jenna was in the supply room, checking inventory.

The hallway lights dimmed. Visiting hours were long over, and the peace and quiet of the setting sun had descended. That was another big plus to the place. It was so much more family-oriented and friendly.

Sicily stopped in Norman's room first. As always, he was

wide awake.

He watched her come in and smiled. "Did you bring my sleeping pills?"

She chuckled. "You should try yoga." She handed him his medication and a fresh glass of water.

He took the little paper cup and tossed back the pills, returning the cup to her. "I'd consider yoga if I thought I could do any of those moves," he said. "Big guys like me don't bend so easy."

They'd been on this conversation merry-go-round over his entire stay, so she knew there wouldn't be a change now either.

She grinned. "Every inch is an improvement." With a small wave, she walked out and headed to the next room.

Her rounds usually took about forty minutes. By the time she walked into Elliot's room to check on him, no lights were on, and the covers were pulled over his shoulders. She stood in the doorway for a moment.

"I'm awake," he whispered.

She walked in. "That's too bad. I was hoping you were sleeping."

"Not yet, but hopefully soon." He rolled over and yawned, his eyes only partially open. "Anything new and different happen today?"

She realized she had something he might like to hear. "We're considering adding horse therapy for the patients. I think that would be good for you."

"Sounds good," he muttered in a low voice, then slid deeper under the covers.

She was worried about how he was doing, but there was no sound, so hopefully he slept.

She tiptoed out and continued to her office.

She still had some notes to read from the day shift. With the need to have somebody on twenty-four hours a day, they ran three shifts, and it was important for her to keep up with the information on all patients. She made herself a small pot of coffee and sat down at her computer desk.

Minutes later her alarm went off. She checked the room number and realized it was Elliot's. In an instant, she was already in the hallway, dashing toward his room. Although she was fully equipped to handle most emergencies, and they did have crash cart here, she could call on only a few people if it were a true medical emergency, like a heart attack. A doctor was always on call, but it would take them at least five minutes to get here.

Jenna was only minutes away as well.

Sicily usually got an alarm like this once or twice a week, and it was rarely life-threatening. She burst into Elliot's room to see him thrashing on the bed, his covers on the floor, and his huge muscled body arching, his arms clenched as if fighting off an unseen enemy. His features were twisted with rage.

In a low, soothing voice, she spoke. "Elliot, it's Sicily. You're having a nightmare. Slowly come back out, please. Relax and take it easy."

She knew better than to touch him. He could just as easily see her as the unseen enemy and attack. She assessed his condition and realized he was lying on the nurses' call button. It was wall-mounted but with a longer cord for those who struggled to reach it. Somehow it had been caught underneath him, triggering the alarm.

Realizing it wasn't worse than it was—and it was already bad enough—she relaxed slightly and continued to talk to him in a low voice. She walked over to the small dresser where he had a portable radio and put on some music. Peaceful, calm, and joyful instrumental sounds filled the room. She continued to talk to him for a long moment, trying to get through to him.

Then his body collapsed against the bed, and his arms dropped to his sides. His eyes flashed open. He bolted into an upright position and cried out at the pain.

She placed a hand on his shoulder. "Take it easy, Elliot. You're coming out of another bad dream."

He stared up at her, pain and torment in his eyes. "When will it stop?"

She shook her head wordlessly and then clasped his hand with both of hers and held it tight. "I don't know. I can't tell you that. But they are getting better."

He stared at her in disbelief. "How can you say that?"

She smiled. "Because lots of nights you don't have these. I don't know what brought this on tonight, but if we could figure out what triggers them, maybe we could stop them."

"The doctor says I'm avoiding looking at something."

"That could be part of it. It doesn't mean you did something wrong or you saw something so horrific. Everything you experienced over there was terrible. Separating that life from the life you have now, that's what's important. Finding a way to compartmentalize that history and to put it away would be a good thing."

Slowly his breathing relaxed. He lay back down on the bed, wincing as he finally made it to the prone position. She picked up his water glass.

"I'll get you a fresh glass." She walked outside into the hallway where they had an ice machine and filled it for him. When she returned, he had the light on, and the soft glow filled the room. She understood. Some of the men could never sleep in the dark again. Some of them could never sleep in the light. Every man's experience of what he'd gone through was different.

When he was calm again, she asked him, "Do you need anything? Are you hungry, or do you want to sit and read for a little bit?"

He smiled. "I'll be fine. I'll read or turn on my laptop."

"If you want a hot cup of tea or something, just let me know."

He tilted his head in acknowledgment. "Maybe later."

With nothing else to do, she slowly backed from his room and returned to her station. She wished she could do something for him. She had been correct in that his nightmares were improving. But when you were the one caught up in the nightmare, progress seemed so far off.

THE SKIN FINALLY dried. One of the worst things was waking up drenched in sweat.

He knew the doctors meant well, and they said he needed to rest, but every time he closed his eyes, he was sent back to the same frontlines, being unable to save his friend ... His continuing reaction seemed like a weakness to him. Every time he tried to strong-arm his mind into bypassing all the scenarios, it refused and dug down deeper. He shifted so he sat up in bed. From his window, he could see the stars outside. It would be a beautiful evening.

He checked his watch and gave a broken laugh. "Actually," he muttered quietly to himself, "it's already midnight, so the evening's long gone."

Slowly he shifted to his feet and grabbed his robe and his

crutches and carefully made his way to the dining room. He could make himself a cup of tea, but what he wanted was to sit outside on the deck. Feel the cool air pass over his heated body and breathe in the scents of normality outside. He put on the kettle, filling it with water from the jug, and when it was ready, he brewed some tea.

He did not care what kind of tea it was as long as it wet his throat and warmed his chilled body. His body was a mixture of conflicting emotions and sensations. He couldn't explain it. Moving slowly, he made his way through the doorway out to the deck.

Once outside, he made it to the far end of the deck and sat down. He laid his head against the railing and closed his eyes.

He was so damn tired. And he was so damned scared to fall asleep. Instead he sat and watched the night fall away. When he did crash, morning light was already breaking through the clouds in the sky.

Chapter 7

OVER THE NEXT few days, Sicily sent out several emails regarding the horse therapy idea. She'd discussed the matter with several of the physiotherapists. They had all been open to the idea of bringing in horses for specific exercises. Although several of the horses here were broken to ride, they didn't have the right disposition for this kind of work rehabbing patients. Most of the horses were rescues themselves. They were in need of human interaction but not in this way.

Several days after her first inquiries, she got an exciting email. She printed it off and walked to Dani's office. Dani had already left for the day, but Sicily placed the copy of the email in the center of Dani's desk, so it would be the first thing she saw. Then Sicily dashed off emails to both Shane and Sidney. She wrote Might Be the Best Answer in the subject line and then copied all the parts of the email so they could see how far she'd gotten.

It appeared somebody was willing to come to the property with two of her horses once a week for a few hours to work with several of the patients. The prices seemed reasonable to Sicily, but that part was up to Dani.

Finally Sicily felt she had accomplished something with this event, and she shut down her email program and went back to her rounds. It was five o'clock in the morning, and her shift was almost over. Several people were stirring, but if given the chance, they would roll over and fall asleep again. When she came to Elliot's room, she stopped in the doorway and checked to see how deep his breathing was. He'd had several bad nights. Whatever time she'd come in, he had been staring blindly at the wall across from her. He'd been past the point of pretending to be asleep. He was so exhausted he couldn't complete most of his daily schedule.

She walked in. "How are you doing this morning?"

He rolled over and gave her a half smile. "I think I slept for a couple hours."

"Excellent." She beamed, delighted for him. "Do you think you can deal with your schedule today?"

They were all concerned because he was here to make progress, and so far, they were still dealing with getting him physically strong enough to get through the programs set up for him.

"I think so. After the workout with Shane a couple days ago I fell into a very deep sleep. I was wondering if it's possible to get more massages in a day."

She nodded. "What about the pool or the hot tub?"

He shrugged. "The pool is great. I haven't tried the hot tub yet, but it doesn't sound like a bad idea. Particularly at bedtime."

She frowned. "I'm not sure how late it's open. However, if it's something you want, I could probably arrange it, and I could be there with you to make sure you're okay."

He sighed, his shoulders slumping. Sicily partially understood the reason. It was a hit to his pride to be babysat at every turn. It was so damned important for him to keep his pride too. "Not that I want to babysit you or anything," she teased lightly. "The liability issue would be horrific if you didn't have somebody with you and if something happened."

"Of course. I'd be happy to have you stay with me." He flashed a big grin at her.

Not for the first time she recognized the grin coming her way. It both warmed her heart and made her feel special. Then again he *was* special. He was a good man, and she was honored to know him. He was going through a very difficult time right now, and that was hard on him, but he withstood the pressure like a trooper.

"I can ask too." He snagged his tablet and made a few clicks. "I am sending Dani a message right now."

She grinned. "While I'm walking around, checking on everyone, do you want a cup of coffee, or do you want to sleep?"

"Sleep's done for the night," he announced. "The therapist has me doing some meditation for the next little bit. Maybe coffee around six?" he asked, glancing up at her, his tone hopeful. "You're off then, right?"

"I am, indeed, and yes, for coffee. I love my caffeine."

He nodded, a smile spreading across his face. "I do too. This is a habit I'd get up for every day."

She gave him a shy smile, feeling the color wash over her face as she hurried away. As it was, she'd spent a good ten to fifteen minutes with him. But she'd already been ahead on her schedule, and she loved her time with Elliot.

Sandra was in the office by the time Sicily finished her rounds. Jenna was logging off the computer. The three compared notes. By the time Sicily was done, she realized she was late. She winced and stood up. "I'm late for a coffee meeting. Got to run. Any questions?"

"No, I'm good." Sandra said. "Go."

Jenna waved her away.

She grabbed her sweater and headed to the dining hall.
She stood there for a long moment, studying everyone, but
there was no sign of Elliot. She headed back to his room, but
the door was closed, and she didn't know what to do. She
pulled out her phone and sent a text. **I was late this
morning. Are we still doing coffee?**

She walked the hallway for a few minutes, then returned
to the dining room, waiting for a response. When she didn't
get one and saw no sign of Elliot anywhere, she headed to
the pool to see if he happened to be there. Again, nothing.
Feeling out of sorts, she realized there could be any number
of reasons why he hadn't shown up. She hoped it was
because he slept.

She headed to her own room, feeling disappointed. She
hadn't had breakfast, and she'd missed out on the coffee. It
felt like she'd missed something special. Her apartment felt
cramped and closed in. She wasn't tired enough to go to bed,
so she slumped on the couch and groaned. "Now what the
hell will I do?"

She had some running around to do in town, then realized sitting here wouldn't give her any answers. She couldn't
get in contact with Elliot, so the best thing she could do was
get something else done. With that, she changed out of her
uniform into a T-shirt and jeans, grabbed her keys and wallet
and headed out.

In town, she realized she hadn't asked Dani about the
hot tub. She finished up her shopping, stopping to get a
coffee shop muffin and coffee, and headed back to Hathaway. She checked the time. It was almost eleven. If she went
to bed, she might miss Dani.

She walked to Dani's office. Thankfully she was in, so
Sicily waited in the doorway for Dani to notice her. When

she lifted her head, Sicily stepped in.

"There you are," Dani said. "That was an interesting email you left me."

Sicily nodded. "I don't know if there is any room in the budget for something like that, but since we were talking about it, I wanted to do the research and see if it was even a possibility."

"It's a heck of a good idea," Dani said with a pleasant smile. "I'll give her a call this afternoon. Of course no decisions on budget until we know more."

"Right. That makes sense." Sicily shifted her weight on her feet. "Did you get an email from Elliot?"

Dani nodded. "Something about wanting to use the hot tub at night." She frowned. "He's still having problems sleeping, isn't he?"

Sicily nodded. "Yes, he is. He's awake most of the night. I stop in and talk to him on a regular basis to see how he's doing. He's tried some sleep aids, but they did more harm than good, so he's gotten off of them. We're looking into other avenues to help him sleep. Massages and the hot tub were some things he suggested."

Dani frowned and nodded. "Massages need work to re-schedule. The hot tub …"

"If I took him down and let him have, say, forty minutes, I could stay there and do my paperwork and then bring him back up. That way, he wouldn't be alone or unsupervised."

"No, of course not." Dani studied Sicily with a curious gaze. "Would you go in the hot tub with him?"

Sicily chuckled. "Elliot suggested it." She shook her head. "But I would consider that very unprofessional. I'm on shift, and I have a lot of other patients. I don't see how he can go in the hot tub without supervision. It's not open at that hour of the night, but if he is up, he's often in a lot of pain with muscle spasms."

"It's the staffing issue that I'm worried about. If you're at the hot tub with him, then you won't be looking in on the other patients. So you'll coordinate with the other nurse, and they must know where you are at all times in case something arose."

"Agreed. But I also get a half-hour break. So in theory, I could take that break to bring him to the hot tub."

Dani tapped her pen on the table for a long moment. "Let me think about this. Lots of side issues could arise with something like this."

"Not the least of which is other patients' knowing." Sicily nodded. "I do understand the problem."

"Two orderlies are on night shift as well. Maybe one of them could work it into their schedule."

"That would be great." Sicily smiled. "Elliot might want me to be there, but I think it's more important that he get the water relaxation."

"Is there something developing between the two of you?"

Sicily started at the question. "I don't know," she said slowly. "Maybe?"

Dani gave a burst of laughter. "Well, that's nice and decisive."

Sicily chuckled. "It's not an easy thing to answer. I spend a lot of time with him because he is awake at night. And definitely something is there. But as to what it is, I have no idea."

"Let me think about it and get back to you later this afternoon." Dani glanced at her watch. "You shouldn't even be in here. You're off shift."

"Right. I went to town and did some errands, and then I normally go to bed, but I realized I'd miss you, and I wanted to discuss this first."

Dani nodded. "You know you can contact me anytime in the evenings, right?"

Sicily was already in the doorway and nodded. "Understood. Like the rest of us, you try to keep your private life and work routine separate. I hate to cross that line. There will be times that I must, and I know I can. But if it's something I can take care of during my work hours, then I will do so."

"Much appreciated."

"By the way, is Aaron coming back anytime soon?"

"He is at the vet school right now finishing his first term." Then she grinned. "He should be back in a few days for a short break."

"Well, good luck to him. That's an awesome career."

"I think so too. He's excited. Stan is also, as he's hoping to have Aaron come on board here."

"The best of both worlds for you. The rest of us are figuring out how to make relationships work when some are at a serious crossroad in our lives."

"I am a firm believer in Mother Nature and faith taking a hand. See how it plays out. Be true to yourself and true to him, and everything will work out."

SO WHY WASN'T she there? Elliot ran a hand through his hair, feeling at least one hundred years old. Since these nightmares had started, he'd struggled to get a handle on who and what he was. Now it looked like he couldn't even manage a coffee date. Instantly a voice inside said anything could have happened and to not judge until he knew more. He'd been tossing her absence over and over in his mind for hours.

But in truth, why would she want to spend time with him?

"Good morning," Shane said from the doorway. "How is our night owl?"

"Wishing he was sleeping," Elliot retorted. He tried to keep the pain and that sense of defeat out of his voice but knew he'd failed when Shane's gaze sharpened.

Shane lifted his tablet and tapped on the surface a couple times.

"*Great.* Telling the rest of the team that I'm still suffering?"

"The team already knows. What we don't know is how to make you sleep. I was hoping a workout and a massage would give you a few hours."

Elliot brightened. "That would be great. I did send an email to Dani asking if it was possible to get more massages and to use the hot tub when I wake up in the night."

"I'll speak to the doctor about that," Shane replied. "I want you on muscle relaxants too. The last thing we want is for you to finally fall completely asleep only to be woken up by muscle cramps. But also, you cannot be swimming or in the hot tub while taking the relaxants. Not without somebody with you at all times."

As Elliot watched, Shane clicked away on his tablet. He looked around his room as he waited for Shane to finish. "I'm not even dressed for a workout."

"Do it now then," Shane said, lifting his head to look at Elliot. "Meet me in the big room in about ten minutes, okay?"

Elliot nodded. But that was the last thing he wanted. All he wanted to do was lie here until his body went back to sleep again. It was like he'd been awake for weeks. His eyes burned like sandpaper. He dragged himself off the bed to get changed. When he was done, he collapsed into the wheelchair and said out loud, "Sorry, but I'm wheeling down to the therapy room. I'm too damn tired for anything else. My back is throbbing."

He wheeled himself to the appropriate room, parked his chair and waited for Shane to arrive. When there was no sign of him after a couple minutes, Elliot leaned his head back and drifted in and out of sleep, yet never quite got to where he'd like. He was no longer in danger here at Hathaway House—he wasn't watching anybody else or worrying about being captured or fired on. He was safe, and he didn't understand why his body wasn't getting the message. He didn't know how much longer he could go on like this.

He suspected that if he could resolve this situation, he'd fall asleep and stay under for a couple days. He needed to cross whatever fine line was stopping him. He'd had high hopes it would happen today, but instead his nights were still restless, and even when he started to doze, he became uneasy. Before sleep claimed him, he'd jolt awake as if knowing that as soon as he slept, the nightmares would come.

Maybe what he needed was an answer for the nightmares, not for the lack of sleep. That would take him back to his therapist again. He picked up his tablet and jotted down a few notes to bring up with her.

Shane walked in at that moment, his gaze critical as he studied Elliot. "I'd hoped we would get a full workout from you today, but it looks like that's not happening."

For some reason, that brought Elliot's competitive spirit

to the surface. He shook his head at Shane. "I'm not that bad. You've got plans? Bring it on. As long as you promise a massage afterward, I'm willing to go the distance."

Shane chuckled and rubbed his hands together. "In that case, let's go. Remember your words because you'll regret saying them."

And the physical therapy session started.

Chapter 8

S EVERAL DAYS LATER Sicily worked quietly, writing up notes from the long shift she was about to complete. She looked up to see Dani walking toward her with two mugs of coffee.

"Not sure if you wanted coffee or if you're ready to hit the sack," Dani said with a smile. "I understand it was a tough night."

Sicily nodded and leaned back in her chair. She motioned to the coffee. "That won't stop me from sleeping. Plus I need to unwind for a bit. It's pretty hard coming off a shift and going straight to sleep."

Dani settled down in the chair across from her. "I wanted to tell you that we are bringing in the horse therapist next week for one afternoon. I'd like a list of how many patients you think would benefit from this. Therapy sessions will run for approximately one hour each, and in some cases, perhaps less. A lot of different muscles will be used. The therapist wants an idea of which patients we're looking at having her work with, and she needs to know about some of their injuries, so she can make adaptations to her program."

Sicily brightened. "Oh, that's great news. We can certainly put Elliot on the list, but I have several others who would like the opportunity."

"Good, get five who you think are ready and talk with

them to see if they're interested. If they are, we will make that happen next week. If it's a good session, we can try again the next week. I'm certainly not promising to do this on a weekly basis, but maybe every couple months we can bring her in for a program of a few consecutive weeks." She got back to her feet. "Sandra should be here any moment. After that, you can crash. You're looking a little peaked."

Sicily looked at her empty coffee cup. A little peaked? She was exhausted. She'd had to call two separate doctors for patients during the night. She could go weeks without having to call anyone, but last night hadn't been an easy night. But that was what she was here for.

Sandra walked in with a bright, cheerful smile on her face, which made Sicily feel like she was seventy years old and ready for retirement.

"Hey, how you are doing?"

Sicily shook her head. "Now that I'm off shift, I'm much better." She glanced at her clock to double-check the time. She still needed to go over the night's events, but she sure wasn't looking to do much more than that.

Sandra sat down beside her. "Sorry, I'm running a bit late myself this morning. Let's go over what we need to, and you can go to bed."

Sicily went through her notes, spending extra time going over the two patients who had required extra care during the night. "When the doctors come in for rounds, can you make sure you get clear direction as to what they want to do moving forward."

Sandra nodded. She wrote out several notes for herself on a scratch pad. They updated the files on the patients, and then Sicily stood.

"I'm so done."

Sandra waved her off. "Go have something to eat. It will you make you feel a ton better."

With her empty coffee cup in hand, Sicily walked toward the dining hall and out onto the sunny deck. Sandra's idea wasn't half bad. The next time Sicily saw Elliot, she'd apologize for missing their coffee date. Whenever she'd seen him recently, he had seemed normal, but they never spoke about the missed connection. But neither had they tried to make another coffee date. Maybe they both had their feelings hurt. Past time to discuss it then, to try again. Today was not a good day for either though. She was too damned tired and wanted to go to bed.

As she walked toward the stairs, she heard his voice. She turned to see Elliot sitting at a table on the far side of the deck. Instantly her spirits brightened. She changed direction and walked toward him. "I didn't expect to see you here."

"I'm often here in the mornings," he responded quietly. "Most of the time hoping to see you before you go home."

That startled a laugh from her. She pulled out a chair and sat down, a little more heavily than she intended. "Sometimes I'm perfectly fine to have coffee. Then other times, like right now, I feel like I'll barely make it to my apartment and crash." She could feel the intensity of his gaze, but there was no criticism.

Then he asked, "Is that why you didn't meet me here the other morning?"

She shook her head. "I was caught up with work. I couldn't leave when I needed to, and when I came here, there was no sign of you. I sent you a text. I figured you'd either gotten tired of waiting or had fallen asleep."

"That figures. But you're here now, so maybe you're not too tired to have a cup of coffee with me?"

He asked the question so hopefully she propped her chin up on her hands and placed her elbows on the table. "As long as you don't require scintillating conversation because I warn you, I might fall asleep."

He chuckled. "I know the value of sleep, so I wouldn't wake you."

"When I checked on you last night, you were sleeping," she said. "Not sure what brought on the change, but it sounds like it's working."

"Meditation and yoga and muscle relaxants." He winced. "I'm still not entirely convinced, but it seems to be working out okay. I certainly can't do three-quarters of the yoga moves they show on the videos, but something about the breathing exercises and stretches seem to ease up the muscle cramps."

"And the nightmares?" she prompted.

She watched as his gaze dropped to the table then he smiled. "I can say they're better as they don't appear to be as intense."

"Oh, that's a good thing then."

He nodded. "That's what I was thinking."

"By the way, I spoke with Dani, and we have a horse therapist coming next week for one afternoon session. It would be a good idea for you. It would help you sit longer, and of course, work on the damaged back muscles."

"I don't remember any such discussion." He stared at her with a look akin to dread. Then he gave a hard shake of his head. "Nice idea, wrong patient."

Her jaw dropped. "Are you serious?"

He nodded.

"I set it up for you." Then she bit her lip and hastily corrected her words as he'd been falling asleep at the time she spoke to him, so maybe he didn't remember. "I set it up with you in mind."

He raised an eyebrow. "Then I guess you should've asked first," he said, his voice hard.

She settled back, stunned. After all the work she'd put into it and finally getting Dani's approval, here was the one patient she had done it for. But not only was he disinterested but he appeared to be completely against the entire concept. "Why?"

He stared moodily out at the pasture. "Because horses belong behind fences," he said finally.

She sat and stared. She hadn't considered he might be afraid of horses. Certainly a lot of people were. But it never occurred to her that a big bad best-of-the-best military guy would be one of those. It made her pause. As much as she might know he was afraid, she didn't want to force him to admit it. His self-confidence was very important to the healing process. She leaned forward. "Do me one favor and don't be completely against it. Keep an open mind."

Elliot half snorted. "My mind is open. It's not for me."

She stood and put down her coffee cup. "Okay, I'm heading to bed. But of all the things I would like for you to do, the topmost is to consider the prospect. It would be hugely helpful for your back." She gave him a smile and turned and walked away. She couldn't deal with it now. She was too tired and her mind too foggy to wrap itself around the fact he was completely against horse therapy. It was so disappointing. She thought he'd love the idea, but instead …

ELLIOT WATCHED HER walk away. How could she have

done something like that for him without discussing it with him first? He'd been very good at hiding how he felt about horses. He was okay with dogs and cats or any small animals. Horses were a different case altogether. He'd gone riding as a young boy and had a bad accident. His first time on a horse and his last. As a SEAL in the military, he was supposed be good at everything, strong and brave and able to face all kinds of trauma. Yet here he was, terrified to get back on a horse. He had been here weeks, and it had never been an issue. They hadn't had horse therapy before—not until Sicily got it into her mind he needed it in order to get better.

He appreciated the thought. He appreciated that she cared. But she needed to find some other way to help. That was the one thing he couldn't do. Yet something nagged at him ... He couldn't remember the details of the accident. But it had been traumatizing ... And the last thing he needed was more stress ...

So no way in hell was he getting on a horse. Therapy be damned. He didn't know if he should talk to Dani about it or wait and see what happened. He had enough to deal with now. He didn't want the trauma of worrying about being on a horse to work its way into his head too. It made him feel like a coward, and he didn't need that. He didn't want to feel worse than he did already. Yet here he had one more thing on his plate to contend with. Plus he was afraid he'd hurt Sicily's feelings. At the very least he'd disappointed her, and that was the last thing he wanted to do. He liked her, and it was hard knowing she'd now see him in a different light. Weak, cowardly.

Shane walked over to him. "Hey, man. You're up early again."

Elliot glanced up at Shane. "Did you hear they are

bringing in horse therapy?"

Shane sat down in the seat Sicily had vacated. "I'd heard some discussion about it. I think it's a great idea."

Of course he did. He was a therapist. Why wouldn't he be happy about horse therapy? Elliot could see the benefits for others, if not himself. Moodily Elliot stared down at his now-empty coffee cup, turning it around in his hand.

"You don't have to if you don't want to," Shane said.

"Good, because no way am I getting on the back of a horse," Elliot snapped. He narrowed his gaze and added, "But apparently Sicily arranged it because she thought it would be good for me."

Shane settled into his seat. "So you don't want to disappoint her, but at the same time, you don't want to do something you don't want to do."

"Something I *can't* do," he stressed, his voice hard and angry. He hated even having to explain himself.

"The last thing we need is for you to be under more stress. So forget about the horse therapy. I can talk to her and tell her you're not ready."

"That sounds workable." Elliot's face eased back with relief. He lifted his coffee cup. "Maybe I'll get a second cup."

Shane smiled. "Let me." He stood, and ignoring Elliot's protests, walked over and refilled their cups.

Elliot shifted carefully in the chair to study the crowd slowly filtering in for an early shift, grabbing a coffee and leaving while others came in for a bite to eat. He couldn't imagine working in a kitchen like this. There were a lot of people to keep track of, and of course, the cooking would continue all day long.

Shane brought back the coffee and placed one cup in front of Elliot. "I'm heading to a meeting, so I will see you later this morning." Shane turned and walked over to the other side of the dining area where a number of other therapists were already seated at a table.

Elliot had to admit that one of the things bothering him was his lack of purpose, a job, a reason to get up every day. He had a lot of healing to do. Inside, a lot was happening, but until he could get some optimal rest and then deal with the nightmares, it was hard to heal.

Just that Shane was being so amiable about it all, pissed him off more and made him ashamed. Like a coward. They just didn't know ... they didn't understand what he'd been through ...

He stared at the hot coffee and realized he didn't want it. Right now all he wanted to do was hide in his room.

A room where he understood what was expected of him and where he wasn't pressured or stressed to go outside of his comfort zone. He already knew how that could be disastrous. So why go there?

It was good he'd told her he wasn't interested from the get-go, and she could deal with the fallout. If she wanted to do this for him, then she should have spoken to him first. And made sure he heard her, not talk to him when he was almost asleep.

He'd have told her the truth then—no way in hell was he getting on a horse. That one time had been more than enough.

Chapter 9

T READING LIGHTLY, SICILY headed to the coffee station in the dining hall. She plugged in the small teakettle on the side, and while she waited for the water to boil, her eyes wandered around the large space, empty at this time of the night. Only running lights shone around the coffee station— a soft glowing ambient light. When the kettle was ready, she made herself a hot cup of tea, snagged a cookie and slowly made her way back to the office.

There was always work for her to do, always medicines to check, inventory to update and an ongoing order list she kept track of. Some suppliers only sent certain drugs, and other suppliers sent others. She tried to focus on the files that needed updating, but for some reason today, it was hard to even figure out what she needed to do. She closed the database so she wouldn't make any foolish errors that would impact their supply.

Sicily settled into her chair and closed her eyes. She'd been so focused on making something special happen for Elliot that maybe she hadn't done enough for the others. Instantly she was ashamed of herself. Had she overlooked somebody else who was more in need of her attention? She didn't think that was the case, but she quickly went through her case files to make sure. Often she had nights where nobody needed her at all.

Elliot was the only one with nighttime problems now. Lots of the others took pills to sleep better while some pushed themselves to exhaustion through their physiotherapy and exercise. But even if they woke up, they usually got up, went to the bathroom and returned to roll over and fall asleep again. Then there was Elliot. Reassured that she hadn't overlooked anybody, she still found it difficult to focus on anything else.

Then again, he'd barely been civil since she'd told him about the horses. She knew multitudes of people who would jump at the chance. She also knew several people who wouldn't go near horses, thanks to fear. She lifted her gaze and stared blankly at the empty doorway. Was that Elliot's case?

Was he scared of the horses? He hadn't said so. She'd assumed he was, but she'd only seen anger. Well, he'd very clearly and effectively gotten out of it. Not just the horse-back-riding therapy, but now it felt like he was pushing her away too.

If he was pushing her away to avoid spending any time with the horses, that wasn't good either. She didn't want him to be so threatened he felt he had to isolate himself to get out of this. If he didn't want to do it, then he didn't have to. But if fear was holding him back … maybe it was something he just *should* do.

She considered her options and jotted down a few notes. The team would discuss this case in their upcoming meeting, and as she wouldn't be there, her notes needed to speak for her. She attended one every second week but that wasn't this week. When she was done, she felt better. She closed the file and shifted to sorting through the paper files.

Because she often had a lot of time on her hands in the

evening, the other staff left a lot of the paperwork to her. She got up and walked to the large wall cabinets and put away the patient files. Elliot's was on her desk. She opened it to see if anything was new. Their online filing system showed her if any new notations had been made by any of the team members, but she'd yet to see his actual paper file. She flipped through, not seeing anything new or different. There were several notes from his intake and original interview, which she quickly read through. He had been a SEAL, badly injured on a mission and would never return to active duty—but again nothing that was new. Not once did it say he was terrified of horses, for example.

There was no note saying he had been bitten by a horse or trampled by a horse or had anything against large animals. But then she didn't expect a military man would allow his fears to become public. They were all about the big macho hero aspect. They wouldn't let their insecurities and childhood fears be on written record somewhere. Still, she was stumped and disturbed. And if she were honest, hurt.

ELLIOT FOUND THE next few days to be the hardest yet. His nights were completely nonexistent in terms of sleep, and his body had worn down to the point where he could barely function. But he also knew the comfort coming from the nights of seeing Sicily wasn't an option anymore. He'd killed that. "Not sure what to do anymore, but I can't keep this up."

"You're deteriorating from a lack of sleep. Without that rest …" Shane's voice trailed off.

Elliot nodded. "I need to sleep."

"That's why I came to give you a massage. Maybe it will knock you out for a little bit, so your body can heal. This is an ugly cycle your system's on, and we must shake it off."

Elliot rolled over at Shane's instructions. He groaned when the strong fingers worked at the tension and knots in his back.

"Hey, this is way worse than last time. Are you upset about something?"

Elliot winced. He stayed quiet. This wasn't a good place to be upset about anything. Everybody would know.

"You don't have to tell me the details, but we do need to know if something is upsetting you."

He shook his head but stayed quiet.

"We've seen it all here. Heard it all too, so no one will judge you. That's one thing you need to understand. It's usually your ego, your pride, your vision of who you think you should be that comes into play every step of the way. When I put you on the spot, you expect to maintain or even achieve a certain level. It's a day-to-day push, and slowly but surely, you see progress. So the sudden lack of progress … well, that's a concern."

The words tumbled around in the back of his head. Elliot understood what Shane was doing, and in a way, it was working. The timbre of his voice slowly lured Elliot seductively toward sleep. If anything, he was exhausted. It was not about the nightmares. It wasn't about the horse therapy. It was about having hurt Sicily. The divide that had opened between them. She'd come by, deliver his medicine and walk out. Rational, competent, cool. It was no longer the warm visits over tea, ensuring he ate or a little social stop to see how he was doing. He missed her.

"Maybe you need to talk to the doctor again," Shane

said.

"Won't help," Elliot mumbled.

"Has something happened here? Because you can't keep doing this. Since being here, your progress has been stalled. We must find a way to break through whatever is bothering you—even if it is only a little breakthrough." After that, Shane didn't say any more, but he continued working on Elliot's back.

Elliot lay there, shame and pain rolling through him. Everybody had such wonderful experiences at Hathaway, and here he was, unresponsive. The last thing he wanted to do was fail. It would be hard enough to accept that of himself. But to be Hathaway House's latest failure …

After Shane was done, Elliot lay in a quiet stupor, figuring out how to shut off his mind.

"If there was any one single thing you could do right now, what would that be?" Shane's question came out of the blue.

Without thinking, Elliot murmured, "Apologize to Sicily."

A moment of shocked silence followed, but apparently Shane caught on quickly. "Here I thought you would say something like, return to the time before your accident. Or heal faster. But this is good. At least I know what's bothering you." He walked to the doorway and called back, "I'll tell her you need to see her." He let himself out.

Elliot mumbled curses under his breath. If he hadn't been so tired, he never would have said that. Maybe it was for the best. At least he could apologize for the way he had treated her and move on. Although she dealt with difficult patients all the time. He doubted he was any different. At the same time, that wasn't how he wanted her to see him. It wasn't how he wanted to leave here and to have people remember him. And it wasn't how he wanted his relationship with Sicily to be. But he'd been the one who put a stop to their growing friendship, so he was the one who had to fix it. At least having made that step, or knowing it was coming, he could relax a little bit. As he did relax, sleep caught him sideways and took him out. Maybe confession was good for the soul after all.

Chapter 10

S ICILY WALKED INTO the office that evening to find a note from Shane. She read his handwriting with one eyebrow raised.

Elliot needs to see you. When asked if there was one single thing he could do right now, he said, "Apologize to you." He's been having a particularly difficult time and not sleeping these last few days. If you can do anything to help him make peace with you, it needs to happen. No point in having him here, taking up space, if he is caught up in turmoil and not progressing. Particularly if his progress is related to one of the staff.

"That doesn't sound good," she mumbled to herself. She pulled out her phone. It was already past ten—too late to call Shane. She sent him a quick text instead. **I'll talk to Elliot.**

His response was immediate. **Good. Go easy on him. He fell asleep after I was there today. He was exhausted to the point of a physical breakdown. As far as I'm concerned, he needs to be knocked out for the next five days. He's not doing well.**

Worried and upset, Sicily put away her phone and set up the medications for her next rounds. She took care of everybody else first and then walked to Elliot's room. The door was closed. She gave a small tap but got no response. She turned the handle and pushed the door open.

Elliot was curled on his side, facing the window.

"Elliot?"

He twisted slightly at the sound of her voice.

She walked in, quietly placed his medicine on the table. "How are you doing?"

"I'm fine." But his voice was hesitant.

She waited a long moment. "Shane said you needed to speak with me about something?"

He gave a strangled laugh, followed by a heavy, sad sigh. "I need to apologize. It's been eating away at me. Stopping what little actual sleep I've been getting."

Ouch.

"I'm sorry," he said abruptly. "I didn't mean to hurt you. You went through a lot of work to set up the horseback riding, and I was pretty harsh in my refusal."

"Care to explain?"

"No," he snapped. "Not at all."

"Do you think you are the only person who is afraid of horses?" she asked, taking a stab in the dark. "Everyone has fears to deal with, of one kind or another. If I'd known in the beginning, I wouldn't have gone this far down this route."

He glared at her but stayed quiet.

She groaned. "I get that pride is important. But ..."

His glare deepened. Then his words rushed out. "It's not so much about pride or ego as much as it's about admitting to having a weakness."

"I suppose, in the military, all weakness is frowned upon," she guessed.

He stared at her for a long moment, then gave a clipped nod.

She didn't know how to get through that wall. She'd

seen aspects of this type of personality before. People came here with all kinds of issues. Showing weakness was one of them. Anything that pricked that pride and ego got a man's back up against the wall. It made her want to do the exact opposite with a problem. She hadn't come across anything like this.

"I had no intention of forcing you," she said calmly. "Would I have pursued it earlier if you'd told me the truth ahead of time?" She shook her head. "I'm not sure. So in this case, having this set up for at least one session, some of the other patients will get the benefit. However, I would at least like you to come out and maybe watch while the others do their therapy."

She watched his face shut down. She added, "I'm not saying touch the animals. I'm not saying be in the pasture with them. I'm saying be in the area outside the fence, so at least you can see the others go through the paces."

He tilted his head to the side, then gave a second sharp nod. "I can do that much."

She smiled. "Good. I'll let you know ahead of time. No pressure."

"What did you think it would have done?" he asked her.

"Hopefully strengthen your back muscles to help you sit up for longer periods of time. Yet maybe nothing. If it makes you feel better to see other people will be helped, that would be good too."

She walked to the door and as she was about to step through, he called out, "You forgive me?"

Startled, she turned to look at him, and then walked back inside the room. "Of course. This isn't something unforgivable. It was a lack of communication. You had a fear I didn't know about. I pushed your button. You pushed mine." She shrugged. "I guess that's what friends are for."

He grinned. "Okay, so we're back to being friends?"

"We were never *not* friends. As with all relationships, there are ups and downs. If you are concerned about something, I'd much rather you told me about it before our communication got worse instead of better. It's also a good lesson for me. Maybe I didn't ask enough questions. I was looking to help you, but that doesn't mean horse therapy won't help other people. Maybe that's where my priorities should've been, with everyone and not just you."

Elliot winced. "It's not that I don't like the fact you did this for me. I feel guilty as hell because I could use whatever therapy sessions are set up, but could they be with anything other than a horse?"

She chuckled. "Speaking of which, maybe you need to spend some time downstairs again. Some smaller animals could use some love."

"I haven't been down there on my own yet."

She glanced at her watch. "That's the problem with me working nights. I can't take you down either. Everyone's asleep or settled in for the night."

"I'm sure you don't want to be there during nonworking hours of course."

"I work with Stan quite a bit," she said. "There are never enough hands to do all the work needed."

"So if I go down there tomorrow, is there any chance you'd be there?"

She shrugged. "No idea. Depends on how good a night's sleep I get."

"Right, sleep. Something I don't get much of."

Then a muscle had him twisting in pain. She walked closer and could see his shoulders tensing into a big hard walnut. She gently massaged his back, lessening the tension around the knot. When the pain finally passed, she stepped in front of him.

"Look. I have a bit of a break in my routine. I can give you a back massage to work out some of those other knots. It might help."

He looked at her in surprise.

She smiled.

"I would love that," he said gratefully. "I must admit, almost every time you or Shane give me a massage, I fall right to sleep."

"I can't guarantee that every time, but I might be able to help." She checked her watch and looked at her tablet. "Give me about twenty minutes, okay?" She turned and walked out. She quickly finished her rounds. Back at her office, she walked to the counter and picked up a special cream to ease the pain of sore muscles and a small hand towel. Then she headed back to his room.

Elliot lay on his stomach, his sheet draped over his hips. She stepped quietly through the doorway and waited a moment. If he was asleep already, she wouldn't disturb him.

"Come on in. Not asleep."

"Too bad," she said, walking closer. She put some cream on his back and gently coated her fingers and then went to work. Muscle cramps weren't easy to get out, but she could help ease them for a few hours. She made a mental note to add this nighttime massage to his file as she continued to work the muscles across his back and his shoulder blades. His back had taken quite a beating. Some muscle mass was missing, and the scar tissue ran across the lower side. One shoulder appeared to be slightly higher than the other one.

She worked gently and steadily for twenty minutes, feeling the muscles finally relax under her fingertips. She never said a word but kept working from one side to the other, then down through the center of the spine and back up again. Her approach was different from that of a massage therapist. She was working out the tension to give him relief from the pain more than anything else. By the time she was done, gentle soft breathing came from Elliot. She hoped he had dropped off to sleep.

She stepped back and wiped her hands, closed the tube of cream and tiptoed from the room.

She waited outside the door for a moment, but she heard no other sounds. She smiled and returned to her office. It hadn't taken long, and it had given him some measure of peace. That made it totally worth it.

Now to catch up on her paperwork.

WHEN ELLIOT OPENED his eyes, he blinked rapidly at the bright sunshine streaming in through the window. He didn't move for a long moment, feeling peace and a sense of awareness in his system he hadn't had in a long time. He'd slept last night. He didn't know what time it was that Sicily had come in and given him the massage, but since that point, he'd been out like a light. He didn't even remember her leaving. He wondered how often he could get her to give him a massage. He didn't want to take advantage of her, but it was becoming very clear that massages were one of the few things that helped put him out. On the other hand, if he could make the hot tub thing work, that might do the same job.

His body felt so heavy, he wanted to lie in bed and relax.

There was a knock at his door and then it opened. Shane stepped in and raised both eyebrows. "Well, I didn't expect to see you still in bed."

Elliot smiled. "I literally just woke up."

"Waking up means you slept, so that is freaking awesome." Shane glanced at his watch. "You know? You're already late for your therapy this morning, so I suggest we have a pool session instead."

Elliot sat up in shock. "Are you saying I missed breakfast?"

Shane laughed. "You missed most of this morning. It's after 11:00 a.m. already."

Elliot stared at Shane in surprise. "Holy crap, I haven't slept like that in a long time." He slowly rotated his shoulders and his neck. "Sicily gave me a massage after my back seized in the night, and I fell asleep and slept right through."

"In that case, you'd better talk to her about getting another one tonight," Shane said. "Massages appear to be the answer for you."

"I also asked Dani if it was possible to hit the hot tub during the night. Because the heat would definitely help also. I haven't heard an answer yet."

Shane nodded. "As long as an orderly is with you, I think that'd be a good idea."

Elliot stood up slowly. "Should I shower first and then go to the pool? Or do we want to do the pool first? I'm not hungry yet, but I doubt I can go for long on an empty stomach."

"I suggest we hit the pool for a bit. Then you can have a shower and lunch around one o'clock. Your schedule's been cleared until two-thirty this afternoon."

Elliot looked out of the window and blinked, still adjusting to being awake. "Did you do that?"

"Yes. Better you sleep first, then get some physical exercise second and finally food." He walked from the room. "Meet me at the pool in ten minutes." Shane gave Elliot a big grin. "Congrats on getting some sleep."

And damn if it didn't feel like an accomplishment. Although he owed Sicily for that success.

Elliot brushed his teeth, got into his swim trunks and made his way to the elevator. He was a couple minutes late. He dropped his towel on a bench, went to the deep end of the pool and dove in. As soon as the water closed over his head, he smiled and broke through the surface and struck out strong.

Shane waited at the other side.

Instead of a physical workout in the weight room, it would be a physical workout in the pool. For the first time in a long time, Elliot felt he could handle that. Although, by the time his hour was done, he felt shaky and worn down physically already. Still, he felt decent mentally and emotionally.

As he walked to the bench where his towel lay, Shane joined him. "Got to say Elliot, that was a hell of a workout. If that's what sleep does for you, we need to find out how to get you more of it."

Elliot grabbed his towel and rubbed his head down and wiped his face clear of the droplets. "I feel good. I'm hungry, but I feel strong for a change—even though you wore me out."

"That's what we want here. Same time tomorrow. Let's see if you can get some more sleep, and then we'll get you back into the pool. After a few days of this, we can move to the gym and do some very specific exercises." On that note,

Shane took off for lunch.

Elliot wasn't quite as full of energy as he had been when he first made it downstairs, so getting back to his room and getting changed took a lot longer. But he showered and got dressed, then stopped at his bed, wondering if he should take the wheelchair to save some energy. Then, deciding he was okay, he grabbed his crutches and made his way very slowly to the kitchen. The dining hall was mostly full, but there were plenty of spaces with both staff and patients eating inside and out.

As he walked along the buffet to see what was on offer, Dennis smiled up at him. "Hey, don't you look a whole lot better?"

"I have no reason to be better at all," Elliot joked. "I finished a session in the pool with Shane. That's brutal."

Dennis nodded. "But just think—at least you made it through the session. It wasn't all that long ago you wouldn't have made it even halfway through." He quickly served up a big plateful of food and then walked around the buffet to stand beside Elliot. "Do you want this tray inside or outside?" Dennis scooped up the tray, a juice and a water and at Elliot's request, a cup of coffee, and then led the way to one of the small tables on the deck in the sunshine.

Elliot followed much more slowly. But he knew that today, even slow was still progress. As Dennis had said, a few weeks ago Elliot had looked a lot worse. For the first time in a long time, he was filled with excitement and optimism. He sat in his chair and realized his first meal of the day would be fried chicken, and he couldn't wait. He set the crutches off to the side and dug in.

Chapter 11

S ICILY WOKE UP to find it was already four o'clock. She'd had a lot of trouble sleeping but had managed it eventually. Wishing she could have gone to the pool and the hot tub herself, but not wanting to interfere with the patients' daytime therapies, she'd stayed in her room, tossing and turning until she finally nodded off. She got up and grabbed a bathing suit and went for a swim. The pool wasn't empty, but it wasn't crammed with people either. She dove into the water and proceeded to do laps. When she had done thirty, she pulled herself out and sat down on one of the chairs and lounged in the sun. Now, if she had a coffee and a glass of orange juice, things would be perfect. She closed her eyes and rested.

"There you are."

She jumped at the familiar voice, and then she opened her eyes and smiled up at Shane. "Hey, how are you doing?"

"Good. I wanted to thank you for seeing Elliot yesterday. He had a marvelous night and is a completely different man. It's amazing what sleep can do."

"That's awesome." She raised her eyebrows. "His back's muscle spasms last night were pretty bad. I gave him a short massage to help ease the tension. I wasn't sure if he was asleep or not when I left, but if he wasn't, he certainly was out before too long."

"Also his soul feels a little bit better. Confession and apologies are good for that."

She chuckled. "He had nothing to apologize for, but I put his worries to rest anyway."

"The combination was good. He had a much better night, which made today much better."

She beamed. It made her feel good to think she had helped Elliot in some way. "I'm glad to hear that. He's a good guy."

"He is, at that."

She shook her head and then glanced around to make sure nobody was close enough to overhear. "Maybe you can help me with something. He's afraid of horses and is refusing to have anything to do with the sessions other than possibly watching part of one session from the other side of the fence. There could be more behind it but he's not ready to go there yet."

Shane's mouth formed an O of surprise, and then he shrugged. "He mentioned the horse thing to me. It's too bad, but it's his choice. We can't deal with everything. At least some of the other patients can give it a try."

"True. At least if he could see what the others are doing, I think it might help him."

Shane nodded. "I'm looking forward to seeing what the horse therapist can do. Let me know when it's all scheduled, so I can fit it into my day."

"Will do." She watched as he walked away. She got up and grabbed her towel, wrapped it around herself and headed back to her place. She had to shower and change and then head into town for a few things. Maybe even include a walk in the park for a change of scenery.

Suddenly she remembered she needed to speak to Dani

again about the hot tub. That could potentially be another answer for Elliot.

She dressed quickly and headed to the office. As she reached the main office area, she watched as Dani and several other members of the medical staff exited the small meeting room. Sicily waved at her. "Hey, Dani, may I see you for a moment?"

Dani nodded and motioned to her office. "Perfect timing." She said a few quick goodbyes to the other staff as Sicily entered the small office. Dani shut the door and walked around her desk and sat down. "Would you rather grab a coffee and go for a walk outside?" she asked.

"I'm fine here for the moment. I wanted to check if you decided on the hot tub issue?"

"That came up in the meeting a few minutes ago." Dani leaned back. "There are a few concerns. One is more patients might want to have the same treatment, and we don't have the staff to watch over them."

"That's a definite concern, but as a night nurse, I can tell you I only ever talk to three patients who are awake at night, and one usually falls asleep easily. The other one hates water. Everyone else is asleep, except Elliot."

Dani pursed her lips. "The doctors and therapists agree with the suggestion in theory. Others are concerned about the intimacy of the setting."

That threw Sicily. She stared at Dani in shock. "Are they thinking something inappropriate would happen during that time?"

"They are concerned that *it could*," Dani stressed.

"I'm not as well thought of as I'd hoped then," she said with a frown. "I'm officially at work. The hot tub area is under camera surveillance, and as much as I might be friends with Elliot, I certainly wouldn't cross the line and have a tawdry sexual encounter with a man in the hot tub." The longer she sat here the angrier she got.

"Exactly what I told them, but the discussion needed to be out in the open." Dani smiled. "I'll speak to both Edward and Paul and let them know their assistance would be needed to get Elliot in and out of the hot tub during their night shifts."

"Right." Still a little dazed, hurt and quite royally pissed off, Sicily stood. "I'm sorry. This has thrown me. I'll leave and try to enjoy the rest of my day before I return to work. Somehow that thought is no longer quite as appealing as it was an hour ago."

Dani stood with her. She held up a hand, indicating caution. "I didn't tell you that to upset you. I wanted you to know that the topic was brought up and was discussed, and it was dismissed as not being something we needed to worry about. I wouldn't be doing my job if we kept it under the table. It's always better to have subjects like this in the open."

Sicily nodded. "But why would it even be under consideration?"

"Rules about relationships between staff and patients have changed over the past while and have become a bit more of a concern than before. I understand that you and Elliot may not be at that point. But intimacy in any surroundings moves relationships forward. We wanted to make sure that wouldn't be a problem." Dani laughed. "Particularly with the fact that the video cameras are on, I can't imagine it being an issue."

Sicily could feel the heat crawling up her skin. She shook her head. "No, I'm not into videos." She stumbled to the doorway. "But I hadn't considered that something personal, private and special, especially in its early stages, was something that all the staff discussed."

"Oh, they aren't," Dani rushed to reassure her. She stepped closer and reached out a hand, clasping Sicily's in her own. "Don't think that. We were not sitting there gossiping about you. It was an ethical, professional discussion—that's it. Let me share this bit of backstory with you, because it applies here, and I know you'll keep it confidential. Since you've always worked the night shift over your five years with us, you may not have heard about this. But Sidney and Brock had a passionate kiss in the pool, which Marsha saw and recounted as something much more. We don't want a repeat of that."

Sicily studied Dani's gaze, feeling something settle inside. Finally, she nodded. "For the record, I respect Sidney. But just because she kissed Brock in the pool doesn't automatically mean I will kiss Elliot in the pool or hot tub or wherever. I feel like I should be judged on my own merit, not based on Sidney or Marsha or anyone else for that matter."

Dani nodded. "I'll make sure to mention your concerns in the very next meeting. I'm sorry you are being judged based on the actions of others. It is not fair to you. I'll make certain that kind of thinking is stopped at the outset from now on."

"Okay, that makes me feel a bit better." Sicily shook her head. "But I must admit I was thrown there for a moment."

"I would be too," Dani exclaimed, "if I thought that's what our staff was doing. But it wasn't anything like that."

Sicily took a deep breath and walked toward the closed office door. Dani's voice stopped her.

"We also discussed the equine therapy sessions."

Sicily faced her. "Any issue with it?"

Dani smiled. "No, not at all. But I do understand that Elliot might have one. Is that correct?"

"Apparently, he's afraid of horses. He doesn't want anybody to know and is not prepared to do much about handling it."

"Of course not. He has enough on his plate."

"I did get him to agree to at least *see* some of the therapy in action. I told him he didn't have to touch a horse or even get close to the horses, but if he could understand it's not such a scary thing, I thought it would be a step in the right direction."

"Potentially. But as he's under a lot of stress now, I wouldn't want him to feel pressured even to do that much."

Sicily winced. "You are right. I'll mention it to him the next time I see him." She headed to the door again, then turned back. "I think it would be better if you told him about the hot tub. Also, when is the horse therapist coming?"

"She's booked for next Thursday, at one in the afternoon. She's just bringing one therapy horse this time. She'll arrive early to give the horse time to get comfortable. Then we'll bring down some patients for her to work with."

Sicily nodded. "That sounds great." She walked out of Dani's office. She had been planning on stopping by Elliot's room, but after the conversation with Dani, she went back to her place and headed into town instead. She could use a break. As much as she loved being at Hathaway, she didn't quite have that warm, fuzzy feeling about her workplace after what she'd just heard. An hour later she settled into a coffee shop in town. She'd gone to the drugstore and picked up a few essentials as well as the latest novel by her favorite author. At the coffee shop, she ordered a latte and a sandwich and sat back to read. When her phone went off a few minutes later, she frowned and pulled it out.

It was a text from Elliot. **Any chance of meeting for coffee or having dinner together tonight?**

She stared at her sandwich, which had looked so appetizing until she got this message. She wasn't sure how to respond, so she decided to think about it for a few minutes, but the phone rang. She picked it up again to see it was Elliot. Frowning, she answered the call. "What's up, Elliot?"

"I was wondering if you are avoiding me," he said without any preamble.

"No, not at all. I'm in town. Why?"

"I had a talk with Dani about the hot tub option and about the horses. I understand she had a meeting with you today, so I wasn't sure if that was a problem. I don't want to cause problems."

"No problem," she said lightly. "I was getting out for a bit."

"That makes sense. Will you be back in time for dinner, even if it's late?" he asked, hope in his voice.

She stared at the sandwich. The fact that Elliot wanted to be with her made some of her world start to feel right again. She smiled. "I might be back in the next hour. Is that early enough?"

"It's only six-thirty now, so if you're back anywhere between seven and eight, that would be perfect. I'm sure there will be leftovers available, or we could get something from Dennis or the kitchen staff. Besides, I'm not that hungry yet anyway."

She glanced at her watch. "Okay, I'll try to get back within the hour." She hung up the phone and called a waitress over and asked her to wrap up her sandwich to-go.

She finished her coffee and packed up. She still had to hit the grocery store for a few special snacks and treats to keep in her room. It only took her about twenty minutes to finish the things on her list. She was doing well on time as she drove to her last stop for fuel.

She walked into her place, unloaded her purchases and took a few minutes to check her email messages. She washed up and then headed to the main center. On the way, she pulled out her phone and sent Elliot a message. **Where are you?**

In my room. Where are you?

Heading to the dining hall.

His response came right away. **I'll meet you there in five.**

She laughed, her heart light. So nice to know she had somebody to meet. Somebody who cared. Somebody who wanted to be with her. He really was a special person.

She stood in the doorway to the dining hall and scanned the room. Only a handful of people still sat here. Elliot hadn't arrived yet.

She grabbed a cup of coffee and stepped outside on the deck where the day's heat still hit her like a brick wall. She decided it was a good night to eat inside for a change. She chose a table for two off to the side and sat so she could watch the entranceway. She didn't wait long before Elliot walked through the door.

He made his way slowly toward her on his crutches. He was walking but with a bad limp.

She motioned to his leg. "Is that much worse?"

"No, but I've got some chafed spots on my sole from putting too much pressure on it." He pulled out the chair and sat down, tucking the crutches off to the side. Then he covered her hand with his and said, "Are you okay?"

She raised her eyebrows and smiled warmly. "Of course I'm okay. Why wouldn't I be?"

He shrugged and sat back, letting go of her hand. "You went to beg for me to use the hot tub, and you went through all the trouble of getting a horse therapist to come in. I want you to know I appreciate that, and I hope something wasn't said to upset you over it all."

She shook her head. "Not at all. I have a great working relationship with Dani. We can talk about most issues. In fact, she told me not to pressure you about the horse therapy as you have enough on your plate to focus on. And I totally agree with her. So I'm sorry that I pushed you about even watching the therapy."

"No problem," he said, visibly relieved, "but thank you for that. I'm excited because she told me the hot tub would be an option if I felt I needed it. She also said I wasn't to abuse the system because only two orderlies are on duty at that hour, and they also have other duties to perform. But this is huge to know that when I wake up in the night full of knots, I'm free to use the hot tub."

She nodded. "Maybe tonight that'll be something we can look at."

He smiled. "I don't want to look forward to it because that also means I'm waking up in severe pain." He laughed. "On the other hand, it sounds like a really nice benefit for me, and I appreciate it." He glanced around and said, "Shall we get some food before we can't anymore?" He grabbed his crutches, and together they slowly walked to the buffet area. Dennis waited there with trays already loaded for them.

Sicily smiled. It had been Italian night, and she was very partial to lasagna. Without thinking, she picked up her tray and returned to the table. She set it down and realized he hadn't followed. She walked back over as he placed a cup of coffee on his tray.

"You might've tried the tray before you put down the coffee," she said jokingly. "Once the coffee is on there, that makes it so much harder." She picked it up and carried it ahead of him. She didn't wait to see if he was upset or not at her taking his tray and stepping out in front with no discussion. But she hoped he'd take it the way it had been intended.

As she sat down again with him, he placed the crutches on the floor beside them.

"Thanks," he said quietly. "I always think I can do more that I can. If I'd tried to carry that, I would have ended up falling on my face."

"It wouldn't have mattered, except you might have hurt yourself."

He nodded but didn't say anything.

"Accepting help can be difficult. There are enough times when you have to do things on your own that you should consider the help when it's available. Remember that."

He gave a short nod and dug into his meal.

So often relationships were all about this, working through each other's buttons that were pushed and finding a happy place in the middle. As she had done with Dani earlier. Sicily chuckled and leaned back, and when he stared at her, she said, "We're starting to sound like an old married couple."

Surprise lit the depths of his eyes. "Why's that?" he asked lightly. He put down his fork and picked up his glass of water and took a drink, but he studied her.

She smiled. "Helping each other without needing to be

asked or told and understanding each other's moods and perceived contrariness. Understanding when somebody's upset and giving them a moment." She pointed at him. "Somewhere along the way, we crossed a line from being patient and employee to friends." She gestured with her arm in a wide arc. "Did you ever notice how all the employees tend to sit on the other side of the room, and all the patients are on this side?"

He turned and looked around, a thoughtful expression coming over his face. He nodded. "I've never noticed that before. He glanced at her. "Does it bother you?"

She shook her head. "No, but I realized today that other people have talked about us. Not gossiping but it's been noticed."

Elliot nodded. "I imagine they have, for no other reason than concern for a trend starting here with so many relationships forming. What is it now? Five?"

"Counting us, yes." She smiled—a bright, truly happy smile. Because if she did like one thing, it was the thought that her relationship with Elliot might end up growing into something special, the way Sandra's, Hannah's, Sidney's and Dani's had. "You know? I'm good with that."

HELL, HE WAS more than good with that. He'd been perturbed, not ashamed, but his self-confidence had taken a hit when he realized he couldn't carry the dinner tray while walking with crutches. He'd carried one yesterday with only a single cinnamon bun on a dessert plate. It was a small step forward, but he hadn't even considered that earlier success when he was in line at the buffet with Sicily now. Yet she'd come back, picked up his tray and carried it, saving his pride at the same time. Then she had even joked about it. Yeah, she was his kind of girl.

He smiled at the thought. He raised his gaze as she cut into her lasagna. There was something about her ... She was the take-home-to-Mom kind of girl. She was also a nurse, a professional who cared about people, and she had no trouble stepping out of the role and being a friend to one in need.

"What are you looking at?" she asked self-consciously. "Do I have pasta sauce on my face?" She wiped her mouth with her napkin.

That sinfully rich mouth. He sighed, forcing his gaze away from those plump lips. "No, you don't," he said gently. "You're perfect."

She stared in surprise, and he realized how much emotion he'd conveyed in those few words. He gave a big happy sigh and added, "I meant it."

Heat washed up her cheeks.

He'd never seen anyone blush the way she did. It was heartwarming and fascinating.

"Thank you," she mumbled, but she dropped her head to hide her embarrassment.

He chuckled, feeling more alive and younger than he had any right to feel. "I do like my life right now."

Her head shot up, and she stared at him, then gave him a slow dawning smile that came from deep inside, and by the time it bloomed fully, he was even more under her spell.

Her smile was so endearing and honest ... Well, he'd already been sliding down that slippery slope of attraction, but now—he'd fallen hard. He knew there was no going back after this.

If he couldn't convince her they were meant to be together, then there would be a lot less joy in his forever-after.

The problem was, he didn't have much to offer. At least not yet.

Chapter 12

THE NEXT THURSDAY Sicily left her office, excited that the day for the horse therapist had arrived. She raced back to her apartment, had a shower and dove into bed. She hadn't expected to feel such excitement buzzing through her. The horse therapist would be here around one o'clock, and that gave Sicily plenty of time to sleep. Well, at least, she hoped. The patients were excited too. She was grateful for that. Five had signed up, and that was about all the horse therapist could handle today. Depending on how this first session went, Dani and the horse therapist and the medical staff here at Hathaway House would see how much more they did after this. There was no real way to know until they went through the process.

She hadn't brought it up with Elliot again after telling him how she wouldn't pressure him further on that topic. She had earlier placed strings on his attending, and that wasn't fair. She hadn't meant to, but that had been the end result. Through most of his life he had kept that scared-of-horses secret under wraps. It wasn't like there was any right way to go through life. Everybody had some kind of weakness.

Her alarm woke her up at noon. She got dressed and grabbed a cup of coffee at the cafeteria, then headed outside to the pasture where the session would take place. Nobody was here yet. She checked her watch and frowned, but when she glanced up, a horse trailer slowly made its way toward her down the drive. She grinned—right on time.

Word must've gone out that the horse therapist had arrived because by the time the trailer pulled up and parked, Dani, Stan, and several of the patients had made their way outside. Excitement filled the air. She chuckled when she saw the anticipation on Dani's face.

"Anything to do with horses and I'm happy," Dani said, almost dancing in place.

Stan chuckled. "Very much so."

Sicily waited until the therapist hopped from the truck and walked over to Dani. The two women exchanged handshakes. Sicily stayed close enough that she was part of the group. She introduced herself to Amy, the horse therapist, after the pleasantries were exchanged.

Amy motioned to the trailer behind her and said, "I'll get Copper out." She returned to the horse trailer and brought out a beautiful chestnut gelding.

"This is Copper. He's eight years old and has been doing this for about four years now."

Dani stepped up and introduced herself to the animal.

Sicily watched a look of complete adoration come over her boss's face. It was beautiful to see. Sicily stepped up beside Dani, and the horse lifted his beautiful soft velvet nose. Copper sniffed Sicily's hand as she stroked his long nose. "He's beautiful," Sicily said.

Amy laughed. "Yes, he is, and he knows it. He has quite a vain streak."

The women laughed. "He deserves it," Dani said.

Amy looked around at the other horses standing by the fence and smiled. "You've got quite a few of your own here too, don't you?"

Dani smiled. "And if you don't already know, there is always room for one or two more."

"At least you have the space for them. I do hate to see horses in small pastures without room to run." She led the gelding into the pasture set aside for the day's session and walked him around for several minutes, letting him get used to the feel and the change in the area. "He's used to traveling a fair bit. But it's always a good idea to let him have a couple minutes on his own." She unhooked his lead and let him go.

Sicily was surprised. "Won't it be hard to catch him again?"

Amy laughed. "No, not Copper. He will come when he's called. He loves people. So the minute another person arrives, he'll be here to greet them."

Sicily watched Amy check her watch. They did have ten to fifteen minutes before the first person was scheduled. A second truck pulled in. Amy said, "That's one of my helpers. You can never have enough hands when you're working with horses."

"Or when working with patients," Dani added with a smile. With the new arrival, things got a little busier. They had a specific ramp set up for patients to mount the horse. They had the list of patients to get ready. Sicily was fascinated. She stepped out of the way as she wasn't even on duty, and Dani already had the staff on hand, ready to help.

Charles was the first patient. He had lost his full leg from the hip and part of an arm. He was also struggling with some spinal injuries. He had made phenomenal progress, but he'd also been at Hathaway for months.

Sicily hopped onto the fence and sat on top, watching as Charles was helped onto the horse and secured with some strapping she hadn't seen before, then was slowly led around the yard. She was surprised when a second horse was brought into the pasture, not having seen it inside the horse trailer with Copper. The assistant hopped onto its back and rode up beside Charles. A discussion ensued between the three of them, then Amy walked along as she took Copper and Charles for a slow, steady walk down the fence line. Amy kept an eye on Charles's posture, and from the look of pure happiness on his face, he appeared to be enjoying himself thoroughly.

Before Sicily realized it, the hours slipped away. Patients came. Patients went. Not everybody walked up to the fence line and spent their time on the horse, like Charles did. Shane was here when they brought out Andrew. He had both arms, but his back injuries made it difficult for him to lift his huge frame. Shane, on the other hand, quickly helped the large man into the saddle. Amy's assistant got off her horse and walked to the side of Andrew and helped navigate him and Copper through the pasture.

Sicily joined Dani, who had remained to watch the entire afternoon, and asked, "How do you think it's working?"

A big smile washed over Dani's face. "Wonderful. Some of the men will be quite sore tomorrow."

"As long as they are up to being sore."

"Exactly. It's all about balance."

By the end of the afternoon, there were smiles, a whole lot of happy people with no accidents, no spills, and no injuries. Including Sicily. Amy and Dani were having a private discussion by the time Copper and his buddy were loaded up. Sicily wandered back to the dining hall to find dozens of staff and patients lined up along the deck railing, watching.

Sidney walked over to join Sicily. "I'm so jealous. They looked like they were having so much fun out there."

Sicily nodded. "They seemed to be happy. There were a lot of smiling faces out there."

"It's about connecting to the animals and having a chance to ride. Most of these people have probably never ridden a horse before. This is not exactly an easy introduction to it, but even emotionally their spirits should be so much happier after this."

Sicily nodded. "I think that's what it's all about. Making them feel good. Making their muscles work in a different way."

"Anything we can do to make the body engage is huge. People don't realize it, but even shifting chairs forces muscles to work. When you sit in the same chair over a long period of time, the body gets accustomed to it. It doesn't like change, and then, when you do shift to a new chair, it can complain pretty loudly."

"Hopefully these guys won't have too much pain from their afternoon ride."

As Sicily found out later that night, not only were there no ill effects on the riders, but those who had had some prior trouble sleeping fell asleep like babies with smiles on their faces. She caught one before he was nodding off to give him his medicine. His smile said it all.

"Riding the horse today," he said, "was just magical."

"Then I'm glad we set this up," she said.

He rolled over and closed his eyes. She turned off the light on her way out. Inside, she found it hard not to be pleased and delighted. She'd helped bring this about, and that was a good thing. She carried on down the hall, finishing her rounds at Elliot's room. "Hey, how are you doing?"

she asked as she walked inside.

He raised his gaze, but it was dark and shuttered.

She stopped and studied him. "You okay?"

He nodded. "I'm fine."

She walked over and placed his medicine on his night table. "Did you get a chance to see the horses arrive?"

He nodded. "I saw them arrive, but that's all."

Letting him know he was off the hook, she sat down and said, "Even a few minutes is more than you would've done before, so I thank you for that."

After a few more moments of small talk, she could tell he was still out of sorts, so she stood again. "I'll head back to work and check on you later." With a breezy smile, she walked out. He didn't stop her—he didn't call to her in any way. She wasn't sure what she was to do when he was like this. She figured doing nothing was probably the best. Not everybody liked everything every day. Today might've been a little more difficult for him because of the horses, because of the reminder of what that meant to him. For that, she was sorry. She wanted him to get better, not to feel bad about anything. The others were right. Enough was enough.

She popped her head back into his doorway. "And I shouldn't have asked you to show up for the horses. That was my bad. I'm sorry."

He stared at her, his gaze still dark and fathomless, and gave her a clipped nod. "Good. I wasn't going anyway."

She grinned. "At least now you don't have to worry about it."

HOW DID THAT work? He stared at this woman, so loving

and giving. She never complained. She never argued. Instead she went out of her way to do even more for people. She had such a positive attitude to life.

Look at the horse therapy and getting him access to the hot tub. The horses just weren't for him. As much as he'd like to think she was doing something special for him that she wasn't doing for other people, he knew that wasn't fair. It was not professional, and if there was one thing she always was, it was pro.

He sighed. She was always doing her best.

Unlike him.

Even when she was wrong to do so, she took the high road. Whereas, he'd fallen off fast and taken the low road as soon as he could.

She'd already figured out how to let him off the hook with the horses, going above what she needed to do, because she wanted to make him feel good even when she'd been right.

He hadn't admitted to his weakness in a long time. But since he'd finally told her, he felt better—and worse. Better for clearing the air but now worse as she'd been so damn good at forgiving him and letting him off the hook.

She was doing her best.

And he wasn't.

He didn't like himself much at this point.

Chapter 13

NOW THAT SICILY was back on more settled ground with Elliot, the days passed happily as the two slowly regained their footing and surged ahead. She had a good feeling about their relationship. He'd learned they could move on. It was all good. Several days later, while working on her files, she got a phone call from Elliot. "What are you doing awake?"

"Muscle knots," he gasped.

She bolted from her chair, phone in hand. "I'm on my way. Hang tight." She could give him certain medications to relax the muscles. But he reacted badly to so many of the drugs, so doing anything natural was easier. It was less stress on him physically.

When she walked into his room, he was twisted on the bed, his shoulders back and his face frozen into a grimace.

"No drugs."

She grabbed the bottle of cream from the side table and coated her fingers. She knelt on the bed and went to work. "I didn't say I would give you any." She shook her head. "But you need to talk to the doctor about this. There should be something you can take."

As her fingers touched his skin, he said, "The worst is past." His voice was tired.

"Good," she said. "This should work pretty fast. But you

still must talk to the doctor tomorrow. The spasms are getting worse, but that's also a good thing. It means life is returning to the muscles with all the work you are doing. Don't overdo it."

He lay quietly as she worked, her fingers sliding up and down each of the muscle bands, coaxing them to relax.

"I doubt I'll sleep again tonight," he said with a heavy sigh.

"You want to try the hot tub afterward?"

He lifted his head a few inches to look at her. "You think that would work?"

She pulled out her phone and contacted the orderly. While waiting for him to come, she continued to work on the rest of Elliot's muscle bands. When the orderly arrived, she smiled at him. "Let's see if we can get him to the hot tub."

It took a few minutes to get Elliot into the wheelchair, with a blanket around his shoulders, and the trio moved slowly to the hot tub area. It was off to the side of the pool, under cover. The night was balmy and warm, so she didn't see any point in closing the doors. They rarely closed them, unless a big storm or an unexpected cooler period was coming in.

With the orderly's help, Elliot made his way into the hot tub. As soon as he sank into the warm water, he groaned. "Oh God, that feels so good."

She stood at the edge of the tub and studied him. His color was almost back to normal, and although he was exhausted, the stress lines had eased. The furrows of pain on his forehead had relaxed. She nodded at the orderly. "How's your schedule? You okay to stay with him for the next half an hour or so?"

He nodded. "I can be here for a bit. If I get called away, I'll have you come down and replace me first."

She nodded. With a smile at Elliot, she said, "Relax and use some of the yoga exercises you were taught to stretch out those muscles. Don't do too much. A little bit will help ease the tightness. I'll come back and check on you in about twenty minutes."

He barely opened his eyes, but he gave her a small finger wave from the top of the water and sank deeper into the bubbles. With a smile, she headed upstairs to his room. His sheets were drenched, so she did a quick linen change for him, then flipped back the covers so when he returned from the hot tub, he could crawl right back inside. Afterward she walked to the coffee station and made herself a cup of tea. Dennis often left out a few snacks for the nighttime staff.

If one of them was even hungrier, they had a fridge of leftovers to choose from as well. She only occasionally did that. She usually had a sandwich that she brought from her own place, or she packed up something from dinner to have later.

At that moment another patient called for her, so she headed there to help reposition the bed and realign him so his pain was eased. He didn't need any sleeping pills—he needed help rotating his body. So often that was the case. Sometimes in the night the muscles locked up, and it was so hard with their patients' recent injuries to get into a position that wouldn't hurt.

By the time she was done there, it was past time to check on Elliot. She walked to the hot tub as he slowly sat down in the wheelchair. He looked much more at peace. The orderly was drying him off, and Elliot held a towel, scrubbing down his hair. She stepped in front of them. "How do you feel now?"

He gave her a smile. "That's a magical cure."

She laughed. "Nothing magical about it. Just heat." When they were ready, she walked beside him on his way back to his room, and Elliot got into bed.

He moaned as he sank into the fresh bedding and smiled. "I'm so tired," he whispered.

"Good, sleep." She shut off the light beside his bed. "I'll check on you in an hour or so," she said. The orderly stepped out into the hallway to carry on with his duties. Sicily watched and waited, but sure enough, Elliot closed his eyes and fell into a deep sleep. With a smile, she returned to her office. Inside, she felt great. From the looks of Elliot, the hot tub might be a magical answer after all.

ELLIOT WOKE THE next morning feeling rested and at peace. Waking up screaming in pain hadn't been much fun. He wasn't sure why the muscle spasms had been so bad lately, but they were. He'd read somewhere about nerve endings and muscles finally coming to life again. They needed time to adapt. In those cases, muscle spasms weren't unusual. The use of magnesium, calcium and something else could help prevent the muscle spasms. He'd ask the doctor about it today. He didn't like taking even muscle relaxants, although given the pain he had been in last night, he'd do a lot to avoid that again. He'd always been sensitive to drugs. He couldn't even take aspirin most of the time, without getting shortness of breath and perspiration-like sweat attacks.

He sat up slowly. His skin felt odd, but then he had been in the hot tub and not showered afterward. He stood up straight and stretched. He checked his clock and realized it was almost breakfast time. After a quick shower, he slowly made his way to the cafeteria on his own two legs. He wasn't full of energy, but he wasn't dragging his feet either. Weeks of sleepless nights weren't made up for in a couple good nights, but it sure was a healthy start to fixing the problem. As he walked into the cafeteria, he ended up behind Dani in line.

She studied his face for a moment and smiled. "Hi, Elliot. You look better this morning."

He nodded. "I am. I feel great today."

"That's good to hear. I'm really pleased."

He nodded. "I'll talk to the doctor today about changing my nutritional supplements."

Dani inclined her head. "Good idea." She accepted a plateful of omelet from Dennis on the other side of the buffet. "Looks great, Dennis."

He chuckled. "You're easy to please." Dennis turned to Elliot. "What about you, big man? What can I get you this morning?"

Elliot studied the array of food in front of them. "I'm hungry."

"Meat it is then. Especially for a growing healing boy. Sausages, bacon and eggs. Toast and hash browns."

Elliot surveyed the platter, shoved high with food, and smiled. "Normally I wouldn't get through half of this, but today it looks about right." He moved on to the end and grabbed a fresh juice and milk. At least there was calcium in the milk—that might help too. Although he was fooling himself to think a single glass of milk would make a big difference. He headed off to the sunshine-washed deck, only to find Sicily sitting there, hugging a cup of coffee, waiting for him. Dennis brought Elliot's tray behind him.

He approached her quietly. "May I join you?"

She nodded and gave him a small smile.

It was a beautiful morning. He felt better, but she looked tired.

"Thanks," she said to Dennis as he placed the tray down and left.

It had to be hard to work the night shift. "Do you like working that shift?"

She shrugged. "Sometimes I think about asking for a shift change, but I like it most of the time. It's peaceful, and it's quiet."

"What do you do on your break?"

"I usually sit in the office. Sometimes I walk around because I need the exercise and to get out of the four-walls type of thing. I might go out on the deck for a few minutes, but I always have my phone in case anything comes up."

"So you're never off, are you?"

"It doesn't matter." She shrugged again. "It works for me."

"It's not like working in a normal hospital, is it?"

"No, it's a completely different environment." She sipped her coffee. "Here I get to help people. It's like giving back in a way, as well as doing a job."

He was wondering if he could do something to give back. Elliot glanced at the buffet as Dennis, back again behind the counter, smiled at the people moving along in front of him. It reminded Elliot how helpful Dennis was.

That gave Elliot the glimmer of an idea. Only it wasn't one that would work every day. She'd done so much for him. He wished he could do something to give back to others—especially to her.

Chapter 14

TWO NIGHTS LATER, she got a call at three a.m. from Elliot.

Expecting the worst, she was already up and out of her chair, heading toward him at top speed with her phone still in her hand. "Elliot, what's up?" She tried to keep her voice level, but his last call in the night had ended up with them massaging out the knots on his back and followed up with a hot tub visit, so she was expecting something similar. She had almost reached his door before he answered.

"I was wondering if you could come here for a moment," he said. "Have you had your break yet?"

"No, it's been too busy for that. I'm almost at your room. Hang on." She shut off her phone and pocketed it. At his door, she knocked, walked inside and came to a complete standstill. He was sitting up in bed with a big grin on his face. But beside him were several food trays on a cart she would normally have used to carry her medicines and another food tray was on his small table. She frowned, not quite understanding. "What's this? Are you hungry or something?"

He motioned at the chair sitting beside the cart. "This is me trying to pay you back for all your loving kindness and care," he said with a big smile. "You haven't had your break, so I arranged with Dennis to set this up."

Her mouth dropped open, but no words came out.

He chuckled. "Well, it's nice to see you're shocked into silence, but I hope it's a good surprise," he said quietly, his gaze searching hers.

She turned shocked eyes to him and then beamed. "I can't remember the last time anybody did something like this for me." She approached hesitantly, her gaze going from the pot of tea to juice, sandwiches, muffins and cookies and a bowl of fresh fruit salad. "This is a veritable feast," she exclaimed.

"It is, so I hope you're hungry."

She laughed. "It's my break, but that doesn't mean it's yours."

"I don't know about that. I'm always happy to eat big meals three times a day and another one during the night."

She chuckled and took her seat. "Having time to eat can be a problem. But if I don't eat in my eight hour shift, it's hard to stay awake."

"We can't have that happening," he said. "Sit down and pick what you'd like to start with."

She stared in wonder. "This all looks so wonderful." She picked up the bowl of fresh fruit salad. "But I'll start with this."

"And here I thought it would be dessert first," he joked.

She pointed at the cinnamon buns and muffins and cookies. "There's enough dessert here for half a dozen people."

Elliot shook his head, picking up a cinnamon bun and a cup of tea. "Not if I'm eating too. I'm starting with dessert."

That set the tone for the next half hour. By the time her break was over, she was very comfortably full. "I'm so sorry," she said regretfully, "but I must get back to work now."

He nodded and smiled. "I know. I didn't expect you to stay past your break time. But you are allowed a coffee break, so if I'm still awake, feel free to come back."

She looked at the food still on the tray. "I was wondering about taking some of this back to my station."

His grin widened. "I'd be happy for you to do so." He consolidated the food from the two trays onto one. "I'm more than ready to try for some sleep, so take the cart with you, and I'll see you tomorrow sometime."

She stopped before she walked out the doorway, pushing the cart, and turned to look at him. "Thank you for doing this," she said with a big smile. "It was very much appreciated."

He was already curled up on the bed with the lights out. "We can't exactly go on a date," he murmured, his voice drowsy, "so this was what I could come up with."

Then he fell silent. Slowly, she pushed the cart to her office. A date night—that was how he looked at it. In a way, it certainly was. People in situations like this had to make do with whatever they could manage. As far she was concerned, he'd done a heckuva job. She'd never been happier.

She wandered past the orderlies, sitting down having coffee, and offered them the rest of the desserts. Both accepted thankfully. She grinned, then brought the cart back to the kitchen, where she dropped it off, but not before collecting the remaining half sandwich and the last of the fruit salad. Both of those she would take care of before the end of her shift. She must remember to thank Dennis for his contribution to her surprise. Although he'd probably just grin at her and tell her to let others do something for her for a change. With a big smile on her face, she finished the rest of her night filled with a quiet happiness.

ELLIOT WOKE THE next morning feeling bright and happy, only to realize it was a horse therapy day. He rolled onto his back and wondered what he could do. What was he prepared to do? What was even reasonable to try to do? He lay there quietly, thinking about how far he'd come in so many ways and how far he still wanted to go. The progress was for him but also for Sicily. She was a very special person, and he was happy with the way their "evening" had turned out. It was unusual to sit here and have a date at three o'clock in the morning, but given their circumstances, it had been perfect.

He'd spoken to his therapist about what was on his mind, but he hadn't mentioned it to Shane. As Elliot made his way to his daily session with Shane, he held his tongue as Shane put him through his paces. When they took a break, he brought up the subject of the horses.

Shane cast him a sharp look. "Anytime you want to try, you tell me, and I'll make it happen."

Elliot nodded. "That all sounds good in practice." He shook his head. "But making something happen is a lot more than just talking about it, and I'm not sure I can do what I want to do."

"Then start with coming down and seeing everyone. Start by meeting the horses. They're great big beautiful animals, looking for love and attention, the same as we are."

Elliot smiled at the imagery. "Hardly. They are huge, and they can be vicious."

"Sure." Shane nodded. "But humans can be much more vicious. Keep that in mind."

Elliot brought up the subject again at the end of his session. "Can I go down to the corral on my own to watch for the last half hour or something?"

Shane nodded. "It's this afternoon, so you can make your way on your own, or you can let me know, and I'll come get you."

"I'll think about it," Elliot said hurriedly, backing off again. Every time he even thought about committing to such a step, it made his stomach heave.

As it was, he made it to the top of the deck and watched from his wheelchair, but he certainly didn't go down below. Still, he remained there for the whole time that afternoon, missing out on two appointments because he had a morbid fascination with what went on below. He was supposed to be more engaged in it all, but instead he was separated from it because of his own actions and his own fears. He wanted to get down there, but so far, he couldn't force himself.

Before the end of the day, Shane came up beside him.

"Do you want to take a run down to meet the horses?"

Instantly a refusal came to his lips. He shook his head, but when he opened his mouth, he said, "Yes." He stared at Shane in astonishment. "I didn't mean that."

Shane chuckled and grabbed the handles of Elliot's wheelchair and took him to the elevator. "If you were on crutches or walking, I wouldn't do this," he said with a smile. "But you're exhausted today, so the wheelchair means I get to push you around like I want to."

"Unless I don't want to go out there," Elliot protested. "Which I don't."

"But you've already said yes. So what we have here is a very conflicted mind-set. I'll take you outside, but we won't push it. We'll see how close you can get to the horses."

Outside, in the bright sunshine, he could feel himself knotting up the closer he got to the huge animals. Until he saw something he completely hadn't expected. Dani was with the tiny baby horse. Dani looked at Elliot and smiled, glancing at the little horse she had at the end of a rope. The little horse gently walked closer to Elliot.

"I don't know if little Molly here counts as a full-size horse or not," Dani said, "but she's a bright filly, and she very much likes people. Plus she's very gentle."

In fact, Molly stepped up to say hi to Elliot.

He was fascinated. "She's not much bigger than a huge dog."

Instinctively he reached out to touch her soft neck and her velvety nose. Molly nuzzled his hand, her lips working away at the sleeve of his shirt. He chuckled. "If all horses were this size, I wouldn't have a problem. But she'll grow up to be one big badass mother."

Molly nickered slightly, as if laughing at his comment.

"Actually," Dani said. "She's already over a year old."

Molly stayed at Elliot's side while he gently stroked up and down her face. For the first time he could see why people fell in love with these animals. Such intelligence was evident in her huge brown eyes, and she was so gentle. Shane motioned toward the others, saying, "Come on. Maybe we should walk Molly over to where the other horses are."

Elliot nodded.

Dani led Molly to meet the horses arriving for therapy day. "It's good for her to see other horses."

Slowly their group made their way to where the therapy horses stood. Amy was walking along with Copper. It was stupid that Elliot remembered the names of the horses and the people involved in this new therapy. He couldn't see where Sicily was because he couldn't pull his attention away from the huge horse. The gelding rose up high above him, as if he knew that Elliot was afraid. Amy stepped forward and shook Elliot's hand.

"Hi, this is Copper. He does very well with people—including those who don't like him."

Elliot winced. "Does he know I don't like horses?"

"He'll like you anyway." She carefully walked Copper a couple steps closer to Elliot. She watched Elliot's reaction, so she could tell when he stiffened, and she slowed her pace. "Reach out a hand."

No way Elliot could do that. He was so damned sure the horse would take it off.

Shane offered his hand instead and took a half step forward. Copper sniffed and then gently played with Shane's fingers. Shane scratched his long nose and under his chin. Copper looked to be almost drooling.

Elliot stared in fascination. "I've never seen that side of a horse."

"These are tame horses," Amy explained. "You can never completely trust any animal to be like a stuffed toy. They are animals after all, and they do have their bad sides, like people do. But in this case, Copper is very well-trained. He's met thousands of people, and despite it all, he still likes us."

Copper stretched his long neck closer to Elliot. Everybody waited to see what Elliot would do. He hated the pressure, but at the same time, he felt like he was letting everybody down if he didn't at least try. Gently he stretched out a hand until Copper could smell it. Instantly Copper blew his warm breath all over Elliot's hand. Elliot took another moment, but slowly he scratched Copper underneath the chin, loving the soft, velvety texture of the few hairs underneath his fingers. He slid his hand up and around the long brow. "He's beautiful."

"Yes, he is. He's beautiful inside as well, and that makes a huge difference."

Feeling emboldened, Elliot leaned forward, and Copper took a step toward him as well until they met in the middle, and gently they got to know each other.

When Copper stepped back to nuzzle Molly, who had walked up closer to him, Elliot dropped his hand with a happy sigh. "Thank you for that," he said quietly to Amy.

She flashed him a bright look. "No problem. Maybe next week we'll get you up on him."

Elliot shook his head. "Oh, I don't think that'll happen."

Amy smiled. "You'd be surprised what you can do. One step at a time."

Only he knew how impossible that hope was. But he kept it to himself. In the back of his mind, a small voice said, *Never say never.* Because he'd done and achieved so much more already today that he didn't think was possible. Maybe riding a horse wasn't so far off reality either. And then he remembered the accident ... his lips pinched tight. It was just as far off as ever.

Chapter 15

T HE NEXT WEEK passed in a blur of activity for Sicily. Several patients had completed their stay at Hathaway House, and several new ones were coming in. The nights were busier, and when she got off shift every morning, she tended to head straight to bed. She had missed the second horse therapy session, as she'd been sleeping. Disappointed, she got up in time to see everybody dispersing from the horse area. She made her way to the balcony and grabbed a coffee, still rubbing the sleep from her eyes. Nobody said anything to her, so she presumed she hadn't been missed. That was the problem with working nights. Sometimes she felt she missed out on so much.

When she went on shift that night and completed her rounds, she stopped at Elliot's room.

"How are you today?" She studied him carefully. He showed definite signs of progress. They'd had one hot tub session during the week, but that was it. He looked hesitant, as if he wanted to say something. She waited a bit. When he didn't speak, she asked, "Do you think you'll sleep tonight?"

"Yes, I think so. Things are calming down somewhat," he said with a smile.

She brightened. "That's nice to hear." She wheeled her cart into the hallway.

He called back and asked, "Want to have your break

with me tonight?"

"Maybe, but I'd rather you slept."

"Oh."

She turned to catch him staring out the window. She smiled and said, "I'll come back and check. If you happen to be awake, I'll stay. How's that?"

He gave her a smile. "Sure."

As it went, it was another busy night. She didn't get a break after all but neither did Elliot call her. So she considered that a decent trade-off.

By the time she had completed her shift at six in the morning, she was tired and restless. She needed to swim away some of her stress in the pool. She walked down the hallway to see if Elliot was awake, thinking maybe they could do coffee, but his door was shut. She headed to her place and changed into a bathing suit and then made her way to the pool.

As she dove in, and the cool water enveloped her whole body, she almost cried with pleasure. These last few days had been rough. She almost missed the long boring nights. She would much prefer something to do, but at a level between having something to do and too much to do—a kind of balance—that she needed to find. She swam hard and then relaxed and floated gently. Finally, she pulled herself from the pool. She grabbed her towel and walked over to one of the chairs in the sun and sat down.

A shadow blocked out some of the rays. She looked up to see Elliot. She smiled, delighted to see him. "There you are," she teased. "I was wondering if you were avoiding me."

"Why would I be doing that?"

She shook her head, feeling foolish. "It's just that I'm so busy on shift right now, and I sleep when you're awake, that

I never get a chance to see you."

"We need to rearrange it slightly, so that it works better for us. But you're right, I am sleeping better." He smiled a boyish look that made her heart melt. "And you're the one who's so busy right now. I was hoping for coffee this morning, but when I came to the office, Sandra said you'd already gone, and you looked like you were heading for bed."

Surprised and pleased, she said, "I went past your room this morning, but your door was shut. I had the same thought. Mine was maybe coffee or breakfast before I crash."

He motioned at the pool. "Instead, a swim?"

She nodded. "I needed to work out. It was a pretty long night."

"So how about coffee and breakfast now?"

He reached out a hand, and she placed hers in his, and they sat there for a long moment, enjoying being together.

"I need to get dressed before we eat," she said.

"As long as you don't take too long. I'm afraid you'll crash and not get up again."

She shook her head. "I won't be long." She stood and walked to her place where she stripped out of her wet suit and put on shorts and a T-shirt. She could collapse after breakfast. Their time together was short—she didn't want to waste any that they had available together. After nine o'clock, possibly even eight o'clock, his schedule for the rest of the day could be full. Dressed, she went out to find him still sitting where she'd left him.

His face brightened at the sight of her. "Good." He stood, and together they made their way up the stairs.

She marveled at how much better he was doing. "Seems like sleep is the magic formula for you."

"Sleep and Shane and hot tubs and your late-night massages. I've come a long way. Yet, it's not just those things, it's the whole package."

"That's great."

Upstairs, they walked to the dining hall as breakfast was served. When they had full trays, they sat back outside in the sunshine. She tilted her face up to the rays and the blue sky and smiled. "It's a lovely place to work and live."

"And to recuperate."

She gave him a happy smile.

When they were eating, he said, "You missed horse therapy yesterday."

She nodded. "I was so exhausted I went to bed and slept through it." As she picked up her cup, a thought crossed her mind. She froze and lifted her gaze to him. "How did you know I missed it?"

"I made it down to see the horses," he confessed.

She brightened, her heart warming. "My God, that's wonderful," she cried.

He shrugged. "It's nothing."

"No, it's progress, and progress is good."

He smiled. "Especially this type of progress."

After breakfast, she made her way to her room again as Elliot went to start his day. She walked into her room, stripped off her clothes and crawled into her pajamas, lay down on the bed and crashed. The last thought in her mind was how well Elliot was doing. If he continued like that, he'd be better soon, and he'd be discharged.

Then what would she do?

ELLIOT WORKED HARD for the next several days, and Shane

noticed.

"You've made an about-turn. You appear to be improving in leaps and bounds here."

"I'm sleeping better at night, and the sessions leave me with more energy," Elliot agreed. "I'm more relaxed and stronger."

"All of that's good stuff."

"Of course Sicily helps too." He gave Shane a smile, knowing he'd understand.

"Oh, yes. Sicily's a big part of that." Shane put Elliot through his paces for a while longer. "Okay, we need to do a different set of exercises coming up. The horse therapy would help—at least one time—for you to see the muscle groups affected." He shifted some equipment out of the way so he could show Elliot exactly what Shane wanted to do.

"Well, the horses could quite possibly be helpful, but there's not enough hours in the horse session to do any good, is there?"

"It's not just a physical thing," Shane explained. "It's a physical-spiritual bonding type of thing. But what it will also do is isolate some of the muscles you need to work on because they're kind of hard to access without that. When you ride the horse the first time, your body will initiate movement in those muscles. Those are the ones you'll want to access afterward, but it's hard to isolate them so you understand where they are. We can stimulate them in a different way." He said, "Sit down on the medicine ball, and let's do core work."

They worked with him balancing on top of the ball, sitting with his legs on either side. Shane forced Elliot's body to react and to recover to keep his balance with each movement.

After ten minutes, he could feel the muscle fatigue setting in. "Well, okay, that already hurts."

"Exactly. It'll be quite different on a horse, in that you won't be afraid of falling because you'll be in the saddle. At the same time, you'll access the same muscles but differently. Riding is also excellent for your thighs and lower back."

"I made it down to visit the horses, but I sure haven't made it to the point of wanting to get on one."

"If it is something that you want to try for, we have another two sessions booked. Copper is a beautiful animal."

"He is, indeed." Those simple movements might have done a lot to open up his awareness of his body, but he still had a long way to go to embrace riding a horse. Yet the thought nagged at him. So did his accident. He'd never talked about it. Maybe he should.

Later that night, his body wasn't too interested in platitudes when he woke up knotted in agony. Sicily quickly arranged for the hot tub while she worked on his muscles.

By the time Elliot got into the hot water, he felt marginally better, and the heat of the hot tub made a major improvement. He sank into the water, groaning in joy. He didn't even notice when Sicily finished talking to the orderly and quietly disappeared. By the time Elliot made his way back to bed again, he realized how much his taut muscles benefited from the hot tub. After exercise, particularly if he overdid it, he was sore within hours. It was as if he'd woken up nerves and muscles from a long sleep, and they weren't happy about it. Shane would say this was progress.

Elliot hoped so. Because he also knew his time here was passing quickly. He had another month at Hathaway House, but that wasn't very long. He hoped to maximize as much healing as he could in that time. He knew he would be very disappointed in himself if he couldn't make it on the horse. He had to figure out how to get there.

He wanted to experience it, to know he'd beaten that fear. To say he'd done it. But wanting something didn't always mean getting it.

Chapter 16

S ICILY WOKE UP tired and groggy and feeling blue. She lay in bed for a long moment, wondering exactly what had hit her emotionally. She realized thinking of Elliot leaving before falling asleep had her waking up feeling lonely. In all the years she'd been at Hathaway, she hadn't connected with a patient like she had with him, and she didn't want him to leave. Just the thought brought tears to her eyes and made her heart ache.

Relationships beyond here were difficult. And were made all that much more difficult because of her night shifts. She had contemplated whether she wanted to continue with her night shifts several times over the last five years. Indeed, if she wanted to stay in this job, there were so many good things about it that continuing to work this night shift had always been an easy answer.

By doing night shifts, she also avoided a lot of people. There was only a skeleton staff, and the patients were mostly asleep while she hardly had to deal with any service staff. When she did see them, she wasn't on duty. She lay in bed and realized how much she had avoided a lot of life's pressures and stress by simplifying her schedule to a night shift. She certainly worked hard, and she had no problem with her work, but it was easier at night because she only dealt with two or three other staff people.

She hadn't been looking for a relationship with her move here but only to step back out of the craziness that came with working in an ER in Detroit. A craziness that permeated her relationships there. In that sense, coming here had certainly done that. But how would that work for her moving forward? Elliot had shown her the hole in her life. She'd been missing something and hadn't realized it, and now she didn't want to do without it.

He was a special guy, and she did not want to lose him. It was silly to say, but one of the reasons she'd gotten to know him was because of his health. Because he couldn't sleep, they had had more time to get to know each other. A lot of quiet private time. As he healed and started to sleep through the night, there'd been less and less of those interactions. She could sleep while he met the requirements of his daytime schedule and then got to spend some time with him in the afternoons. Night shift certainly didn't stop her from having a relationship. She had been happy doing her night shift work before Elliot, but she'd been cocooning.

When she'd applied for the job, it had seemed like such a massive change to move to night shift. It had taken her a long time to settle down, but she had done this for so long now she'd forgotten how traumatizing that period of life was. It had been such a relief to know here she wouldn't be put under the same pressure. The pressure here was on an hour-to-hour basis.

Back in Detroit she had had so many things going on, but here she had a chance to step back and remember to live a little. She had settled in—to a comfort level she hadn't expected, in fact. Because now it felt like it was too comfortable. She had to assess what she wanted to do. Because the thought of losing Elliot was truly discomfiting. Maybe it was time to make another career change? Or at least a shift change?

She rose from bed, sad and somewhat melancholy. Where had the last five years gone? They had slipped away in peace, and she was delighted to have had that. But in a way, she hadn't been living—she knew that. After she showered, her mood improved slightly but not a whole lot.

She talked herself into going to the dining hall, even though she wasn't ready for food, but so she could visit the coffee station where she poured herself a cup. The place hummed with activity. Sicily took a chair off to the side, in the back, where she simply sat and watched. She realized how much of her last five years she had spent on the outside. Plenty of people were here if she had wanted to connect with someone, but she hadn't wanted to.

Sicily glanced up to see Dani walking toward her. She smiled. "Good afternoon."

"Good afternoon. How are you doing?" Dani asked. "You look kind of sad."

Sicily raised her eyebrows. With a smile, she shook her head. "Not sad, melancholy."

"Why?" Dani sat down with her coffee, really wanting an answer.

She tried to explain, she really did, she gave it a couple attempts, and then finally she shrugged. "Change. Change that I hadn't seen coming. Change I wasn't sure I was ready for. Somehow the situation that brought me here healed a long time ago, and I didn't even notice."

Dani chuckled. "Healing happens here and not just for the patients," she said. "Everything around here is about the state of healing. It's good for us all."

"I hadn't expected to look back and see how far I've

come in some ways and yet, in others, not at all."

"Judgment—that's always an easy pitfall. One of the interesting things for me is when I look back on all the years since I started Hathaway House with my father, and I see how much we've accomplished, I suddenly feel sad to see how fast those years have passed by. It's like they disappeared so quickly that we didn't have a chance to take note or to mark on a calendar all the individual shifts as they happened." Dani settled back in her chair and lifted her coffee cup. "I've started to think we should institute a monthly honoring system. Keep track of the little bits and pieces, the big and small milestones, so when we look back on the year, we know where it went and how we passed the time. I don't think we do much *passing of the time* here. It's time passing over us as we're too busy doing."

Sicily laughed. "True enough. One of the things I have been looking at was the passing of time. I've been here five years."

Dani jerked forward. "You're not thinking of quitting, are you?" she asked in a low voice.

Sicily shook her head. "No, I'm not. I came from a job that was incredibly stressful and incredibly difficult emotionally, and after arriving here, it seems like I've spent the last five years in a cocoon. I've been all wrapped up in a bubble of serenity and peacefulness with a thick layer between me and the reality of what kind of work I used to do. That's been really good."

Dani waited a moment and then slowly nudged her. "And? Are you ready for a change?"

"I'm not sure what I'm saying. I woke up this morning with a sense that something needed to shift."

"Night shift is not necessarily good for people," Dani

said. "I've read lots of research. It's not harmful for a certain amount of time, but over the long-term, your body rhythm gets out of sync. Maybe that's what this is all about."

"I think night shift is a part of it, but I think it's more the reasons why I've stayed with night shift. You've given me lots of opportunities to switch out, but it was an easy way to live. I didn't deal with the day-shift frictions. When I first got here, that was ideal, and that's what I needed. But over these last few weeks, something made me realize how much I have maybe isolated myself. How much I was hiding from the world. During the daytime"—she waved her arm at the full dining hall—"I can see people all I want. But I chose the option of not seeing people because my job is fairly alone, so I'm not forced to deal with people on a regular basis." Then she leaned back in her chair and took several sips of her coffee, staring at Dani over the rim of her cup.

In a quiet voice Dani asked, "How much does this have to do with Elliot?"

Sicily gave Dani a half smile, Sicily's lips crooking more in sadness than in joy. "Quite a lot. When he leaves, I'll be alone. He gave me a unique insight into my world. Because most of the patients here sleep through the night, I'll see every one of them only very briefly at some point between ten and six, on the odd occasion multiple times, but it's only been Elliot who, until recently, was up all night long, and I spent a lot of time with him." She told Dani about what Elliot had done for her break.

"Oh my, that's beautiful. What a nice thought." Dani shook her head. "I never even thought about what your breaks must be like. Is it that you're alone?"

"There's always a second nurse on, but we take our breaks at different times for obvious reasons," Sicily said with a shrug. "Until Elliot, I was totally happy being alone."

The two women shared a smile, both understanding.

"Men are responsible for making us think through a lot of things," Dani said. "I believe that's a good thing. At the same time, it can also be difficult to go through the process and see how they've made us grow and change."

"I'm not sure I have. I think he's awakened me to the fact I'm still hiding."

Dani's eyebrows rose. "What would you like to do?"

Sicily shook her head. "I'm not sure. One possibility is to switch out of night shift, maybe a little farther down the road."

Dani leaned forward. "Down the road as in, when Elliot's gone?"

Sicily took a deep breath. "Maybe a little earlier. He has started to sleep through the nights now."

"Ah," Dani said in understanding. "And as he heals and gets stronger, you're losing time with him. And the time lost at night is intimate time. It's the two of you wrapped up in a bubble of a world created by the circumstances. That's all shifting now that he's sleeping. While you're loving that improvement in his health, it has changed your world and not necessarily for the better."

"And yet, here I sit, thinking it's not for the worse."

"Good idea," Dani said. "Because here it doesn't matter which way you turn or which way you go. You have choices. Let me know what you want, and I'll see what I can arrange. I don't want to lose you. I know you don't want to lose Elliot, and I am certain Elliot doesn't want to lose you, so let's figure out what works for all of us."

Sicily nodded and smiled. "Thanks, Dani."

"Don't thank me," Dani said. "I'm thanking you for five

years of night shifts." On that note, she rose, grabbed her coffee cup and left.

And even though Dani left Sicily sitting there alone, she no longer felt lonely.

ELLIOT HAD LOTS to think about.

The thing about phobias was no one cared but the affected person. It didn't matter to anyone else but to him that he got on that horse. That made this self-imposed pressure stupid. Why was he doing this?

Because it felt like a weakness. With so much he couldn't change, that was one thing he felt he could—if he was brave enough. Another problem though was that he didn't want to do this to impress Sicily because what if he failed? Then he would have failed twice. Once for not getting on the damn horse and then for disappointing Sicily on top of it all. He understood in theory this needed to be done because he wanted to do it. To regain control of his life, even if it was just in some small measure—yet finding a visible sign of long-term success in something that had bothered him for years.

Having a phobia like this was easy to ignore, if he stayed away from horses ...

However, he did want to be the man who Sicily thought he could be. Maybe he was, maybe he wasn't, because part of him felt like a fraud. Part of him felt like he had strung her along because of the circumstances. Because he wanted that boost, that friendship, and that sense of knowing he wasn't alone. But what if this was all a facade? What if, when he left this place and went back out into the real world, he couldn't handle it? What if everything in his world crashed and burned, and he was back to being the mess of the man he had been when he woke up after the surgeries? He wouldn't wish that on anybody.

He didn't want to drag another person down with him. Especially not when he cared about Sicily. And he did care about Sicily. She was very special in so many ways. It was hard to consider she might be better off without him. Yet in some stupid way, it felt that way. Because if he couldn't handle something like a horse, how was he expected to handle the bigger issues? Things like getting a job and rebuilding his future?

He settled back into the deck chair and looked out across the fields. He could see the horses, and that was fine when they were out there, and he was up here, but when they got close, well, that was a different story.

"Heavy thoughts?"

He turned, startled to find Dani standing beside him, a quizzical look on her face.

He shrugged. "Wondering how one deals with big fears that can be ignored most of the time."

Understanding crossed her face. "The horses?" She pulled up a chair and sat down next to him. "I know a lot of people afraid of horses. In your case, I'm not so sure it's a fear as much as an uncertainty because you haven't been around them so much. You came up to them, and you touched them. And let them smell you."

He shook his head. "But what you didn't see was the terrified person on the inside."

"Don't you think we all have that same person inside? Whether it's at a job interview or on a first date or facing a dog that's way bigger than we're used to?"

He stared at her. "This is different."

She chuckled. "Of course it is because it's *your* fear. That makes it very scary."

He crossed his arms and leaned back, not sure he particularly liked the direction of the conversation.

She leaned in closer. "You think I'm making light of your feelings, but I'm not. I've seen people scream at the thought of being *this* close to the horses."

Complete astonishment came over him. "You're kidding me."

She shook her head and laughed softly. "Although it's something that really bothers you, I think you can manage it."

He frowned, his gaze sliding to the pasture where the horses walked calmly in the morning sun, stopping to munch here and there. "They're beautiful—at a distance."

"They're beautiful up close too," Dani said. "As you've already found out."

"But that doesn't mean I'm ready to ride," he said hurriedly.

"Of course not. Nobody says you have to ride them."

He took a deep breath and let the words fall out. "I had a riding accident when I was eight."

She leaned forward. "I'm sorry. That must have been difficult. Is that why you can't get close to a horse now?"

He started at her, then slowly nodded. "It was bad."

"Tell me about it."

Shudders wracked his body as if in complete revolt over the idea, yet he knew it was time. It was past time. He took a deep breath. "I was riding my uncle's horse." He stopped as slowly the memories filtered back in. "We were all out there together, but I was falling behind. The horse was big and placid. An old farm horse. But there was a massive explosion and the horse bolted." He stopped, struggled with his breathing, before he managed to say, "I was tossed and landed against a small shed that collapsed on top of me."

He looked down to see Dani holding his hands gently. "That's more important than you can possibly imagine," she said. "That sounds very much like what happened to you in the military incident? Was it?"

Memories rolled through his brain, taking the first incident and laying it over the second. They had similarities. The second obviously much more damaging, yet to that young boy, that horse incident had been terrifying. He'd had nightmares for months ... just like he was having worse nightmares now. "They were both bad to the person I was at the time," he whispered. "I wonder if that's all related to why I'm struggling with my PTSD now."

"Of course it is. Everything in our life experience is related. You're not just that boy and this man but that boy *grew* up into this man, so everything that happened since is built on the foundation of that boy's experiences."

"So then why do I feel like a failure?" There, he had said it. And yet inside he had to admit he felt different. Freer. As if the act of sharing had loosened up something held tight. Sicily was right, weakness wasn't something he'd ever discussed in the military.

Dani's eyebrows arched. "No need to feel like a failure. We have over 100 patients here, and yet how many rode that horse?"

He shook his head. "But that doesn't matter because I feel like I was the one who should have gone, and I couldn't."

"Can you now?" This time she crossed her arms over her

chest and eyed him carefully. "Consider this … What would it take to have you get on that horse?"

He stared at her, swallowing hard. "I'm not sure. I'm wondering that same thing."

"It can't be for somebody else," she warned.

He didn't dare glance at her. "I know," he said quietly. "But Sicily put this program together with me in mind."

"That's not a big deal because it's a good idea for most of our patients here, and I would never put a program in place for just one person."

Elliot did feel a little relief then, easing the knots in his stomach. "Well, that's good to know. I knew that, but I didn't *know* if you understood what I meant."

"Of course I do. The thing is, anytime you want to try, you let me know. I do think it would be rewarding—if for no other reason than it will help you take control of something and change it. Remember that little boy was a long time ago," Dani stood up with a smile. "Think about it."

"I will." He watched as she walked away.

By the time the horse session came around the following week, Elliot was one more week stronger, one more week longer at Hathaway House and one more week further into a relationship with Sicily. But one more week closer to his check-out time too. Still, there had been improvements. His nightmares had eased slightly, he was understanding himself that much more. Even Shane seemed happier with his progress.

His relationship with Sicily continued to grow and develop. He knew he was a lucky man and there was a chance this was real and true and honest. But it was that *honest* part that bothered him.

After the session, he called Dani over once she walked

away from the horse trailer. "Put me down for next week."

A delighted smile lit up her face. Then she stopped and studied him carefully. "The thing is, if I do, I need you to show up. Because you'd be taking a spot somebody else could use. Of course the spot is there for you if you want it. But what I don't want is to have you back out."

He winced.

"At the same time, if you find that when you get out here, you can't do it, then we will let you off the hook. How's that?" she said.

"No pressure?" he joked.

"No pressure."

"Also I have another request."

She waited quietly.

"Any chance we can make sure Sicily is *not* there when I'm with the horses?"

A really quiet silence followed. "*Not* there?" she asked, a frown forming between her eyes and wrinkling her forehead. "That's an interesting request." She stared off in the distance and then gave a clipped nod. "I can request she not show up for that time, but I can hardly order her. It's her free time."

Instantly he felt better. "Right, I forgot it was her free time. Maybe she'd like to go into town or something that afternoon," he joked. "Anywhere else but here."

"So she's not here to see you fail?"

He winced, his body shifting with the blow. "I wasn't planning on failing."

"No," she said with a gentle smile, "but you weren't planning on succeeding either."

Chapter 17

THE DAYS FELL into a lovely pattern as Sicily understood more and more about herself and where she was going in life. She had a few decisions to make, yet she was no closer to making them as part of her really enjoyed the night shift. She also understood this stage of her life was coming to an end, along with several other things.

Later that night Elliot was once again soaking in the hot tub. Sicily and the orderly moved him downstairs in an organized fashion. They had this whole routine down pat now. He usually needed about twenty to twenty-five minutes in the water and then to be helped back out again. The extent of her involvement had been getting him to the orderly. Tonight he seemed to be a little more stressed-out than usual.

The orderly had called her after he'd helped Elliot back to his room. "He's still not in great shape. You may want to see what's bothering him."

She picked up a fresh cup of coffee and walked to Elliot's room. He was in bed with the blanket up over his shoulders and appeared chilled. She studied his face for a moment. "You want a heated blanket?"

He shook his head. "No thanks, I'm fine. Just not a good night."

"I can see that." She waited a few seconds and then

asked, "Is there anything I can do?"

He gave her a weak smile. "I'll be fine. I'll lie here and see if I can fall asleep."

She had her doubts as to whether that would work, but she'd give him a chance. She walked back to her office, checking on several of the patients as she went. It was a relatively calm night. She had patients checking out the next day and their files to update. One was going for a round of intensive reconstructive surgery, and another lucky person was going home.

She loved the idea of patients going home. John was leaving and returning to his family. His wife had been in to see him several times, along with his kids. Everyone at the center was delighted to know he was going home. It would be a huge adjustment for him, but he had a support network and the love that was very important for him to succeed.

"Unlike Elliot," she murmured. Elliot was alone as far as she understood. So his entry into a single's world and the reality of living on his own would be much harder. What little of his former life remained now sat in a storage locker, waiting to be shipped. By the time she started her final rounds the next morning, she noticed a change she hadn't noticed the previous night. Usually she was comfortable with the peace and quiet and the aloneness. But now it was more a sense of being alone that, for the first time, she didn't particularly like. With all the other changes going on in her world five years earlier, it had seemed like *that* was one less thing she had to contend with, and it wasn't like it was a big change.

But now it was time for *her* to get back into the real world. She planned to change to day shifts and slowly reintegrate into a more mainstream work environment for herself. Not for Elliot but for herself. She'd been hiding long enough.

After meeting with Sandra, who relieved her shift, Sicily headed to breakfast, feeling slightly uneasy but not knowing why. Grabbing a coffee, she walked out into the sunshine, loving the early morning. Today was horse therapy day. She looked forward to it. But if she wanted to be there, she had to get to bed soon, or she wouldn't get enough sleep before the session started. She sat, mulling over her options, tired but not quite ready to go to bed when she looked up to see Dani standing in front of her. Sicily smiled. "How's the boss doing?"

With a chuckle Dani sat down. "She's fine. But she has an odd request that she needs to ask of you."

Sicily looked at her, curious. "Sure. What's up?"

"I'm asking on behalf of someone else for you to not show up for the horse therapy today."

Sicily looked at her in surprise. "I was figuring out how to arrange my sleep so I could be there this afternoon. Why shouldn't I be?"

"Somebody has requested it," Dani said calmly. "That might sound hurtful, but I do understand the reasoning."

Too surprised to even answer her, Sicily stared for a long moment. "Somebody's asked that I not show up? Somebody doesn't want me to be there?"

Dani nodded slowly. "But not for the reason you think."

"What do I think?" she cried. "All I can think is why someone would not want me there when they're there." She hated that. "How else can I take that?"

"If I could tell you who made the request, maybe you would understand. Or maybe it would hurt you. I don't know. But I can't because I promised. So all I can say is that, this afternoon, can you please avoid the horse therapy session? It is your free time, and I don't have any right to ask you or to tell you what to do in your spare time, but this is important to somebody, and they felt like they needed to ask."

Sicily sat back in her chair, feeling thoroughly defeated. After coming off a shift—where she had figured she was ready to go into the real world and bring more people into her life—somebody was asking her to butt out. She shook her head. "I don't even know what to say."

"Say that you'll skip today."

"And next week?"

Dani smiled. "I don't think it will be an issue next week. I'm hoping it won't be an issue today, but it was a request."

When Sicily stayed quiet, Dani added, "It has to do with someone's progress, and for that, we always do everything we can to move them forward."

"So for the progress of somebody, I can't be around the horses." She shook her head. "Wow. Am I happy about it? Hell, no. Like you said, it's to help the patients move forward, but it hurts." She stood. "On that note, I'll head to bed." She forced a smile, turned and walked away. This was not at all how she felt her day would go.

Back in her own space, she showered and got ready for bed. She couldn't stop pondering who might've requested such a thing. Even though she was tucked in bed, sleep felt a long way away. She was tired, but her mind wouldn't let it go. Finally, after much rolling, tossing and turning, she felt herself slowly drift off. As she was about to go under, one name surfaced—Elliot. He would try to get on the horse today.

Instantly she was wide awake. She stared at the ceiling,

worried, and wondered, *Could it be?* And if so, why didn't he want her around for his first time?

HE COULD HARDLY breathe. He was outside the doors and *only* outside because the damn doors opened automatically. On the lower floor, the horses were around the corner, and nobody could see Elliot yet. He knew Dani was expecting him, and he knew he was on the roster, plus he knew she'd said something to Sicily. But dear God, why had he thought he could do this? He stared at his hands. He'd deliberately come with the wheelchair, knowing that nerves would be a huge factor. He was already trembling. He sat for a long moment, waiting, his eyes closed, hoping maybe they would carry on without him.

Behind him, he heard a noise.

He stiffened as Stan's voice washed over him. "Elliot? You okay?"

Slowly he shook his head. "No. I bit off more than I can chew."

He heard footsteps as Stan walked closer.

"Sometimes we don't need to chew all that we bite off. Sometimes if we hold it in our mouth, it dissolves. Sometimes we can take it out and try for a smaller bite." His voice was compassionate and understanding. "And sometimes we realize that our fears really are just hangovers from our childhood and it's time to let them all go."

That made Elliot feel all that much worse. "Sometimes we can't do something in life, and that's the way it is."

"If you are talking about sitting on Copper's back today, I can promise not only would it go very well but you'll feel like a whole new man just having achieved it." As he spoke, he stepped in front of Elliot.

Elliot looked up at the vet, who'd seen too much to be surprised by much. "How does one deal with fear?" Elliot hated to hear the tremor in his voice.

"By facing it head-on. By diving in and doing the best you can."

"That's how I felt last week. I'm not feeling that today," Elliot admitted and shared a little of his accident. Stan seemed to take it in stride as if he assumed it was something like that.

"Last week you weren't on the roster. Last week it was a concept. This week you've committed, and having made a commitment, you don't want to let anybody down, but at the same time, you getting out there and doing the job is a whole different story." Stan grabbed the back of the wheelchair firmly and pushed Elliot around the corner before he had a chance to protest.

"You don't have to do this," Elliot hissed.

Stan laughed. "No, it's you who doesn't have to do this. But if you take yourself off the roster, then you need to 'fess up and tell these people they can give somebody else a chance. This is what Amy needs to make it worth her while. We want her to keep doing this, so therefore, to the best of our ability, we get the people who are registered for the sessions to show up."

"Showing up is not the problem," Elliot snapped, feeling pressured. He could feel himself stiffening, pushing back into the chair the closer they got to the horses.

"Do you trust me?" Stan asked.

"You already know I trust you. The problem is me being around animals that can hurt me. Again."

Stan chuckled. "Fair enough. Do you trust Dani? And a more important question, do you trust Sicily? They all believe in you."

"That makes me feel all that much worse," he cried in frustration. "I want to be the tough person who can get up on that horse. But I don't think I can."

"Stop fooling yourself. Why would you set yourself up for failure like that?" Stan's voice seemed curious, as if he didn't understand.

They were almost within hearing distance of the others. Elliot caught the look of relief on Dani's face, realizing she'd been afraid he wouldn't show up. No time to answer Stan quietly anymore. Whatever Elliot said now, it would be heard by everyone. He stood up in front of Dani.

"I don't know that I can do this."

She nodded. "Maybe not, but you're here. So let's go through the process and see."

He opened his mouth to protest, and Amy, who was a big strapping woman, came and stood beside him with her assistant. Together with Stan, they had him at the top of the ramp in no time. He was too shocked at the speed of which it all happened to get a coherent protest past his lips. He stared at the huge animal, now standing slightly below him. Copper turned and looked up at Elliot. The look in his eye was maybe kindness but also nonchalance. As if to say, "So are you ready to do this?"

Oddly enough, the look in the horse's eyes made Elliot realize this could be doable, yet he was terrified to think he'd have all that horsepower between his knees. Then panic filled him once more. He took a deep breath and shook his head. "I don't think I can do this," he whispered.

But whether they didn't hear him or misunderstood him

or were ignoring him, he didn't know because the next thing he did know was he was on the back of the horse. Copper whinnied as if to say, "Ha! Got you."

Elliot grabbed the small horn of the saddle with a white-knuckled grip. He wanted to shift, but he was petrified to try. What if Copper didn't like it? He wanted to cry out—in panic maybe—in joy maybe—but definitely in shock. He could already feel the strain in his back. Slowly he released his pent-up breath …

Dani, a huge smile on her face, beamed with joy.

Elliot shook his head. "This isn't a good thing."

She chuckled. "It *is* a good thing. Trust me. It's something you must do. When you were in the military, you had your brothers. They were there, and they had your back. While you're here, we're your team. *We* have your back. It's time to let this fear go …"

He stared at her for a long moment, and then realized that one of the main team members in his world wasn't here. She didn't have his back because he wouldn't let her. He settled slightly on the seat and voiced his concern. "But Sicily is not here."

Understanding crossed Dani's face. "I can fix that, real fast."

He glanced at her with hope. "She might be mad at me."

"She might be overjoyed." Dani already had her phone in her hand. She held it up and looked questioningly at him. "You say the word."

He took a deep breath. "Call her."

Then he was busy listening to Amy and her assistant as they went over how to shift his position for comfort and what that shifting would do to the horse. How to hold the reins and what holding the reins meant. And then they said they would take a walk. Startled, he stared at them. "What? You can't leave me."

The women chuckled. Amy's assistant went several feet away to the second horse, hopped onto the horse's back and then came over toward Copper. She made a clicking sound. Copper's ears perked forward, and his head came up at the sound. He walked behind the assistant. Terrified, his body rigid, Elliot knew that was not the purpose of this, but it was so damn hard to relax when all he could do was hold on to the saddle and not fall.

Amy's voice reached him. "You can't fall. Once you understand that, you'll relax."

He stared down at her, walking beside him and Copper, but it was hard to have her words match what he felt. She instructed him to push his butt back into the saddle to settle his position better.

Slowly following her instructions, he found a place on the big animal for himself.

But it wasn't easy.

And it wasn't fun.

But he did it. And he didn't fall. Nor did he get thrown.

When he was finally led back to the special ramp, he could almost breathe normally. He had no idea how long he'd been out here—his entire body was stiff and locked in pain. He'd be sore tomorrow. Hell, he'd be lucky to get through the night without painkillers. On the other hand he knew he'd sleep a lot better tonight. And every night. Something had slipped from his soul, an age-old pain, a fear that never quite left. The same fear of this echoing in his life had repeated with his injuries. At least the incidences were now separated in his mind. Each to be released when he was ready. Well the one he was definitely ready, and the other ...

he was almost there. He'd make it now. Somehow this little incident had made all the difference. He wasn't that little boy any more ...

Then he looked up and saw Sicily—with the biggest, most caring look on her face that he'd ever imagined—and with tears in her eyes.

He realized it didn't matter what his night was like or how sore he would be tomorrow. It was all worth it to see that look on her face.

When he was finally standing, albeit a little shaky on the ground again, she raced into his arms, bawling.

He crushed her close to his heart, feeling his own eyes burn. "Thank you."

She shook her head, and when she finally could, she lifted her face to his, tears glimmering in her eyes, and she whispered, "No thanks needed. This was all on you."

He grinned. "It was, wasn't it? Still, I wouldn't be here if it weren't for you. I didn't even know I needed to be here. But I did, and I remembered a few other things I'd forgotten, some I'm ready to let go of forever, and also who and what were important to me."

One elegant eyebrow arched. "Oh?"

He smiled, placed his hand at the back of her head to hold her in place and lowered his head. Before his lips touched hers, he whispered, "But I know now. And I know it's you. You're the most important thing in my life today, tomorrow and all the tomorrows after that."

She gasped in joy.

And ignoring the smiles and curious looks of all those around them, he kissed her.

A kiss of longing. Of shared joy. A kiss of promise for a wonderful future—together.

Epilogue

F INN WAITED FOR the ambulance ride to take him to
Hathaway House. He couldn't believe the emails he'd
received from Elliot.

They had to be fiction. Surely he didn't have a girlfriend
and not just a girlfriend but like a wedding in the near
future. And then there was his health, which was not only
doing incredibly well but his PTSD symptoms had eased
back tremendously. As in he was a new man, with a bright
future, having finally turned the corner on his past ...

How could that be? And so fast?

Finn knew that a lot of good women would take on a
man less than whole, but Elliot sounded like a completely
different person. One who acknowledged that scars existed
but no longer held power over him. Originally Finn had
tossed it off as infatuation but now, months down the road,
apparently not. He'd told Elliot about applying for a
transfer, but Finn's multiple surgeries had pushed that back.

And rightly so, but as he lay on the bed, worn out and so
done with doctors and the hospital, he realized maybe this
was the right time now.

He was at a crossroad. This was the end of the surgeries,
and now it was all about making the best of who and what
he was today.

There was no need to transfer to another center to get

that, but he wanted a change of faces, smells and scenery. And Hathaway House sounded divine. He'd been raised on a ranch in Texas. That alone made him want to go. Any chance to go home—particularly at this stage of his life—was good.

A text came in. He lifted his phone and checked the message. It was from Elliot.

Put in a request. They have beds opening up and a cancellation. No better time than right now.

This was the right time for a lot of reasons. But instead of filling out the request form, he dialed a number he'd looked at many times.

When a woman answered, he said, "Dani? It's Finn. Any chance you've got a bed there?"

"For you, I'll find one. How soon can you come?"

"As soon as you can make it happen," he said with a silly grin on his face. It would be good to see her again. He'd met her years ago when he was friends with Levi and Stone. They'd kept in touch, but it had only been through Elliot that Finn had realized who was running the center.

Lord, it would be good to go home.

Finn

Hathaway House, Book 6

Dale Mayer

Chapter 1

INN MACGREGOR, WITH the help of the aide behind him, slowly pushed his way up the ramp in his wheelchair. He could see that, over time, this ramp would be a lot easier, just like so many other ramps in his life. Being in a wheelchair sucked. He'd had high hopes of getting out of it at the beginning, and that hope had faded over time. But now that he was at Hathaway House, his friend Dani's place, with Elliot, another friend, here to cheer him on, Finn had reinvested into that same hope again.

He knew it was a bit foolish, but, when a man was down and out, hope was one of the biggest things that kept him going.

The aide pushed a little harder behind Finn. When they reached the top of the gradual slope, Finn twisted and looked up at the big man behind him, smiled and said, "Thanks."

His voice cheerful, as if he'd done this many times before, the man replied, "No problem. Next time you can do it all on your own. You did pretty well getting here as it is."

The name tag on the man's shirt read Malcolm. "Well, Malcolm, hopefully it won't take too long to make that kind of progress."

"It won't," Malcolm said. "All kinds of miracles happen here."

Finn straightened up as the huge double doors opened,

letting Malcolm push him into the front reception area. Finn stopped and stared at the massive open space and all the long hallways that conjoined right at the reception area. An office was off to the side, light music played and absolutely nothing was institutional about this place. More like the lounge of a bed-and-breakfast.

Finn frowned. "Are you sure this is the right place?" he joked.

Malcolm, a big yet quiet smile on his face, nodded and said, "Not only is it the right place but that person has been waiting for you." He pointed to a woman walking quickly toward Finn.

He stared at her and felt a shock of recognition. "Dani?"

She let out a peal of laughter, opened her arms wide, bent down and gave him a big hug.

He wrapped his arms around her as best he could. Just feeling her arms tighten around him made his eyes leak a bit. "Damn," he said, "I should have tried to get here earlier."

"I told you to," she said, "but I must wait until people are ready. Ready to make that kind of move. It's not easy to do, and I'm really proud of you for having made it."

Again he felt that light prick of pride inside. He had to remind himself that pride went before the fall, and he'd already had enough falls in his life. He glanced around and said, "Honestly, I thought Elliot was off his rocker with everything he's been telling me about your place here, and I'm so proud of you for having done what you've done. This place is huge."

"It is, indeed," she said, "and getting bigger every day. We are adding a wing up and down. Here for the humans and downstairs for the animals' vet."

Finn nodded. Elliot had filled him in on how this rehab

center catered to both injured animals and humans. They had a massive veterans clinic and rehab center here, where veterans came home with more than a few health issues, had gone through surgeries, and now needed specialized care to get them back on their feet. This wasn't a long-term facility for people who had no improvements to be made. This was a place where people came to get their strength back and to learn how to become mobile with whatever body parts they had replaced—or, in some cases, didn't have replaced.

Finn stared at his missing lower leg and frowned.

"Not to worry about your leg," Dani said, her gaze following his. "You're just one of many here."

He winced at that. "Somehow that's not reassuring."

"It will be," she said. She walked behind the reception area, picked up a file and then said, "Come on. Let's get you to your room. The sooner we get you settled, the sooner we can start having fun."

As they headed down the hall, he asked her, "How long have you guys been open now?"

"Seven years," she replied. "But, of course, getting the word out is a whole different story. This last year has been incredible though," she admitted.

"Sounds like it's well-deserved with the kind of success Elliot has been spouting off about. If it's even one-tenth as good as what he's been telling me," he said, "it's got to be fantastic."

"We've had a lot of really good successes," Dani said with a bright smile. "But with all that comes one case which just gives you no end of trouble. And we've had a couple people who have come here and then decided it was not for them and left."

"I think that goes for everything in life," Finn said. "We

are not all geared for the same things."

She turned to Malcolm and said, "We're heading for 212."

Malcolm nodded. They took the next corner, went down a short hall and turned Finn's wheelchair to face the door with big black numbers proclaiming 212.

Dani opened the door, and Malcolm pushed Finn through the extra-wide doorway. The room was large. Had his own private bathroom. There was a dresser and a large double bed with all the equipment that went with his disabilities. He stared at all the hooks and chains and winced. "I sure hope I don't ever need those," he said, motioning at the apparatus above the bed.

She walked over, and, with the push of a button, the apparatus retracted against the wall. "I'd be happy to never have to touch that again for you," she said cheerfully. "But it's there if you need it. Physiotherapy specialists and doctors will decide how much of that you might need."

He nodded, staring up at it. "Very high-tech," he murmured.

"We try," she said. "Do you want to get into bed right now?"

He hesitated.

"Otherwise, we can go over the paperwork. I'll give you your iPad and then I can take you for a tour, and we can sit out on the deck with a cup of coffee."

He brightened at that. "That sounds much more informal and more my style."

She grinned. "Here's your iPad with your schedule and more information, if you're curious. I want you to flick through it all. Your team has been assigned to you, and they are all available for messaging on that tablet, custom designed for us. You'll see all the names of everybody who will be working with you. I'll leave this paperwork here. You can take a look at it when we get back and you're on your own. Obviously, you have some personal effects coming."

Malcolm stood by the doorway and said, "I'll grab his stuff at reception."

Dani smiled up at him. "Thanks, Malcolm."

She turned toward Finn. "When we get back after coffee, you can put your stuff away, so that it feels more like home. Let's head down, and I'll show you around."

As they wheeled out with her pushing him, he said, "I can wheel myself, you know?"

"Good," she said, "but sometimes it's nice to be wheeled around. You're tired and stressed with your travels, and I need to make sure that your stress levels are minimized. So how about letting your old friend push you around?"

He sagged into the wheelchair, his back easing because, of course, it *did* hurt his back to do the wheeling. It was one of the things that his prior doctors had not been happy about. He was missing a big swath of muscle along one side, not to mention the kidney on the right side, and of course, the shrapnel had eaten away part of the muscles around it. After the act of removing that shrapnel, they had put as much of Finn back together as possible. Multiple surgeries later, he was as good as he would get, but he was weak on one side. That was his job to fix now.

She whispered, "Good way to start."

He chuckled. "We go way back, kiddo. I can't believe we're at this stage of our lives."

"Not sure about you," she said, "but I'm engaged to be married. Remember Dad? He's here too."

"The major?" Finn asked with a laugh. "Man, back then

I wasn't so sure he would make it."

"Neither was I," Dani said, all her laughter falling away. "He started this center, I think, more as a project to help himself and to help his buddies, but since then he's a completely different person. We'd have been lost without this center all these years."

Finn watched as they headed down the short hallway and into the main hallway, and almost immediately she turned a corner, and there it opened up a huge section, the entrance to a large eating area. He stared to see tables and chairs and couches, more like little community sitting areas.

"We redid part of this area so that it was a more of a sitting room," she said. "Pretty happy with the way it worked out." She carried on, pushing him forward into what opened up to a massive cafeteria.

He stared in surprise. "Wow. I was expecting little trays on hospital trolleys."

"That can be arranged too," she said. "If you need a meal in your room, then don't hesitate to ask. When you've had enough of the people or the physical work, or you're just too damn tired, or you're just too depressed, and you don't want to make the effort to come in for a meal, we'd all appreciate it if you would at least call for a meal so that somebody can come and check up on you and bring you something hot to eat."

"I'll remember that," he said in surprise.

"We're much more of a family here," she said. "You'll get to know the characters around the place fairly quickly."

"Looks like it." He watched several people at the cafeteria counter pushing trays in front of them, some with legs, some on crutches, some in wheelchairs.

She pushed him into the line, pulled a tray down and

placed it beside him as they moved along. "Are you hungry?" she asked.

He flushed and shook his head. "No. Just coffee will be fine."

"Right," she said. "I forgot, but I have to add a couple notes on that for your PT to consider."

"What notes?" he asked gruffly.

"Notes about your system," she said. "Not that you have allergies but you have a lot of food sensitivities."

He shrugged. What he was sensitive to was the way his food had to travel. Who knew that he would lose most of his bowels and need a colostomy bag? How embarrassing was that? He'd heard lots of other people say it made no bloody difference, but Finn had yet to come to that point. Who liked to poop out of their side? That was just gross. And every time he ate food, it reminded him that it had to go in one way and come out another.

Almost as if she understood what he was thinking about, she bent and said, "I guess you don't want a bran muffin with too much fiber then, do you?"

He glared at her. She smiled, a secretive smile, as if she knew something he didn't.

She pushed him up to the coffee station. There, she poured two cups and said, "If you don't want anything to eat, I'll grab a muffin." She placed it on the tray with butter and a knife and then looked around and said, "Where would you like to sit? Inside or out?" She pointed to a whole wall that opened up to an outdoor section of the cafeteria.

"Outdoors," he said instantly.

She placed the tray in his lap and said, "You get to look after that."

She wheeled him past several other groups of men out in

the sunshine. As Finn studied the inside area, he thought he caught a glimpse of a dog. Maybe a therapy dog? As they shifted into the hot sun, he tilted his head back and smiled. There was something absolutely glorious about having the sun on his face.

She removed the tray to place it on the table before pushing him up close and taking a seat across from him. He didn't even want to face her; he was enjoying the morning sunshine so much.

"There's something just so wrong about being in an institution for so long," she murmured. "Getting out in the sun and feeling it deep in your soul is so very healing." Just then she called out, "Elliot!"

Instantly Finn's eyes opened. He twisted to see her pointing at somebody. He twisted around a little more, almost crying out, barely stifling the gasp of pain as he took the motion too far and settled back, gasping at first, then trying to breathe deeply to ease the pain. She waited calmly at his side. When he could, he said, "Sorry, that was foolish of me."

"Limitations of the body are not something any of us ever like to admit," she said calmly.

"I guess you're used to it, aren't you?"

"Nobody ever gets used to somebody's pain," she said with the gentlest of smiles that he remembered so well.

She had always been all heart, this girl.

"And living in a place where every person lives with pain helps me to realize how grateful I am to be pain-free."

"Good point," he said. He shifted in the wheelchair to ease the pain in his back when he felt a hand clap on his shoulder. He looked up to see Elliot Carver, an old friend, standing above him. Finn reached up to shake his hand, but

Elliot bent and hugged him hard.

"Damn, I'm glad to see you finally here," he said with a big smile. He looked at Dani and back over at Finn. "Do you mind if I grab a chair and sit down?"

"Hell no," he said. "Please, join us."

Elliot grabbed a chair and dropped into it at Finn's side.

Just the ease of Elliot's movement and how comfortable he was in his own body now struck Finn as odd. Not so much odd, just ... so natural and so graceful. It made Finn realize how awkward he was in his own physical state. He was unappreciative of his body, and, in some ways, it felt as if he'd been paired up with a brand-new partner in the military and they hadn't had time to work out their idiosyncrasies to blend together. It had never been like that before. He'd always been a perfectly fit physical specimen.

Until the accident.

And now, well, now it was as if he hated his body and his body hated him.

"You look absolutely fantastic," Finn said to Elliot.

Elliot grinned. "Well, besides the fact that I'm healing at an incredibly fast rate—and Dani here would say that emotional and physical and mental healing also has to happen in order for us to move forward in leaps and bounds," he said, "I am happy. I'm fit. I feel good, and, for the first time in a long time, it feels as if life isn't like I pulled the short straw."

Finn immediately recognized the feeling. "Right," he said, "and I'm still stuck not only with the short straw but it's way shorter than it was originally."

Elliot burst out laughing at that. "Oh, I do remember feeling that too," he said. "There's only so much in life that we can really blame others for before we have to deal with the reality of what we're stuck with." He motioned at the missing lower leg on Finn's right stump and asked, "Have you been fitted for prosthetics yet?"

"They had to do more surgery to change the way the stump was because the prosthetics were soring me up," he said, "I haven't had a chance to try again. I'm hoping to do that while I'm here." He glanced at Dani with one eyebrow raised.

Dani immediately nodded. "That'll be one of the first things we try to get you into, but, in the meantime, you'll have crutches."

He winced at that. "The back and the right shoulder don't like crutches," he said apologetically.

She gave him a serene smile that immediately made him suspicious.

Finn glanced at Elliot, who was also grinning. "I'll get crutches and will have to suffer through it, won't I?" he asked glumly.

"You will," Elliot said. "Hathaway House doesn't do too much on the babysitting level here, and you'll be glad for it. It's a tough journey to start. Yet it's an absolutely wonderful journey when you get to your destination."

"How much longer are you here for?" Finn asked, already worried. "I hope you're not leaving too quickly because it's partly because of you that I'm here," he said, glancing between Dani and Elliot.

"I'm here for one or two more months, but I think I get to graduate soon," Elliot said. "Just some fine-tuning now."

Immediately Finn felt lost, knowing he would be here much longer. He still had Dani, whom he knew, but Elliot had been somebody who knew him in his old life, understood what he'd gone through and understood what shit he was dealing with now. "Well, obviously I wish you all the best," he said lightly.

"No sending me away yet," Elliot said. "I'm still here for a while. Don't you worry. Besides, I'm likely to settle close to town."

At that, Finn frowned. "Why? Your family is back West, aren't they?"

"Not exactly sure where I'll end up yet," he said, "because I have some new family that really matters to me. So I'm not ready to pull up roots from here and go back there again."

"Just make sure it isn't an attachment to the recovery process," Finn warned.

Elliot laughed and laughed. "Oh my, I'm so glad you said that. Because you really need to have that mindset when it comes to dealing with the stuff you're going through here," he said as he turned to look at Dani. Elliot smiled. "Isn't that right, Dani?"

Dani smiled and nodded. She picked up half of her muffin and offered it to Finn.

He stared at it, his stomach grumbling. "But it's bran," he said. And then he winced. "You have no idea what bran does to an already damaged digestive system."

"Sometimes it's supposed to be the best thing," Dani said with a shrug. "But we have many other options, from carrot to chocolate chip."

At the words *chocolate chip*, his eyes lit up.

Elliot chuckled. "I'll go get myself one. Do you want one?"

Finn nodded slowly. "Well, I have to eat sometime," he said.

Dani agreed. "We have lots of other food choices here, if

you want something other than a muffin."

He remembered seeing all kinds of hot dishes inside, and he realized that, with the stress of moving, he had hardly eaten breakfast. Besides, the hospital food had been pallid, lukewarm and tasted like flat Jell-O. "Maybe," he said.

Elliot smiled and said, "How about I pick you out something? Do you promise to try it?"

Finn nodded. "Maybe not breakfast this time. A sandwich maybe? Nothing fancy," he said. "I'm not super hungry."

"I'll be back in a minute."

Finn watched as Elliot casually walked through the dining room as if he owned the world. "It's hard to believe the condition he's in," Finn said.

"True enough," Dani said. "All kinds of improvements are being made on many levels with every patient here. Don't judge anybody else or yourself. The scale doesn't slide evenly, and it doesn't slide in only one direction." At that, she stood and waved at somebody else. She leaned over and said, "Excuse me. I have to speak to somebody," and she disappeared around his back.

He sat here for a long moment, thinking about her words, acknowledging just how much truth was behind them. It had been the same in his recovery. Six SEALs had been in Finn's original team. Two had died during the mission—one more had taken his own life—and, of the three left, he would have considered himself to have been hurt the worst and showing the least amount of progress.

But he doubted the others would agree with him.

FIONA SMITHERS PICKED up two coffees and walked over to join the nurses at their favorite table before Fiona started her morning shift. She sat down to see Dani waving at her. She stood again, murmuring to the group, "Sorry. I need to talk to Dani." She walked across the cafeteria, holding a coffee in her hand, as Dani met her halfway.

"Hey, glad to have you back again," Dani said. "I forgot you were due in today."

Fiona chuckled. "How could you possibly have forgotten? Like I could leave this place for very long," she said affectionately. She gave Dani an awkward one-armed hug, making sure not to spill any coffee on her.

Of course, she'd come close to leaving a little while ago after a patient had perceived a personal relationship that wasn't there. The scenario had an ugly end, and she was still smarting from it. But life moved on, and the patient had left—thankfully—and the ensuing weeks had been calm and peaceful.

"I wanted to introduce you to my friend and a new resident here," Dani said.

"Only you would call them *residents*," Fiona said. "Nobody wants to live here. You know that, right?"

"Well, I'm a resident, and I live here," Dani said, chuckling, walking slowly to give Fiona some background on Finn. "His name is Finn. I knew him back in the first year after high school," Dani said. "We were volunteers for several animal organizations and used to do the Walk for Paws things to raise money. He went into the military at the end of that year, but we've bonded quite well during that time. When he needed a place for rehab, I offered it to him, but he wasn't ready. Finally, he gave me a quick call a couple days ago when we happened to have an empty bed, and I brought him in."

"Sounds like it was perfect timing," Fiona said. She wondered at the wisdom of bringing in friends to a place like this, but, so far, Dani had been very good about keeping personal relationships and paying clients on a very good balance. "Is he a good, *good* friend?"

Dani slid her a look and then chuckled. "He's a good friend but only a friend."

"I'm sure Aaron's relieved to hear that," Fiona said with a smirk.

Dani flushed. "Aaron trusts me, and I trust him," she said with a big smile. "We can't wait to get married."

"Good," Fiona said. "And that should be pretty darn soon, shouldn't it?"

"Potentially. We haven't really set a date and don't want to make too big a deal out of it. We might just get married in town and call it done," Dani said. "Life is busy, and I can't really have a wedding at home with everybody here. That's more than I want to put on people, so I might just do something small in town."

"Invite me when you do," Fiona said. "If I'm not working, I'd love to come."

Dani gave her a smile. "Will do," she said. "That's another issue. Whoever we invite will have to get others to cover their shifts, and I don't want hard feelings. So it's back to that whole 'might just do a few people in town' thing."

"Makes sense. We can always have a big reception afterward here. I'm sure the kitchen staff would be happy to put on something to celebrate the day, like we do for any other big holiday."

"You know what? That's not a bad idea," Dani said thoughtfully. "Aaron is coming home at Christmas time and

Thanksgiving."

"How's he doing in school?"

"I think it's rougher than he thought it would be," Dani said comfortably. "But it's his passion, and he's getting phenomenal grades. I think it's the toll of the daily studying and the exams and reports," she said with a smile. "And, of course, he wants to come home."

"Right," Fiona said. "I tried a long-distance relationship when I was in nursing school, but it wasn't for me."

"It's not for everyone," Dani said. "When you think about it, it's hard to be separated from the one you love." She approached the table where Finn sat and motioned at him.

Fiona looked at him and saw a shock of red hair that made her grin. Tall, lean, with freckles across his face that made him younger looking than he was, because she could see the world-weariness in his eyes, and the pain in his body as he held himself stiffly on one side. She recognized some of the aftermath of his injuries but was interested to hear what else was going on.

As Dani came around the table, she smiled at Finn. "Here's somebody I want you to meet. This is Fiona Smithers," she said, "one of our nurses here. You'll see her a fair bit. She's assigned to your team too."

Finn held out a hand, and Fiona shook it gently.

"Hi, nice to meet you," she said.

"Wow, somebody from the Old Country," Finn said.

"Maybe originally," Fiona said, "but it was generations ago."

"Well, I was born here too," Finn said, "but my mother's from Ireland."

That helped break the ice a little bit. He seemed to relax,

but she noted the pain up and down his spine just from the way he was trying to settle in his wheelchair. She glanced back at Dani. "Has he had all the intros to the place yet?"

"No," Dani said, "we got sidetracked here with coffee. Elliot's bringing him a sandwich."

Fiona nodded and kept her next comment to herself.

Elliot appeared then with a big sandwich.

Fiona looked at it and laughed. "If you can eat all that, you're doing pretty well."

Finn looked at the sandwich in shock. "Good Lord," but Elliot sat down beside him with one of equal size.

"I cut it in half in case you can't eat it all," Elliot said. He picked up his first half and chomped his way through it.

Finn looked at the food, looked at the ladies and said, "I'm not used to eating this much."

"Your body needs the nutrients," Fiona said. "Go ahead and eat. I'll talk to you later." And she turned and walked away.

As she did, she glanced back, caught Dani's eyes and smiled.

Dani always worried about everybody in the place, but those she knew personally before coming here she worried about even more.

Fiona didn't know why she was worried about Finn. What was going on with Finn that she either didn't like or didn't think Finn would like?

Chapter 2

FIONA APPEARED SHORTLY thereafter for her shift, bright and cheerful as always. She'd enjoyed her week off, but something about getting back home again felt so right. She really loved working here, loved the people, both staff and patients. It was always upsetting to come back and find that somebody had left, and that was the case this time. She studied the charts, looked over at Mina and asked, "What happened to Fred's chart?"

Mina smiled and said, "He took an early discharge. Transferred to his hometown. He and his girlfriend are now engaged, and he wanted to be closer." Her tone was so delighted that Fiona realized it was good news all around.

"I'm sorry I didn't get a chance to say goodbye," she exclaimed. "I really liked him."

"And he really liked you too," Mina said, sorting through paperwork. "I think he left you a note. Aha." She pulled out an envelope with Fiona's name on the front. "He did."

Fiona smiled and reached for it, pulled out the folded piece of paper and read out loud the few lines. "*Dear Fiona, I wouldn't have come as far without your help or your care. Thanks so much for holding my hand on the days when I couldn't hold my own. Much love and progress in your bright future.*" Fiona showed it to Mina. "Isn't it nice when we have success stories?" she said.

Mina nodded and tapped the note. "You should frame that," she said in all seriousness. "That's a lovely goodbye."

"I know," Fiona said as she folded it and tucked it away in her pocket. "I'll figure out what to do with it later. But I'm back to work and reporting as scheduled," she said with a chuckle. She waved goodbye and headed into the nurses' station. She was still a couple minutes early, and that was good because she could catch up with her new patients and see about the progress on the ones she had left behind. A week here when she was on duty often seemed to take forever from Monday to Friday, but, when she was gone, it seemed like so much happened that it always shocked her. She walked in and smiled at Anna. "Hey there," she said. "How are you doing?"

"I'm doing just fine," Anna said, smiling. "And don't you look all bright and cheerful."

"Hey, a week off, you know what that's like."

"Not enough," Anna said, laughing. "But I leave on Monday."

"Right, I forgot about that," Fiona said. "In that case, you better catch me up before you leave because, after it starts to get busy here, I may not see you again today."

With that, they sat down with the stack of files and went through the progress on the patients. They split up the center by hallways and tried to keep a fairly even workload per nurse, but everybody always had one patient who caused trouble. It wasn't the same trouble that they would often have in a normal hospital because everybody was here by choice, but there were still problematic people. It didn't matter where you went or what setting you were in, there would almost always be at least *one*.

Anna tapped the top file and said, "So, this is Jerry. He was admitted last Monday, the first day you left. He's progressing and adapting slowly. As you can see, he's got extensive physical issues, and we haven't started his physiotherapy yet because, as soon as he arrived, he had a medical setback. He has pulled through at the moment, so, outside of keeping a tight watch and making sure the medications are working, the doctors are on it. By Monday we can start him on physiotherapy."

Fiona nodded thoughtfully. "It's funny how that happens, isn't it? They get here all excited, and then it seems, in some cases, they have a complete relapse, and it's back to the beginning again."

"I wonder how much of it is all the shock and excitement of getting here or how much effort it took and if it was too much for the body," Anna said. "The thing is, he's doing fine now."

"And I see we have another new patient today," Fiona said.

Anna smiled. "Yes. Finn, he's a friend of Dani's. He's also a friend of Elliot's."

"I just had coffee with them. Or, I should say, I just met them while they were all having coffee," she said. "So, Elliot, I presume, gave us a good reference to bring Finn in, and Dani, being the friend that she is, found him a spot."

"Dani always tries to get everybody in who asks," Anna said. "You know that."

"She does, indeed. And it seems like she and Aaron are making a go of it, so I'm really happy for her. But, of course, her heart is so big, all she wants to do is help heal the world."

"We need more people like her," Anna said. "Just think how much nicer the world would be to live in if we had people like her running the country."

Fiona chuckled. "Can you imagine?" she said. "Then again, we would all be healthy. We'd all be educated. We'd be treating each other nicely. And the world is so not like that."

Anna looked at her watch and said, "I'll introduce you to Jerry, and then we'll see how Finn has settled in."

"Sounds good," Fiona said as she picked up her stack of files, put them on the table and then took her tablet. "I'm sure glad we're digital here. I hear from friends in other places where they're really behind and nobody wants to spend the budget money and pieces of paper are all over the place."

"Well, we do both, don't we?" Anna said, "We have paper and digital, but I think digital is the way of the future. It also helps keep track of what the doctors are up to."

"True enough," Fiona said. "Sometimes I wish I'd become a doctor."

"Not me," Anna said. "This is the level I'm happiest at. I'm great as a supporting staff, but I wouldn't want to be the one making the frontline decisions."

Fiona chuckled. "I hear you there," she said. "So maybe I'm happy as a nurse and not a doctor after all."

They walked into Jerry's room to find him dressed and lying on top of his covers.

Fiona smiled and said, "That's always a good sign."

Anna walked up and greeted him gently. "I see you had a bit of a rough weekend," she said.

He glanced up at her smile and said, "It's nothing compared to when I first arrived. I was just trying to not do too much again."

Fiona stepped up, gave him a finger shake and said,

FINN

"You should know better by now," she said.

He grinned at her and said, "You're new."

She nodded. "I'm Fiona. I was gone for a week's holiday, but I'm back now, and I'll be taking over for Anna."

Immediately his smile fell away, and he glanced at Anna. "Where are you going?"

"I'm on holiday starting Monday," she said cheerfully. "Don't worry though. I'll be back the following Monday."

"Well, I can tell you right now," he said, "I'll still be here." And then he laughed and laughed.

Fiona grinned. "Glad to see you have such a great sense of humor," she said. She quickly took his vitals, and, when she checked his blood pressure, she frowned.

He shook his head at her. "Don't tell the doc," he said, "but I had some potato chips yesterday, and that salt always sends my blood pressure way up."

"Then you know not to eat them, don't you?" she said, putting the note down on her file.

He watched her and frowned. "Are you tattling on me?"

"If you ate so many that your blood pressure's affected, yes," she said with a serene smile. "Next time, show some restraint and have half the amount."

With Jerry still protesting, they walked out of the room to his laughter. In the hallway, Fiona said, "Where's he getting that stash of potato chips from?"

"We'll have to talk to the kitchen," Anna said. "He's definitely got a weight issue that we need to work on too."

"Yeah, that's slowing his progress. Physiotherapy will have a heyday with him."

"Let's hope he has some fun and us too," Anna said, and that set the tone for the rest of the morning as they went through everybody in their quarter. By the time they made it

343

back to the nurses' station, Fiona felt like she'd never left.

"Why don't you get your lunch first?" Anna asked. "I'll go afterward."

"Sounds good," Fiona said. Then she stopped and said, "We didn't go to Finn's room."

"No, he's being assessed by the doctors all morning," Anna said. "We'll have to tackle him after lunch."

"Right," she said. She headed to the kitchen, but so many people were there that she thought maybe, just maybe, she would push that back a little bit and grab something to eat at her desk when Anna was gone.

With that thought in mind, she escaped the crowd and headed downstairs into the veterinarian clinic. She walked into the main reception area to see Mavis sitting there.

Mavis took one look, stood and opened her arms. Fiona chuckled and gave the woman a big hug. "It seems like you've been gone forever," Mavis said.

"Oh, no," Fiona said. "Just a week. And right now, it feels like I never even got that."

"There's nothing like leaving, but, when you come back, there's nothing like being home again," Mavis said comfortably. "Stan is just about to take a break if you want to have a coffee with him."

"If he's around," she said, "I'd love to see him."

At that, Stan stepped out, saying goodbye to another patient. Fiona chuckled as a Chihuahua walked forward stiffly, eager to get away from the vet. She looked at him, and Stan grinned at her. "Welcome back."

"What happened to the little guy?" she asked, motioning at the woman leading the Chihuahua out to the parking lot.

"Greenstick fracture on the back leg," he explained. "He'll be fine."

"I haven't seen Chickie since I came back," she said. "Granted, I've only been on my corner all morning, but I miss the little guy."

"Chickie and Helga are doing fine," Stan said. "Plus, we have a couple new recruits here too."

"Ones staying or ones you're fostering?" she asked curiously.

He walked her down the hallway toward the barn. Stan stopped at one of the horse stalls, and there in front of her was a small llama. She stared at it and cried out, "Oh my."

"She was surrendered to one of the animal centers," he said, "and they were trying to find somebody to keep her when one of Dani's friends called here." He gave her a lopsided grin. "For some reason, Dani seems to think this little girl belongs here."

"How old is she?"

"That's the problem," he said. "She's only six months old, and she's fairly attached to this guy." He pointed deeper into the stall at an Appaloosa horse. Fiona looked at him, and he said, "Yes, they were raised together. This one is two years old, but, ever since the llama came to visit, the two have been inseparable."

"And anybody with a horse that needs a home, of course, Dani's all over it," she said, laughing.

"When it came with a sidekick like this one, absolutely."

"And what are their names?"

Stan laughed and laughed. "Well, the Appaloosa is, of course, named Appie," he said, "because people are so original. And the llama? … Can you guess?"

She looked at him, stared and said, "Oh, please no. Not Lammie?"

He shook his head and laughed. "It's almost as bad. Her

name is Lovely."

"Oh, that's lovely," she said.

The llama's ears twitched. She looked right at Fiona and took several hesitant steps toward Stan, who opened the stall door and motioned for Fiona to come inside. "She's very friendly."

"What about Appie?" she asked, eyeing the big gelding a little more warily. "He might be young, but he's big."

"Yes, something else is in his heritage," he said. "Appaloosa, of course, refers to the coloring and the breed but generally not of this size. And he's young, so he's potentially still not done growing." He crouched in front of Lovely and gently stroked her long neck and scratched around her ears.

"So how long do they have to stay in the stall?" she asked. "It's a beautiful sunny day. I imagine they want out."

He laughed. "That's what I was just about to do on my lunch hour. We'll put them in a pen by themselves and see how they adjust first before we mix them in with the other horses." He held up a halter, which he quickly slipped over Lovely's nose and face. "Do you want to take Lovely out?" He walked over to Appie, hooked a lead to his halter and walked out into the front pasture. Appie wasn't too sure about going until he saw Lovely following him.

Fiona marveled at the bond between the two, yet it was just like humans. Everything was easier if you weren't alone. Out into the sunshine they stepped, and she followed Stan as he led Appie to one of the pastures close by. Just as she was about to join him, she heard sounds of a wheelchair.

She turned to look, and there was Dani with Finn. Fiona stopped and smiled. "Finn, you want to meet this guy?"

Finn said, "Sure."

Dani called out, "I do. Stan, are they ready to go out to

the pasture?"

He nodded and brought Appie over to be introduced as well. Appie behaved himself beautifully, bending down to let Finn gently rub his nose.

"He's beautiful," Finn said sincerely. And then he looked at the llama and smiled. "But there is beautiful, and then there's absolutely adorable."

Stan quickly explained their ages and the medical problems each had. But Finn was head-over-heels in love, cuddling little Lovely. "Hard to believe she'll grow to be the same size as Appie here."

Stan said, "Not quite the same, but close."

Finn looked at the little one, then up at the big horse and shook his head. "It's almost a shame. She's so adorable right now."

They walked them to the pasture, with Finn and Dani watching, and then took off the leads, leaving the halters on.

"Shouldn't we take it off the little one?" Fiona worried about the material chafing the baby's skin.

"Yes, you can take it off Lovely," he said. "They're quite easy to catch, apparently."

Dani walked in, leaving Finn sitting in the wheelchair just off to the side. She walked up, unclipped the halter from Appie. "It's best for him to get used to being free and to trust us in that way too," she said, handing the halter to Stan. She reached up scratched Appie along the face where the halter had rested.

Appie nuzzled her gently and then took a few steps away. Realizing he had his freedom, he danced off to the side, then picked up steam and ran. Lovely immediately followed. They raced around the pasture several times before slowly coming to a walk and strolling toward the group of people again.

Stan stood beside Dani and said, "Let's hope they were right about being easy to catch."

"If not, we'll bring in a wrangler." Dani laughed, stretching out an arm to encompass the nearby pastures where her other horses—Midnight, Molly and Maggie—grazed contentedly. "But we know that trust is everything. Especially here."

FINN LISTENED TO her words and realized that Dani really was living what she believed. He wanted to believe it would have the same effect on him that it had on Elliot, and Finn could already see that Appie was amazed at his newfound freedom. Lovely was just beyond adorable though. He watched and smiled at the llama's antics as it dashed under Appie's belly and came up on the other side. The two of them played, danced around and nuzzled, and, when Dani whistled, Appie came immediately.

She scratched him on the face and said, "Good boy." She gave him a treat that she must have had in her pocket and then watched as Stan fed him a few more. They then gave Lovely a couple treats more suited to llamas.

Dani stepped out of the pasture, turned and said, "Go and enjoy, guys."

Appie, realizing he was once again free, took off with Lovely at his side. Finn stared at the two animals, realizing just how much mobility played into everybody's life. He stared at his missing leg and thought about all the things that he had bitched about and how absolutely meaningless they were at this point in time. He knew he could get a prosthetic that would fit, particularly after the surgery he just had. It would take a bit, and he'd have to start with some pretty rough stuff, but he knew he'd get there. And, just like Appie and Lovely ahead of him, he was pretty darn sure he could enjoy the same freedom with the same exuberance that they had just shown.

Dani walked over and smiled at Finn. "Aren't they beautiful?" she exclaimed, her face bright and so happy.

He nodded and smiled back. "They are, indeed."

Just then his gaze caught on Fiona's face as she stared at the animals racing across the green hills. There was such a serenity and a deep sense of contentment on her face. Whereas Dani's expression was full of joy, Fiona's was different, a quieter happiness. He smiled up at her. "You two are both so lovely," he said. "Don't think I've seen any women more beautiful."

Fiona laughed. "That's the Blarney Stone you've been kissing."

He grinned at her. "I thought you would be my nurse," he said, "but I've yet to see you."

"We were at your room this morning," she said, "or at least you were on my roster, but I understood you were still consulting with the doctors. But, if you're done, we can always start after lunch."

"Lunch," he said in mock horror. "Have I missed it?"

"No," she said, "I haven't had mine either."

Dani motioned at Finn and asked, "Fiona, would you mind taking him through the cafeteria then? I've got to get to my office for a meeting at one." She waved goodbye and quickly dashed off.

"She's special, isn't she?" Fiona asked, watching Dani run off.

He beamed up at her. "She always has been," he said.

"And a very good friend. I'm blessed."

"We all are," she said, motioning to Stan, who was still standing and staring at the horses. "Whether four-legged animals or two-legged humans," she said, "we've all been blessed by Dani's vision."

"Do you know the major?" he asked. "I knew him when I was friends with Dani a long time ago, but he was a pretty difficult person back then."

"Well, that's changed too," Fiona said, stepping behind Finn and pushing the wheelchair. "Now let's get some lunch. Then we can start with you afterward."

"Oh, is it back to business already?" he asked with a mock grin.

"Everything here is blended," she said, "some business and some pleasure."

"Right. Well, I am hungry," he admitted. "The thing is, I hate eating."

"Yeah, because of the colostomy?"

He sank inward slightly and then realized that, as his nurse, of course, she'd seen his file. He nodded slowly. "It's very unsexy," he announced.

At that, she laughed and laughed.

And yet, he didn't feel like she was laughing at him. He twisted to look up at her. "It's not *that* funny," he said crossly.

"Nope," she said, "it's not that funny. It's the way you said it, as if that was the epitome of your world's woes right now," she said. "I can think of a lot of things that could be so much worse."

"I know, and, in a place like this, I feel bad for bitching," he said. "I'm sure other guys with colostomies are here too." He looked at her hopefully.

She smiled but didn't say anything.

He sighed. "It's pretty bad to realize now how much that's bothered me. But I don't know why."

"It's a fact of life," she said calmly. "You took major damage to your intestines and your colon, so that's part of it. The fact that we have medical surgeries that can fix it so you can still function as a normal, healthy human being and still eat normally," she said, "that's another miracle."

"And the leg?"

She just waved her hand.

He realized that, for her, it was just that simple.

"You'll fix that in no time," she said. "I understand you recently had surgery, and the stump is pretty raw because they had to go in and make a few changes to the blood vessels and the tendons. It will make life so much easier when you get a proper prosthetic. Once you're standing on your own two feet," she said, "the change, mentally and emotionally, is amazing."

He nodded slowly. "I felt that the one or two times when I was being fitted. To be able to walk ... Humans weren't meant to always be sitting," he admitted. "And just something about taking back control ..."

"Exactly," she said. "However, in your case, I would think your back is the bigger issue."

At that, he fell silent. "I try to ignore it," he said. "I haven't started PT yet, so ..."

"And you'll hate your therapists at the beginning," she said, her voice calm but cheerful. "But they'll make for an incredible difference at the end of it all."

"We can't strengthen what is gone, though," he said. "So there are no miracles in my world."

"You'd be surprised how the body can compensate," Fiona said. "So come on. Let's see if we can fill that colostomy bag."

Chapter 3

F IONA GRINNED AT Finn's response, but she was serious; there were things in life to be worried about, and there were others that just weren't worth all that energy. He had a lot to learn here, but, at the end of the day, his priorities would be realigned, and he'd be happy. Getting him there, well, maybe not so much.

She understood another aspect. Everybody assumed that because they were in a rehab center like this that only the residents had health issues, and that wasn't the case. Several of the staff had health challenges of their own. But it wasn't the time or the place for that discussion. Finn wasn't ready to hear about anybody else because he was still stuck on *poor me*.

Just wanting to know that he wasn't alone with a colostomy bag was one of those signs. He needed to know that he wasn't the only one who's had such a hard time. She thought a colostomy bag was a huge invention and a medical step forward, and it was so much easier to deal with than he likely realized. But he would over time. This was still new to him.

Back upstairs at the cafeteria she pushed him into the line and said, "Do you want to try this yourself, or do you want help?"

He looked at her and said, "Well, I can't reach the tray, so maybe you could help me with that."

"Gotcha." She put the tray down for him and then walked with him.

As they walked along, he said, "Is there a menu?"

She pointed up to the back wall. He stared up at it and said, "Wow, okay, I want pierogis and cabbage rolls."

On the back side of the counter, Dennis, according to the name tag on his T-shirt, smiled at Finn and said, "Hey, you're new."

Finn grinned. "Are you here so much that you recognize everybody?"

"Been here since Hathaway House opened," he said with a big smirk. "I know every one of you guys. And I'll get your favorites down pretty darn fast."

"Well, that would not be hard," he said. "My favorites are cinnamon buns and a good steak."

Dennis chuckled. "That just makes you male," he said. "Now, what can I get you for lunch?"

Finn quickly gave his order and watched as a huge amount of food was put on his plate. Finn tried to stop Dennis. "Whoa, that's way too much for me."

Dennis looked down and raised an eyebrow but handed over the plate as he said, "Now there's more food, lots of coffee, lots of desserts. Keep moving down the line and grab what you want." He flashed a big grin at Fiona and served her about half the portion he'd given Finn.

Fiona moved Finn along the line to the tea and coffee and asked, "Do you want something to drink now, or do you want it later?"

"I'd love some water," he said, studying the large cooler's selection of cold drinks in front of him.

She pointed ahead and said, "Go grab one."

Dennis came around from the back and said, "Let me

grab the tray for you."

They waited while Finn awkwardly wheeled up to the cooler and tried to open the door. It took several attempts to open it without the wheelchair being in the way, and, at the time, he appeared frustrated and flustered, as if wondering why no one was helping him.

As Fiona and Dennis watched, she smiled and whispered, "Gotta love it when they start."

"It's always tough, isn't it?

They watched as Finn finally pulled back enough to figure out how to open up the door and then wheeled around and grabbed the water, and, just because he was in there, he grabbed three.

Dennis chuckled. "I can see this guy'll make sure he gets what he wants when he wants it."

She smiled, walked past Finn and said, "Come on. Let's go this way. We'll sit outside."

She didn't give him a chance to argue and headed for a table that was half in the sun and half out. She put her tray down, waited for him to roll up beside her, and she asked, "Which side do you want? Sun or without?"

"No sun," he said briskly.

She nodded and removed the chair so he could sit easier. Dennis placed the other tray down, and she sat across from Finn. She grabbed one of the bottles of water and asked, "May I?"

He stared at her resentfully.

She grinned and said, "Around here, the more you can do yourself, the better off you are. Yes, it took you several times to make it, but that's not the issue. Celebrate the wins. You accomplished your task, and you did it very quickly. I was impressed."

He looked at her in surprise, and then, as if realizing she was serious, he smiled, grabbed a bottle of water for himself and said, "I did, didn't I?" He grinned and held up his bottle, and they tapped them together, saying, "Cheers."

FINN HAD TO smile. He hadn't realized just how affected he was by being watched—or, in this case, by appearing stupid, awkward and like he couldn't do anything. It was a completely different thing being in a rehab center like this where everybody appeared to be in similar circumstances. When he was in the hospital, everybody jumped to help. And maybe that hadn't been the best thing for him, but it had been easy and stress-free. The last thing he needed was extra stress.

But somehow he didn't think that same let-me-help-you philosophy would work here. It seemed to him that Fiona watching him and waiting for him to deal with it in that calm, unfazed manner of hers showed a lot about who she was. He wasn't sure that he liked it, but he admired it. He also admired that she didn't seem to care whether he approved or not.

She smiled at him. "Not quite what you were expecting, was it?"

He shook his head quietly. "No. I'm used to people jumping up and helping."

"I get that," she said cheerfully. "But think about the advantages of us not doing that."

He frowned at her, but her grin widened. His shoulders sagged as he agreed. "I still don't like feeling like a fool."

She stared at him, her gaze gentle. "The only fool is a fool who doesn't try," she said.

His brows came together as he thought about that. "I'm sure there's something very philosophical about that," he muttered. "But I'm not really seeing it."

She smiled. "Appearances matter to you, don't they? You have this view of who you are and what you should be, and, anything different than that, you're not willing to accept."

"Is anybody?" he asked, wanting to challenge her on that. He shifted uncomfortably. "Besides, you're my nurse, not my shrink."

She settled back and looked around.

He wondered if he'd hurt her and immediately felt bad. "I'm sorry," he muttered.

"No need to be."

"Yes, there is," he said. "I didn't mean to come across as an arrogant asshole. Apparently, I've been doing a little bit too much of that lately."

"Or, you are somebody desperate for the same chance that you see everybody else getting," she murmured. "The thing is, when you're desperate, it doesn't happen."

Her words were like a sock to his gut because so much truth was behind them, but how did she know? He stared down at his water bottle, wondering.

"Everybody comes here with that same look," she explained, her voice once again cool but warm. "And you have every right to it. This is your life. This is your physical body. This is your future. You have to want this change, to be the best you can be. You have to be hungry for it," she said. "But you have to be willing to do the work to get there. And the work is not always the work that you think it'll be."

He stared back at her. He didn't even necessarily want to go down that train of thought. But what she was offering him was tantalizing. "Is that part of your shrink duties?" he asked, but he tried to keep the sarcasm out of it.

"We're all shrinks here," she said, "because we're all people who walk this world called life. None of us are any better than you. None of us are any worse. We're all here on this journey. We're all at different stages. Just because I'm healthy and seemingly whole and have a job where I get to help people become healthy and whole doesn't mean I'm ahead of you. On the contrary," she said, "I've learned so much on a day-to-day basis from each and every one of you that I know that I'm further behind."

She almost took his breath away. He took a sip, trying to gather his thoughts as he considered her words. "I guess you've seen it all, haven't you?"

"I keep thinking I have, and then I get a new patient with a new set of problems and a new set of beliefs and a new set of handicaps, and I realize that, yet again, somebody new with something different has presented which I haven't seen before, and it's another opportunity to learn."

Her words were hard-hitting, and yet, so damn meaningful that it made him feel small. "It seems like, every time you open your mouth right now, you come out with something incredibly prophetic, and it makes me feel even smaller," he admitted. "I had no idea my insecurity was such an issue."

"What I've found," she said in a conversational tone, leaning forward and linking her fingers loosely in front of her, "is that whenever we're up against a new challenge—in your case, your physical disabilities—it makes us all feel very insecure because it's different. We don't experience a stable footing to stand on. We don't know what we're up against, so we don't have the confidence to know if we can handle it. It's as if the mountain seems to be so big that you just don't have the coping skills, so everything falls apart. And the first thing to go is your sense of confidence, your sense of security, your ability *to do* versus *maybe I can do.*" She cut her roll in half and offered him half.

He stared at it and then nodded. He leaned forward, wincing only a little at his back as it twinged with the movement.

"Did you lose that kidney too?" she asked, her tone so normal and commonplace.

He laughed and said, "I did. That and a bunch of other stuff." He picked up the half of her roll, took a bite and slowly savored it.

She nodded and said, "You haven't allowed yourself much in the way of food, have you?"

Instinctively he gazed at his waist.

She nodded, "Because whatever goes in has to come out, and you've been avoiding what comes out."

He flushed, looking around, wishing she kept her voice low.

"If I were to stand on this tabletop and yell out to everybody that you have a colostomy bag," she said comfortably, "not one person here would give a shit or be fazed by it."

"How do you know?" he asked in horrified fascination. "Do you do that to all the newbies who come here?"

She stared at him in surprise for a moment and then went off in a peal of laughter. When she finally calmed down, she wiped the tears from her eyes, still chuckling, and said, "Oh, that was great," she said. "No, I don't. I should though, shouldn't I?" Still chuckling, she checked her watch and said, "Not sure what time your next appointment is, but I have to get going."

"What time is it?" he asked.

"One."

He nodded. "I should go too. I'm not exactly sure how anything works here, but it seems like it's not really been set up yet."

"That's normal until everybody on the team gets up to speed," she said, standing. "Do you want a hand back?"

"I think the answer that I'm supposed to give you," he said, "is, *No, I'll do it myself.* But the honest truth is, I would. I'm quite tired." He lifted a hand to see it trembling.

She gave a decisive nod. "I'm taking my lunch back to my desk. Let's get your drink and your lunch and bring it back with you." She quickly packed up a tray, put it on his lap, walked behind him, pushing him toward his room.

"Are you supposed to see me this afternoon?"

"Yes, I am," she said. "Will you be there, or will you run away?"

"I was thinking that I really wanted to see you," he said. "You have a take on life that's refreshing."

"It's because I like to take life by the hand and give it a good shake and see what falls out," she said, still laughing.

"Like I said, refreshing."

Chapter 4

A S SOON AS Fiona got Finn back to his room, with
assurances that he was fully capable of getting onto his
bed and that he should lay here and close his eyes for a bit,
she placed his tray of food on the night table and headed
back to the nurses' station with her lunch. She was still
chuckling about his comment, asking if that's how she
introduced all newbies to the center, because it wasn't a bad
idea.

From the very start, get over the embarrassment, get over
that humiliation, get over the unseen worry that people were
whispering behind their backs, so that everybody knew
upfront exactly what the problem was, and then they could
get on with it. They could move past all the initial hurdles
with a modicum of effort.

She was all about being transparent, about being out-
spoken, but she'd learned that one had to tread carefully
because most men's egos were fragile. She'd also found that
men made the worst patients if they still expected to be a big,
strong, hunky he-man type.

In this place, sometimes they needed to cry like a baby.
Sometimes the fear, the worries, the pain were just too much
for the he-man image. They broke down, and they always
felt embarrassed afterward. They always felt like they had
somehow broken some male pledge to be strong forever. It

took time for them to adjust to the fact that this was normal behavior and that not everybody could be strong all the time. Not only that but it sometimes took the strongest of men to let out that pain, let out that grief, so they could wake up the next day and start all over again.

She'd seen some of the PT sessions that were absolutely, unbearably painful. And it was her job to help ease that pain in whatever way she could so that the patient could get up the next day and do it all over again. Eventually, over time, it got easier. Eventually, over time, the pain diminished; and eventually, over time, they didn't need her. That was both a sad and a great moment. Because they could sleep on their own then. Having seen the progress, having seen that momentous change was the tipping point in their recovery.

Everybody went through a process, but everybody's process was different. It's not enough to think that everybody processed things differently, because, of course, they did, but everybody experienced things differently too. That meant everybody's tipping point was different.

Wouldn't it be nice if she could say, "Five days of doing this and you'll hit that tipping point. When you wake up on day six, it'll be as if you scaled that mountain. You'll feel like you are David who killed Goliath." But it wasn't like that. Sometimes the tipping point came at six months; sometimes it came at three months, and sometimes, for some people, it took years.

She'd had one patient who was here for six months. He went home not quite as healed as much as they all expected for him, and, when he came back almost a year and a half later, he'd walked into the center as a visitor, visibly healed in body and mind. Not in a wheelchair but standing straight and tall, wearing casual jeans and a T-shirt, and she'd been shocked and delighted to see him. She'd walked forward, held out her hand, shook his and said, "Wow."

He grinned and said, "And that's why I came back. When I left, I was a mess, and I wasn't ready to listen to anything you had to say. I wasn't ready to hear anything you wanted me to hear. I was a slow learner. But I did get the message—finally. I'm here in town, and I deliberately made this trip just so I could see you and could let you know that I finally found that tipping point. For *me*."

Tears had come to her eyes, and she'd flung herself into his arms and hugged him hard. It had been mutual, and, when he'd left, there had been more tears in his eyes too, but he'd become a whole man, a healthy man, and she'd never ever seen anything better.

Even now she could feel the tears in her eyes, that sense of joy, that beautiful sense of accomplishment of knowing that that broken man had reached that point in time. They still corresponded. He was back out West again. She knew that she wasn't important in his life now, but she'd been important then, and she'd been important up to the point that he had needed her to be. And, once he didn't need her anymore, he'd moved on, and that was the way it should be.

Was it her fault that she gave a little bit of her heart to each and every one of her patients? Maybe that's why she had no relationship now—because she'd given away so many pieces of her heart to these men who had shown her just what a real man was.

She didn't want the jocks. She didn't want the slick businessmen, and she certainly didn't want the successful millionaires because money didn't matter. She saw money here every damn day. Money made no difference because money didn't give you the spirit to get up in the morning.

Money didn't give you the courage to crawl out of bed to face PT when you knew it would hurt and it would send you crawling back in tears, wishing you could die so you didn't have to face another day. Money didn't do a damn bit of good when you had to crawl inside yourself to find out who you really were, because, at the end of the day, we were all poor unless we had built up our own riches, and we had that bank account of self-reliance to draw on in times of need.

Like the real men she'd seen here had done.

That was the kind of man she wanted.

TWO DAYS LATER Finn slowly worked himself out of bed and did several loosening-up exercises, as he'd been instructed. When he was done, he pulled out his tablet to check what was on his list today. As he sorted it out in his head, he dropped into his wheelchair, headed to the bathroom, quickly went through his morning ritual. By the time he made his way back to the bed, he could already feel a sense of exhaustion. He was never big on routine. It was necessary for many parts of life, but he'd always found it was a difficult thing for him to get into in his personal life.

But he didn't have much choice here. He literally tapped items off his list as he went through everything, and the list was extensive, as if they knew that he might skip one of every two items on his list. He also knew that tablet sent the same tally in real-time so that everybody else on his team could see what he'd done—or tried or skipped—at any time.

Sure, he could lie and tap and say he'd done all these things, but that wasn't who he was. And just staring at the list was both empowering and terrifying.

He slowly dressed, wondering when he could get fitted for another prosthetic. That would make a huge difference to his mental state. He stared at the wheelchair and wondered if he was ready to go with crutches. He'd done a lot of work on crutches before, but his back …

He grabbed the crutches and walked to the doorway, awkwardly opening it, and stepped out. He took several deep breaths as he looked around and realized that the cafeteria hadn't looked quite so far away when he was in his wheel-chair, but, now that he was on crutches, it looked miles away. It shouldn't matter. He'd been there and back many times. It was amazing how being on crutches made the world look different. Still, he figured he could go for breakfast, maybe not make a fool of himself, then could come back and switch into the wheelchair for his first PT session.

He wasn't looking forward to it, and he was waffling as to whether he should even eat beforehand. The last thing he wanted was the embarrassment of having this colostomy bag filling while he was in a PT session, and yet, he knew it probably wouldn't be the first time for his therapist. It would just be Finn's first time. Muttering, "There will be a lot of first times coming up," he slowly worked his way to the cafeteria, happy to feel his body getting into the swing of things a little easier than he thought. But he also knew how damn easy it was to overdo things.

At the cafeteria, he'd managed to get a tray off the stack and onto the runner, and, as he hobbled along, he saw Dennis at the end. He beamed when he saw the crutches. "Moving up in the world, are you?"

Finn grinned back at the wonderfully even-tempered man and said, "Maybe, but I could fall flat on my face trying to get to a table with a full tray."

"I've got your back there, not a problem. What can I get you for breakfast?"

Finn settled on a nice omelet stuffed with veggies, a big glass of juice and a little bit of fruit. As he got his tray to the coffee station, he studied the tray and wondered how he would ever make that trip to the table. He'd seen others do it easily enough, but he figured he'd dump everything on the floor.

While he was still frowning, Dennis came, snatched the tray from in front of him and said, "Lead on."

Laughing, he hobbled his way forward so he was out on the deck again. Dennis placed the tray on the table in front of him and said, "Enjoy."

He disappeared without giving Finn a chance to even say thank-you, but he called it out anyway. Just because Dennis couldn't hear it didn't mean Finn didn't need to thank him for the help. He laughed because he figured that was also something that Fiona would agree with. That thought uppermost, he tucked into his breakfast and settled back with his coffee. He was thinking a refill would be really nice, but it was too damn far away. He watched as some other guy walked with a tray, while on two crutches and talking to his buddy. Amazingly the man made it to his table, sat down and never spilled a drop. Finn shook his head in amazement.

"You'll be doing that in no time," a familiar voice said.

He looked up to see Fiona walking toward him, two cups of coffee in her hand.

He grinned and asked, "Is one of those for me?"

"It so is," she said with a grin. She motioned to the man he'd watched. "Don't worry. You'll be doing that soon too. It just takes time and practice."

"I can't imagine," he said. "Dennis helped me this morning."

"Dennis will help you anytime you need it," she said. "He's a very giving person."

"He is, at that," Finn said. "I was figuring out whether I should eat before therapy or not."

"It's your first session?"

"Well, we've done the testing," he said with a half nod. "Today is the start of the exercises."

"Well, they won't go too crazy on you then," she said. "I'll stop by afterward at the end of my shift to see how you're holding up."

"So you can cheer me on or hold my hand in commiseration?"

"To see if you need pain meds," she corrected with a half laugh.

He winced at that. "It'll be bad, won't it?"

"Maybe not," she said. "But, if you didn't need help, you wouldn't be here."

"It's my back," he admitted.

"It won't be just your back then," she said. "Once a muscle is damaged, other muscles are called into play. In this case, you've got a lot of back injuries that pretty well affect your entire body."

"Right," he nodded. "And what do I do if I have an accident?" he asked bluntly. There was silence for a moment. He glanced up to see her studying him and again found that warm glow. He flushed. "Yes, I'm worried about humiliating myself," he muttered. "Yes, I'm worried about acting like a fool. And, yes, I'm afraid of making a mess and having to get help," he said. "Is that so wrong?"

"Not only is it *not* wrong," she said, "I'm really happy you managed to voice that."

He could feel the heat getting stronger on his cheeks. He shrugged uncomfortably.

She chuckled. "And, like so many men, you don't like to talk about such things."

"No," he said, "I prefer to avoid those conversations than to talk about them."

"So you can either tell your therapist that you have a colostomy bag, so that you're both not surprised, or you can expect that they will have done their job and will have read your chart," she said firmly, "and will be expecting that bag to be there and will also be working on the muscles that are required to keep the bag functioning properly."

"I don't know how much is required," he muttered. "I'm just worrying."

"About leakage?" she asked.

He hated to even discuss it, but he nodded quietly.

"And again, doing the exercises, you could find that is a problem."

"Which is exactly why I brought it up," he said. "You know, if it was a guy I was talking to now, it wouldn't be quite so bad."

At that, she laughed. "We have lots of male therapists," she said, "but I don't think you'll be that lucky."

Finn groaned and asked, "Why?"

"Because you have one of our new therapists. She's tiny. She's bouncy. She's bubbly, and she's got a mean streak in her."

He stared at Fiona in shock. "So that really won't help my cause, will it?"

"Part of being here is to get adjusted and to be happy and to understand where you are physically," she said. "You cannot hide from this forever."

"I don't want to hide from it," he said. "I want to hide *it* from everyone else."

She nodded. "Heard and understood. But don't expect miracles."

And then, realizing the time, he struggled to his feet, grabbed his crutches and said, "Wish me luck."

"You won't need it," she said in a gentle tone of voice. "Remember. It's a bodily function, and it's also one of the greatest gifts you got. That surgery saved your life. Learn to work with it, not against it." And, on that note, she sat back and sipped her coffee.

Chapter 5

FIONA STOPPED BY late in the afternoon to find Finn in his room, sitting on his bed, despondent, covered in sweat and looking like hell. She rapped on the open door and stepped inside.

He looked up at her, flashed her a half smile and said, "If you want conversation, I don't have it in me." He shifted on the bed and collapsed flat, his head on his pillow. "I'm done," he whispered. "Just bury me now."

She chuckled out loud. "If I had a dollar for every time I heard a patient say something similar ..."

He lifted a hand and waved it at her. "I know. You'd be a millionaire by now, right?"

"Absolutely," she whispered. "So, do you need pain meds."

"Well, I don't know," he said. "It's more muscle cramps than pain."

"Where?" she asked, stepping to his side.

He shifted, rolled over until he was sideways and said, "My back."

She could actually see the knots cramping. He groaned as one spiked and bunched up under her fingers. She gently helped him so he lay on his stomach, then straightened out his frame so that she could get at the muscles and gently started massaging. Using pressure and tension, she pulled and stretched out the knots. When she was done, she asked, "Anything else?"

But there was no answer. She leaned over to see his breathing was strong and steady, his eyes closed. She smiled and stepped back. She'd check on him later and see if he needed anything. For the moment, what he really needed was rest and recuperation. He might also miss dinner, which may or may not be a good thing in this case. She headed to the cafeteria, grabbed herself a half sandwich and a salad and said to Dennis, "Finn crashed. He might be looking for food a bit later."

"Okay," he said. "It's always tough when they first get here, isn't it?"

"Sometimes I think it's tough right through to the day they leave," she admitted. She smiled, her gaze meeting Dennis's with the same understanding that he showed everybody else. He'd been here a long time, and so had she. Not quite as long but almost. Smiling, she took her dinner to a table and sat down.

Almost immediately Dani sat down beside her. She smiled at her friend.

"I hardly ever see you these days," Fiona said teasingly.

Dani just rolled her eyes. "We have so many people coming and going," she said. "It's getting crazy."

"Plus the addition in progress," Fiona reminded her friend.

"And the addition," Dani agreed. "How is Finn doing?" she asked bluntly.

Fiona smiled. "As far as I can tell, it's been a bit of a shock arriving here," she said carefully. "I just gave him a massage and helped him to crash. He had his first real PT this afternoon, and he's exhausted. I just warned Dennis that he might need food in a bit."

Dani's face immediately closed down, slightly pinched with worry. "He's been a good friend. I offered him a bed a while ago, but he wasn't ready."

"I'm not sure he's ready now either," she said bluntly, "but he's trying to get up to snuff fast."

"He's always been like that," Dani said. "Came from behind and took over very quickly. I know that he always had a bit of a self-confidence issue, so I think his injuries probably made it a lot worse."

"I think his colostomy bag is his biggest hang-up," Fiona said. "I've known several women with them, but I haven't really had personal experience with too many men."

"And yet, it's such a marvel of modern medicine," Dani said with a smile. "I guess it's that whole male-ego thing again, isn't it?"

"I would think so. But, as he becomes more comfortable dealing with the changes to his body, I think he'll become a little more comfortable around other people too."

"And, of course, being in a place like this, we're fairly blasé about it," Dani said. "But, for him, he's not quite to that level yet."

"No, but I think the faster he gets there, the better off he'll be," she said. "Bodily functions are bodily functions, and there isn't an easy way to deal with them when things mess up."

"Isn't that the truth," Dani said. "Maybe I'll check in on him after I eat and see how he's doing."

"And maybe take him back down to the animals, if you have a chance," Fiona said. "Or I should. Let's see how he is when he wakes up. I know he was pretty exhausted when I found him, not to mention had lots of muscle cramps."

"The animals are a huge help," Dani said with a tender smile as she looked across the deck. "Lovely is absolutely lovely," she emphasized.

"I think the animals would help Finn too. Animals are so very natural in their own skin," Fiona said. "It would make a massive difference if people could be the same."

"More than that," Dani said, "the more that he realizes we don't care about his supposed limitations and that we accept him for who he is, I think the better off he'll be all around."

"Only when he starts to accept it for himself," Fiona corrected. "Then he'll be perfect."

AS THE DAYS had gone by, Finn was wrapped up in this roller coaster of tears, burning depression, feelings of hopelessness. There were smaller triumphs too but also more defeats. Only his visits with Elliot kept Finn from sinking too deep. So far he'd kept the depth of his emotions from his friend, but it had been hard. Sometimes almost impossible.

When he woke up on his one-month anniversary, it almost blew him away with what he'd accomplished, but it highlighted just how much he still had yet to do. His team had spent the last few weeks doing one thing: strengthening a specific set of muscles in his back so that he could sit properly. He hadn't realized how much he was forcing the rest of his body to compensate for the weak muscles until they'd taken pictures and shown him how he slouched to the side while sitting.

He'd thought nothing of it, only that he was finding a comfortable spot. It was odd now, as if he were finding a place for all his organs so that they would rest naturally inside. He was missing a few parts, and others weren't quite the same anymore. It had never occurred to him how much overall adjustment was needed for that. But he'd managed for a half hour to sit straight, not even conscious of what he was doing, before he started to slump.

And then his therapist had come along and had given him a hard poke, reminding him that his posture was once again falling. He'd straightened but had hurt himself in the process. The only damn good thing about his time here were the massages.

That had to be the best benefit of being injured. He didn't know if other places did them, and he hadn't gotten anything like that at the hospital. But here, after a heavy workout, his therapist gave him a hard rubdown. Several times he'd had muscle cramps, and a couple times he'd fallen asleep on her.

He'd been embarrassed at the time, but she never said anything, making him realize she was used to that reaction. Same with Fiona. It almost made him sad. He wanted to be special, and yet, he didn't want to be special in a needy way. He didn't want to be special in an injured way. He wanted to be like a special man. And all that seemed so damn far away. He wasn't even sure it was something he could feel.

When Fiona came in that morning and took his blood pressure, she frowned at it and said, "Looks like you didn't wake up on the right side of the bed."

"Just woke up feeling a little bit happy and then immediately depressed," he said, giving her a small smile and turning his gaze out the window. "It's been a month since I've been here. Do I ever get a couple days off?"

"In the beginning, you'll get half days off," she said, "unless you overdo it or are recuperating from something. In that case, your team will shift your schedule."

He nodded and continued to stare outside.

She clipped her notebook together and placed her tablet down with such force that it had his head coming around. "You look depressed," she said. "Why don't we go outside and visit with the animals?"

His gaze went back to the window, where the early morning sun was dappling across the trees. He nodded. "I can get out there myself though," he said. "Go do your shift."

"I can do my shift if and when I want to," she said, her arms slowly crossing over her chest. She studied him for a long moment. "This isn't a pity request."

At that, he frowned. "I never thought that you were saying that out of pity," he said carefully. "That would be a really terrible thing."

"It would, wouldn't it?" she said cheerfully. "I just thought that maybe you would feel a little happier if you could get outside in the sunshine." She quickly whipped his wheelchair up to the side of his bed and said, "Come on. Let's go. We'll play hooky for an hour."

He grinned at her. "Only if it comes with coffee."

"That can be arranged," she said.

He still wasn't dressed—he was in his boxers as he slipped into the wheelchair.

She looked at him and said, "You'll be cold."

He snagged his T-shirt from the top of the dresser and some shorts, putting them on quickly, and then rolled his way to the hallway. "Are you coming?" he called back, laughing.

She grinned. He caught the bright twitch of her lips as

he went around the corner. That made him feel better. If he could make her feel better, maybe it would make him feel better. Then he realized that she was probably trying to make him feel better, and that would make her feel better too. He sighed, and it came out a little too heavy.

"No, none of that," she said.

"I just realized you didn't look like you had a good morning either," he said.

"Nope, I didn't," she said. "One patient who I have worked with for six months thought he was going home this week, and he found out last night he has to stay for another two weeks. He's pretty upset."

"I can imagine," Finn said with feeling. "It's hard enough being here, but, if your family's on the other side of the country and you're looking to go home, well …"

"Exactly the problem with him," she said. "He's got two little girls and a wife. They've flown out once, but they don't have the money to keep making the trip."

"Ouch," he said. "That hurts. Kids grow up so fast, and six months is huge."

"So true," she said. "So he was very off this morning. I tried to cheer him up, but he'll take a little bit of time to get out of this funk."

"And, of course, his funk affects your funk."

At that, she laughed out loud. "Well, I wasn't in such a funk. I didn't sleep well last night."

"Why not?" he asked.

"I don't know," she said cheerfully. She spun his wheelchair with a backstep, turned him at the corner and said, "Let's go get coffee." Instead of going into the line, like he'd been heading, she wheeled him around to the far corner where the coffee service was, and there they stopped, picked up two hot cups of fresh brew, and she motioned him outside.

They went down a long ramp, and he said, "I've never even been in the pool yet."

"No," she said, "you don't get to go into the pool until the therapists say you're cleared for it."

"That's a bummer," he said as he studied the clean blue water. "It looks absolutely perfect right now."

"Talk to your therapist," she said. "Chances are you could go in now."

"It's supposed to be good for sore muscles, isn't it?"

She laughed. "It's not me you're trying to convince. Convince your therapist," she said. "I don't have the right to give you permission to go in there."

"Drat," he said amiably. "I'm talking to the wrong person."

"You are," she said. "Now, if the hot tub would calm you down and ease some of your back pain, then maybe, but that's not really your problem."

"Muscle knots," he said instantly. "It would help with the muscle knots."

She laughed. "Now, if you'd said that first, I'd have jumped on it immediately."

He was still carrying both cups of coffee as they went past the pool and patio area around to the back where there was a heavy gravel path. It went all the way around the building so that people could come for a walk, whether rolling along on wheelchairs or on crutches. Using whatever mobility they could, this was a space for them. "A lot of thought's gone into this place, hasn't it?"

"You have no idea," she said. "Dani and her father have done so much here."

"Speaking of which, where's the major?" he asked. "I saw him the first day across the room, and I haven't seen him since."

"He was at a conference," she said. "He should be back today."

"Good, I want to see him," he said. "I doubt he remembers me, but I certainly remember him."

"Was he already back from the war then?"

"Yes," Finn said, his voice dropping. "He was a very angry man with a lot of issues."

"Good, then you should see him now," she said. "He's completely different."

They stopped at the side where the horses dotted the fields on the hillside.

He asked, "How many does she have right now?"

"Hi," Dani said from off to one side, where he hadn't seen her. "Five, and I'm boarding four right now."

He grinned at her. "Aren't you a sight for sore eyes?" He looked and motioned at her jeans. "Have you been out riding or just communing with the horses?"

"Communing with the horses," she said, "and Lovely." She pointed out the small llama that was, as always, beside Appie. "She's such a beautiful addition to the place."

"But she will grow up," he warned her. "She'll grow up into a big spitting llama."

At that, Dani went off in peals of laughter. "And I'm okay with that too," she said warmly. "There's room for all of God's creatures."

"Even spiders?" he teased.

She nodded. "Even spiders." She looked at the coffee he was holding for him and Fiona. "Enjoy your early morning outing," she said. "I've got to have a shower and get ready for work." And she disappeared up the pasture.

He stared at the landscape until he noted a beautiful house up on the hillside. He glanced back at Fiona. "Is that Dani's place?"

"It is," she said. "Too many nights she doesn't even get that far. Lots of times you have to wake her up in her office and send her home because she's been working too hard."

"I think that's the problem when you have a business like this," he said. "A business which is a burning passion. She was always all about helping others."

"She still is," she said. "She met Aaron, her fiancé, here."

"I heard about that," he said. "I think Elliot mentioned it in one of his emails."

"Well, they're doing really well together," she said. "He's off in vet school. Like you, he was missing some body parts and wanted to find out what to do with his life."

"Yeah, that's another big thing. We all have funding from our time in the service. There's apparently a fair bit of it, if we want to go back to school and get new training, although I don't imagine all of it's covered," he said, "but certainly enough of it that most of us can get retrained as we need to."

"There are definitely some budgetary guidelines," she said. "We've come across it with a few of our patients. But most men have found a way to make it work."

"I haven't even thought about my future," he said. "For a long time, all I felt was that I had absolutely nothing to offer anymore. Feeling I couldn't work a job and, therefore, wasn't a man."

"And now?"

"Now I feel like there's got to be all kinds of things that I *could* do," he said. "I just don't know what I *want* to do."

"And that's a huge difference, isn't it?" she asked with a bright smile. She stepped in front of him, took one of the coffees from his hand, walked a few feet away to a large rock on the side of the pathway and sat down.

"Will you get in trouble for being here with me?" He frowned at the thought. He loved spending time with her but hated to think it'd cause her trouble.

She shook her head. "No, I was on duty early this morning anyway, and they don't clock-watch here, which is really good."

"They probably can't," he said. "It seems like you guys are always around."

"Because it's not just a job," she said. "Everyone becomes part of our family."

He nodded, instantly understanding what she meant. "That's good," he said. "That's the way it should be. That's the way it was in the military, and I guess I'm hoping to find something similar."

"Well, we had three friends who were here all at the same time, although most of them have left by now but have stayed close in town. I know that they were getting together and doing some things as a group," she said. "Building up that supportive brotherhood bond."

"But they probably already had that bond before they left the military, didn't they?"

She nodded. "I believe so. I think they were all part of the same team."

"Ouch," he said, "to have three injured to the extent that they have to be here means it was pretty ugly."

"I think that's a very mild word for it," she said with a half smile. "What kinds of things would you like to do?"

He looked at her in surprise. "Well, sometimes I think

about working with animals, and then I think I can't make a living doing that. Sometimes I think I should get back to my art, and then I talk myself out of that and think I can't do that anymore. I really have no idea. I do have an electrician's license," he said. "I did get a trade when I was in the military, but I'm not sure I want to do that anymore."

"You're an artist?"

Of course, she'd glommed onto that one. "I used to sketch," he said. "I don't know that I do anymore."

She studied both his hands and asked, "Were your arms affected?"

"No," he said, lifting his hands, wiggling his fingers around. "They're perfectly capable of drawing. It's just the disconnect between my mind and my heart. I used to sketch from my heart, and, right now, all I see are images of accidents and war. I used to see animals all the time. It's one of the connections that I had with Dani. She loved her horses, and I used to sketch her horses for her. All kinds of poses, sometimes cartoony. But I haven't done it for years now." He looked at his hands and said, "I don't even know if I still can."

Chapter 6

FIONA WOULD HAVE to talk to Dani about that, see just how talented Finn really was because maybe something was there that he could do as a full-time career. She'd seen people with little talent take off. She still didn't understand some of the more modernistic stuff, but it wasn't for her to judge. If Finn could do something that Dani would appreciate in terms of horses, then he was certainly in the right part of the country for it. "I don't know about a full-time living," she said quietly, "but art can certainly be a huge passion and an outlet for healing."

His lips quirked. "You see? That's how I always know that you're in the right field," he said. "Even when you're not at work, you're at work."

She chuckled at that. "Just because artwork is great for the soul and helps you to heal and all kinds of things," she said, "that doesn't mean that I'm on duty." She looked at her watch and sighed. "But it does mean I have to get back on duty pretty soon."

He looked at his empty cup and then at her and smiled. "Thanks for this," he said. "It really did help."

"Good," she said, standing. "Let's take the long way around. I could use a little bit more exercise."

"Don't you swim in the pool?"

"I do," she said. "Definitely I do. Just haven't been in

since I've gotten back from vacation. But I should. Just doing a few laps helps me let go of my day."

"What about horseback riding?"

"Not my thing," she said. "I wouldn't mind running alongside them, but I can't say that I particularly want to ride them."

"Do you jog?"

"Again I used to," she said, "but somehow it seems to have been something I let slip away. But I do love it," she said thoughtfully. "Maybe that is something I should get back into."

"You've got beautiful trails here to jog."

"There're trails all across the property," she said. "It's one of the reasons I got into running. There was so much to see, and it is just such a beautiful geographical region to step out and get exercise and breathe fresh air and enjoy my surroundings," she said. "But time is like that. It gets away from you, and you stop doing something one day. The next thing you know, it's been a week or two, and you're way behind."

"Agreed," he said. "That's like my artwork."

"Well, I tell you what. I'll start jogging again if you start drawing again."

He laughed. "I don't have any supplies here. You just need runners, and then you can go."

"Well," she said as she pushed him around the pathway, "I'll check around to see what we have hidden away and see what we might come up with."

"Well, if you can," he said doubtfully, "and to keep you exercising and in good health, I agree."

She was still laughing about his comment when her shift was over, but he'd kept her smiling all day, and it hadn't been a terribly easy day either. When she walked out to the front reception area at the end of her shift, she talked to Mandy and asked, "Hey, do we have any art supplies here?"

Mandy, harried and in the middle of answering multiple phone calls, looked up at her and said, "Talk to Dani."

Fiona stepped off to the side and saw Dani sitting in her office, her feet on the desk and the phone to her ear, and figured it probably wasn't the right time. Fiona walked down the hallway to the supply room and stood staring at the items in front of her, but she didn't know what Finn might need.

"Fiona, did you need me?" Dani called out to her.

She retraced her steps to Dani's office and saw she was done with her call. "Hey, I didn't want to disturb you," she said. "I was just looking for something."

"What is it you need?"

Fiona plunked herself down on the chair across from Dani and said, "Something I'm trying to get Finn back to doing," she said, so she told Dani about their deal.

At that, Dani's face brightened. "You have no idea how talented he is," she exclaimed. "I mean, like seriously talented. He could be doing this as a full-time career."

"Well, he's looking for some idea of what to do with his life but says that he's not even sure he can draw anymore."

Dani walked around and closed the door, then pointed out a sketch of wild horses racing across rough terrain. "He did that in about ten minutes flat."

Fiona gasped. She stood and stared. "That's Finn's work?"

Dani stood beside her and nodded. "It so is. I was having a really crappy day back then, and I had these pieces of paper I was supposed to be doing summary reports on. Anyway, he snatched one of my pages and made me really mad. Well, I sat here, having a cup of coffee, trying to calm down. When he lifted up the sketch, I could just feel all the pain and anguish and frustration drain away. He's that talented. Just look at the detail."

Fiona couldn't stop staring. Five horses streamed across the field, but he'd done it with minimum strokes. The detail was there, and yet, it wasn't the whole of the picture. It was just marvelous. "It's like they're part of the wind," she whispered.

"That's exactly it," Dani said with a heartfelt sigh. "So, anything to get Finn back to drawing is money I'm quite happy to spend."

"I don't know what he needs though," she said. "He seemed to think that we wouldn't have any supplies here, and I don't think he's looking for just a couple pieces of printer paper."

"No, we need sketchbooks for him. I think we have an excursion going into town Thursday," she said, reaching for her calendar. "Maybe I'll run in myself."

"Can you spare the time?" Fiona asked, puzzled. Normally Dani didn't do personal trips like this.

Dani flashed her a smile. "For Finn? To get him back to his art? Absolutely."

Fiona was delighted that she'd brought it up. "I may have to go get new running shoes then too because the other half of the deal is that I start jogging again," she said with a laugh. "It's something that I used to always love, but somehow, like so many things in life, it fell away, along with the rest of my schedule."

Dani nodded solemnly. "Which is why I was out there this morning, just to trample around with the horses. I want to get back to riding on a more regular basis too, but, like you and the jogging, and Finn and the drawing, it's something you have to work at to keep in your life. And it makes no sense because it's what brings us joy. Yet so many other things we label as priorities, and the things that bring us pure joy end up not even making the list."

Fiona was still thinking about Dani's words as she walked back to her on-site rooms. Like many of the other staff here, she had a small apartment to herself. She didn't have a kitchenette because she didn't need it. She had all the food she could want at Hathaway House. And anytime she wanted a special meal, she already knew the chefs personally, and they were more than happy to accommodate her. It was easy to live here. It was easy to enjoy the food at the cafeteria. It was easy to accept the lifestyle and let everything else slide.

She did her job—usually more than the thirty-five hours a week she was paid for—but again that's because they were family.

But she hadn't gone in the pool lately. She hadn't gone for her walks. She hadn't gone for her runs. And she didn't have any friends in town anymore. For a while, she used to meet up with a group for lunch every once in a while and catch a movie, but now it seemed they'd all gone their different directions.

She checked her watch and realized that dinner was about to start pretty soon. She either wanted to go early or wanted to go late to miss the rush. So today she would go late. She walked back to her place, quickly switched out of her uniform and had a hot shower. There, with her hair freshly braided, noticing the length and realizing a haircut was something else she needed to do, she dressed in a soft cotton dress that flowed around her legs. It helped the patients to see her out of uniform, how she was a normal person, not just a staff member. Ready for her dinner, she stepped out of her place, closed the door behind her and saw Stan standing off to one side, staring up the hills. She walked over to him. "Wow, don't you look like you're lost."

He gave her a half-smile, but it was a teary smile.

"I'm sorry. I guess you lost somebody today."

He nodded slowly. "Yes, I did. I tried hard, but I couldn't make it happen." He gave half a whistle, and Helga, the great big three-legged Newfoundlander dog, came racing toward them. Fiona bent down and gave her a big cuddle. "You keeping them close? I don't think Finn has even met these guys."

"Well, Racer's pretty well hard to track down at any one given time in the day," he said. "Helga here had a little bit of trouble with her back legs, so I've mostly kept her downstairs where I can keep an eye on her."

"Is she okay now?" she asked in concern.

Stan reached down and affectionately scratched her long back. "She is. Now if we could stop everybody from feeding her," he said, "she'd do much better."

"She looks like a big girl, but I hardly think she needs to go on a diet."

"No, she probably doesn't, but too much human food isn't good for her either."

"At least most of the residents here know not to feed Chickie," she said with a laugh.

"Well, the repercussions on that one are pretty instantaneous," he said. "One guy fed him when you were gone. Poor Chickie chucked almost immediately all over him. He didn't try it again after that."

"Serves him right," she said. "These animals have already got enough physical problems. The reason they live as long as they do is because we follow strict rules with them."

"It's not like Chickie's getting any exercise either," he said with a smile. "Everybody carries that poor little dog around."

"Well, I don't think Helga has the same issue. She's too big to carry," she said.

Helga lifted her head and woofed at her.

She reached down, patted her gently and asked Stan, "Are you coming up for dinner?"

Stan stuffed his hands in his pockets and nodded. "Yes, I should." He looked at her, smiled and said, "You're looking very pretty tonight."

"Just one of the things that I was thinking about today," she said as they walked slowly toward the cafeteria. "Living here becomes too hard to separate our private lives from work. How often do we not bother getting changed out of our scrubs? We stick around, have dinner in our work clothes and then go home and change." She shook her head. "I should be going home, getting changed so that I feel like my workday ends and that I have a personal life again."

"It's part of that whole syndrome of living here, isn't it?" he asked. "You try to separate it, but it doesn't really happen."

"True enough," she said. "Are you sitting with anybody for dinner?"

"With you, if you'll let me," he said, holding her arm.

She chuckled, tucked her hand in the crook of his elbow and said, "I'd be pleased. Thank you very much, sir."

"You should be dating some of these young bucks, not hanging around with an oldie, like me."

"I think you're a whole ten years older than I am," she joked. "You're just having a rough day."

"Some days are like that," he admitted.

"On the other hand," she said with a smile, "Lovely looks lovely."

He burst out laughing. "Can you imagine someone named her that?"

"Can you imagine keeping her named like that?" she teased.

He just rolled his eyes at her. "As far as Dani is concerned, it's a *lovely* name."

Fiona chuckled. They made their way to where the plates were stacked to see Dennis waiting for them. She said, "You're another one who never seems to leave his job."

Dennis's face split, his white teeth flashing in a huge grin, and he said, "Nope, this is where I belong."

"Hardly," she said, "but I've never seen you sitting down and eating out here."

"That's because we have lots of tables in the back," he said. "We're a big family back here too, so we like to sit together."

"As long as you don't feel like you're not allowed to sit out here, that you can't sit out here or that you're not welcome to sit out here," she said.

"Nope, that's the last thing we feel," he said. "Now, what will you have for dinner?"

She looked down and said, "Chicken pot pies. Are they homemade?"

"Is today Sunday?" he asked with a teasing grin. "Of course they're homemade. I made them myself."

"In that case, I want one," she said, "and a big salad."

"You've got to eat something besides salad," he said.

"Oh, I will," she said with a big grin. "I fully intend to eat a slice of apple pie with it."

FIVE DAYS LATER, Finn found himself crippled with cramps again. Fiona had brought Chickie with her to stop by his room, but the tiny dog was staying because he wanted to.

Finn's heart broke when he thought about how small this little dog was, curled up against his chest like he was home. "How old is Chickie?"

"I have forgotten, actually," she said. "I think he's four or five. Stan has done a lot to keep him alive and thriving. But we have a very strict rule about not feeding him because the wrong food will upset his stomach immediately."

"Which is just another problem along with his back legs," he said.

"Right. But he is a well-loved mascot," she said as she worked Finn's leg.

At one particular spot, he gasped and rolled his face into the pillow, feeling the pain shuddering up and down his back.

She whispered, "Sorry. It's really not wanting to loosen up." Finally, she stopped, and she said, "You're in your boxers. How about we get you into a bathing suit and get you to the hot tub. I can keep working on it down there."

He rolled over, gasping. "Just the thought of getting into the hot tub …"

"Not a problem. I'll help you," she said. She walked over to his chest of drawers, pulled out a pair of swim trunks and held them out. He nodded, reaching for them. She walked over and snagged the wheelchair, came back and said, "Do you need help getting changed?"

"Nope. I'm done," he said, throwing off the covers and picking up Chickie again.

She helped him, half-lifting, half-sliding him into the wheelchair. And, with him still hanging on to little Chickie in his arms, she quickly wheeled him down the hallway. But she didn't go the normal way. He was surprised to find himself inside an elevator. He looked up at her. "I didn't even know you could go this way."

"Normally we can't," she said, "but this time I think it's necessary."

"Good," he said, "the faster, the better."

Before the doors even opened, he realized he was already at the pool level and close to it. She walked up to the nearby hot tub, parked the wheelchair, put on the brakes, lifted the little dog from his lap and put him on a pile of towels at the side. Chickie hopped off immediately, running to the edge of the water at the pool.

Fiona said, "Now, slowly, I want you to get up and get into this warm water." She helped him up the hot tub steps and then, stumbling, half-falling, he let himself collapse into the hot tub. He groaned as the warm water eased up over his body and splashed his face. He let himself sink to the bottom for a moment before coming up slowly to get a breath. He opened his eyes to see her staring at him.

"Glad you came up when you did," she said. "I did not want to have to go in after you, fully dressed."

He smiled and asked, "Can you come in?"

"I can if I need to," she said, "and, if we keep working those legs, I might have to." She glanced around and said, "But I can't leave you alone."

He looked at her in surprise.

She said, "There are rules."

Just then a big male walked over. He looked at Finn, smiled and said, "I'm Shane. I'll stand watch, if you want,

Fiona. Actually, I'm already dressed for the water, if you want me to go to work on those legs." He took a couple steps, already in a bathing suit, sat down on the edge of the hot tub and said, "I could see from the way you went in how your legs are all twisted up in pain."

Finn nodded, gasping. "I guess therapy was too much."

"Well, I'm a therapist too," Shane said, scolding him. "You have to tell your therapist this. Otherwise, there's no way for us to know. We can adjust your treatments."

"I've already told him that," Fiona said from the side. She watched as Shane carefully worked on Finn's legs. She nodded, seeing some of the tight lines on Finn's face relax, and asked, "You okay?"

He nodded, gasping, and said, "I will be now. This water's heaven-sent."

"It's perfect for this," Shane said. He carefully worked out the knots; then he looked over at Fiona and said, "We're good here. I'll get him back up to his room."

Finn lifted a hand, waved at her and said, "Thanks." He watched as she walked away. When he could, he sighed deeply and tried to shift his position, feeling the pain once again jarring his back. "It's my back and my legs," he whispered.

"Yep," Shane said. "We don't get simple injuries here. And everything is connected. People tend to forget that."

"I think it's my fault," Finn said. "I was pretty eager to get through my therapy today, and I pushed it."

"*Pushing it* to a certain extent is what we want. But *overdoing it* is the opposite of what we want."

"It's a fine line though," Finn said. And then, to his embarrassment, he felt and remembered his colostomy bag. "Oh, no." He reached down and said, "I don't think this is supposed to get wet."

Shane looked at it, shrugged and said, "Why not? Everybody else does."

Finn felt the shock run through him. "Everyone else?"

"I think we've got six guys here with them right now," he said. "A couple are permanent. Others are waiting for their guts to heal until they can have surgery to fix things permanently. They are what they are." He was completely casual about it all.

As this was the first time Finn had been in water since he'd had the colostomy, Finn stared at the bag laying against his skin and said, "It's pretty ugly."

Shane looked up at him in surprise. "Not really," he said. "It's pretty normal. There are different bags you can get. Ones that aren't quite so big, ones that aren't quite so obvious maybe," he said, "but honestly, it's a miracle."

"Everybody keeps saying that," Finn said, "but it still seems like quite an eyesore. And, for anybody who's not used to it, it's pretty embarrassing."

Shane grinned at him. "You mean, it's embarrassing for you. Nobody here'll care. They've all got their own problems, missing pieces and body parts that have been redirected. That"—he nodded toward the colostomy bag— "that's nothing."

Relaxing, Finn sank back and said, "Yeah, but I wonder if the women think so."

"My buddy is married, and he's got one," Shane said with a laugh. "I don't think he gave a damn, and I know his wife sure as heck doesn't."

Finn loved to hear that. "I think, when you get to that stage, you're probably okay," he said, "but I imagine accidents are pretty embarrassing."

"Accidents can happen no matter where your feces exit your body," he said. "Sure, to you it's not sexy, but that doesn't mean that a woman will look at it the same way."

Finn didn't want to keep thinking about it. "The stump is bad enough," he said.

"Around here it's not like you even got a war wound if you don't have a stump," Shane said with a laugh. He started to rub long, lean strokes up and down the rippled muscles of Finn's leg. "See if you can stretch that out a little bit now."

Finn gently extended his leg, waiting for the pain to surface. But, when fully extended and his toes pointed, expecting it every second, he realized no cramp waited around the corner.

"Wow," Shane said. "That is so much better. Let's get the other one into the same shape. You can't have just one leg massaged. Gotta do the other one too."

"Well, the other one doesn't cramp," he said, shifting so he could get out the leg that had the stump. "I don't know why."

"Because it's not connected at the other end," Shane said, chuckling. "The leg that cramps, the tendons and muscles have connections at both sides. Here, they're damaged at the one end, so it won't cramp the same way. But that doesn't mean that they cannot be stiff and sore." He gently dug his fingers in, working the muscle all along the length, trying to ease up some of the stress. "And part of the problem is because that leg's tense, you tighten up on the good leg to compensate."

"I guess," he said. "I never thought of it that way."

"Your body is a fantastic machine," Shane said, "and it will do what it needs to do. The trouble is, if we interfere, we get emotions that make us react, and, as soon as we do that, the body has to compensate. It's a fine-tuned machine, and, as soon as it gets out of tune, then things have to happen in order to get it back to being a well-maintained body again."

"Got it," Finn said with a smile. "It's amazing just how much more normal that feels now." He shifted his other leg and then extended his leg at the knee. "Wow, I hadn't realized just how bad that cramp was."

"Who's your therapist?"

"Nicole," he said, "but it's not her fault."

"Well, it is, and it isn't," Shane said. "I'll have a talk with her."

"I don't want to get her in trouble," Finn argued.

"But, if you don't tell her the kind of aftereffects you're having," Shane said, "you're the one who's in trouble."

As it was, they didn't have to tell Nicole anything. She walked along the pool on the other side and saw Finn in the hot tub. She came racing over as her gaze went to Shane massaging the one leg. "Finn, are you okay?" She crouched at the hot tub.

Shane quickly explained. She shook her head. "You should have told me," she scolded.

"So everybody keeps telling me," Finn said with a half a smile. "I figured I was doing fine. Didn't realize that the cramps were something I was supposed to let you know about."

"Has it happened before?"

"Yes, every day."

There was a moment of silence, and then she just swore at him. Very gently, very politely, she said, "You have to tell me these things."

He waved a hand at her. "Consider yourself told," he said. "I gather the therapy is too much, and I'm weaker than

I thought."

"No," she said, "that's not it at all. It has to do entirely with the exercises we do, and that's something I need to know."

He nodded and smiled.

"I'll get you a drink and some relaxants to help those muscles," she said. "I'll be back in a minute."

"Make it a whiskey," he called out.

She laughed and said, "In your dreams."

He grinned and said to Shane, "One of the nice things about being here is the casualness of it all. The fact that I can tease her and sit here in a hot tub like this, it's huge."

"It is," Shane said. "I've been here for years, and I can't say there's any other place I'd want to work."

"You're lucky," he said, closing his eyes. "I don't know what I want to do anymore."

"But you're the artist, aren't you?"

Finn's gaze popped open. "I don't know who told you that," he said. "I used to dabble, but I don't know that I'm any good at it. And I haven't done it for years, so I'm sure that I'm beyond rusty."

"Uh-huh." Shane didn't say anything more but started working on a different muscle path that had Finn crying out. "Yeah," Shane said, "I'll ease up, but these knots need working out. You'll feel the next one since we're getting closer to the knee."

He kept working while Finn twisted in reaction. When he could, he gasped. "How come it's okay for you to hurt me, but it's not okay for the cramps themselves to hurt me?"

Shane laughed. "Because I know what I'm doing. The cramps are a reaction to the previous work. You won't get cramps from this. I'm taking the cramps away. Besides, no matter how odd this feels, I'm not really hurting you."

"I didn't know I had knots in there," he gasped out, grabbing his knee as Shane worked lightly right up against the bone.

Finally, Shane was done. He shifted back slightly and said, "Now kick your legs out as if you're swimming."

Finn tried to kick and was surprised to find how fluidly his legs moved. He stared at them in surprise. "Wow, that's amazing."

"Your structural integrity is compromised too," Shane said with a frown. "Has anybody worked on that?"

"I don't even know what you're talking about, so I'll say *no*," he said.

"In that case, we book you for it too," Shane said. He stepped up, held out his hand and said, "I want you to stand normally."

So, in the middle of the hot tub on his one good leg, he stood. But because they were in the water, it wasn't an effort to balance.

Shane said, "Now close your eyes and just stand, relaxed."

Finn did feel a little odd, but Shane walked around him several times and said, "Open your eyes now."

Finn did.

"Now I want you to try to take a step forward."

"You mean, a hop?"

"Yes and no," he said. "Imagine that you had your foot there, and I want you to take a step and then quickly take another step. Because you're in water you should be okay."

He did as he was instructed.

"Okay, now raise your arms out to the side." And with Finn's arms up parallel, Shane once again walked around him and took a look. "I want you to sit here and rest a bit," he said. "I'll grab a tablet so I can take some notes, and I'll take some photos too."

Finn looked at him in surprise. "Photos while I'm sitting here?"

"Yes, but then we'll do some more when you're standing upright. And I'll show you how you're compensating."

"Well, of course, I have to compensate," he said. "I'm missing my lower leg, for crying out loud."

"Yep, you sure are," Shane said. "But you're compensating for a whole lot more, so hang on. I'll show you in a minute."

Chapter 7

F IONA WALKED AWAY, determined to check on the men later. But she had other rounds to do—plus medications to sort, shipments to open up and inventory to mark off. While she stood here with a clipboard in her hand, going over the medications and checking them against her digital database, Dani came in. Fiona looked up and smiled.

Dani held up a large sketchbook and another smaller one.

"Oh, wow, are those for Finn?"

"They so are," Dani said. "I also picked up a case of pencils for him."

"A case?" she asked cautiously. "Not one?"

"I remember Finn having favorites," she said, "something about not all pencils being equal when it comes to sketching."

"Well, I don't sketch and don't know anyone who does," Fiona said, "so I bow to your expertise. Maybe we can deliver these to him later. I left him in Shane's care. He was having a lot of muscle knots so we got him to the hot tub."

"Oh, good," Dani said. "That hot tub has come in handy for a lot of people."

"Isn't that the truth. And, if we know Shane at all, he'll be all over Finn for his *structural integrity*."

"Right, Shane just came back from his latest course, and,

if he can help at all, then I'm sure Finn wouldn't mind."

"I'm sure it's more than a case of *wouldn't mind*," Fiona said. "I think Finn is eager to do whatever needs to be done, and that's probably how he ended up in trouble in the first place. A little too anxious, a little too eager, and working a little too hard, without letting people know where he stood."

"That's common here," Dani said. "Way too common."

"Right? Anyway, if you want, you can give him the art supplies," Fiona said.

Dani shook her head. "No, I think you should." She turned and walked out again.

Fiona waited until the end of her shift because she still had lots of work to do, and, even then, she didn't get it all done. She signed off after her shift, consulting with her replacement over a couple files.

As she stood to leave, she smiled and said, "I have one delivery to make." She picked up the sketchbooks and the pencils and walked out. She had no idea how Finn would take this and wasn't sure if she should say it was from Dani or not but figured it couldn't hurt. Fiona didn't know if, at this point, he'd get angry or be happy about it. She knocked on his closed door but got no answer. She frowned and walked to the cafeteria to see if he was there and then headed over to the railing, where she could study the pool and the hot tub below to see if maybe Finn just hadn't made it back to his room yet. Shane was there, but he was working with a different patient. She called out to him. "How's Finn doing?"

"He's fine," he said. "He went to have a shower and a nap."

She nodded and realized he was likely still asleep. She didn't want to disturb him, but he might be just resting at this point. At his door, she tapped again ever-so-lightly and listened, but still, she heard no answer. She carried the sketchbooks back to her place, dropped them on the couch and then went for a quick shower and a change herself.

He'd be awake for dinner so she could see him then. She dressed up particularly nicely in a dress again and braided her hair and then stepped outside to visit with the beautiful little Lovely. She gently stroked the llama's soft ears, loving the trusting soul so eager for affection. Appie was a little more distant but came over anyway. Fiona didn't have any treats for them, and she definitely didn't have any feed for them.

She wondered who looked after that, but nobody was around to ask. She could ask Stan, but that would mean going back inside, and that almost felt like work. Instead, she went for a long walk in the pasture as Appie and Lovely walked beside her. It was so nice to be outside to enjoy the green grass and the sunshine. She sat on a large rock, perfect for sitting, and enjoyed the beautiful view. It was really a special location.

She should have brought a cup of coffee with her, something to help her relax and destress from her day. Today wasn't that bad; it was just work, and sometimes work was, ... well, work.

Inventory was always irritating because she kept missing bottles and then would find them in places where people hadn't put them back. And, of course, as soon as medications went missing, alarm bells went off. Missing medication was something they had to keep a strict eye on. Of course, all the medicine cabinets were locked, but she knew perfectly well that many of the men in her care could unlock it easily. These patients came with such a varied set of skills that the staff made sure to keep track of medications a little closely than they might at another location, and there would always be at least one difficult patient.

Thankfully it wasn't Finn. Although she was pretty sad to see the way his body had reacted to the physical therapy, with Shane on it now, she knew that Finn's assigned therapist, Nicole, would have her methods questioned, and Finn's medical team would have further consultations to make sure that Finn wasn't going through unnecessary pain. A certain amount of pain in order to push through limits and break through barriers was one thing, but pain afterward to the point of cramping up and down his legs and his back was something else. He should have been given medication to help relax the muscles too. Then again Finn was stubborn and might have refused. She heard a voice and looked out across the field to see somebody in a wheelchair waving up at her. She waved back at Finn.

She hopped off her rock and walked slowly down the hill, the animals once again following her. As she got to the fence, she smiled at him. "What are you doing?"

"Did you knock on my door?" he asked. "I thought I heard somebody, and I came and checked and kept on going until I was already up and outside. I saw you in the field here when I was grabbing a cup of coffee," he said, "and it looked too nice to leave you alone." He apologized, saying, "I'm sorry if you wanted the alone time though."

She smiled, shook her head and said, "Time with you is always welcome."

"I hope you mean that," he said. "It's hard enough being in a place like this, but, when you find somebody you truly connect with, that makes it very special. But it's easy to overstep the bounds and misunderstand what that relationship truly is."

That stopped her for a moment. She tilted her head to the side and asked, "Do you need to analyze it?" She could see him hesitate, and she nodded. "You do."

She sat on the top of the fence, stared down at him and said, "The least you could have done was brought a second coffee," she complained good-naturedly.

"True," he said. "I could have. Didn't think of it. I'm sorry."

"Don't be." She waited a second and then said, "And I can tell that you're avoiding the conversation."

He nodded. "So I guess that's my answer."

"Nope," she said, "it isn't your answer. You surprised me, but I shouldn't have been surprised because I could see something was between us, but again I have to be a little more careful, being a nurse. I mean, I'm your medical caregiver. One of many, true, but it's something that we're always much more aware of."

"Are relationships not allowed here?" he asked lightly.

"Well, if that were the case, a lot of people would be in trouble," she said, chuckling. "And Dani started it anyway. Aaron was one of the patients here."

"Right," he said. "I guess in my mind I hadn't put that two and two together, but, of course, if she says it's okay …"

"It's frowned on in most centers just because it's easy to misunderstand the boundaries of where patient medical care stops and gratitude, emotional dependency starts with a personal relationship."

"Got it," he said.

"However, on my side," she said, "I'm quite happy to see you after work hours."

"Which is right now, correct?"

"Absolutely," she said. "Besides, I have a present for

you."

That stopped him for a moment. "I can't remember the last time I had a present," he said, in surprise.

"Well, it's from both me and Dani," she said. "Come on. We can go to my place, and I'll give it to you."

"If I can roll over to your place," he said, "that would be fine. I'm still dealing with the aftereffects of all the cramping earlier."

"Did you take the muscle relaxants I left on your night table?"

"I found them, yes, thanks. And the note."

"If you need more, tell me," she said. "Plus, I'm sure some changes will be made to your PT schedule after this."

"Well, there'll definitely be some changes on the exercises," he said. "I'm not sure how much value any of this is doing to my back, as it seems like we help one body part and the next part screams."

"And I think that's what Shane was talking about regarding your structural integrity," she said. "Because, if your skeleton itself isn't standing straight, everything else is working to compensate. In your case, because you're missing so many back muscles and you're missing part of a leg, all along your right side, then your body is forced to compensate a lot. Shane will likely add in some extra stuff for you."

"My schedule is pretty booked as it is," he said with a bit of life in his voice. "It's hard to find time for anything else in the day."

"This is your job right now," she said, her voice serious. "Everything to do with you and your health is your job *and* your hobby."

"Got it. But afterward," he said, "when therapy's over, it's nice to step away and to spend some time outside, forgetting that this is why I'm here."

"Absolutely," she said. "And, if we get to do it with a friend, it's even better." She smiled and tousled his hair. When he laughed, she stepped away and said, "Come on, this way." And she picked up the pace. She knew he was forced to wheel a little faster, but she wouldn't totally compensate for his injuries. Once you started doing that, there was no end to it.

At her place, she left the door open so he could wheel in, and she walked to the couch, picked up the art supplies and turned around. His gaze went to the sketchbooks, and his eyebrows shot up.

"I know you don't think you can draw anymore, but sometimes in the evening, sometimes in the morning, maybe when you just want something different to do," she said, "I think it might be good for your soul if you try it again. Besides, we made a deal." She held out the two sketchbooks.

He took them slowly. "You know what? There's something very special about having a clean page in front of you." He opened the big pad, pulling the cover piece back and folding it under his hands, gently stroking across the slightly rough surface. "And this paper is perfect."

"Is there a difference in paper?" she asked curiously.

"A lot of difference," he said. "I'll have to find some pencils."

Immediately she held out the case that she had in her hand.

He looked at it, smiled and asked, "Dani is behind this, isn't she?"

"I was behind it, and then Dani went to town, brought everything, and I'm delivering. According to Dani, pencils aren't created equal either," she said.

"No," he said, "they definitely aren't." He opened the box and shook a few out into his hand. He smiled and said, "This is the best thing anybody could have gotten me. I don't guarantee to create anything worth keeping, and I certainly am not promising any finished prints," he said, "but it would be nice to see what my fingers can create. Just maybe doodle a little bit."

"And that's all that's asked of you," she said. "They're gifts. They don't come with strings."

"And that's the best kind of gift," he said.

"It's the only kind of gift," she said. "Everything else then becomes a barter. So, why don't we take this back to your room, and then we can go get dinner together."

"Is that like a date?" he teased, waggling his eyebrows.

She chuckled. "Absolutely," she said, "as much of a date as we can have, considering we both live here."

"But it's about making every day and every meeting special," he said. "Dates don't have to be anything more than a cup of coffee in a field. It's just an appointed time to spend our moments together."

"I like that," she said, thinking about it. "It's a nice definition. And, in that case, yes," she said. "This is definitely a date. We get to have a meal together where we can talk."

"Good," he said, "but please, not about muscle cramps anymore. I'm so over those."

After stopping by his room, she headed into the cafeteria with him at her side, laughing cheerfully. "At least you have a sense of humor," she said smiling.

"I do have that," he said. "And honestly, I've needed it."

FINN WENT TO bed with a smile on his face and woke up in the middle of the night, almost screaming in agony. He tried to stifle his cries, but it was hard. Very quickly, muted lights were turned on as people came running in. He tried to tell them he was okay, but he could only gasp in pain. It was his back, not his legs this time, as his back muscles were coming alive and were working harder than they ever had before.

Now they screamed with pain and cramped from an overwhelming amount of built-up acid. He lay here, desperately trying not to bawl as warm hands laid hot cloths on his back, trying to calm the agonizing muscle spasms. That eased the immediate pain. Hands coated in cream gently massaged the insertion point of each of the muscle bands, then smoothed down their lengths, trying to relax the knots.

Finally, when he could, he gasped out, "Thank you."

"Do you want anything for the pain?" a woman asked.

He twisted his head. "Fiona, is that you?"

"Yes," she said, "I'm doing a nightshift to help out a friend."

"Lucky you," he said. And then he groaned as she worked on one muscle deep in his back.

"Yes," she said, "lucky me." She gently worked his back muscles, her tone even and calm, as she helped reduce the stress on his system until finally, he could straighten again, and he rolled over onto his back.

"This isn't exactly how I would want my night to be with you," he said.

"Me either," she said cheerfully. "We had dinner and a lovely evening, and now you're having a rough night. Did you expect me not to come help?"

"I just wish there wasn't the need for it," he said softly.

In all honesty, the sheet was soaked underneath him too, but he wouldn't mention that to her. Finally, she gently stretched out his calves, pulling them up tight against his chest and doing several exercises to try to relax the rest of his body that had tensed with the initial shocking pain. After he'd done those, he lay here, shaking, but it was mostly a slight tremor now. He whispered, "That's much better, thank you."

"No problem," she said. "Now I'll get you to sit in your wheelchair, and I'll quickly change your bedding."

"No," he said, embarrassed. "Just leave it."

"Of course, I'm not leaving it," she said. "Come on. Get up and into the chair with you." He sat up and then realized that he hadn't made any attempt to hide his colostomy bag. He stared down at it suddenly, but his silence had already alerted her. She looked at it and smiled and said, "Prissy, one of the nurses here, has purple and pink polka-dot bags."

He looked at her in surprise. "One of the staff has one of these?"

"Of course," she said. "Why wouldn't they? Depending on the health issues, this is a hell of an answer." She helped him gently sit in the chair.

He said, "It's located in an odd space. My belt fits underneath it, but I want it to be below that."

"Then your pants won't fit," she said. "I think they put it where it worked the best for your particular issues."

"I know," he said. "It's just ..." And his voice petered out.

"You're worrying too much," she said, "but I can get you a hot pink and purple one, if you'd rather."

At that, he burst out laughing. "That'll dent my manhood even more," he said.

She stopped, walked around in front of him and said, "You're not really afraid that that colostomy bag will affect how women view you, are you?" Her ominous tone made him realize she took offense on behalf of all womankind.

"I don't know how women will take it," he said carefully, trying to explain. "I can only tell you how I'm taking it, and, to me, it's an eyesore. It's an embarrassment, and it's something I would prefer not to show anybody."

"Well, it's a good thing that your date tonight was with me, and I've already seen that," she said blithely as she went over to the bed, seemingly now completely unconcerned with his words as she stripped off the bedsheets. She quickly removed the pillowcases as well and, within minutes, had his bed made up for him with crisp clean linens. She took the others out to the hallway and tossed them somewhere that he couldn't see. When she returned, she asked, "Now can you sleep? Would you like something else, like a hot cup of tea?"

"Actually," he said, "that's not a half-bad idea." He got up and made his way awkwardly with his crutches to the bathroom, and, when he was done and came back out again, he felt better but now more awake. "Can't wait to get a prosthetic on this stump again," he said.

"You had one before, didn't you?" she asked, pulling back the sheets and the blankets so he could get into bed. As soon as he lay down, she pulled the covers up to his waist.

"I did," he said, "but I kept soring up, and then I got an infection from it. So they changed something on the skin flaps to give me a little bit more cushion and did something to one of the veins that was too close to the surface."

"So it was a relatively minor surgery, but hopefully one that, once it's healed, will make a major difference," she said.

He looked up at her. "I like the way you think," he said.

"It was minor surgery, but, of course, no surgery is minor."

"Exactly," she said. "If you're okay now"—she switched on his bedside lamp, then walked over to turn off the overhead light—"I'll put the teakettle on. Then I'll do rounds and will bring you a hot cup of something. A Sleepytime chamomile or a hot lemon. What would you like?"

"One of my favorites, honestly," he said, "is a hot lemon. But only half the honey."

"You got it," she said. "Have you got a book to read or something?"

He nodded. "I'll be fine. I've got my phone, and I'll surf the web."

"Back in a few minutes then," she said, and, just like that, she was gone.

He lay in bed and thought about her reaction to his colostomy and then her comment about having seen it before. And, of course, she had. He hadn't even thought anything of it because she was a nurse. She'd seen things like this all the time. But, as a girlfriend, or a potential one, it was different. Or he thought it would be. Did that make her one-in-a-million because it didn't bother her? Or did that just make him an idiot for thinking it would bother everyone? Sure, a lot of women wouldn't like it. A lot of women would be turned off by it, but, just because a lot of women were, didn't mean that every woman would be.

Chapter 8

FIONA QUICKLY FINISHED her rounds, made him a cup of tea and stopped back in his room. She half expected him to be asleep again, but instead, he lay here, staring through his window at the dark night, his cell phone on his waist, his eyes open as if deep in thought.

"Penny?"

His lips twitched. He rolled over, smiled at her and said, "It's worth a dollar at least."

"Watch it," she teased. "I have a dollar in my wallet."

His smile widened. "You're a really nice person, you know that?"

"That's usually a brush-off," she said. She could see the surprise in his eyes. "It's what you tell somebody when you don't want to go out with them. *You're really nice, but ...*"

"Except for one thing," he said. "I never said *but*."

"That's true," she said with a smile. "Is that because I didn't give you a chance?"

"You're a really nice person, *and* I like you a lot," he said firmly.

She laughed at that. "Well, in that case, I think you're a very nice person. I like you too."

"See? Now we've already said that we like each other, and we've already had our first date, and we've already met at midnight to do all kinds of things to my body," he said with a snicker, "so what's next in our unique relationship?"

She shook her head. "Not sure there's any preset one-size-fits-all pathway when it comes to relationships."

"You're sure you're allowed to have them here?" he asked, no longer teasing.

"Of course," she said. "As long as there's no hanky-panky," she added with a twinkle in her eye, "because that's definitely not allowed here."

"Of course not," he said, "that would cause all kinds of chaos because everybody'll want some for themselves."

At that, she laughed. "Well, we're not exactly a brothel," she said, "and we don't accommodate families or partners. So it's definitely not that type of a home."

"Understood," he said, "but you can't blame a guy for thinking."

"Not at all," she said. She headed toward his sketch-books and pencils. "If you can't go to sleep right now, why don't you do some sketching?"

It was almost like a switch turned off in him. He nodded slowly and said, "I think I'm tired."

She took that as her permission to leave. "Do you want me to turn off your night-light?"

"I'll be fine," he said, his tone almost brusque. He slipped down into the bed and reached over and turned off the light.

"See you in the morning," she said.

"Wait, what? You won't be here in the morning too, will you?"

"Yes," she said. "I'll grab a few hours' sleep in the mean-time. I'm doing a double shift."

"I've been through enough of those myself. They're not fun."

"Maybe not," she said, "but, trying to help a friend, well, that makes a difference."

"Lucky friend," he called out softly.

"All my friends are lucky," she said, and then she closed his door.

She stood here for a long moment, wondering why the mention of the sketchbooks had brought on that reaction from Finn. She frowned, walked back to her office and jotted a small note about this in his file. It was hard to know with these guys sometimes just what was going on behind that tough-guy facade. They'd been through so much mental stress, so much physical trauma, that you never really understood sometimes who and what these people were on the inside.

So far, Finn had shown himself to be amiable, hard-working, going the extra distance to help himself, to the point that he'd even refused to comment when it was too much. She'd seen the damage afterward. She also knew that Shane was once again working on Finn as well and that structural-integrity stuff was happening. Speaking of, she needed to put a note in the file about his back. She quickly updated his file online and took care of a bunch of paper-work.

She glanced at her watch. The woman she'd relieved for the first part of her shift was coming on soon, and then Fiona herself would head home for a couple hours before showing up for her eight o'clock morning shift. She started to yawn and got up and walked around a little bit to keep her brain active. She did another pass through the hallways, but everything was calm and quiet. It was one of the reasons she didn't particularly like the night shift—she preferred to have something to do all the time.

But then again, she was still here at Hathaway House because it was way less busy than a regular hospital nursing job. She loved the family scenario here so much. She really didn't see herself changing locations anytime soon.

But Finn had brought up an interesting point, even though it's not one he'd meant to. What about a relationship? Was she still hiding? She'd caught her best friend and boyfriend in bed, and that had been enough for her. It had been years ago. It's not that she was horribly religious, but she did expect loyalty and not infidelity while they were together.

Her boyfriend apparently hadn't expected it out of himself at all, just from her.

It had tainted her view of relationships and friendships. She and her girlfriend were obviously no longer friends, and that her boyfriend and her girlfriend had been carrying on behind Fiona's back for months just made it that much more hurtful.

As she sat here in her chair, she wondered about Finn. There was so much to like about him. He'd found a spot in the back of her heart, settled in, made himself at home. Did she like him enough? Or did she not want to go down that pathway? Was it fear of the path? She was very aware of patient-nurse relationships.

One patient had become a little too attached to her, and it had been very painful to separate. He'd taken it terribly when she'd finally been forced to confront him very bluntly with Dani at her side as to what was going on. The shrinks had worked with him for quite a while afterward, but he'd taken it hard.

So now, with her own personal history and the professional history of her relationship with a patient where he had misinterpreted her feelings for him, Finn worried her. Yet she didn't see any similarities between her previous patient and Finn. Maybe she should talk to Dani about it.

With that thought in mind, she sent herself a reminder email to talk to Dani. Fiona should also maybe talk to Dani about the sketchbooks and Finn's odd reaction. Then Fiona heard footsteps in the hallway.

She stepped out to see Becky, her replacement, rushing toward her. The beaming smile of happiness on her face made it all worthwhile. When she held up her finger and flashed the new diamond ring on it, Fiona realized how special Becky's night had been. Becky threw herself into Fiona's arms, and they hugged tight.

"Oh, my goodness. Oh, my goodness," Becky cried out. "We're engaged. We're engaged!"

She was trying to keep her voice down, but, at the same time, she was so ecstatic that it was almost impossible to be quiet. Fiona caught her up into her arms and hugged her again. They moved inside the nurses' station and closed the door, so they wouldn't wake anybody, and Fiona immediately demanded details.

Becky chuckled and said, "We haven't set a date. We don't know anything, except look," and she squealed again. On that note, Fiona couldn't leave right away. She was too hyped, and so was Becky. So Fiona made tea for both of them, but hers was to help her to sleep. They sat and discussed the dinner and the proposal and how special it was. It was obvious that Becky was completely over the moon.

Finally, Fiona gave her friend an extra hug and said, "Now I'm gone. I'll be back in five hours to do my regular shift."

"Go, go, go," Becky said. "And I owe you one big-time."

Fiona waved it off and headed home to her rooms. She was absolutely overjoyed for Becky. She and her beau had been going out for years. They had often talked about marriage but had never come to that sticking point, but now it was almost too good to be true. He worked in town, and Becky worked here, so they had options where they wanted to live, but chances were she would live in town. She would probably not want to do night shifts either if she's newly married.

But that was for Becky and her fiancé to work out. Fiona was thrilled for both of them. She quickly changed into her pajamas, brushed her teeth and crawled into bed. Even though she'd had that last bit of excitement, she fell asleep with a smile on her face. And also with a little pang of loneliness in her heart.

SEVERAL DAYS LATER Finn finally had a few hours to himself and wasn't exhausted enough that he just wanted to lie in bed and cry. It had taken a long time to get here—more than six weeks now—but the last two nights he hadn't woken up in pain, and that had been the best thing ever.

The difference that a good night's sleep made had been astronomical, and, with that, today had been that much easier. He'd had several meetings with his therapist over some of the work that Finn had been doing and whether it was working or not. His medical team members were all really delighted with his progress, whereas Finn couldn't see it except that he was sleeping better now, and he wasn't dealing with as much pain.

Now he had an hour before dinner, and, if he didn't

want to go early to avoid the rush, for the first time in a long time, he wondered what to do with that spare time.

His gaze landed on the sketchbooks to his side. When Fiona had asked him about it earlier, he hadn't known what to say. He hadn't even opened the sketchpad since they'd been purchased and gifted to him.

How terrible was that?

His instant reaction had been guilt and a need to brush it off and to not disclose that he had yet to do anything.

Fear was one of those terrible things that just sat there and ate away at your soul, even for the little things. He remembered being in school and having to do presentations in front of the class, and he couldn't sleep for days as they got closer and closer to the event. He stood up there and stammered, his face turning red, and he'd looked like a fool. It was probably way more embarrassing for everybody else than for him. He was in so much shock that he never did get half of his presentations out. He had the worst stage fright and panic attacks in the world, but he'd grown out of it eventually.

Except when Fiona had questioned him about his art, he'd been back in school again, and the teacher had picked him to answer a question he didn't have an answer for. Such a weird sense of being an adolescent again.

He got up and, using his crutches, brought the sketchbooks and the pencils over to his bed. He tried with his knees up. One knee up. He propped the other one up to use it as a bit of a table. No matter what he did though, it wasn't working. Frustrated, he finally grabbed one of the pillows and put that underneath his sketch pad, and that worked.

He opened to the first page and got out one of his favorite pencils. He'd always preferred a 2B. It wasn't everybody's favorite, but it was his. They were nicely sharpened, but he didn't know quite what to draw. He sat here aimlessly, letting his fingers hold the pencil for a bit, getting used to the feel of it in his hands. And then, closing his eyes, he smiled and let his fingers do their thing. He didn't know how long he sketched—at least ten to fifteen minutes.

He reached for a bottle of water, had a sip and went back to it. Finally, he could see the shape, the turn of the nose, the glint in the eyes. He chuckled. It's not what he had expected to be sketching right now. And certainly it was a rough piece, but at least it was something. He kept working away for another good half hour, and finally, his arms got a little bit on the sore side. He dropped his pencil and shook his hand out.

Needing to move, he got up and hobbled on crutches around the room. He always had to remember to get up and to move, even just a quick turn around the room and several deep breaths in order to keep his muscles fluid. He didn't know how office workers did it. Sitting at a computer all day had to be brutal. Finally, he sat back down again and looked at the sketch. As he studied the face in front of him, he had to admit it wasn't half-bad. It wasn't great. But as a first attempt in ... what? Ten years? It wasn't bad at all.

"So there you are," Dani said, walking in. He held the sketchbook against his chest. She smiled and said, "I'm glad to see you using those."

He studied her face, but, as always, Dani was sheer, wholehearted warmth and a lovely personality. "How could I not?" he asked. "Most of the time I'm so tired. I haven't had any energy to even think about it."

"May I see what you're working on?"

He winced. "You've seen my good pictures," he warned.

"This is nothing like that."

"I've seen some pretty awful sketches that you started out with and tossed, and I've seen some absolutely fantastic pieces you hated that you ripped into shreds," she said with a grin. "And I know you haven't done this for years, so I don't really expect it to be very good. I'm just curious to see what you would choose to draw."

At that, he laughed. "I'm not sure I should be drawing this," he said. "The fact of the matter is, I didn't expect to. But, when I put pencil to paper, that's what came up."

"Tell me more," she said, hitching a hip to rest on his bed. "That sounds like something even better."

He handed it to her. She studied his face for a long moment and then turned to look at the image. Her eyes widened as he watched, and a smile immediately lit up her face. "Wow," she said. "I understand how hard you are on yourself, so I expected you to say it's not very good, but you certainly caught the essence of her."

"That's what I was thinking," he said. "I don't know if it's a picture I want to keep working on or not," he said, "but there's just that light, that little bit that makes Fiona caught right there," he said. "I don't even know how."

"Oh, I do," Dani said lightly, still studying the paper. "You have exceptional talent. I've told you that for years. This is unbelievably good."

"I just forgot everything around me," he said. "There's such a sense of satisfaction when taking something in your mind and putting it on paper."

"Absolutely," she said. "This is fantastic." She handed it back to him. "And you have no idea how happy you've made me to see you sketching again."

"You were behind the sketchbooks anyway," he said. "I

figured that I should do something with them. Otherwise, you'd consider it a waste of money."

"Not really," she said. "I figured that, when you were ready, you'd get there." She tilted her head toward the sketchbook. "And that just proves I was right."

"Ouch," he said with a laugh. "Don't tell her I did this, please."

"No, I won't," she said. "That's personal."

He nodded. "Very."

She smiled and said, "Why don't you start drawing the things that really bug you too? You used to do that way back whenever situations bothered you. You put them down on paper, and sometimes you even ripped them up until you could deal with them."

He looked at her thoughtfully. "I'd forgotten all about that."

"Yeah, remember that scar you had? You kept drawing all these faces, all these self-portraits with the scar, every new one making it bigger and badder and meaner and uglier, as if by putting all that poison from your mind onto the paper, you could dispel some of it. As I recall, it worked too." She hopped off his bed and asked, "Are you coming in for dinner?"

He nodded slowly. "I am. Are you going yourself or are you heading to your house?"

"My dad's finally home. He's been traveling around but is back now."

"The major?" He said, "I have yet to see him."

She spun around and stared at him. "What? Come on then," she said. "Let's go."

Laughing, he hopped up, grabbed his slipper and his crutches, and together they walked to the cafeteria. "Are you sure?" he asked. "He'll probably be surrounded by people."

"My dad is always surrounded by people," she said, sending Finn a sideways look. "He's a very different person than before."

"So I've heard," he said. "It's one of the reasons I really want to see him. I remember what he was like. I also remember how difficult it was to live with him and how sad you always were."

She smiled. "I was. But it's amazing how much he's changed and how much I've changed."

"Well, you have Aaron," Finn said teasingly. "Has your dad got a partner?"

"No, he doesn't, but he does like to tease all the women."

"That's a side I didn't see before either." They got to the double-wide cafeteria doors to hear a cheerful, happy crowd at the food line, but instead, she led him to the deck outside. "You okay to sit out here?"

"Of course," he said. "Why not? It's beautiful out."

She marched him to a large table and said, "Grab a spot where you can get in and out easily, and we'll sit here and wait till the rush arrives. When the crowd goes down, then we can go get some food."

He liked that idea. He propped his crutches beside him and waited until, all of a sudden, a whole group of men came over, and one of them slammed a tray down right beside Finn, making him start.

"Finn?" a loud voice roared.

He looked up in shock. Well, it was the major all right. But not the major who Finn knew. He stood up shakily. "Oh my," he said, staring at the burly man with a huge grin on his face. "Is this really possible? I don't think I ever remember you with a smile before," he joked.

Almost immediately the major's smile fell away. He looked at Dani, back at Finn, nodded and said, "And those days are firmly behind me. Now I smile all the time and I don't even have to try." He reached out and swept Finn into a great big bear hug. Finn hugged him back because he understood those crappy circumstances.

When he finally released him, the major looked at him and shook his head. "Wow. I'm sad to say it, but I'm also very glad that you're here. It's really good to see you, son."

Chapter 9

FIONA WATCHED THE large party at the table just ahead and to the side of her. They all looked to be having so much fun, though a part of her was infinitely jealous, and yet, also very happy for Finn. He seemed to get along with a lot of people very easily. Elliot was even there. Then again, she'd seen the two of them together a lot. And that was good. It was right. Finn needed a buddy. His life was tough enough without that camaraderie those two had. She wondered if she was one of many or if she was special in Finn's mind. From their discussions, it seemed she was special, but …

She'd been taken in before. But Finn wasn't the kind to be deceitful. Her own insecurities led her down that pathway. She didn't have a problem with any of his physical—as he would say—abnormalities. As a nurse, she'd seen so much in her life, and yet, she saw the human courage, that ability to get back up even when you're knocked down, that always amazed her and made her look at people in admiration. Finn more than most. But maybe that's because she had a soft spot for him.

Anna booted her gently under the table. "What are you thinking?"

Fiona pulled herself back to her dinner table and smiled at her friend. "Nothing much," she said smoothly.

But Anna wasn't having any of it. She twisted around so she could see where Fiona had been looking. "Dani looks to be having a fun time tonight. The major is always the life of the party."

Fiona nodded. "I think the major knows Finn."

"Well, that would explain it," Anna said. "How come you're not over there?"

"Why would I be?" Fiona asked.

"Because you and Finn have a thing," Anna said with a great big smile. "Everybody knows it."

"Everybody but me, apparently." She gave a half laugh. "That's not fair. *Something* is between us," she said, "but it's too early to tell just what that is."

"No, that's not quite true," Anna said. "You already know you're in that lovely stage of *Does he, or doesn't he?*" At that, she grinned.

Fiona let out a peal of laughter. She knew she'd been a little too loud when both Dani and Finn turned to look at her. She immediately quieted her voice and gasped, "Oh, my goodness, is it that bad?"

"Absolutely, it is," Anna said. "Just think about it. You mope around all the time when he's not available, and, when you're with him, you light up. He's the first person you want to tell something about your day."

Fiona sat back slightly and nodded. "I hadn't really considered these points. Or that I'm so obvious," she admitted. "I mean, I like him as a person. I like him as a friend. We had a date," she added with a smile, "and I love spending time with him ..."

"And you want him as more than a friend," Anna said with a nod. "And it doesn't matter how much I tell you that it's there, you still won't believe me unless he says something."

"Exactly, and, of course, I'm a little bit distrustful of the patient-nurse relationship," she said, drawing that out to make it more humorous. "And he does have a self-image issue compounding that."

"I think that's one of the biggest things that we find here," Anna said. "Men come in, beaten up by life, and they were all big healthy strapping men beforehand, and who they are now is a completely different person, at least on the outside. Most of the time they have to find that inner strength to fall in love with themselves all over again, as the best person they can be right now."

"And Finn's not there yet," she said.

"The colostomy?"

Fiona nodded. "That's part of it. I think the missing leg is another part but minor. He seems to think the colostomy is very unsexy."

"So, as the girl who potentially could end up sharing his bed, how do you find it?" Only simple curiosity could be heard in Anna's voice.

And, for that reason alone, Fiona answered her. "I couldn't care less," she said. "He's missing a big chunk of muscle from his back and a couple ribs too, but that doesn't make me feel any differently. He's missing his lower right leg. That doesn't make me feel any differently. I'm a nurse," she said with a shrug. "I've seen it all, and I'm not looking for physical perfection. I'm looking for inner strength."

"And we have heard from multiple people with colostomies how they feel about it. You know Sarah here has one, right?"

Fiona nodded. "Yes, I do, and she's adapted well to it by now."

"I think she feels her surgery was a gift, in a way. She's pain-free. She's happy. She's married, and her husband obviously doesn't have a problem with it. You and I both know the world doesn't want to contemplate bodily functions, let alone talk about them, but they're an essential part of healthy living. When bodily functions mess up, it has a drastic effect on us. Honestly, Finn should be grateful. He'd be dead without that colostomy."

"It's so different in our medical world. We talk about this freely. And he is alive today because he had that colostomy. And telling him that is *so* not gonna be helpful," Fiona said with a chuckle. "Although I've said more or less the same thing to him."

Anna nodded. "Again, back to that 'have to work it out themselves' issue."

"Dani bought him some sketchbooks and pencils," Fiona said. "I hope he's started drawing something but no clue. It might take him time."

"And, of course, you're not gonna pry."

"Of course not," she said. "And I'm not even sure that he *is* sketching. It's just that the sketchbooks used to always be off to the side, but he's moved them closer. Maybe I'm wrong. Maybe I'm just hoping he's started drawing again."

"It'd be good for him," Anna said. "Everybody needs an outlet here."

"Right," she said, "it's even more important here."

"I would just keep on the way you're going," Anna said. "He'll get the message."

"Oh, I think he has the message," Fiona said, her lips twitching. "But it takes time, you know."

"Not around here, it doesn't. Not when we all know too well about the fragility of life," Anna said with a smirk. "And not with you. There's no need for time. You're so picky, and yet, you already know you care about Finn. You're a wise woman, probably ready to settle down, yes? You're in your early thirties, and what is he, early to mid-thirties? It's the perfect time for two people, wise to the world, to make better choices now. And, if you want to be together, why would you waste any more moments being apart?" At that, Anna stood, grabbed her tray and said, "I'll see you later."

Fiona nodded. She sat here nursing her cup of coffee as she leaned back and relaxed. It was dinnertime and her evening off. The sun was still high in the sky, creating yet another gorgeous Texas day. It seemed like this was God's country. She looked at the rolling hills, the animals, and caught sight of Stan coming up the stairs. She watched the veterinarian as he came up the far side. He looked more tired than usual. She lifted a hand in greeting, catching his eye.

He smiled and walked over.

"Long day?" she asked.

He nodded. "Long, stressful and sad. I'm gonna grab some food. Do you mind if I join you?"

"Please do," she said. She waited for him to return, feeling better just having somebody here at her table to talk to. She was surrounded by people but had felt very alone for a moment, and there was no need for it because Anna had just left.

It was because of the twenty feet that separated her from Finn. And yet, it wasn't twenty feet—it was miles. Miles of emotional expanse. She didn't know where they were going—*if* they were going anywhere—but she hoped so. She was wondering how long it would take for her to get over her doubts about whether Finn's feelings for her were real or not. She also had to avoid judging him based on her ex's behavior.

She'd been distant with patients, cordial, of course, but never too friendly. Until now. She'd had no choice with him as something between them just clicked. And this time, it was *her* heart that would likely get hurt.

Just then Stan sat down across from her with a plate of roast beef, mashed potatoes, and Yorkshire pudding.

She looked at it and smiled. "I saw all that food, but I just wanted a salad tonight."

"I'm tired and worn out. I have to go back down and check on a very difficult case from this afternoon," he said. "I need the energy." He forked up his first bite of roast beef and sat back as he chewed, a picture of sheer bliss on his face.

She chuckled. "Well, it's nice to know that you're enjoying it."

"I get that, in a lot of medical institutions, the food is one of the biggest complaints. Here, Dani runs a really great cafeteria. And we never ever get shafted on the quality of the food."

"I don't think Dennis would allow it," she said, smiling. "Just think about it. This kitchen's his domain."

"And yet, other chefs are in the back, and he's more the face of the kitchen," Stan muttered around a mouthful of food.

"Exactly," she said.

Just then Dennis appeared at her side. "Hey, did I hear my name called?" He topped off her coffee.

She chuckled. "You did but all good things," she said, "always all good things."

He stopped and watched as Stan had another bite and then asked, "How is it?"

Stan couldn't even answer. He just picked up his free

hand and pinched his thumb and forefinger together in a circle to say, *A-okay.*

Dennis nodded with satisfaction and disappeared again.

"He doesn't need to be collecting dishes, but he's always out here," she said, "always filling up waters and coffees and helping the patients. Just generally being a nice guy."

"And that's what he is," Stan said, "just a generally nice guy. We need more like him in this world."

"True enough," she said. "And it's always hard to know what's going on inside a person versus outside too."

"You're talking about Finn?"

She frowned and then let her irritation slide away. "Yes." She caught the twinkle in Stan's gaze. "Does everybody know?"

"Sure. Why not?" he said. "We do love to see people matched up happily."

"Well, it's too early to be that," she said.

"Nope, not at all," he said. "But you're going through that really interesting kinda-sorta-boyfriend-girlfriend-but-not-quite-there-yet stage," he said. "I find that fascinating. It's like when two animals come together but walk away only to return as if they have absolutely no choice—like magnets. That's you and Finn. I've seen it many times before, and I hope to see it many times again," he said. "And here, with you two, it's definitely obvious. You guys have that electrical surge around you when you come together."

"And it's not just physical?" she murmured in a low tone.

All seriousness fell from Stan's gaze, and he shook his head slowly. "I can see you're feeling very insecure, and, of course, the only way to feel any better about that," he said, "is to talk to him and see if you can work through some of this. And, I imagine, you feel like it's way too early for that."

She gave him a luminous smile and said, "Very wise of you."

"I didn't earn my gray hairs for nothing," he said with a smile.

"So, what's this terrible case downstairs?"

"I've got a female lab that was hit by a vehicle," he said, "and she was pregnant. I had to do a C-section right off the bat because the babies were almost full-term. Then more surgery to try to save her life. Now, of course, we're hand-feeding the pups while we see if the mom can survive and if she'll produce any milk. And also keeping the puppies close to her so that they know who Mom is."

Fiona's heart broke at the thought. "Oh my," she said. "May I come down and see them?"

"Absolutely," he said. "As soon as I finish eating, I have to check on them. I'll be staying close by all night. She's touch-and-go at the moment."

"In which case, you're gonna have puppies to bottle-feed and often," she said.

"Five of them," he said with a smile. "Five wiggly small black newborns that deserve a chance at life."

"Exactly." Then she compulsively said, "If you need somebody to help bottle-feed …"

"Accepted," he said instantly. At the suddenness of his response, she looked at him and said, "Did you set me up?"

He gave her a bland smile and said, "I always knew that you were a warm, caring, loving person who would do whatever was needed to help. Besides, you won't be alone, and it would be every two hours."

The thought of every two hours made her cringe. It was hard to get a good night's sleep when it was interrupted so often.

He said, "If we have enough people to handle every four hours, you'd only have to get up once in the night."

She smiled at that. "Will you get any sleep?"

"Depends on how many volunteers I get," he said craftily. "And the mom is also a major part of my concern because life will be so much easier on those pups if Mom survives too."

"I can't imagine," she said. She settled back, sipped her second cup of coffee and waited until he was done.

As soon as he was, he hopped to his feet and said, "Ready?"

She nodded and quickly grabbed his and her trays, carried them to Dennis, who met her halfway across the room to take them from her. Then Stan came over and said, "Come on. Let's go." He didn't slow his pace. She gave a wave to Finn as she walked past, but she raced to keep up with Stan.

Dani noticed and called out, "Stan, any update?"

"Five pups. Mom's in tough condition." And then he was gone.

Fiona could hear Dani giving an explanation to her dinner companions, obviously having heard the news earlier.

Then Fiona got really busy as she walked into the back of the vet clinic and was immediately handed a tiny black wiggly-worm pup that wasn't any bigger than her hand and a minuscule dropper and was asked to start feeding. And with now two of these guys tucked up against her, she fed them both with eyedroppers, then she closed her eyes and cuddled them close.

"DO YOU THINK Stan would mind if I go down?" Finn asked Dani in a low voice.

She smiled, leaned over and whispered, "He's probably dying to get volunteers if it's puppy-feeding time. Over the years, I've helped many, many times," she admitted. "Sometimes we have kittens, sometimes puppies, sometimes ducklings. He takes in anything that needs help, and, in this case, the mother is badly in need of help." She motioned downstairs. "Go if you want to."

He nodded and shifted his chair back.

She leaned closer and whispered, "By the way, are you going for Fiona or for the puppies?"

His lips twitched. "Maybe both?"

Her laughter rang out across the table. "I'm delighted to hear that," she said. "Go have fun." She turned back to her father.

Finn realized the discussion at the table didn't include him now and struggled to his feet with his crutches and then made his way downstairs, wondering if he could seriously do anything to help Stan or Fiona or the mother dog or if he would be in the way. The stairs were a challenge, so he took the elevator and dropped down to the veterinarian clinic. When he made his way in through the double doors, he stopped, stunned to see Fiona curled up in a corner with two of the tiniest black puppies possible in her arms, sleeping. Eyedroppers were beside her.

He turned to one of the vet assistants and said, "I heard helping hands were needed."

The woman—her uniform name tag read Babette—looked up at him and smiled. "I think all five puppies are okay for the moment, but, if you want to come and love one," she said, "we're more than happy to have that happen.

Then we're gonna tuck them back up against Mom."

He glanced over to see Fiona's eyes open, staring at him, the depth of her gaze full of love and emotion from seeing and holding these puppies.

He accepted the tiny bundle as soon as he was seated beside her. He cuddled it close and whispered to it constantly. "It's okay, little one. It's been a rough beginning, but you'll make it." The little guy didn't even murmur. He just curled up as much as he could, seeking warmth, and slept. Finn glanced at the puppies nestled high on Fiona's bosom and smiled. "Your two look very happy."

"They're adorable," she said in the softest of voices. "New life like this, it's so precious."

"I can't argue with that," he said. "They've had a rough time of it, but, with any luck, they'll be fine."

"I'm hoping so," she said, reaching up to gently stroke one, then the other. "They don't take in very much food at a time, so they have to be fed on a regular basis."

"Are you gonna get up and come down later and feed them?"

"I think I will," she said. "It depends on how many volunteers they need. I'll come back before bed anyway and do one more round and then see."

"Do all five have to be done at once, or can they be done in rounds?"

Babette answered, "Two of us can handle five babies," she said. "They don't take very long to feed. So, if need be, I can do it myself."

"And Stan said he was gonna stick around close because of Mom?" Fiona said.

Babette nodded. "Mom's really struggling. She may have to go back into surgery, but we're gonna do our best to not have to."

Just then Stan came back out, looked at the puppies and smiled. "That's what they need, warmth, love, food, and as much time as they can have."

"How is she?"

"She's holding," he said. "I'm cautiously hopeful. Depends if she can make it through tonight."

"Right," Fiona said. She looked over at the little guy in Finn's arms. "This guy seems quite content too."

Finn stared down at the little one. He was curled up in the crook of Finn's arm, high on his chest. It wasn't the most comfortable position for him, but he couldn't have cared less while gently stroking the velvety-soft ears, looking at the tiny little face. "Hard to believe these guys are gonna be labs."

"They're just all wrinkled-up pieces of love at the moment," Stan said. "If you guys want to give them back to Babette, I'll put them in with Mom."

"Is it safe to leave her with them?"

"In this case, yes, and Babette will sit in there and will do her work beside Mom and babies. Babette can keep an eye on Mom. These little guys won't really move much right now, and the closer they are to Mom, the better."

Babette came out so they could hand off the puppies to her. Finn looked at the huge female black lab, tubes coming and going from her, obvious stitches showing on her shaven belly, and even a cast on a back leg. She looked to be in seriously rough shape, but it was almost like something about her softened when the puppies were tucked up against her. He imagined that, if she was aware in any way, she'd consider this part of the reward for trying to survive. He looked at Babette. "Do we know anything about what happened?"

"No," she said. "Somebody saw her get hit by a vehicle. They picked her up, put her in the truck bed and brought her in. The fact that we got her as soon as we did is the good news, but we haven't located an owner yet."

"If there is one," Fiona said.

"Too often there isn't, or, if there is, they don't want to admit it, in case they get stuck with the vet bill."

"And do you run a lot of charity work through here?" Finn asked.

"We do, indeed, and Dani funnels a lot of financial assistance to us as well," Babette said. "It's the only way to help those who don't have anybody to help them."

As soon as he handed his pup off, Finn felt bereft.

Fiona gave a heavy sigh. "I didn't want to hand them over," she confessed as soon as Babette disappeared with her two.

"I know," he said, "I was just thinking that. Like there's a hole in my heart already."

She looked up and smiled. "Sad, isn't it?"

"I think it's good," he said in all seriousness. "Think about it. Somebody needs to love these little guys."

"They all deserve love. We all do," she said firmly. She moved toward the door. "Are you coming, or are you staying here?"

"I'm coming," he said. With his crutches once again under his arms, he followed her down the hallway. She stopped, looked outside and said, "I don't know where you're going, but I'm gonna go outside and visit with Lovely and Appie. They're right there at the fence again."

"Perfect idea," he said. His mind buzzed with the picture that he'd seen of Fiona holding the babies. Part of him itched to return to his room and sketch her in that pose, but drawing a picture of her versus spending time with her? Well, there was really no contest. Outside with the animals, he laughed at Lovely's antics as she danced with joy at seeing them. As soon as they were close, she came over and shoved her face through the rails. Appie, not to be outdone, came too.

"We don't have any treats," he said.

"No, but we have long grass." She bent and snapped off several big clumps and handed it to the critters. Both of them immediately accepted their treat with joy. She smiled, her arms crossed on top of the railing and said, "It's so beautiful to see them here."

"Having the animal interaction," he said, "makes this a very special place."

"Doesn't it? Now you know why I am so happy to work here."

"And here I thought it was because of the patients," he teased.

She laughed. "Most patients, yes. Some patients are special, and some are special in other ways," she said, her tone turning wry. "But, on the whole, we've been very blessed. Dani has had good luck in bringing in people who are at the right stage of life to take advantage of what we have to offer."

"I guess that's the trick, isn't it? If you're not ready, it doesn't matter what you are offered here because you don't accept it." He was thinking about how long it had taken him to ask Dani for a bed, how it had taken Elliot to come to that path ahead of Finn to show him the way and why that was surprising because he always used to be a bit of a trendsetter. In this case, it seemed like he was behind the curve.

And then he realized it wasn't that he was behind the

curve—he was literally just behind. Insecure, worried about his future, having trouble dealing with progress. He worried about his progress—or lack of it. He couldn't do a whole lot back then about moving forward faster, but he was grateful that Elliot had convinced him to come because Finn couldn't imagine being anywhere else now.

"Now that you've been here for as long as you have," she said, "how are you?"

"Much, much better," he said. "The night cramps have eased, and that's made it much easier to sleep, which makes the days much nicer too."

"Of course," she said, "and physiotherapy will continue to help you to improve."

"I think the thing about physio here is everything seems so much worse before it ever gets better. So I'm definitely not at the better stage yet," he admitted. "But I'm in a nice place to be as I no longer feel worse every day."

On that note, there was an awkward silence as they both stood here, elbow to elbow, but not quite touching as they stared out at the landscape around them.

"Dani's built something very special," he said, almost as if filling the gap of silence.

"She has."

"Do you think you'll stay here forever?"

"Not forever," she said with a smile. "I'd like to have a family one day. But I'm certainly here until my life changes."

"Sometimes you have to move in order to make a change," he murmured.

"That's very true," she said. "And, if that's the case, I'm in no hurry. There's lots for me to learn and to do, and to feel rewarded by my work here, and by the people I meet. I don't have to be always doing something or feeling like I'm appreciated, but it's lovely to be a part of a big machine like this that can still do so much good for everyone."

"Very true."

"What about you?" she asked. "What are your plans?"

"I'm not exactly sure I have any," he said. "I'm still here for at least another two months—I presume anyway. I haven't had an update from my medical team, but I don't really have any plans afterward. I was hoping that maybe, when I came here, I would find enlightenment in some way or form that would lead me down the right path for me now, after the navy," he said with a mocking tone. "And so far it hasn't happened."

"Give it time," she said with a smile. "You never know what might happen while you're here."

"Yeah?" he said, looking at her. "Like what?"

She just gave him a mysterious smile that hit him right in the heart and said, "Maybe wait and see."

Chapter 10

FIONA HAD NO real reason for leading him on except that she truly believed in the power of healing. When people healed their physical bodies, they also helped to heal their emotional and mental bodies—and vice versa—and that led to making decisions and seeing clarity in their lives. She had no doubt Finn would sort himself out, just like every other person she'd met here. And she'd met hundreds by now. It was amazing as she looked back along the years of all the patients who had come through Hathaway House's doors and just how well so many had done here.

Days later, when she walked into his room to see him quickly closing his sketchbook and putting it beside him, she realized he truly was back at his artwork. She smiled brightly at him and said, "Do those pencils work well for you?"

"They do," he said noncommittally.

She had to do a full checkup on him. By the time she had written down her notes, she said, "I didn't get to see you yesterday," she murmured.

"No," he said, "my therapy has switched again, and I have to admit to it being pretty rough." But there was no strain in his voice, and he was still as friendly as ever.

She motioned at his belly. "Any problems with the colostomy?"

"Only that it exists," he said, but a new teasing tone was

in his voice, as if he might be finally coming to terms with it.

"At least you only have one," she said. "It could be worse. You could have two."

"And I've only just recently come to understand that," he said. "Who knew you could have two bags, not just one?"

She chuckled. "I'll still get you a pink polka-dot one."

"*Yuck.*" He shook his head. "Unless there's something macho male out there that'll help, don't bother," he said with a smile.

"As more and more people end up with this problem," she said, "someone will get creative and will make all kinds of designs."

"Right, and I guess I'll never get rid of this, will I?"

"They do these temporarily for some patients, while other areas of the body heal or have to be reconstructed. I'm not sure what the situation is in your case, but I suspect this is permanent."

"My surgeon said it was permanent, but I keep hoping ..."

"You can hope," she said, "but stay within the realm of reality."

"Right," he said, "and that means this is permanent."

She studied his face for a long moment, but he didn't appear to be anywhere near as down and depressed about it. "Sounds like you may be getting used to the fact that it exists."

"Well, I'm not screaming and depressed and crying about it, if that's what you mean," he said briskly. "And, as I improve in other areas, it is easier to look at something like that and realize that I've done everything I can and that I can't improve it anymore, so I'll have to live with it."

"Good," she said. "Speaking of which, I understand the

prosthetic fitting is happening in the next week."

"I hope so," he said. "I'll finally see how this latest surgery did."

"Well, here's to hoping," she said. "I know sometimes it takes a couple attempts, but it would make such a huge difference in your mobility."

"It always did," he said. "Even though my stump swelled up, I didn't want to let go of it."

She motioned to the sketchbook. "How's the drawing going?" At that, she could feel him withdrawing again.

He shrugged and said, "As ugly as I expected it to be."

She smiled, picked up her tablet and said, "You'll just get better," she said, "like with everything else."

And she walked out. There was something very secretive about him and his sketchbook, as if he didn't want her to see it. Having seen the drawing he'd done in Dani's office, Fiona couldn't imagine it being very ugly. But, if he was using his drawing as a therapy that could rid him of some of his depression, then maybe he wasn't drawing pretty pictures either. He needed time alone to do his thing.

As she walked down the hallway, Dani walked toward her. "How are you doing?"

"I'm fine," she said, "but you look serious."

"The one patient we had who gave you some issues," she said, "do you remember him—Ziegler? He sent a letter and a lawyer's note."

Fiona froze. "A lawyer's note?"

"He's attempting to sue us for our handling of the situation."

Her stomach sank. "He's the one who got a little too infatuated with me. I didn't know how to get out of it," she said. She reached up a hand, rubbed her forehead and said,

"What was I supposed to do?"

"Our lawyers will handle it," Dani said gently. "I just wanted to let you know that this was in progress."

"And that's likely to stop me from ever being friendly with anyone again," she cried out. "What a horrible turn of events."

"No," Dani said firmly. "Some people—like Finn—need it."

"The trouble with Finn," she said, her voice harsher than she wanted it to be, "is I don't want him to see me in that light. I really care about him." Lowering her voice, she said, "Finn is not like Ziegler at all. I didn't see him as anything other than a patient. But Finn's different."

"And Finn would handle the situation differently. Ziegler was dealing with more than rejection, and my lawyers will make that very clear. He received the best treatment he could possibly get here, and he wanted a whole lot more than he got. That's the end of it."

She said it so firmly that Fiona wanted to believe her. To a certain extent she did, but it was depressing, nonetheless. "Well, I hope he doesn't cause any more trouble, and that can be the end of it," she said slowly. "Has it ever happened before?"

Dani shook her head. "No, it's the first case."

"But it does set a precedent for all of us now to look at our relationships with the patients and worry that we'll be taken in the wrong way."

"One in hundreds," Dani said. "Really, that's about to be expected. We can't expect to walk away from something like that scot-free. We would love it if it would never happen, but you know what the world's like."

"I know," Fiona said, "but I can't tell you how much I

regret that happening in the first place."

"And we all know that," Dani said. "Anyway, carry on with your rounds. I've got to go back to the office."

Fiona stood in the hallway and watched as Dani headed to the reception area. Suddenly feeling more depressed and bereft, she walked to the front to see if Racer was there. Surprise, surprise, he was. His little tail wagged like crazy when he saw her.

She picked up his basket, petting him with her free hand, and asked, "How do you feel about coming to visit with me?" She had a lot of notes to enter, and having him around would be a help. She carried him back and placed him on the desk beside her. He just lay here, his huge eyes blinking at her as she gently stroked his ears. She spent a few minutes cuddling him before working on her notes.

When she looked up, Dani sneaked in, taking one look at Racer and snagging him for herself. "Another patient needs him." And she disappeared.

Fiona chuckled. "It was definitely a huge plus with him being here."

On that note, a grumbling *meow* came from the doorway, and she looked around to see the latest addition to the therapy animals—the three-legged cat, a big Maine coon that had his ways fixed, sat and stared at her. It reminded her of the puppies. Fiona had been at the clinic several days in a row, helping out, but hadn't been needed thereafter. She'd sent a message to Stan asking for an update. She didn't expect to hear anytime soon, but she should probably make it there on her lunch hour and see if she could visit with them.

Finally, she was done with the paperwork, and it was time to do another round again. She started at the other end so she would end up at Finn's. By the time she was done, a couple patients taking longer than normal, she was tired and ready to be done with her day. When she finally entered Finn's room, he had his sketchbook open across his lap, and he'd nodded off. She hesitated at the doorway. If he didn't want her to see his sketchbooks, then she didn't want to look, but she needed to wake him up.

Keeping her eyes averted, she walked up to him, gently picked up his arm and took his blood pressure. He woke up with a jerk and stared at her, blinking owlishly. She smiled at him. "Just rounds."

He nodded, closed the sketchbook and shifted. "I didn't realize I was so tired."

"Apparently," she said. "Are you sure you're not doing too much?"

"I probably am," he admitted. "But, once you start seeing those first signs of progress, you just want to get to the end as fast as you can."

"This is definitely a case where the turtle wins the race," she warned.

"And you know you can tell me that until you're blue in the face, and it still won't make a difference as to how I feel."

She smiled gently at him. "You and everybody else in this place."

He chuckled and said, "I'm also very hungry. Is it almost dinnertime?"

"Almost," she said. "I'm off now."

"Will you have dinner with me?" he asked in a rush.

She looked at him, smiled and said, "Sure. I'll go home, get changed and what? Meet you in the dining room?"

He nodded. "If we're early, we can always have coffee first."

She checked her watch and said, "How about we meet in forty-five minutes?"

"Good, and, if I start now, I might make it on time," he joked.

She grinned and turned and walked away, but her footsteps were lighter. She wasn't exactly sure what she'd caught sight of in his sketch, and she didn't really want to analyze it because he'd closed it as soon as he'd been aware of it, but it had been the start of a woman's face. She just didn't know what woman. Fiona suspected Dani, but who knew? Fiona hoped he didn't have any intentions for Dani because Dani's heart was definitely locked with Aaron's. Those two were a perfect match.

But Finn and Dani went way back, so who knew just how deep the heart went? And maybe they were just good friends. Still, it bothered Fiona. It bothered her a lot. She couldn't stop thinking of anything else when she showered and got dressed in another summer dress. As she headed out from her place to meet him in the dining room, she tried to let it go, but, as she walked up, Finn already was seated with Dani at his side. Dani looked at Fiona, smiled, then leaned over, kissed Finn on the cheek, and got up and left. At that way-too-friendly gesture, Fiona's heart sank.

"YOU LOOK ABSOLUTELY stunning," Finn said in admiration. "That dress with the blues and greens flowing around you is gorgeous."

"Thank you," she said with a smile. "I didn't realize you and Dani were that close."

"Not that close," he said. "But we've been friends for

decades. Or at least it seems like that. I don't want to count too close to see if it really is that long or not."

"Maybe two decades," she said.

"Okay, but it feels longer," he said with a smile. "And I know how happy she is with Aaron."

"She is, indeed," Fiona said, taking a seat beside him. "Have you checked out what's on the menu tonight?"

"Greek," he said. "These theme nights are absolutely to die for."

"Dani has always done a great job with the food budget here," she said. "And Dennis keeps us all coming back for more."

"A happy tummy is a happy system," he said. "Do you want to sit for a bit, or do you want to eat first?"

"You were the one who was starving earlier."

"I am, that's why I'm having the coffee, to try and take that sting back a bit."

"Then we'll sit and wait until you finish your coffee," she said. "I'm in no rush." She looked over at the sideboard and said, "Actually, there's fresh juice. Do you want one?"

"SURE," HE SAID. He watched as she walked over to get water first. The dress flowed freely around her, wrapping her curves and showing off her long legs. He wondered at her questions about his relationship with Dani and realized Fiona had probably seen the kiss Dani had given him. But there'd been a reason for that. Dani was cheering him on in every aspect of his life. She always had. Matter of fact, she was one of the best cheerleaders he'd ever met. But he didn't want Fiona to get the wrong idea.

At the same time, Dani had also explained about the problem with the one patient, and he realized just how much of an issue him liking Fiona might be for her. To think that a pending lawsuit would add to her sense of guilt, that bothered him. It was just more crap for her and Dani to deal with that wasn't necessary. When she returned with two glasses of water and then disappeared again, he watched, loving every step she took and the way the dress molded to her body.

"Dresses like that should be banned," he decided. "But I'm glad they haven't been." They were way too sultry, and she had the body for it. And with her hair braided down the center of her back like that, she was very beautiful.

When she returned with two large glasses of juice and sat down again, she looked at him, a puzzled look on her face, and asked, "What's the matter?"

He lifted both eyebrows. "The only thing that matters," he said, "is you're too beautiful to believe."

She stared at him, pleased. "Thank you, I think," she said. "But what you see is what you get."

"I wish," he muttered. He caught her sudden surprised look. He shrugged and said, "You know I care for you."

"Well, I know something is there between us," she said lightly. "It's just a matter of what that is."

"Dani told me about that lawsuit." He could see her expression dim.

"It's one of the low points in my life," she said quietly. "I would never deliberately lead anybody on, and I would never wish such emotional pain on anyone."

"And yet, I think we're all forgetting the fact that, because of that, he healed and worked harder and faster than he ever could have before. Of course, he's only thinking that the carrot he expected was pulled away by you, instead of giving the carrot to him, but the real plus here is the fact that he did so very well."

"Maybe," she said, "but I'm no carrot for anyone, and the fact that he thought I was a prize at the end of his day makes me feel quite icky."

"I didn't mean it that way," he said gently. "But knowing that you were there is what helped him to heal so much faster."

"Maybe." But her gaze turned almost inward, and he kicked himself for having mentioned it. "Just in case," he said suddenly, "I don't want you to compare the fact that I really like being around you and really enjoy spending time with you as similar to his problem."

And once again, he could feel her shuttering back and closing off. "Seriously," he said in an attempt to regain lost ground.

She nodded and said, "It's a painful topic. Let's change it. Are you ready for dinner?"

He accepted the change of conversation and nodded. And, in his wheelchair, he twisted and headed over toward the entrance line to the food. Dennis was there. As he smiled up at the other man, he asked, "Are you ever not here?"

"Sometimes," he said. "I always try to be here for dinner-time. My mama didn't raise any fools." At that, he cracked up laughing. The dinner looked so good, and, by the time Dennis had set up Finn with a nice portion of souvlaki and Greek potatoes, he was looking forward to getting back to his table and diving in. He could have seconds or thirds if he wanted to, and tonight he might.

Traveling carefully with the tray on his lap, he headed back to his table. As he turned to look around the corner to see where Fiona was, she still talked to Dennis, his face lit up even more as he spoke to Fiona, making Finn's own heart clamp down. She knew so many people here, was friendly with so many people that he sometimes felt a little out of the loop. But, then again, that's probably how she felt about the relationship between him and Dani. And how was he to explain what that longtime friendship was actually like?

He knew he wanted to continue this discussion, but he also knew it wouldn't be that easy. When he looked up the second time, she wound her way toward him, carrying her own tray. He quickly emptied his tray, much preferring to eat off the table, like a real dining room. She did the same and then moved both trays to the side. As she sat back down, she sniffed her plate and smiled. "I do love Dennis's cooking."

"Maybe you should marry him," he said, half joking.

She shot him an odd look. "That wouldn't work out so well," she said quietly. "Dennis has been here for a long time. He's a good friend."

Feeling small for his comment—when he'd intended it as a joke, but it had fallen flat—he just nodded. He had to wonder if one of the reasons they fed the patients so well here was, by feeding one appetite, it helped to keep another at bay. He was no saint, and he'd loved many women in his lifetime, but he also knew that the time for short-term relationships were long over for him. That's not who he was anymore, and it hadn't been who he was for a long time. Across from him, Fiona sat, elegant, and yet, sweet, classy and funny. There was just so much to like about her, and he felt like a grumbling teenager.

"You've stopped eating," she said lightly.

With a start, he pulled himself back to his plate, grinned

and said, "Well, that will never do. Dennis might be insulted." He dove back in.

"Have you been in the pool yet?"

He shook his head and forked up another bite. "I've been in the hot tub a couple times a week for the muscle knots, until they eased up, but I haven't had a chance to do hydrotherapy yet. I really want to."

"It's probably coming soon then," she said. "Just talk to your therapist about it."

"I keep forgetting," he said. "It just seems now that I'm a little busier how I lose track of things I want to do."

She seemed to let that slide for a moment; then she looked at him, her head cocked slightly to the side, and in a quizzical voice asked, "So much to do?"

He nodded. "I haven't really told you much," he said, "but the more of my artwork I get back into doing, the more I feel like doing, and it becomes all-consuming. I had that problem before. I could sit in front of a movie, and I'd sketch away, but, by the end of the movie, I wouldn't remember anything of what had gone on because I'd become so involved in my artwork."

"That sounds wonderful," she said. "Isn't that a good thing?"

"I'm not sure it is," he said slowly. "Sometimes it seemed like hours would go by. I hadn't thought I'd ever get back to it again, and I'm not sure I want to get back into it that intently," he said. "But it is an incredible feeling when you come back out of that fugue to realize what you've created."

"I don't have a creative bone in my body," she announced. "And so I'm incredibly envious of what you can do."

"You don't know anything I can do yet," he said, laughing.

"Not quite," she said. "Dani has a picture that you did of the horses on the back of her office door."

That stopped him for a moment. He stared at her and asked, "Really?"

She nodded. "Absolutely."

He frowned. "I don't remember doing it for her."

"Well, it's there," she said. "Whenever you get back to her office, you can take a look."

"I'll do that," he said. "So, did you like it?"

"No," she said, teasing. "I loved it. The freedom the horses personify—it's as if they came alive off the page. You could just see them moving across the wall. It was really spectacular."

He settled back with a smile at the corner of his lips. "I was wondering about going pro," he said, "but always that voice inside my head said I wasn't that good."

"You are beyond good enough," she said. "I don't know how one does something like going pro, especially in this digital age," she said, "but, if there was any way you could, wow."

"I've tried some digital art," he said, "it doesn't give me the same satisfaction as with a pencil."

"Makes sense to me," she said. "I mean, I used to love Lego blocks. Yet the computer games based on them don't appeal the same to me. Still, the younger generation, I guess they seem to take to it just fine."

He nodded. "I've always been so busy that I didn't have much time for video games."

"And it's never been something I ever wanted to do. I sit at the computer enough during the day. In the evening," she admitted, "I'd rather go for a swim."

"Speaking of which," he said, "I think when I return to my room, I'll send a couple emails to see if I can get the pool added to my options. In the evenings, it would be really lovely to go for a swim."

"And there's no reason you shouldn't," she said. "There are rules, like regarding safety, but, other than that, you should be free to use the pool as you want."

He nodded and then thought about something and slowly lowered his fork. "What about the colostomy?"

She nodded. "You're not stopped from all water sports just because you have that."

"But it might be visible," he said, almost blanching at the thought.

She gazed at him steadily. "And? Your stump will be too."

He frowned at that, thought about it, and nodded. "I guess that's what it's all about, isn't it? My body is no longer what it used to be."

"No," she said, "it's better. It's a survivor. What happened to it had knocked it down, but it didn't stay down. You got back up again, and you're still taking steps forward. That's what counts."

He smiled at her and said, "I knew there was a reason I liked you."

Chapter 11

FIONA REMEMBERED FINN'S words long after she'd gone to bed. She lay here under her blankets, wondering. It was a thought that she kept with her through the night and even when she got up the next morning to start work again. She wondered if he would go to Dani's office and take a look at the picture to see if he remembered it now that Fiona had described it. As it was, she didn't have the chance of doing much thinking throughout the day because she was so busy. And maybe that was a good thing.

By the time her shift was done, she sank back in her office chair, stared up at Helen, who was coming in for the late afternoon shift and said, "Wow, I haven't even had a chance to take a breather."

Helen nodded. "Hopefully you took care of it all," she said, smiling broadly, "so my shift's easier."

"Maybe," she said. "We had two people move out today. We had one new arrival, and one is coming in tomorrow. The new arrival is somebody to keep an eye on." They quickly went over his file, and, as soon as that was done, Fiona stood, stretched and said, "You know what? I think I'll go for a swim."

"They were introducing a bunch of patients to the pool today," Helen said. "I saw them as I walked across."

"Was Finn there?"

Helen looked thoughtful. "I'm not sure if he was or not."

"He was going to ask for permission to go in the pool," she said. "Hopefully he got it."

It was on her mind as she headed downstairs and past the pool. She kept a close eye on it to see if a session was going on. She was allowed to swim after-hours, but, if some of the patients were there working, she didn't want to interrupt them. She didn't see Finn when she walked over to her place, so she decided that the cool splash and the gentle movement of the water was exactly what she needed. She was tired and just stressed enough after her rough day so that a swim would be a perfect answer.

Back at her place, she changed into her bathing suit, grabbed her pullover dress and her towel, and put sandals on her feet. As she headed back to the pool, she could feel her body already craving the cool sensation of the water and the peacefulness of floating. She dropped her towel on one of the benches, kicked off her shoes, pulled her dress over her head and headed toward the shallow end. Her hair was still in a braid, which was perfect for swimming. She stepped down slowly, looking around; a couple people were at the far end. As she hit the bottom step, she noted somebody at the side too. She glanced over to see Finn. She stopped in delight. "I see you got permission to come in the pool."

He nodded slowly, his gaze studying her face. She quickly ducked under the water, suddenly feeling shy. When she swam closer, he said, "Yes, I got permission today, and I'm glad I came. I was tired, almost too tired to make the effort, but I wouldn't have missed that vision for the world."

FINN WATCHED THE wash of color rise up her face before she quickly sank into the water. Not only was she beautiful inside but she was stunning outside. A gorgeous face with a long slim body and she swam like a fish. Even though he was a hell of a swimmer himself, he took time to admire her form as she moved through the water, her arms cutting cleanly as they rose to the surface and back in again.

He was already tired from his PT workout in the pool and was enjoying floating and moving around. It was amazing how easy it was to navigate in the water. It buoyed him and made him feel so much more capable, even with his colostomy bag. The stoma had a space ring to connect the bags he used to his body, but even then it was perfectly safe to be in a shower or the pool. He was a little self-conscious about it, but other people hadn't even made a comment. This was a beautiful place to be, and, if this is what rehab was, he didn't want to leave. Finally, he stroked through the water and then paddled toward her.

"It's good to see you here," she said quietly as she treaded water. "Also good that you're out in the open and not trying to hide."

He knew what she meant. "It was awkward at first," he admitted. "Everything above the waist is in better shape," he said, "but at the waistline and below the knee?" He shook his head.

"Neither matter," she said gently.

"And I'm slowly realizing that," he said. "For that, I appreciate this place and what Dani's built here. The joy and the healing she's brought to everyone. It's been a pretty incredible time here already."

"And that's why so many people have great experiences here. You've learned to become much more open, much more accepting. As soon as you become more accepting, others do too."

"And I would have said, as soon as they became more accepting, then I did too," he said humorously.

"But you know that's not true," she said. "It's the other way around." She hopped up to sit on the edge of the pool beside him, water dripping down her silky skin.

He deliberately looked away.

"As soon as you learn to love yourself, you learn to become more open," she said. She looked up and waved at Dennis.

"What is he doing?" Finn asked in amusement.

"Looks like he's taking orders," she said.

"Surely not."

"Dennis is one of those people who absolutely loves being here," she said. "He goes over, above and beyond the call of duty at all times. And it's incredibly lovely to see."

"You're not kidding," he said. "Like, wow. What do you think he's taking orders for?"

"I rather imagine something cool and wet, and, if we're lucky, treats to go with it."

He looked at her. "You wouldn't tease me about that, would you?"

She started to laugh.

Dennis looked at her and said, "Nice to see you in a good mood."

"I'm sorry. I've been a little down lately," she said, her laughter slowing, "but I'm doing better."

"You should know that the lawsuit was dropped."

She stared at him in surprise. "Seriously?"

It wasn't much of a surprise to Finn that everybody knew about it because the medical personnel and others here were apparently a tight-knit family, and he kept seeing the proof of it every day. He looked at her and said, "Would that make you feel better?"

"It would make me feel a lot better," she said. "I desperately tried not to do anything wrong here," she said in a low tone. "And, when something like that happens, it completely wipes you out. You don't know how you could have done things differently. I didn't want to hurt him. I really didn't."

"No, and I think the bottom line is, he did so much better because you were here," Dennis stated. "He'll get over it."

She nodded. "Maybe, but I'd just as soon not get into that scenario in the first place."

"Just so you know," Finn said, "I'm stating again that I'm not part of that same scenario."

Startled, she turned to look at him, and he caught the nervousness in her gaze, knowing that maybe she had been thinking that.

He grabbed her hand and said, "I'm not. I'm perfectly capable of understanding who and what is responsible for where I'm at, how I've improved and how I haven't improved, and where I need to improve. And it has nothing to do with an improper emotional connection to you. I know exactly how I feel about you, and it's not related to my health."

He watched as the smile bloomed across her face, making his heart beat rapidly. She leaned across, kissed him gently on his cheek and said, "I hope so."

Just then Dennis interrupted. "None of that. Those of us without partners suffer terribly when we watch all this lovey-dovey stuff happening around us."

She chuckled, smiled and changed the subject. "So, what are you taking orders for?"

"What do you want?" he asked.

"I want coffee, if possible," Finn asked. "And, if there happens to be any treats, I won't turn those down either."

Dennis chuckled. "Do you need a light treat, like a muffin or cinnamon bun, or do you need like a triple-decker sandwich kind of treat?"

"Oh, man," Finn said. He looked at the clock and then shook his head. "It's already almost five, maybe we shouldn't have anything."

"Nonsense," Dennis said. "I'll bring you a sweet treat and a cup of coffee. And then, when you guys eat around sixish, if you want more dessert, you can have that afterward." And, with that, he took off.

She turned to face Finn and said, "As you can tell, he's a happy camper here."

"I really love that," he said. "There's absolutely no sense of being in a position that's beneath him or feeling like he's a servant. I really, really appreciate that attitude."

"That's definitely not how Dennis views his world here." She smiled and stretched back, leaving her legs in the water, but her body was stretched out on the concrete behind her.

"Don't you want something to protect your skin?" he asked.

"No," she said, "I just want to stretch out and feel the wind and the breeze and the sunshine on my body. It's been a really long, hard day."

"I'm sorry if I added to that."

She laughed out loud. "It's been a long hard day because of inventory and catching up on patient records. It's been a long hard day because of filing and documentation management and computers that wouldn't work and keyboards that got coffee spilled on them so they got cranky and a mouse, a cordless mouse that ran out of batteries that I couldn't find. It was just one of those days."

He patted her hand and said, "Then close your eyes and rest."

And that's what she did.

He sat here, beyond content, keeping an eye on her, watching the rest of the world go by. When Dennis returned ten minutes later, he brought over a small table and set it up beside them and plunked down a tray with two large coffees and a plate with the largest darn cinnamon bun Finn had ever seen, cut into four pieces.

Finn smiled and said, "Dennis, I do want to say what a pleasure it is to see your smiling face every day."

"And yours," Dennis said. "Sometimes people arrive here thinking their world has completely collapsed. But, by the time they leave," he said, "it's amazing just how much they have grown and changed."

"And I'm halfway there," Finn said. "I'm not all the way, but I'm getting there." He motioned at Fiona. "Of course, she's a wonderful help in the healing department."

Dennis chuckled. "Any time your heart is touched, it's a help. But, in a place like this, it's always very special." Just then he laughed and pointed and said, "Look at who's here." He gave a slight whistle.

Finn turned to see a large three-legged dog with a prosthetic on her fourth leg, walking toward him. The great big massive black Newfoundlander, her tail wagging, came over to greet Dennis.

"Now does she love you," Finn asked, "because it's you, or does she love you because she knows you're connected to food?"

Dennis bent down, gave her a huge hug, scratched behind her ears and buried his face in her neck. When he lifted his face, he said, "I hope the first, but I know for sure the second is at least part of it. This is Helga," he said.

Finn reached out to greet Helga and laughed when he saw the drool coming off the side of her face. "Wow, look at that," he said.

"She's a bit of a spitter," Dennis said, "but we love her anyway."

"Look at her stump too," Finn said. "She handles that prosthetic really well."

"She does, and, when she doesn't have it, she doesn't seem to care either," Dennis said. He gave her a couple good scratches and stood and said, "And I'm back to work." He disappeared.

Fiona sat up to give Helga a big cuddle, and then Helga laid down right beside her—and half on her. She gave a shriek of laughter.

"Is the dog allowed in the pool?" Finn asked.

"I am not exactly sure about that," she said, tilting her head to the side. "It would probably be really good for her."

"She's probably not welcome in the pool," Stan said, coming up behind them. "She does have access to the creek down there on the property, and, as soon as we take her, the first thing she does is jump into the middle of the water."

"I don't blame her," Finn said. "On a hot day ..."

Helga laid here, panting in the heat, as Fiona gently rubbed her ribs. Stan looked down at the coffee and the cinnamon bun and said, "You guys will ruin your dinner."

"We were just thinking that," Finn said, taking a bite anyway. "I told Dennis that we probably didn't need anything, but he suggested we have this now and then dinner at six."

"You guys do that," Stan said, laughing. "I'm heading up to get real food."

"It's early yet, isn't it?" Fiona asked.

"It is," Stan said, "but I figured, if I could get my dinner now, I could go back down to the puppies."

"How's the mom doing?" Finn asked, hating that he'd forgotten about her.

"She's pulled through," he said, "and she's doing just fine. The babies are with her all the time, and she has milk."

Finn looked over at Fiona. "Do you want to get dressed and get food, or are you content?"

She grabbed his hand, lacing her fingers with his, and whispered, "I'm very content." Then she stretched out again, Helga still laying across her middle.

He had to admit he hadn't had a day like this in months and months. As he looked back on his years of naval service, and then the accident as a defining moment in his world, and all the surgeries and recuperation and hell since then, like her, he realized that this was a special moment.

Chapter 12

L YING HERE UNDER the afternoon sun, resting beside the pool with Finn by her side and Helga across her lap ... was utterly perfect. She didn't want to move. Just to hear that the lawsuit had been dropped was magic to her ears and, indeed, lifted a huge weight off her shoulders. She hadn't even realized how much of a weight it had become. It hadn't been there for long but long enough to destroy her good mood. She was so grateful that the lawsuit wasn't going ahead and that the patient could move on. It let her move on too.

She didn't see Finn in the same light. Finn was independent, strong mentally, very capable and emotionally balanced. The fact that he was out here at the pool, even with his colostomy bag on display, was a massive shift. He was stretched out beside her, patting Helga, enjoying the sun. It was also good for his body.

He whispered, "Don't fall asleep like this, or you'll likely burn."

"I know," she murmured, "but it's so damn nice."

"Good for the stress relief, isn't it?"

"Swimming has always been like that for me," she said. "Floating in the water, I feel everything drain away. It's absolutely the best feeling."

"Agreed," he said with a heavy sigh and stretched out.

Long moments later, a breeze came up. "We need to get changed soon."

"Soon, but not yet."

She chuckled in complete agreement. "Any word on the prosthetic?"

"Two days," he said. "It's coming in two days."

"Perfect," she said, "and, if you don't wear it too long right off the bat, to avoid soring up the stump at all, you should be good to go."

He chuckled. "Yes, *Doctor*."

She flushed. "I didn't mean it that way."

He squeezed her fingers. "And I didn't take it that way. It's what I did last time, so I'm certainly aware that that was a big mistake to avoid this time."

"Good," she said. "I know that you'll find your mobility so much more improved when you have it back again."

"I've become accustomed to the wheelchair," he said. "The crutches still sore up my back sometimes, but that's been coming along a lot better too."

"How is the structural-integrity work going?"

"Amazingly well," he said with surprise. "My shoulders are moving back into the proper posture. I'm holding my head straighter over my spine instead of pushed forward. Shane wants me to get my prosthetic too because having that balance will help me to keep my hips properly positioned over my heels, and everything else will fall into place much easier."

"The human body is a marvel," she whispered, feeling sleep trying to drag her under. "Are you tired right now?"

"Tired but not sleepy."

"If I drift off for a few minutes, can you make sure it's just a few minutes?"

"Sure," he said. "How about ten tops?"

She smiled and let her stress drop down yet another notch. She didn't really fall asleep; she just lay here in her deep state, letting everything wash over her. "Have you seen Lovely lately?" she murmured sleepily.

He chuckled. "I thought you were supposed to be sleeping."

"I'm just drifting. But Lovely is adorable."

"I haven't seen her for a few days now," he said, "or the puppies."

"If they're back with Mom, they'll be good for a while," she said. "Once they start walking and waddling around, they're beyond adorable."

"Right." He said, "I love animals of all kinds." He straightened and looked up toward the deck on the main floor. "I think I hear a louder crowd up top." He smiled and said, "I gather that means it's dinnertime."

Fiona opened her eyes more and said, "It sounds like it."

Then Helga's head popped up. She stood the rest of the way up, stepping on Fiona's stomach, and then the huge dog clambered up the stairway to join everyone gathering in the dining area.

Fiona and Finn laughed at her antics to get more loving and to get more food.

Fiona sighed. "We want to wait for the rush to go by anyway."

"Absolutely." He sat up slowly and said, "Not to mention the fact that it'll take me a bit of time to get back to my room and to get changed."

"Right, me too," she said. She glanced over at him. "Meet back up there in what, thirty minutes?"

He looked at his wheelchair, considered the time frame

and said, "Make it forty, maybe forty-five," he said, "and I'll have a shower too."

"Done," she said. She watched as he hopped along the edge of the pool to his wheelchair and made his way into the seat. When he released the brake and turned himself around, she slid back into the water and did another ten laps. Feeling better and a little more tired, she pulled out at the shallow end and grabbed her towel. She wrapped it around her and headed for her own place.

There, she quickly had a shower and decided to wear one of her flowing dresses again. There was just something so very feminine about wearing these. They felt good for her soul. Dressed again, she quickly rebraided her hair and walked up early, hoping to meet him at his room.

He was just coming out as she walked down the hallway. He looked up at her and smiled. "Fancy meeting you here."

She glanced in at his room and his sketchbooks on the bed. "Do you want to stay and sketch?" she asked.

"No," he said. "I'll come back and sketch again later."

He closed the door firmly, and the two of them headed down for dinner. As soon as they entered the dining room, several people called to them. She looked over and said, "Where do you want to sit?"

"Actually, I wouldn't mind spending time with Elliot. Are you up for that?"

She smiled, delighted to be invited. "Absolutely. Let's get food first."

Finn shouted back at Elliot, then directed them toward the food. "Unless you want to go someplace with your other friends," he said.

"No," she said, "I'm happy to be with you and yours."

IT ALMOST FELT like a date again but more comfortable and cozier. Special maybe. In a way, something was so natural about being with Fiona that Finn knew it probably was obvious to everybody around them—and he didn't care one bit. When he approached to see Dennis standing behind the counter again, Finn grinned. "So what's on tap tonight?"

Dennis reeled off the huge menu, leaving Finn wondering what to choose. But he watched as Fiona picked up several pieces of fried chicken and coleslaw. "Oh, man," he said, "I haven't had good fried chicken in forever."

"My favorite recipe," Dennis said, leaning forward. "And it's really mine and my grandmother's."

"That's an easy choice then," Finn said, holding out his plate.

Dennis took four pieces and then grabbed biscuits and filled the rest of his plate with coleslaw.

"You can fill my plate like this anytime," Finn said, grinning widely. He kept on going but didn't really need any of the other food—and there were plenty more choices. They always had lots of food here. He didn't know whether the staff in the back of the counter got to come in and eat as they wanted to afterward or what the deal was, but Finn was delighted. Finally, with everything collected, they rolled over toward where Elliot sat. He had saved them one space but not two. Finn glanced at him. "Can we get an extra seat?"

Elliot immediately stood, grabbed another table and tucked it up to the side. "There is now," he said. "The day I don't find a space for a pretty lady to join us," he said, "is the day I'm dead."

Fiona laughed and placed her tray down. "You always

did have a sweet-talking way with words."

"Hey, I'm not so bad," he said.

"Or so good," she said, waggling her eyebrows.

At that, the table burst out laughing. He loved the way that Fiona settled in nicely with anybody. She wasn't stuck up; she didn't care who was there, and, as long as people were friendly and nice, she was happy to be a part of it. It said a lot about who she was and what she was after in life. And what she'd been through.

Elliot took one look at Finn's plate and said, "Wow, man, can you eat all that?"

"I'll eat all this and go for seconds," Finn promised. "You know me and fried chicken. It's soul food. Nothing like it." He listened to the conversation, but his focus was on his food, and, at his first bite, he almost moaned in delight. When he opened his eyes, Dennis stood off to the side, pointing at him. He lifted his thumb and forefinger in a circle to say, *Awesome*, and then he resumed eating. When he was done with his plate, he settled back to relax. He really wanted more chicken, except he was pretty full.

Just then Dennis appeared by his side with a platter in front of him. "Take a piece or two," he said, handing him the tongs. "You can't be done yet."

There was a perfect drumstick right in front, so he snagged that and then a wing. And then he held up his hand to say no more and added, "But you can put a half-dozen pieces away for me for later, at least for lunch tomorrow."

"Done," Dennis said. "Anytime you want food saved for you, we handle it." He looked over at Fiona and asked, "What about you? Should we pack up a picnic for two?"

"That's not a bad idea," she said in surprise.

"Isn't it your day off tomorrow?" Finn asked.

"It is," she said, "but I'm not going to town. I'm staying around here, so, if you want, we can take lunch out to the horses and see Lovely again."

"You know something?" he said with a gentle smile. "That would be lovely."

At that, everybody else teased the two of them, while Elliot gave Finn a knowing look. But Dennis, with a big smile of satisfaction, disappeared. Finn had to wonder if Dennis hadn't set that up on purpose. Finn leaned over to Fiona and said, "I think Dennis is a bit of a matchmaker."

"Actually, he's a big matchmaker," she said, chuckling. "But it comes from the heart."

She kept working on her plate. It had been half the size of his, and he'd scarfed his so fast that she was still working on her first plate. He finished his last two pieces of chicken and pushed himself slightly back from the table. "That was fantastic."

Elliot grinned at him. "Aren't you glad I told you to get your ass over here?"

Finn nodded. "Absolutely. Should have listened to Dani from the first."

"You should have," Elliot said. "The minute you knew this place was up and running, and you had a way to get in, you should have been here."

"I was still recovering from my last surgery," Finn said. "At least, that's my excuse, and I'm sticking to it."

Elliot reached out and gave him a light smack on the shoulder. "Damn, it's nice to have you here."

"I hear you," he said. "What about the other friends you made?"

"They've gone home," Elliot said. "Although home is not very far away. They're settling in Houston, and we'll stay in touch, probably go into business together. I got about another month here, and then I'll be good to go too."

"That is awesome," Finn exclaimed. "Time just flew by. I hadn't even realized."

"Yep, that's time here," Elliot said, "and I'm almost done. My team thought I was doing pretty well but then not quite so well."

"Well, you're probably better off to stay as long as you need," Finn said. "At least until you're a hundred percent. It's a big, bad world out there and very unforgiving."

It wasn't long before Elliot and his friends at the table got up and left. When they said their goodbyes, Elliot winked at Finn and said, "Time for you two to sit on the deck over on the far side there," he said, "a perfect spot for a couple. Take a coffee, maybe something a little bit stronger, and enjoy." And he disappeared.

Finn looked over at Fiona. "Something a little stronger?"

She laughed. "You're not cleared for alcohol. Every once in a while, a bottle of bubbly comes out, if somebody's got something major to celebrate. But not very often. Aaron and Dani's engagement celebration, yes. As a regular occasion, no."

"So what's this spot for two?" he asked. "Do you know what they're talking about?"

She nodded. "I do, indeed."

Instant jealousy ripped through him.

She looked at him in surprise. "No, not from personal experience."

He chuckled. "Sorry, that was such an instinctive reaction because I hate to think of you with anybody else."

She smiled and said, "Ditto."

And that's just the way life was between them. As far as he was concerned, that made it perfect.

Chapter 13

A FTER DINNER, FIONA went back to the office to check in on something that she'd forgotten about during the day. She said goodbye to Finn as he headed to his room. As she got to the office, Anna sat there, frowning at folders. "Did I mess up?" she asked lightly.

Anna shook her head. "Not really," she said, "just Finn's folder is missing a bunch of information."

"Then it wasn't me," Fiona said. "I have deliberately kept my hands off that just because of our developing relationship."

Anna chuckled. "I can see why," she said. "That former patient really messed you up, didn't he?"

"I just have to be sure that whatever is going on between Finn and me is real," she said, "so I don't want to even know all the details about his condition."

"Well, his condition is fine, just a bunch of stuff hasn't been printed off properly, and some of these consent forms weren't signed."

"Like what?"

"Like the pool, for one," she said.

Immediately Fiona held out her hand. "Give it to me. Plus anything else. I'll take it to him right now. I just left him at his room as it is."

"Hang on a sec. Let me grab it." She quickly printed off

the three forms that she needed, handed her a clipboard and said, "If you can bring them back to me tonight, that'd be great."

Fiona smiled and nodded and immediately headed back to Finn's room. The door wasn't quite closed. She knocked lightly and pushed it open. "Finn, you here?"

The bed was empty. Sketchbooks were on it; he called from the bathroom. "I'm in here," he said. "I'll be a little bit."

"Not a problem," she said. "I have some consent forms for you to sign."

"Leave them on the bed," he said. "I'll sign them when I get back out."

Figuring he was probably getting ready for a shower, she dropped them on the bed and then noticed the sketchbook was open. She looked down and caught sight of the same woman as before, only this time it was complete. She lifted the sketchbook and stared in both shock and admiration. Moments later she recognized the woman. She froze.

It was her.

Tears filled her eyes. The picture was stunning and made her much more beautiful than she was, but, with a few strokes, he'd caught her nose, her eyes, the look on her face. It was magical. She sank to the bed, stunned to see the talent, that raw skill on the page in front of her like that.

How could he not go pro?

This was beyond belief. She quickly flipped through the pages and realized that every damn page of the sketchbook was filled with pictures of her.

Various stages.

Various poses.

Various looks.

She shook her head in shock, and in the back of her mind came that same ugly suspicion again. She didn't quite know what to do. Over forty drawings of her were here, and yet, she hadn't counted, but the book only held forty-five sheets, and hardly any were blank. Her breath shuddered in her chest at the horrified realization that he was quite likely way too fixated on her, just as Ziegler had been. When she heard him in the bathroom, washing his hands, she quickly dropped the sketchbook and disappeared.

She needed time to think about this. Not going back to Anna, Fiona raced outside to the animals. She stood here, propped up against the fence inside the horse pen, Lovely wandering in front of her, as Fiona tried to calm down, but she was afraid it was way too late for that. After what she'd been through with her other patient, she couldn't go through it again. She'd cared about the other patient but on a strictly professional level.

This patient she cared about on a whole different level. The tears, once they started, just wouldn't stop. She couldn't even begin to gain control. When they finally slowed and came to an end, she found herself curled up on the ground, her back against the post, her arms wrapped on her knees, hugging them tightly. As she lifted her head and stared at the much different panorama around her, she whispered, "Oh, dear God."

She didn't know how long she'd been lying there, but her whole world had collapsed in a wave of fear. She lay here for a long moment as she didn't quite know how to deal with this new reality. A few moments after that, she finally shifted and heard a voice behind her.

"It's not what you think."

She stiffened, recognizing Finn's voice. She didn't know

what to say, but she didn't have to say anything. He knew that wasn't an option here. He must have seen her. But then how long had he been here, watching her cry?

"I know you probably don't want to believe me," he said, his voice coming a little bit closer.

She didn't turn around but could hear the crutches as he made several hops and steps and then worked his way slowly toward the fence. "If you'd looked at the other sketchbook," he said, "you would have seen that it's filled with pictures of Dani."

She stiffened at that and frowned. *Dani?*

"I started doing it for her, thinking that maybe it would be a nice gift for her wedding, if I could capture just the right look. She's done so much for this place, I wanted to have something to give back." His voice was sad, almost apologetic.

Fiona twisted slightly to look and saw him only a few feet from her on the other side of the railings.

"And, while I was drawing some of her, I also started to draw some of you," he said. "There's something very special about your face, the way it caught my pencil, or my pencil caught you," he said. "And I just couldn't stop drawing. Dani hasn't seen the ones of her, but she has seen a couple that I've done of you."

At that, Fiona didn't know what to say. "You know what it looks like, don't you?"

"I know what it looks like to you," he said slowly. "But I don't think it would look that way to anybody else."

"How can it not?" she asked. "I mean, how could I possibly not make the same comparison? The lawsuit itself was just dropped after Dani's lawyers had a talk with Zeigler's legal team. But it was traumatic at the time of our initial confrontation. Then I forgot about it until the whole mess reared up again as a lawsuit. I don't want to be put in that position again."

"I'm not fixated on you," he said, his voice steady. "I'm not making you into somebody who you aren't."

She gave a broken laugh. "And yet, our positions are so very different that I don't know that you understand just how you feel," she said.

"I understand exactly how I feel." This time his voice was stronger. Adamant. And a little bit angry.

Well, she understood that feeling. She hopped to her feet, turned and glared at him. "Don't you understand what this looks like?"

He stared at her in astonishment. "Those photos should tell you more than anything how I feel about you," he said bluntly. "Words don't have anywhere near the same impact as something like that, something that I created from my heart."

At that, she took a step back. Confused, she shoved her hands in her pockets. "I want to believe that's how you see me," she said, "but how am I supposed to separate the patient-nurse relationship?"

"You don't get it, do you?" he asked, tilting his head ever-so-slightly to the side. "Just because the other guy was crazy and co-dependent and needed to know that you were there as that shining beacon in order to make the kind of progress he did, he didn't know how to disassociate from it and to keep it within reality," he said. "I highly doubt you went out and had dinners with him or that you sat out in the fields and had coffee with him, did you?"

"No," she shook her head. "Of course not."

"Of course not," he repeated. "Because that wasn't the

relationship you had with him. The relationship he had with you was in his mind. You had a professional relationship with him. That's all there was, and that's why, when you found out how he felt, it was such a shock. You and I have already been dancing around this for weeks. The fact that I drew those pictures has nothing to do with an obsessed mind or somebody who doesn't know the reality of this relationship," he said quietly. "It's entirely pictures of a man who can't get you out of his mind but for all the right reasons."

She looked at him hesitantly.

He nodded. "I get that that's your past, and it's some of your garbage that you have to toss away, but this is your opportunity to do so. You can't judge what we have by the same brush of the relationship he had in his mind. That wasn't real. What we have is real."

She could feel the tears coming into her eyes again. She wiped them away impatiently.

"The thing is, you have to look at how you feel yourself. Maybe this is something that I'm making up," he said, suddenly backtracking. "Maybe I'm the one who made the mistake here. Maybe you don't care about me." He turned away slightly, looking at the horizon. "Maybe you're right. Maybe I'm the one out to lunch here. In which case I need to pull back in a big way. I was planning a future. I was planning on living together, marriage, the whole nine yards," he said, "but I don't want to be thought of the same way as this Ziegler guy and looked upon the way everybody else here looks upon him. If I'm totally out to lunch," he said, his voice harsh, "then you need to tell me. And I'll stop this now."

Slowly he made his way back to the rehab center.

"It's not," she said.

He froze and shifted slightly so he could look at her. "It's not what?"

She took a deep breath. "It's not like that."

"I need more than that," he said, his face stiff and his shoulders rigid. "I get that you've got a problem with us having a relationship. I get that you're afraid that I don't know what my own mind is. And that, in a way, is very insulting because I do know my own mind. I didn't come here looking for an angel. I didn't come here for any other reason than hoping to heal. I've come further and farther and better than I had even thought possible since arriving here, but one of my greatest joys was also meeting you. I am not in any danger of confusing the two. Are you?"

She walked toward him, feeling a shakiness inside, a sense that she was on the brink of losing something that she would regret forever. "No," she said. "I saw those drawings, and it just brought up all the fear and pain and nightmares I've had for the last few weeks. I didn't compare the two of you. You two are so different. In fact, I went out of my way to avoid doing that, but seeing those sketches ..."

"I get that," he said steadily, his gaze never leaving hers.

She liked that about him. He was always very much a person who stared down trouble. He looked it in the eye and dared it to take over his life. He was the kind to deal with stuff and to not shove it under the rug.

She wasn't so sure that she was.

This conversation was hard. She would have to open herself up even more. She'd spent a lot of time these last few years building up those walls—first due to her cheating boyfriend and later due to her deluded patient—and now she would have to break both those walls down.

"What I feel is real," she said with a heavy sigh. "The

sketches just pushed a button, and all that grief, pain and confusion came out. There's so much fear." She stopped, closed her eyes for a moment and said, "Not about you or about how I feel about you. But that you didn't feel that way about me. That I was making a mistake all over again. That I had inadvertently hurt somebody else, in this case, somebody I cared about very much."

"You need to understand how I feel," he said. "I've tried to make it obvious. I've tried to make this easy. But there's nothing ever easy about relationships. Dani knows how I feel about you. She's also warned me to be careful."

At that, Fiona chuckled. "Yeah, that's Dani. Besides, she wants the world to be happy."

"I'm totally okay with the world being happy too," he said. "In a way, I'd prefer it because it's much easier on all of us. And it's nice, when you're happy, to want everybody around you to be happy. But life isn't always that way. So we're either moving forward, and you're letting this go completely and forever, and you'll never doubt how I feel again," he said, with a note of warning, "or we have to decide that this is not built on reality and not built on trust … because, without trust, there's nothing."

She felt his words almost like arrows to her heart, but she also heard the truth behind them.

"I hear. I understand," she said, "and I do trust you, and I do want to move forward. But you also need to understand that sometimes little things can set off hidden emotions. So, as much as I may never want to be afraid or to not trust you again or to want this to ever rear its ugly head again, I *can't* promise that. I will do my best to deal with it when it comes up, and I will certainly want to talk to you about it then," she said, "but don't ask something of me that is not possible to give."

He looked at her, and a slow smile dawned.

She finally realized he stood here, a crutch under one arm, but his arms were open. She closed the gap between them in seconds. As his arms tightened around her, she burrowed in close, and he whispered, "Good answer. None of us are perfect. None of us can guarantee how we'll react in a given situation. I'm willing to try. And that's all I ask of you."

She squeezed him tight. "Trying is easy," she said. "But doing a really good job at it, that's not quite so easy."

He chuckled. "But you're doing so well at everything else," he said, "I'm sure you'll do fine at this." He kissed her gently on her temple and then her nose. "Feeling better?"

She nodded slightly and tucked her head closer into his neck. "I do have to ask you something though," she whispered. She could feel him stiffen beneath her. She gave him a gentle squeeze and then pulled back. "Do I really look like that to you?"

He winked and said, "Honestly, you look way better. If I thought I could get my fingers to draw you the way I see you, it would be perfect. I keep trying. But you're so very precious," he whispered, "and so very beautiful."

She smiled up at him. "Is that because it was drawn by somebody who—"

He placed a finger against her lips, stopping her words. He leaned forward, and he whispered, "If you're asking, the answer is yes," he said. "I do love you."

Her smile, when it came, blossomed across her face, and her breath caught in her throat. She threw her arms around his neck and whispered, "Well, thank heavens for that."

He chuckled, grasped her chin gently with his fingers

and lowered his head and stared into her eyes. "Now, shall we take a moment and be us and enjoy the journey?"

She nodded. "Yes, please."

And he lowered his head, and he kissed her. Not just for today, not just for tomorrow, but a kiss of love for all the tomorrows flowing forward.

And she'd never ever been happier.

Epilogue

G REGORY PARKINS STARED at the application in his hand and wondered. He'd had this thing printed off and filled out half a dozen times in the last couple weeks, and every time he had balled it up and threw it away. Hathaway House was just one of many other rehab centers that he had thought of going to. He knew he needed to go to this one though, but it wasn't so much for himself but because of the woman he had left behind.

He wouldn't have had a clue that she was even there if not for a write-up about Hathaway House that had hit the internet and gone viral. Something about Dani and her father and what they had accomplished since they built the center. The article had piqued his interest, and he'd gone looking to see what kind of a rehab center it was. His research had led him to photographs of the staff at the center, and there, sure enough, he'd seen the photo that had sent him into a tailspin.

Meredith, the woman he had left behind the last time he had headed off on a mission. It had already been five years, but he'd never forgotten her. Gregory could only hope that she'd never forgotten him either. But the chances were, she'd moved on, was likely married and had a family by now.

But he didn't know that. Should he reach out to her or just ignore this? *Ignore?* His laugh was hollow, completely devoid of emotions. He knew he couldn't ignore her. Wasn't that evident by the number of times he'd filled out the paper applications only to crumple them up and throw them away? He and Meredith had spent three wonderful weeks together, and he thought he'd found *the one*.

When he had finally told her that he was leaving again, she'd been heartbroken. Desolate. Her brother had died overseas, and she didn't want to deal with the same kind of loss again. Gregory understood, but he'd signed up for the navy as soon as he could, right out of school. He'd been honored to join, and his career had fulfilled him every year since. No way would he walk away at that point.

As soon as he left her, he regretted his decision.

He knew he should have turned around and found a way to make this work, but instead, he'd buried himself in his work and had tried to forget her. And, for a time, he'd managed. But then he had been blown up by an IED. Now, if he went to look for her, he would feel like *he* was second-best, like he had only come back to her because he was no longer whole. No longer fit for the navy, so she was his second choice.

Again. Just like before. But for different reasons.

He didn't want that. Nor did he want her to feel that way.

Yet, if she was still at the rehab center and single, they had a chance to work on a whole new level of a relationship. And with so many more problems than they had originally. Even to him, that sounded harsh, but the truth was often harsh. He didn't even know why she would want him back in this state. He'd be offering her less than what he had been before, and yet, he'd walked away from her.

He snorted.

As if he were fully capable of walking away anymore. Because he no longer could. ... Not without crutches, a wheelchair or a prosthetic.

Gregory laid the paperwork off to the side. He had also filled out the online form but hadn't really worked on the last couple questions, determined to at least do that much, as he knew Hathaway House could help him physically if nothing else. Maybe he could walk away from her again and not regret it this time. Maybe, just maybe, he could find a whole new life. Sometimes one had to go through the pain to get to the closure, and eventually, to reach a new life at the other end.

He quickly filled out the last few questions online; then his gaze landed on Meredith's picture once more. Not giving himself much chance to rethink anything, he reviewed the online application—the same as the physical paperwork he had filled out a dozen times—and hit Send.

For better or for worse, his application was in.

This concludes Books 4–6 of Hathaway House.
Read about Hathaway House, Books 7–9

Hathaway House (Books #7—9)

Welcome to Hathaway House, a heartwarming military romance series from USA TODAY best-selling author Dale Mayer. Here you'll meet a whole new group of friends, along with a few favorite characters from Heroes for Hire. Instead of action, you'll find emotion. Instead of suspense, you'll find healing. Instead of romance, … oh, wait. … There is romance—of course!

Welcome to Hathaway House. Rehab Center. Safe Haven. Second chance at life and love.

Gregory

Navy SEAL Gregory Parkins knows he's not so bad off as to need what Hathaway House offers, but he'll do anything to get in. RN Meredith Anderson is there, and Greg loves Meredith. In the time since they split up, his life has been one disaster after another, including the one that ended his career—the career that separated them in the first place.

Meredith was horrified to hear what happened to Gregory. But seeing his file was an even bigger shock. Greg thinks he's basically back to normal, but Meredith knows he has a long way to go. She doesn't know how to tell him, without running the risk of him leaving Hathaway House before his healing can really take place.

But the last thing she wants is for him to walk away from her again. Not if there is any chance that they can find their way back to each other …

Heath

Overjoyed at his transfer to Hathaway House, Heath Jorgenson is anxious to maximize his potential and to get better from the multiple injuries that sidelined him. But rest is necessary for recovery, and Heath's body won't give him any. Even when he buckles under and accepts the need for drugs, his body rejects them. And all the determination in the world won't matter when your own body is working against you.

Just when he's about to give up, respite comes from the unlikeliest of sources. The sound of the cleaning lady slowly and methodically washing the hall floor outside his room lulls him to sleep and allows him to see some of the progress he's desperate for.

Hailee Cisco is grateful for the part-time job of washing floors at Hathaway House. Sure, it isn't glamorous, but it's honest work, and, along with her other job, it's enough to pay the bills—of which Hailee has many. When Dani, the heart of and the partial owner of Hathaway House, offers Hailee a full-time job, Hailee is delighted at the chance to cut back to just one job.

Until she realizes that her change in hours has an unintended impact on Heath's sleep patterns …

Iain

Getting accepted to Hathaway House is the new start Iain MacLeod has been waiting for. His old VA center has put him on the road to recovery, but he's nowhere near where he wants to be. Much work remains to be done, and Iain is determined to do what's necessary to get back to full power. But he has hit the limit of his current professionals' abilities. He needs a new team. New eyes. New methods. He can only hope that Hathaway House has what he needs to keep moving forward.

Robin Carruthers works in the veterinary clinic at Hathaway House. When she connects with Iain, she's his biggest cheerleader and enjoys watching him take steps toward greater recovery. Until she realizes that, while Iain is growing in major ways, ... she isn't. When traumas from her past intrude on the present, and Robin is forced to confront issues of her own, she's afraid she and Iain won't find their way back to each other again ...

Books 7–9 are available now!
To find out more visit Dale Mayer's website.
https://geni.us/DMHH7-9Universal

Author's Note

Thank you for reading Hathaway House, Books 4–6! If you enjoyed the books, please take a moment and leave a short review.

Dear reader,

I love to hear from readers, and you can contact me at my website: www.dalemayer.com or at my Facebook author page. To be informed of new releases and special offers, sign up for my newsletter or follow me on BookBub. And if you are interested in joining Dale Mayer's Reader Group, here is the Facebook sign up page.
http://geni.us/DaleMayerFBGroup

Cheers,
Dale Mayer

About the Author

Dale Mayer is a *USA Today* best-selling author, best known for her SEALs military romances, her Psychic Visions series, and her Lovely Lethal Garden cozy series. Her contemporary romances are raw and full of passion and emotion (Broken But ... Mending, Hathaway House series). Her thrillers will keep you guessing (Kate Morgan, By Death series), and her romantic comedies will keep you giggling (*It's a Dog's Life*, a stand-alone novella; and the Broken Protocols series, starring Charming Marvin, the cat).

Dale honors the stories that come to her—and some of them are crazy, break all the rules and cross multiple genres!

To go with her fiction, she also writes nonfiction in many different fields, with books available on résumé writing, companion gardening, and the US mortgage system. All her books are available in print and ebook format.

Connect with Dale Mayer Online

Dale's Website – www.dalemayer.com
Twitter – @DaleMayer
Facebook Page – geni.us/DaleMayerFBFanPage
Facebook Group – geni.us/DaleMayerFBGroup
BookBub – geni.us/DaleMayerBookbub
Instagram – geni.us/DaleMayerInstagram
Goodreads – geni.us/DaleMayerGoodreads
Newsletter – geni.us/DaleNews

Also by Dale Mayer

Published Adult Books:

Hathaway House
Aaron, Book 1
Brock, Book 2
Cole, Book 3
Denton, Book 4
Elliot, Book 5
Finn, Book 6
Gregory, Book 7
Heath, Book 8
Iain, Book 9
Jaden, Book 10
Keith, Book 11
Lance, Book 12
Melissa, Book 13
Nash, Book 14
Hathaway House, Books 1–3
Hathaway House, Books 4–6
Hathaway House, Books 7–9

The K9 Files
Ethan, Book 1
Pierce, Book 2
Zane, Book 3
Blaze, Book 4
Lucas, Book 5

Parker, Book 6
Carter, Book 7
Weston, Book 8
Greyson, Book 9
Rowan, Book 10
Caleb, Book 11

Lovely Lethal Gardens
Arsenic in the Azaleas, Book 1
Bones in the Begonias, Book 2
Corpse in the Carnations, Book 3
Daggers in the Dahlias, Book 4
Evidence in the Echinacea, Book 5
Footprints in the Ferns, Book 6
Gun in the Gardenias, Book 7
Handcuffs in the Heather, Book 8
Ice Pick in the Ivy, Book 9
Jewels in the Juniper, Book 10
Killer in the Kiwis, Book 11
Lovely Lethal Gardens, Books 1–2
Lovely Lethal Gardens, Books 3–4
Lovely Lethal Gardens, Books 5–6

Psychic Vision Series
Tuesday's Child
Hide 'n Go Seek
Maddy's Floor
Garden of Sorrow
Knock Knock...
Rare Find
Eyes to the Soul
Now You See Her
Shattered

Into the Abyss
Seeds of Malice
Eye of the Falcon
Itsy-Bitsy Spider
Unmasked
Deep Beneath
From the Ashes
Stroke of Death
Ice Maiden
Psychic Visions Books 1–3
Psychic Visions Books 4–6
Psychic Visions Books 7–9

By Death Series
Touched by Death
Haunted by Death
Chilled by Death
By Death Books 1–3

Broken Protocols – Romantic Comedy Series
Cat's Meow
Cat's Pajamas
Cat's Cradle
Cat's Claus
Broken Protocols 1-4

Broken and... Mending
Skin
Scars
Scales (of Justice)
Broken but... Mending 1-3

Glory
Genesis
Tori
Celeste
Glory Trilogy

Biker Blues
Morgan: Biker Blues, Volume 1
Cash: Biker Blues, Volume 2

SEALs of Honor
Mason: SEALs of Honor, Book 1
Hawk: SEALs of Honor, Book 2
Dane: SEALs of Honor, Book 3
Swede: SEALs of Honor, Book 4
Shadow: SEALs of Honor, Book 5
Cooper: SEALs of Honor, Book 6
Markus: SEALs of Honor, Book 7
Evan: SEALs of Honor, Book 8
Mason's Wish: SEALs of Honor, Book 9
Chase: SEALs of Honor, Book 10
Brett: SEALs of Honor, Book 11
Devlin: SEALs of Honor, Book 12
Easton: SEALs of Honor, Book 13
Ryder: SEALs of Honor, Book 14
Macklin: SEALs of Honor, Book 15
Corey: SEALs of Honor, Book 16
Warrick: SEALs of Honor, Book 17
Tanner: SEALs of Honor, Book 18
Jackson: SEALs of Honor, Book 19
Kanen: SEALs of Honor, Book 20
Nelson: SEALs of Honor, Book 21
Taylor: SEALs of Honor, Book 22

Heroes for Hire

Ice's Icing: Heroes for Hire, Book 20
Johan's Joy: Heroes for Hire, Book 21
Galen's Gemma: Heroes for Hire, Book 22
Zack's Zest: Heroes for Hire, Book 23
Heroes for Hire, Books 1–3
Heroes for Hire, Books 4–6
Heroes for Hire, Books 7–9
Heroes for Hire, Books 10–12
Heroes for Hire, Books 13–15

SEALs of Steel
Badger: SEALs of Steel, Book 1
Erick: SEALs of Steel, Book 2
Cade: SEALs of Steel, Book 3
Talon: SEALs of Steel, Book 4
Laszlo: SEALs of Steel, Book 5
Geir: SEALs of Steel, Book 6
Jager: SEALs of Steel, Book 7
The Final Reveal: SEALs of Steel, Book 8
SEALs of Steel, Books 1–4
SEALs of Steel, Books 5–8
SEALs of Steel, Books 1–8

The Mavericks
Kerrick, Book 1
Griffin, Book 2
Jax, Book 3
Beau, Book 4
Asher, Book 5
Ryker, Book 6
Miles, Book 7
Nico, Book 8
Keane, Book 9

Lennox, Book 10
Gavin, Book 11
Shane, Book 12

Bullard's Battle Series
Ryland's Reach, Book 1
Cain's Cross, Book 2
Eton's Escape, Book 3
Garret's Gambit, Book 4
Kano's Keep, Book 5
Fallon's Flaw, Book 6
Quinn's Quest, Book 7
Bullard's Beauty, Book 8

Collections
Dare to Be You…
Dare to Love…
Dare to be Strong…
RomanceX3

Standalone Novellas
It's a Dog's Life
Riana's Revenge
Second Chances

Published Young Adult Books:

Family Blood Ties Series
Vampire in Denial
Vampire in Distress
Vampire in Design
Vampire in Deceit
Vampire in Defiance

Vampire in Conflict
Vampire in Chaos
Vampire in Crisis
Vampire in Control
Vampire in Charge
Family Blood Ties Set 1–3
Family Blood Ties Set 1–5
Family Blood Ties Set 4–6
Family Blood Ties Set 7–9
Sian's Solution, A Family Blood Ties Series Prequel
      Novelette

Design series
Dangerous Designs
Deadly Designs
Darkest Designs
Design Series Trilogy

Standalone
In Cassie's Corner
Gem Stone (a Gemma Stone Mystery)
Time Thieves

Published Non-Fiction Books:

Career Essentials
Career Essentials: The Résumé
Career Essentials: The Cover Letter
Career Essentials: The Interview
Career Essentials: 3 in 1